Book One of the I

The Mist Keeper's Apprentice

E.S. Barrison

Thank you for reviewing + supporting me! Hope you enjoy! —ESB

E.S. Barrison
www.esbarrison-author.com

Publisher's Note: This is a work of fiction. Names, characters, places, and incidents are a product of the author's imagination. Locales and public names are sometimes used for atmospheric purposes. Any resemblance to actual people, living or dead, or to businesses, companies, events, institutions, or locales is completely coincidental.

The Mist Keeper's Apprentice/E.S. Barrison. -- 1st ed.
ISBN 978-1-7343670-2-7

Dedicated to Grandma Rhoda & Grandpa David

To Kainan
Knoll
Hutch's Creek
Newbird's Arm
To Heims Norte
The Capitol
Maedee's Outlook
Ab Aeterno
Grover's Marsh
Opal's Canyon
To Rosada
Stilette
To Volfium
To Heims Sur
To Proveniro
To Perennes
Janis

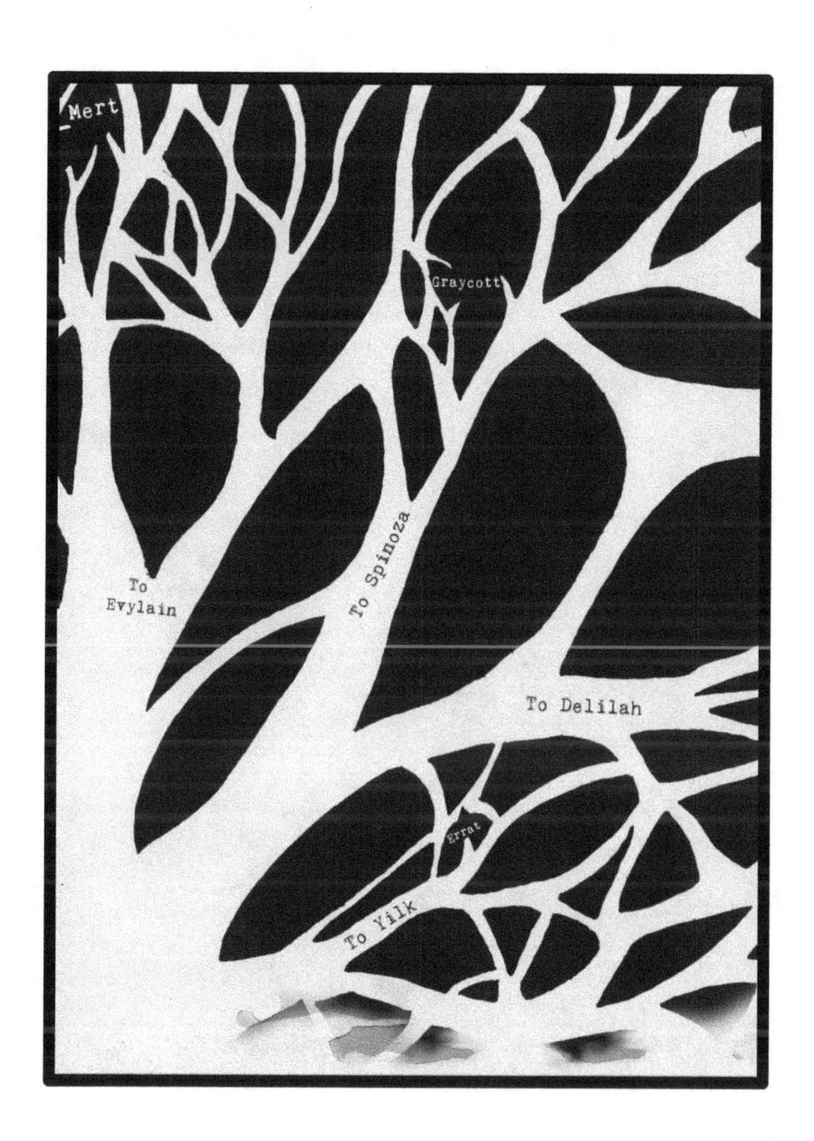
Mert
Graycott
To Evylain
To Spinoza
To Delilah
Errat
To Yilk

CHAPTER ONE

THE STORYTELLER

Brent ducked into the alleyway, leading an entourage of children away from the market to a makeshift stage. He hopped up on the boxes and peered over his audience's heads, waiting for the guard to turn away. Once the path cleared, Brent ushered the children closer, bending his knees to reach their level.

"You ready for a story? Cause I got a good one." He grinned, his audience rapt, and continued, "This is a story about someone you all know: Madame Gonzo!"

"Madame Gonzo!" one child proclaimed. "She's the nice old lady who runs the market square!"

"She gave me a lemon cake yesterday!" another added.

"That's right! But, did you hear she had a granddaughter? There's a story—a rumor, I mean, that Madame Gonzo's granddaughter was born with a flower blossoming on her head." Brent focused as the children's faces lit up. "Haven't you heard? I imagine not! Old Madame Gonzo once had a granddaughter, and well, a beautiful white flower crooned towards the sky at her birth. Her mother, the pernicious witch Angelana, never named the child, but Old Madame Gonzo called her Rhodana, like the song you sing in school.

"The story goes, on a sad-sad note, that the Evil Witch Angelana killed her daughter. But I believe Rhodana is alive! Wouldn't that be something? Wouldn't that be—"

"Mr. Harley!"

Brent shot up. "Cap—Captain Carver!"

The captain grabbed a fist full of Brent's curls and dragged him back into the market, "What have I told you, boy?"

"No stories," Brent muttered.

"I'm sorry?"

"Under statute 19-10-20-B, storytelling by the general populace is prohibited on the counts of hearsay, rumors, malice, and destruction." Brent winced as Captain Carver dug deeper into his hair. "All those over the age of twenty-one will be sent to Newbird's Pit."

"And how old are you, Mr. Harley?"

"I turn twenty-one after Year Birth."

"Then think about where you want to end up." The captain tossed him onto the pavement before marching towards the cadets on the far side of the square.

Brent clutched the ground, digging his fingers into the dirt between each of the cobblestones while clenching his eyes shut. He cursed once, pleading that no one watched; of course, they did. How could they not? How many times had he been tossed to the side after another story? He wasn't even twenty-one yet, so why did it matter?

Because of your stamp. As he sat up, Brent rolled up the sleeve of his coat past where a leather bracelet clamped around his wrist. Beneath it sat two black triangles, connected like an hourglass, upon his wrist. He ran his finger over it, tracing up to the back of his hand where another stenciled image of a single triangle, like a shadow of the stamp on his wrist, rested beneath his knuckles. No one ever noticed this one, not like the black stamp on his wrist, but its mere presence wore heavily on his heart. With it, he lost his ability to love, assigned to another for an empty marriage.

His attention drifted to the wooden fence on the eastern side of the market, blockading Newbird's Pit, the domicile's shantytown harboring all those subjected to vagrancy. It extended down the road to where the Senator's Gardens stood as the precious gem of Newbird's Arm, and up past the square towards the stairs of the Temple of the Effluvium. As the watchful eye of the Order, the Temple gazed upon the town with its ruby embezzled Year Glass, counting down the final moments to the New Year.

Probably two days. When the sun hits the pinnacle in the sky, and the Effluvium is the highest. There we will sing...and a king will —

Shite. Stop thinking up stories. It's no good for you.

Brent rose, coming face-to-face with the lovely Jemma Reds—her hair the color of her name, and brown eyes as scornful as her scowl.

"Jem," Brent gulped. "Hi. Sorry. I—I was...I mean the children wanted a story and I—"

"What am I going to do with you, Brenton?" Jemma tugged him away. A stenciled triangle identical to the one on Brent's hand garnished her hand. "At this rate, you're going to end up in the Pit before I come of age. Can you not contain yourself for a fortnight?"

"What does it matter? Neither of us wants this."

Jemma pinched the bridge of her nose as she led Brent away from the center of town. He hunched his shoulders to hide his face, digging one of his hands into his pocket. People watched. The captain always made a scene at the mere mention of stories, and even with his departure, his stringent words hung in the air. The stamp on Brent's wrist only helped to make him a moving target. The moment he passed his first birthday and his eyes failed to darken from silver, the Order marched onto his family's doorstep. They stamped his wrist black and cleansed him, to protect the Effluvium—the binding mist of life, death, and everything—and keep demons from latching onto his back.

The Effluvium haunted the landscape, descending from the mountains and encapsulating the fields, sifting over the river through town, and decorating the land with malcontent. Dirt spiraled from the roads, and with each gust of wind, the trees trembled.

"Miss Jemma," a shopkeeper called as Brent and Jemma walked past. "Good day to you. A pleasant day, no doubt."

"And in the arms of the Effluvium, and from the mountain, it will continue," Jemma acknowledged. She approached the shop keeper, "Good wares today, I hope. I heard Grover's Marsh avoided another plague this season, so their citrus should be impeccable!"

"Ay, is true Miss Jemma," the shopkeeper beamed. "A new crate of lemons arrived this morning."

"Could I—" Brent mumbled, reaching for a coin in his pocket,

"We don't serve your kind here," the shopkeeper snapped. "Go back to the Pit like the rest of ya vags."

"I'm not—"

"Brent, go," Jemma hissed. "I'll see you later."

"A'ight, fine..." Brent exhaled. He should've been used to Jemma's bluntness by now, but he couldn't help holding out that perhaps she would open her heart.

"Miss Jemma, you are so noble to love a vagrant like him," the shopkeeper remarked. "Not many could handle a man with a black stamp."

Love? Is that the story they're going with now? Brent shook his head.

He plodded into the heart of the town square, ignoring the glares of most shopkeepers. Old Madame Gonzo waved to him from the wicker chair on her porch. On some days, he sat with her and watched the world go by, listening to her so-called *facts*. But were facts not stories of a different nature? Local legends, old wives' tales, rumors, and facts; why did they chastise Brent for similar tales?

Brent waved to Madame Gonzo as he kept moving. Eyes watched him, and he swore murmurs followed with disgust. The orneriest of the guffaws and shouts came from the steps leading towards the Temple, where a group of cadets sat smoking. Heralded by Christof Carver, the captain's son, the cadets threw their dead smokes at him, yelling to get into the Pit. Brent hid in his shoulders, flinching as one of Christof's smokes hit him in the face, scuffling along as fast as he could towards the edge of the market.

Remember the time you got all those smokes stuck in your hair? Brent brushed his curls back and restrained a nervous laugh. *Bria spent all those hours removing them. What a tale...imagine if my head lit on—stop it! No stories!*

Brent shut down his thoughts and diverted his gaze towards a merchant selling wicker baskets. Beside the merchant, his daughter placed flowers in a child's hair, smiling. Brent's heart skipped. The lovely Bria Smidt, with eyes darker than her skin and dimples in her cheeks punctuating her smiles, always stopped him in his tracks. He still dreamed of the nights they walked together through the Senator's Gardens, talking and laughing, smiling and kissing.

Things were different then.

"Brent!" she called as she put the last flower into the child's hair, "You alright?"

Brent shrugged.

Bria frowned, sending the child on their way, before walking over to Brent and placing her hand on his arm, "So no."

"I'm a'ight, really."

Bria saw through it. "I saw Captain Carver make a scene. He's been picking you out more and more lately."

"I'm turning twenty-one soon. I guess I gotta...I mean, I need to start behaving."

"You mean stop telling stories?"

"Yeah."

"That's stupid, though! You love telling stories." Bria kicked the ground. "You should just run—"

"I can't."

"I'll—"

"Harley! What're you doing?" Cadet Christof Carver shouted, marching across the plaza. He mimicked his father's walk, his chest puffed outwards while stomping his feet.

"I'm just...I'm talking." Brent turned, though Bria's fingers stayed on his arm. "I'm allowed to do that, right?"

Christof's nostrils flared, "Not for long."

"Leave him alone. He's not doing anything wrong." Bria glared up at Christof.

"You shouldn't be talking to him, Briannabella. Doesn't look good for you either."

"I said go away, Cadet Carver!"

Christof grabbed her wrist. "You shouldn't talk to me like that, doll. Just 'cause I'm stuck on you now doesn't mean I'll always be."

"I don't care!" she protested, tugging away, "Let go of me!"

"Please stop!" Brent held his hands up and brought his hands to his head. His throat tightened, the anxious gong in his head starting to vibrate as he took a step backward. "I'm—I'm leaving, a'ight? There's no reason to fight. I mean, please...don't."

Before anyone replied, Brent backed into the market. The mist from the mountains had grown heavier around him, but that was far from unusual. Sometimes, Brent wondered if the mist had a way of knowing when someone needed it the most, to become invisible, to hide their sorrow.

Once upon a time, a sad monster lived in the mist. It knitted a cloak out of the fog and walked at night with the clouds. The townsfolk spoke—

He shook his head, and the story vanished, just as he tripped backward into someone.

"Oh! I'm—I'm so sorry. I didn't mean..." He turned. "I'm sorry—"

A pale woman draped in black gawked back at him. She opened her mouth to say something, but as soon as she breathed, a fog trickled over her, and she was gone.

CHAPTER TWO

In the Garden

Brent gawked where the woman stood, blinking away the remnants of mist. A muffled buzzing filled his ears. Had it been another story in his head? It seemed no one else had noticed the woman, resuming their business, shoving by him and tossing glances as due.

"Brent?"

He turned. Bria looked up at him, clutching her basket of flowers to her chest.

"You okay?"

"Yeah. I think...I mean, yeah, I'm fine." He gulped and changed the subject. The last thing he wanted was for Bria to worry the stories had gotten the best of him. "Christof leaving you alone now?"

Bria met his gaze; those pensive brown eyes read him like a book. "I can handle Christof. It's you I'm worried about."

"I'm fine. I thought...I mean..." He paused to choose his words. "I thought I saw something. Just my imagination, a'ight? I'm...it's nothing."

Bria shuffled the flowers in her basket, then turned towards the Senator's Gardens. Travelers often marveled at the Gardens, speaking rumors of the abysmal world beyond the Newbird Mountains. They said only evergreen trees and shrubs, locked in a dust bowl of smoke and ash, lived beyond the town of Newbird's Arm, claiming the world had always been dead. Others blamed the Order's vengeful hand against all magic. Once, after hearing an old traveler rant about the death of the world, Brent concocted a story of a wizard who stole all the greenery, only to have the Forest Queen plant a tree and give life to the world again.

Those were but stories.

Truth-be-told, Brent never ventured beyond the Newbird Mountains. It would be easy enough to hop on a train and leave, but with a black stamp and little money, leaving town might have been a story itself. Besides, he could never leave his ma or sister, or—

"Hey." Bria touched his arm. "I'm going to head home if you want to walk with me...unless you're busy here?"

"Yeah, right, okay," Brent replied. "Let me just find Alexandria."

He scoured the marketplace, over the heads of the patrons, towards where a coterie of children gathered. A young girl with pigtails and gray eyes met his gaze, then bounded towards him with a grin spread from cheek to cheek.

"We going home now?" Alexandria asked.

"Yeah, almost supper time." Brent took his sister's hand. "Bria's gonna walk with us, a'ight?"

"A'ight!"

They walked towards the Senator's Gardens, silence nestling in the air between them. Brent used it to fade out the vulgar calls from the merchants, duck his head away from the guards, and even hide his face from Jemma as she spoke with Brother Roy Al Carver of the Order. The younger brother of Captain Carver stared with serenity behind a pair of rimmed glasses on his thin nose, and whenever he spoke, his lips puckered like a fish. He selected a miniature Year Glass from a merchant table and held it in the air, mimicking the one hanging above the Temple as it counted the final days of the year.

Outside the market square, Brent breathed. The stares on his back vanished. Even Alexandria perked up, hopping along the stones in the river while picking a few wildflowers for Bria to weave into her hair.

"I'm gonna be a flower princess...like Rhodana!" Alexandria beamed at Brent. "How does that story end? You didn't finish it!"

"The one from today, you mean?"

"Yeah! About Madame Gonzo's granddaughter!"

"Oh, right." Brent grinned back at his sister. "Well, I told you, I think Madame Gonzo's granddaughter–the little babe named Rhodana–lived. There is a story that, instead of dying, Rhodana blossomed into Senator Heartz's immortal camellia bushes. You see?" He motioned to the bushes on the side of the road. "Have you noticed how they never die, even when demons turn the wind frigid or when mothers sing the heat into summer? I think, wherever Rhodana is now, she is keeping the camellias alive. They are her children like she was a child long ago...and as long as she thrives, so do they, right?"

Brent glanced back at Bria. She stopped at one of the bushes, picking a flower and holding it up to the sunlight. With the tip of her finger, she grazed the petal, then frowned.

He backtracked to her, "But, I think without help—I mean, without gardeners like Mr. West and Bria...even Rhodana couldn't keep these flowers alive."

"Maybe Rhodana is just a magic gardener?" Alexandria piped.

"Maybe." Brent took Bria's hand. "But most gardeners are magic."

Once again, another smile. Bria reached up and put the camellia behind his ear. "The world could use a bit more magic and fairy tales, not just gardeners."

"At least gardeners are real."

"But gardeners don't have fantastical stories." Her face fell and, after glancing behind her, she placed a hand to Brent's cheek. "It'd be a shame for a storyteller to stop telling stories. If you ran away—"

He removed her hand from his cheek and squeezed between her knuckles. "I can't leave; I don't have money, and I mean, all of *this*...for my ma, for my family...it's the only way to break the cycle."

"Well, it's ridiculous." She turned away to pick another camellia flower.

They reached a fork in the road. The gravel road led towards the barracks, the sight of guards marching in the distance apparent. Another headed straight, branching into the weaving pathways of the Senator's Garden. The last road turned into dirt, trailing towards the border of the Pit. Bria disbanded there, placing one more flower in Alexandria's hair, then vanishing into the Senator's Gardens without looking back.

"Brent?" Alexandria tugged at his sleeve.

"Yeah?"

"When are you and Miss Bria gonna get married?"

"Wha—What!?!" The blood rushed to Brent's ears, "Why would you—what makes you think—why would you say that?"

"You two are in love! Like the story of Prince Sol and Princess Luna you told!" Alexandria crossed her arms, "I saw you *kissing*!"

"Ally-cat, no..." Brent wiped his face. "It's not like that."

"But you are!"

"You know I'm marrying Miss Jemma after Year Birth."

"But why!?! You don't love her!"

Brent guided Alexandria down the dirt pathway, lowering his voice as he spoke. "It's not as simple as love."

"But in your stories—"

"My stories are just that—stories. So, I have to marry Jemma." Brent recalled the day of the betrothal, weeks before his nineteenth birthday. A snowstorm had ravaged the domicile, and he nestled by the fire with Bria, draped in blankets and drinking warm tea. It was then Brent decided he would ask for Bria's hand when she turned eighteen later that year.

He never had the chance. Morning arrived with a knock on the door from his mother, sending Brent's life into another spiral. "Ma and Brother Roy Al came up with the plan that if someone pure like Miss Jemma marries me, then I may not end up in the Pit like Dad. It doesn't matter that we don't love each other; Miss Jemma will be doing what's best for the Order, and I'll do what's best for you and Ma, a'ight?"

Alexandria scowled. "That's dumb."

Brent didn't disagree. While many people thought it was a waste of time, Brother Roy Al wanted to prove the elders of the Order wrong. That Men and women marked with the black stamp did not belong to the demons. There was a cure, he claimed.

But maybe I don't want to be cured. Brent scratched at the triangular betrothal brand on his hand, turning towards his dilapidated home at the end of the cul-de-sac.

His mother waited in the kitchen, stirring a large pot of watery stew, hunched over and mumbling to herself. Clothes hung on the line in the kitchen. When he was younger, he would help deliver the clothes for his mother, pulling in the occasional extra coin, but with age came skeptics, and his black stamp prevented him from helping any longer.

Brent kissed the back of his mother's head then vanished into his narrow bedroom. It was no larger than a closet, with a thin mattress and a single end table. There, he let his magic come to life. Brent kept strips of parchment he'd torn out of newspapers and the three books he had read back-to-cover in his drawer covered by few garments of clothes. He used a fountain pen as his wand, scribbling stories across the papers of a goddess of Camellias, a man with burned eyes, and a woman in black traveling about town whom no one could see.

He paused, ink bleeding through the paper, wracking his brain over the woman again. She'd left in an instant, like the Effluvium marching down the side of the mountain. Brent convinced himself it was his imagination playing tricks again. Only a story, nothing more. Right?

"Brenton?" his mother knocked.

"Ma!" He pushed the strips of paper back in the drawer. "I'm sorry—I didn't...I mean, is supper ready?"

"Was ready hours ago."

"Oh, sorry, I—" He shook his head. "Can I help you clean? Or with the laundry? I can help."

"No, no, it's a'ight." She sat beside him and stroked back his bangs, "I'm just glad you came home tonight."

"Uh, yeah."

Her face fell. "You're going out again, aren't you?"

"Yes."

"Be safe then, a'ight?"

"I'll try—I mean, I will. I promise."

Once the sun set far beneath the mountains and his mother and sister went to bed, Brent snuck into the trees following along the Pit's wall. He hunched his shoulders, hands gripping the scraps of paper in his pocket, keeping to the shadows. The moon hung as a single slither in the sky, and Brent relied on the distant lights from over the Pit's wall to guide him back towards the market.

Brent slipped inside the cracked opening of the Pit's gate. A mirrored version of the market met him. Merchant booths lined the alleyways, and people of the night strode half-dressed through the streets. The guards turned a blind eye as townsfolk entered the gate, bribed by free wares from the dealers, the harlots, and the so-called Magii of the Black Stamp. The Magii sold their fantastical antidotes and spells, blessed with magic long thought eradicated by the Order itself. Yet, while townsfolk entered, the vagrants were not permitted to leave unwarranted.

Brent kept to the side, his head down, not daring to make eye contact. Even when his drunken father swaggered by, Brent didn't call out. *Bite your tongue, keep your head down, and don't attract attention. That's what Ma always says.*

In the Black Market, he listened. Although townsfolk traveled each night into the forbidden tents, harboring of fruit and vices, Brent knew if they spoke his name, the guard would march up to his front door the next day.

So, Brent said not a word as he moved between the vendors. He traded five strips with stories for a bag of lemons. To vagrant named Micca, only a few years older than Brent, he traded seven stories for a pack of smokes and two more for the ones that told his worries goodbye. Micca waved Brent off with a cocky smile, counting the story-strips like currency as he waltzed away.

Even though the stories granted the vendors solace, making the trip all worth it, Brent didn't stay around. Once he bought his wares, he snuck out of the Pit and towards the fields. Cattle slept beneath the oak hammocks. Brent glanced towards a large oak tree, basking in the evening mist. Shadows of the past flashed through his mind; some nights, not too long ago, he had sat with Bria beneath that tree, laughing, touching, and kissing. They sat there and named the cows. He did the same now, blowing smoke towards the field, squeezing a lemon in his hand. *The black one is named Gregory, the brown one is Paula, and the calf is Emily.*

Brent puffed on smoke again. It blew back behind his head, towards the Senator's Garden over the creek. The smoke mingled in the air, spinning about, dancing even, forming a—

He blinked.

No, it's gotta be in my head.

He blinked again. Yet the smoke still gathered around *her.*

The woman in black meandered into the Gardens, her hood up over her face, as spectral as when he first laid his eyes upon her. Her skin glowed like the outline of the moon, or as the snow that tampered with the ground.

Brent stomped out his smoke and followed her from afar. He felt drawn towards her like chains had wrapped around his ankles and dragged him to her. No matter how hard he tried, he could not shake them. How could no one else notice this woman? She was like a bruise against the landscape.

The woman paused by the camellia bushes and picked one flower from it. Upon holding it up, the flower wilted.

Brent ducked behind a bush and shivered. *I'm going crazy. This has gotta be a story. The flowers can't die.*

The woman shook her head, dropping the petals to the ground.

Brent followed from the bushes as she strolled along the edge of the garden where the forest met the flowers. Her stride ceased at a towering oak tree.

When the woman touched the trunk of the tree, the ground swallowed her whole, leaving a trail of mist in her wake.

"What the—" Brent left his hiding spot and rushed over to where she stood. "What the shite? Where did she—I'm going crazy!"

He kicked a root in frustration.

The ground loosened beneath him, and like a door swinging open, it collapsed.

Darkness engulfed him. Seconds later, he hit the ground. The only source of light came from a torch glowing down the tunnel.

Drip.

Drip.

Drip.

Water fell from the stalagmites. On the wall, a lattice of vines bathed in the water, crooning towards the small bit of light hanging in the air.

Brent groaned as he crawled up from the floor, gripping at the ground, then at a shoe.

His gaze trailed upwards.

The woman in black glared back.

CHAPTER THREE

THE GIRL IN THE TUNNELS

Shite!" Brent scrambled backward.

The woman in black jammed her sharp heel into his hand before he could get far. Her shrill voice pierced the silence. "What are you?"

"I, uh...I'm uh—"

The woman thrust him face-first into the wall of vines. "Answer me! What are you?"

"I—I don't—" He cringed. "This can't be real! I'm spent, aren't I? Shite—ow!"

She slammed him against the wall again. Brent gripped the vines, digging into them with the tips of his nails. To his surprise, at his touch, they moved, slithering about his fingers. He stared back at the woman in horror, but as she swiped at him again. The vines retorted by pulling him in the opposite direction and through the wall.

Brent toppled backward into a dark room. The woman in black shrieked as the vines knitted shut behind him. She clawed at them, but the lattice only tightened.

A few lemons and one of his smokes fell out of Brent's coat as he collapsed on the ground. They rolled across the floor, past the dim fire, to the feet of a young woman crouching at the far wall. A gray scarf covered her chin and hair. Yet, even more obscure, what appeared to be tree branches shot out from behind her right ear, encasing her face and twisting into her frizzy hair.

Only her dark left eye remained visible in the firelight.

"What are you doing here?" The scarf muffled the young woman's voice.

"I, uh...I—" Brent winced as the woman shrieked on the other side of the wall. "The woman...I followed her here and I—I mean she attacked me and—"

"What woman?"

"The one out there. She's right there." Blood dribbled from the puncture wound on his skin as he pointed.

"There's no one else down here, though." The young woman peered out of her vines. "You're the first person I've ever seen here."

A knot formed in Brent's throat. It played a song up the back of his spine, into his forehead, where a laughing old man banged a gong in his head. He brought his head to his knees and wheezed. "I'm going crazy...or I'm spent or—or—shite!"

"I don't think you're crazy," the girl whispered.

"But the woman—I mean this—I don't..." Brent gasped for air. "You didn't see her! I should've listened. This is what I get...I should've—"

"You were floating in the air against the wall...and you're bleeding." The girl pulled a kerchief from her satchel and motioned to the side of his face.

Brent took the kerchief and pressed it to his forehead. Blood stained the material instantly.

He sucked in his bottom lip as the woman in black screech once more. "Can't you hear her, though? She's screaming so loud."

"I don't, no."

Brent gritted his teeth and shook his head.

"But I trust you. And you can trust me."

"I don't know who you are, though."

"No, you—" The girl looked away. "Right, no. You can call me Rho."

"Rho..." Brent furrowed his brow. "Okay *Rho*...do you...I mean, where am I?"

"That's a good question," the girl called Rho replied. "I've been trying to figure that out for years now."

"But you live here...don't you?"

"I discovered them by accident, just like you." Rho shrugged. "They're my Tunnels."

"Tunnels..." Brent glanced around at the walls. "Tunnels to where?"

"Anywhere, everywhere. Magic."

"Magic..." Brent's gaze retraced the vines. "So wait, did you do the thing with the vines? That brought me here?"

She nodded.

"So, you're a Magii? But I thought...the Order, I mean. They eradicated magic decades ago."

"I'm something." Rho picked up a lemon and rolled it in her hands. "The tunnels are my hiding place. The Order can't find me here."

"Shite...the Order! If they find out about this...shite I need to go home..."

"Why would you want to?"

"Why would you—" Brent narrowed his eyes, "I mean, why do you care?"

"Forget it." Rho dropped the lemon. As it hit the ground, a tree erupted from the fruit, spiraling up towards the ceiling in the shape of a bark-covered twisting staircase. A few lemons sprouted along its branches.

"What the—"

"Magic." Rho peeled open another lemon, "Go on. That'll lead you home."

"Oh...uh, okay. Thanks." Brent stepped onto the tree-made staircase, "Um, don't tell anyone I was here...please. I mean...yeah, please don't."

"Who would I tell?"

"I—I don't know." Brent glanced once more at Rho. There was something familiar about her, like seeing someone he met in passing. Beneath the layers of sweaters and jackets covering her body, he couldn't tell her actual size. But she did well to avoid his gaze, masked away by the little branch on her face.

Brent climbed up the lemon staircase, clutching the railing and trying his best to ignore the headache ringing in his ears. Yet it never faltered, the gong in his head rippling through his vertebrae.

When he reached the top of the staircase, he crumpled to the ground in the Senator's Garden, where he stayed until the sun rose over the Newbird Mountains to the North.

CHAPTER FOUR

RHO

Rho waited for Brent to leave before collapsing by the fire. All her life, she'd been waiting for someone to join her in her tunnels. She'd wandered them alone since childhood, dreaming of a friend to explore the world and share secrets. Of all the people who had to enter her hideaway, of all the people it could have been, why did it have to be *Brent Harley*? His silver eyes, marked with stress and fear, left a shadow around her. His words weighed heavier.

A woman in black... Rho exhaled. *But it's only ever been me.*

She picked at the seeds inside her fresh peeled lemon. They found a home in her satchel, mixed with an array of other seeds Rho had collected over the years.

It had to be Brent. Of course it did! She inhaled. Nineteen years! She'd been trying to understand these tunnels and her magic since birth. Now Brent Harley had come toppling into her world and admitted to seeing more of the tunnels in those minutes than she ever fathomed. Why didn't the woman in black show herself? How many times had Rho wandered the tunnels searching–no, begging–for answers?

She ran her name over her tongue, foreign to her. After all these years of planning to tell anyone in the tunnels her real name. But when Brent arrived, she panicked, replacing her identity with a hearsay tale.

He's so stupid. How did he not recognize me? Not hard, Brent, not hard.

Rho exhaled and peered out of the vines again. Except for the misplaced foliage, no sign remained of her unexpected visitor.

"Hello?" Rho called as she stepped into the tunnel.

Her muffled echo responded with the wind. The frigid air sent shivers through her body, and she wrapped her cowl tighter around her face. It proved a good disguise from Brent, complemented by the little branch nestled behind her ear.

Her little branch first blossomed behind her ear the day she was born. White camellias bloomed with it, and her mother buried her alive that same day. Instead of withering away, Rho flourished, giving life to the Senator's camellia bushes and sometimes to the flowers in her hair.

Like the stories said.

Yet today, she had no desire to give life to the flowers, sending her little branch back behind her ear as she moved further away from her secret corner.

She followed the tunnel to a junction where many other paths met. At her feet, the vines and root followed, slithering past her to the empty towering northern wall. Rho checked each tunnel; no one loitered but the occasional dripping of water or the lurching blow of the wind.

"Hello?" she called out again, "Is anyone there?"

The wind howled back.

"Please, if anyone is there...answer me...please!"

Silence.

Someone, please...answer me...please.

Rho withered by the empty wall. She forced away the knot in her throat. Why did she bother coming down here anymore? Every time left her vacant and alone. Childhood memories of children mocking her still haunted her years later after a game of Come Find Me with her peers. *Tunnels?!? You're silly! It's just a tree! I see no tunnels.*

That was over ten years ago. So why not just forget it all, live her life as a simple gardener like her family wanted? There was no reason to return to the earth like this.

There was no reason to be Rho.

Besides, no one cared about a girl who talked to plants.

CHAPTER FIVE

The Effluvium's Soul

Brent lay shivering on the cold ground, picking at the weeds. He tried convincing himself it'd been a dream, but the dried blood on his hand and the pounding in his head told him otherwise. He half expected the woman in black to climb out after him and drag him by his feet back into the endless oblivion beneath the surface.

Or maybe that strange girl, Rho, would reconsider.

He didn't move until the sun ascended over the top of the mountains, sending the Effluvium down the mountain to mask the cattle in fog. The only light came from the subtle glow of the Gardener's Hut at the far end of the garden.

Mr. West, the heavy-set, balding gardener with a wide smile, stood on the porch, smoking. He called out to Brent as he walked by, "Brenton! What're you doing about so early? It's hardly sunup!"

"Oh, hi...um—"

"What's going on, Ric? Who is it?" Another man who Brent recognized as Mr. Smidt came to the doorway, placing his hand on Ric's arm as he peered behind him, "Oh! It's that boy...the Brenty-Boy...the boy who—"

"Yes! It's Brenton!"

Brent retreated on himself, bringing his ears to his shoulders. "I was just out for a walk and—"

"Your ma ain't gonna like that." Mr. West shook his head. "Why don't ya come in for tea and biscuits, hm? We can see if Briannabella's around."

"I hope she's home. Wanna talk with her 'bout somethin'," Mr. Smidt mumbled. "Worried she's gonna go running off or something and then..." the man continued to ramble as he retreated back into the house.

"No, no, it's a'ight," Brent gulped. "It's a'ight...she can...I mean, let her sleep. I'll come by another time."

"You sure, boy? You look pale."

"Yeah, yeah, it's a'ight. It's fine."

Before Mr. West could say another word, Brent bolted down the path and out of the garden.

He walked in a haze while the early morning market bustled with vendors setting up their tents. Old Madame Gonzo bumbled between the vendors, her checklist out and taking stock. Brent still remembered the brief time as her apprentice; the numbers eluded him, but he kept the lists tidy and the vendors in check.

Until the merchants withdrew from Newbird's Arm. A boy with demon eyes had no job running the market, after all.

Brent trailed along the side of the Pit. The red-eyed stare of the Temple gazed over him, where early morning service goers gathered at the front steps, waiting for the doors to open. A few guards loitered on the railing, yawning and disinterested, save for Cadet Christof Carver, who peered up at the Year Glass. At the front of the crowd stood Jemma.

"Jem!" Brent called out to her, but she vanished into the Temple before he reached the front. The rest of the congregate whisked him into the Temple.

The Temple's doors opened to a long hall, with crevasses beneath the stained-glass windows. Patrons occupied them, kneeled beneath the array of colors, hands pressed to the smaller Year Glasses on the floor. They didn't move, bodies draped in simple smocks, faces turned downwards as they recited scripture to themselves.

Brent took a seat on a bench in the back and gazed up towards the Year Glass at the top of the atrium. The Year Glass counted each passing second with a metallic red liquid dripping down its sides. On the surrounding walkway, Elder Don Van cast a shadow over the room below. In the back of the room, the guard gathered, heralded by Captain Carver.

Brent's attention shifted when a younger brother of the Order hit a small drum beside the stairwell. It announced the arrival of Brother Roy Al, draped in emerald robes, his long brown hair whisked up by the gentle breeze blowing through the doorway. The young brother with the drum followed behind him, the two men carrying an aura of serenity in their presence.

Brother Roy Al strode to the podium. He lit the candle on its surface. A cloud of smoke filled the air above the congregate, mingling with the flame, and drifting between the colors of gray and blue, ruby and emeralds. The Brother enchanted them all. He was not much older than Brent, but he held the congregate in the palm of his hands, detailing the room with kindness and smiles. With a mere nod, he commanded the congregate to bow their heads. A simple chant turned into a spell, lifting Brent into a cloud of complacency.

Exuberance,

The Year such ends,
A snowfall blesses our dens.
Chilled.
Cold.
So does the air.
The sand counting as the hour's curve.
And as it falls,
So does the snow.

The snow comes like the sun,
She falls.
And Effluvium marches on,
Wraps you tight,
Protects you from the demons.
Dark.
They hide as the night grows nigh.
Alas the Effluvium fights with might,
Pacing those who steal your rights.
The moon stares down as you
As I
Wait for the Effluvium to soothe
Those damned.
The demons, those demons,
They'll fight but fail.
The Effluvium serves the pure,
Those with a soul prevail.

Back demon! Say you be true.
I have a pure soul!

Cast aside those woes,
Those unfortunate woes,
That the demons so desire.
And remember me,
Remember you,
Remember the snowfall,
As been for a thousand years tall.

Remember Effluvium is watching,
It kills the Year clean,
The evil shrivels,
The demons falter,
And you can speak alas.
Say it loud.
Louder.
Say it now.

I shall not be your agent!

Sing it to the dark sky,
And the sun will rise again.

I shall not be your agent!

Repeat it.
Memorize it.
Remember the Year as it bores.

I shall not be your agent!

Why I ask?

Because.

Why?

I am the Effluvium's Soul!

"I am the Effluvium's Soul!" Brent repeated with the congregate. The words fell from empty lips. Brent felt out of place amongst the droves of worshipers, pressing their Year Glass necklaces to their mouths. He curled in on himself, placing his fingers to his leather cusp and black stamp instead.

"We say this prayer every Year," Brother Roy Al preached. "It only seems fitting that the Year ends on another snowfall. It says something about the Year that ends and the Year to come. A thousand Years we have sang this tune, and each Year for those thousand, we reflect on such exuberance. Happiness marked this Year: marriages, babies, vagrants clearing their souls...and the strongest market square we have ever seen! A beautiful end to a beautiful Year, no doubt. And who knows what next Year will bring! We'll hear of our young folk traveling far away to the Capitol or across the sea! More babies will be born, more families made, and a flourishing garden will continue blessing our homes. We'll each begin fresh, yes? So, let's celebrate at the Year Birth Festival tomorrow. The moon may be dark, but we are the Effluvium's soul. So, ban together, pray, and ward the demons away!"

Applause erupted. The words of the Effluvium's Soul teetered around Brent, locking him in place. If the woman in black waltzed through the doors right then, he'd be helpless.

Brother Roy Al's chants cut off Brent's thoughts, "Now, for the last full day until the Year is reborn, let's cross boundaries! Unite with those who stand in the back and forget our—"

"Brother Roy Al!"

From twisted stairway Elder Don Van marched down from the Year Glass. A squat man with silver hair and stark blue eyes, his gaze darted about the atrium, his ruby red cloak skimming the floor. Captain Carver left his post in the back, joining Elder Don Van as he paused a few rows away from Brent.

"Elder Don Van." Brother Roy Al bowed, his glasses almost slipping off his nose. "Service is nearing its conclusion. What do you bring on this lovely morn?"

"The word of the Order, as it shall be." The Elder peered up to the Year Glass and said, "The Year shall bring a fresh cleanse to our populace, yes, yes indeed. But it is only if we choose to be as vigilant as the Effluvium, keeping our promise to watch for those with demons on their backs. Magic is futile, silver eyes belong to Death's demons, and storytellers will bring a plague upon our homes. Lies belong to magic, and magic gives birth to vagrancy. So, Brother Roy Al, I do ask...why did you allow a damn vagrant into the Temple today?"

Brent shrunk into the pews.

"Pardon?" Brother Roy Al straightened his back.

Captain Carver walked into the seats a few rows back and yanked a woman draped in red, the black stamp tattooed across her wrist, to her feet. The Captain dragged her into the center of the aisle. "This is repulsive, *brother*! You let vagrants into your services? Despicable!"

"I believe all should have a chance to enter the Effluvium's arms," Brother Roy Al stated, standing his ground. "Madame Ursula here has not done anything wrong but open her mind."

Elder Don Van waved them away. "Get her out of here, Captain. Brother Roy Al, I expect you in my chambers in the next hour. We have much to discuss." The Elder ventured back up the stairway and towards the Year Glass without looking back.

The atrium dripped with silence.

Then came the loud crack of a whip.

A scream.

And more silence.

Brent's throat tightened at the sound. All else spoke in whispers, leaving the Temple behind with their heads down, never making eye contact.

"Brent?" Jemma's voice caught Brent's attention. "What are you doing here?"

"Jem...oh, hi. I was, um...I needed to—I wanted to—" The words stuck to his tongue, and he looked to the Year Glass above them. *If I tell her, then I'm next.* "I just want to—I mean, if we're going to marry, I thought I'd try to attend...for you. I guess—I mean..." He chewed on his lip. "I'm sorry."

"Oh, well..." Jemma's face softened. "That's kind of you, Brent. But you shouldn't come unless by my side. Otherwise...well, you saw."

Brent nodded.

Jemma took his hand, their identical triangles lining up near-perfectly next to each other, before saying, "I appreciate the efforts, Brent. Really. I do. I know you mean well, but it's best that you stay in the shadows until the Effluvium blesses our union. It's for the best."

"Yeah, I don't know about that..."

"Trust me," She squeezed his hand, then hastened out of the Temple with the rest of the congregate.

Brent followed from the back. Outside, the vagrant from the Temple huddled on the ground, blood dripping from her bare back and her robe draped around her breasts. She gave out a pained sob as Captain Carver walked away from the scene, tightening his whip onto his waist. Cadet Christof Carver and another cadet, a large fellow with an atrocious face like a wide-eyed gecko, shoved the woman back to the Pit.

Brent shook back the gong playing repetitive songs in his head. *Everything is okay...everything is fine. They didn't see what you saw...or if you saw...or that you saw... You're fine!*

Brent hurried from the market, fumbling to light a smoke against the billowing winds. It caught the light as he arrived at the train station. A few beggars and travelers gathered on the steps, singing songs in ancient tongues. He collapsed next to an old woman untangling an old fishing net.

Chewing on the edge of the smoke, Brent picked again at his leather cusp. *You should run,* Bria's voice chimed in his head. It'd be easy. The train chugged from over the mountain. A gold coin, and he'd be free. But then where would he run? Alone, he was helpless. What good was a storyteller in a land where stories were taboo?

Brent blew a puff of smoke. It mingled with the air, sheathing the old woman beside him, growing thick around her face.

Then, she disappeared.

Brent blinked once, looked at his smoke, then back at the space where the woman sat. A misty aura filled the space, trailing off to the bushes across the road.

"What the..." Brent pursued the mist. A buzzing rose in his ears as he hurried.

At last, he saw her again: the woman in black.

CHAPTER SIX

The Woman in Black

Shite!" Brent tripped backward.

"Well, sards," the woman in black hissed.

Brent dropped his smoke on the ground, his knees giving out beneath him. "Are you—are you going to—I mean, are you here to kill me or curse me...or something?"

"Oh great, he's a milksop." The woman motioned to the mist, her voice as shrewd as in the tunnels. "Just what I need."

"You're—you're a demon, aren't you? You're coming for...coming for...shite I should have listened!"

The woman's gazed pierced him, "I am not one of your demons, boy."

"No one can see you and the tunnels—I mean, I—I..." He dug his fingers into the dirt, not daring to look up, and cried, "I'm going crazy."

The woman exhaled, slinging the net over her shoulder and looking past him. In the daylight, she didn't seem as menacing. After all, she was only a few years older than Brent, with blue eyes that pierced the sky, hair as dark as her cloak.

Brent refused to meet her stare, "Why can't anyone see...why am I...what are you?"

"Caroline."

"What—what's a Caroline?"

"No, that is my name, you dolt," she guffawed. "I am Caroline, the Eighth Member of the Council of Mist Keepers, Illusionist to the Second World."

"I—I don't understand what that means."

"Basically," the woman named Caroline paused, twiddling her thumbs, "I am Death."

Brent blinked. He ran the word "death" over his tongue twice, before producing an obscene noise that resembled a pathetic elephant, and then darting back into the market. He rushed past a few vendors, almost tripping over a smaller woman with a trolley of baked goods. When a few toppled off, Brent stopped to pick them up, only to receive a smack of the hand and a few glares. He apologized and shuffled off again, finding a spot behind an oak tree.

"Shite! Shite! Shite! I'm...this is crazy. I'm going crazy!" Brent laughed and wiped his upper lip.

"Yes, it is quite crazy for you to behave like this."

Brent jumped. Once again, Caroline stood beside him.

"You're here. How did you...I don't want to—I..." He bolted again, this time weaving towards the woods. Surely if he kept an irregular path, he'd lose her. He staggered over the roots and along the walls of the Pit, hopping across the rocks in an icy river. Ice and leaves crackled beneath his feet, and the farther he clamored up a foothill and through the dense bushes, the more rampant his breathing grew.

Brent stopped at a fallen tree and glanced down at the path. Anywhere farther than this met dense thickets that blinded even the sharpest eyes.

I'm too young to die. Brent collapsed on the log and gripped his knees, *Go away. Be in my head. Please.*

He snatched a branch from the ground and removed a few pieces of bark. *A hero would fashion this into a blade. Why didn't I take up woodworking? I could fashion this into a knife and then—* He dug his fingers deeper into the branch, watching as the mist thickened again.

He swung the branch at Caroline as she emerged from it.

She caught it easily. "Really? What do you intend to do with this, Brenton?"

"You—you know my name?" Brent gulped, "Are you here to—are you going to...am I gonna die?"

"Consarn it. This is why I hate using the word *death*. It misrepresents everything." Caroline pinched her nose and exhaled. "No, I am not here to *kill* you. It does not work like that. Fate has another destiny for you, it may seem. If you believe in that malarkey."

"You've gotta be...shite, you're in my head, right? You gotta be..." Brent closed his eyes. The gong in his head erupted again. "I should—I mean, I should—I can't—"

"Oh, lovely," Caroline crossed her arms, speaking again to the mist rather than to Brent. "Come, it is obvious you are frightened, but we shall talk. You shall learn."

"I don't know...I mean this...what about—I—"

Before Brent objected further, she pulled him through the mist and into the heart of a tree.

On the other side of the tree, they arrived in the tunnels. They weren't how Brent remembered them, though. Rather than the eerie dripping of water or the slithering vines, the tunnels existed in a rainbow effervescence. Brent blinked when it clicked.

The Effluvium.

It moved with them, dancing in and out of the foliage on the walls, basking in the dim light. It had to be the Effluvium; what else would encase the world in such wonder? Would anything else hide magic but the Order's god?

For a fleeting moment, Brent's mind wandered to that strange girl, hidden as much by the Effluvium as this world. Why couldn't she see Caroline? Who was she? Why did she feel so familiar? He didn't have time to ponder it, as Caroline grabbed him by his arm and marched him down the tunnel.

They moved in silence, Brent's entire body stiff as Caroline guided him. He stammered and shivered as he spoke. "So you're Death? Like if someone dies, you come, Death? The demon—Death thing?"

"We have gone by many names over the years. Currently, we call ourselves the Mist Keepers." Caroline shrugged.

"Mist Keepers..." Brent's thoughts darted again to the Effluvium. "But I'm not dead, right?"

She grimaced. "That is why I have a distaste for the name *Death.* It implies that I control when your heart stops."

"So...so you're not here to...you're not gonna kill me?"

"Nah."

"But then, what are you? I mean, if you're not a demon and you don't kill..." He shook his head. "The stories say you—they say you are the worst demon of them all. That if you see Death, then..." Brent trailed off.

Then there's no hope for you.

"Stories, pah! They're all made up in the end." Caroline plucked a flower off a nearby vine.

"Yeah...a'ight," Brent tittered, "but what do you want?"

"Ah, yes." Caroline slowed and gave him a thoughtful look. "How shall I put this without scaring you off?"

Brent nearly laughed. "I'm already scared. Just tell me."

"Well, it seems that fate has a plan for you...or something. It took me by surprise, hence my attack yesterday. I apologize for that, by the way."

Brent grunted.

"Yes, well...fate has played this game, I find," Caroline continued, beating around the bush, "and has therefore decided I am too old to continue my duties. So, without me even knowing, it decided to find me an apprentice."

"Apprentice?" Brent stopped walking, "*Me*?"

"Oh, look, you have some form of reasoning! This is exciting!"

Brent's mind raced over the past couple years. Every merchant turned down his apprenticeship, every artisan sent him away; but here came strolling a demon with an open opportunity. He gulped. "Me, though? I—I'm stamped. I can't. I mean...no one gave me an apprenticeship. And you're...and I'm—"

"Oh, forget it, his reasoning is gone. What a milksop."

"This can't be...it doesn't—I don't...you can't be!"

Caroline groaned.

"You're *mole* people!"

For a second, Brent thought Caroline would hit him. Instead, she stopped and howled with laughter. "That's a new one!"

"I mean—there're tunnels... like moles." He squirmed. "And mist... misty moles..."

"Oh, Brenton, these tunnels are much more than that. Come."

They rounded a bend and entered a junction. Shaft entries filled the walls, except for to the north, where a pair of smooth-cut wooden doors stretched to the endless ceiling Golden doorknobs shone in the center of a carved tree. As they drew closer, Brent noticed the etchings of tiny warriors, mothers, and stories connected to form the tree. He could hear his own heartbeat as they closed in on it. Or was it the door?

Bu-dump, bu-dump, bu-dump.

His head spun, and his body quaked; maybe he was waking up from a nightmare, and he'd find himself shivering in an infirmary bed. The Order was probably banging on his door to take him away, to cleanse him of these convoluted thoughts.

He didn't wake up, still fixated on the door as it swung open. A soft glow poured out from the doors, and once its light filled the tunnel, Brent laughed with relief.

Books.

More books than Brent ever fathomed. The hallway before him basked in an eternal kaleidoscopic glow from the misty orbs filling the endless ceiling above. It led to a staircase where a row of glass walkways extended above, weaving between shelves and arches like a complex spider web. Mist moved about it, but no one else graced the psychedelic exterior.

Yet, Brent's awe landed on the books. With the dampened scent of the tunnels behind him, the stench of parchment waffled in the air, an aroma so soothing, Brent forgot all his worries. The stories beckoned him, and for a moment he swore every single tale spoke to him at once, shrouding him in an endless blanket of heroism and villainy.

"Welcome to the library of the Council!" Caroline said, pride filling her voice.

Brent continued gawking.

"Oh good, this shut you up." She pushed him forward and urged, "Go on, take a gander."

The mist stroked Brent's skin as he dashed over to the first bookshelf and ran his finger along the spines. The whole experience was nauseating, the mere excitement sending shadow spots over his vision, but he did not let it hinder him. After all, there were so many titles, so many words! His entire life, stories had been reduced to facts in *The History of Rosada, The One Scripture,* and whatever newsprint he managed to get his hands upon. Those words he cradled to his chest. But now there were so many books...in a real library! Not some mendacious bookshelf in the schoolhouse or the Temple! New worlds, new stories...he wouldn't have to make up petty tales for his own entertainment ever again!

He faced Caroline. "You live here?"

"With the rest of the Council of Mist Keepers, yes." Caroline brimmed with joy as she motioned around them. "This library is our palace."

"The rest...so I won't be the first apprentice?"

"No, no, the Council has a history spanning thousands of years. There are eight of us...now nine if you count yourself. I was once in your shoes, Brenton—"

"Brent. I go by Brent."

“Pfft,” Caroline sputtered. “*Brent,* the Mist Keeper, if you insist.”

“What’s so—why are you laughing? Your name is Caroline!”

“At least it has multiple syllables. *Brent.*”

“Fine, call me whatever you want.” Brent picked a book off the shelf with a title he could read, a flat picture book displaying a fairy dancing in the snow.

The Snow Fairy

Brent ran his fingers across the pages. If this was death, at least paradise was indeed a library.

Another bought of nausea interrupted his thoughts, a chartreuse gas passing through the air. The books numbed the confusion, but reality knocked on his skull, tapping in rhythm to the clicking on the staircase.

Tap. Tap. Tap.

He turned to Caroline, gripping tight to the book. “What is that?”

Caroline peered up the staircase and beamed. “Ah! The others!”

“Others? Right...others. A council...”

“Yes, yes!” She ran towards the staircase. There was something odd about watching her move, almost child-like, as she darted up the glass walkway. Two men and a woman waited for her at the top. "Brent, come," Caroline beckoned. "This is my old master, Alojzy," she motioned to the first man, a stout man with a large nose and a receding hairline, whose dark eyes pierced into Brent from where he stood. "And this is Aelia, the second member of the Council. She trained under Ningursu thousands of years ago," she raced on, motioning to the thin, pale birdlike woman with beady eyes and a wide jaw. "And this is—"

"Caroline, slow down. You are overwhelming the poor boy," the final man held up his hand. An ochre scar cut through his sewn-closed right eyelid.

Brent shuddered as another bout of nausea ripped through him and clutched the book like a lifeline.

"I apologize, Tomás, excitement may have gotten the better of me." Caroline turned around to face Brent. "I shall teach you all of this! You'll listen and learn, and you'll be a fantastic Mist Keeper."

"I—I'm sorry...I'm confused..."

"Of course, you are, son, of course," the stout man, Alojzy, said.

Aelia spoke next with a shrill, callous voice. "Caroline, what shall we do with you?"

"Pardon? I did what you asked of me!" Caroline snapped. "I didn't hurt him this time!"

“Yes, but we asked you to wait,” Alojzy added. “We shall talk about this presently.”

“Why? We can talk now!”

“I believe it is best if your apprentice goes home.” Tomás walked over to Brent and placed a hand on his shoulder. His one green eye twinkled. “My boy, you are pale. Go home. Relax...breathe...rest. Do you understand?”

“I, um...” Brent marveled once again at the library.

“The books will be here when you return. Go. You are overwhelmed.”

“I’m not—”

“Yes, you are.” Tomás guided Brent down the steps and towards the doorway. “Go home. Relax. We’ll be with you soon.”

“I—”

Tomás ushered Brent into the tunnels. The door slammed behind him, and a thick fog draped over it, sending the junction plummeting into darkness.

CHAPTER SEVEN

On the Mountain

Rho returned to the tunnels after spending the day in the Capitol, exploring the skyscrapers and stone jungles made from man. She located a small library that once belonged to the Academy of Rosada, hidden away by debris leftover from the Smoke Riots. Before she had a chance to break open the locked door, the guard rounded the bend, sending her fleeing back to the tunnels.

Truth-be-told, it wasn't any different from her other adventures. Some days, the tunnels took her far out east to Yilk, the Land of Giants. Other days, she ventured south to the metallic and glass cities of Proveniro. Just the other day, she even ended up in the Independent City of Mert, marveling at the magic tricks conducted in the streets, unafraid of the Order's watchful gaze. Some days, Rho dreamed of making a life in Mert, free to practice her magic and listen to stories.

No matter how much she yearned to escape her mundane life and keep her adventures alive, she always returned: to her father, who grew distraught if she disappeared for days on end, to her grandmama who made her warm teas, and to the place she called home.

Rho shook her head, repositioning her scarf, so it intermingled with her little branch on her face as she arrived in the tunnels, once again letting the mist enshroud her in its protective embrace. The tunnels sheltered Rho for as long as she could remember from the Order, from the Guard, and from all others who thought magic belonged to demons and demons alone. For over ten years now, she'd learned every nook and cranny of the tunnels. Nothing threatened her. No one dared appear. She was free to practice magic, to be a Magii, as some may have called her, and see the world.

Until Brent.

All day, Rho thought about him, *Brent Harley*, quivering on the floor. Why him? It could have been anyone else on the planet! It had to be *him*.

She kicked the ground in frustration before following her vines back through the tunnels. Once again, they belonged to her. When she was a child, she considered the tunnels her only friends; the branches and bushes gathering on the walls flickered with white camellias to guide her on the next adventure. As she got older, the branches bowed to her as their queen, like that story whispered in the shadows from the Order. Rhodana the Forest Queen, a tale of a warrior who saved her forest from the men who burned rather than give life. Yet, as she grew older, Rho disregarded it. *They're just plants. It's all just a story.* The thoughts belonged to her real self—the girl who behaved and caught no notice from the Guard, the pious girl with a smile that went from cheek to cheek. Her persona beneath the earth didn't belong up there. If she showed her true colors, then the Order would knock on her door and drag her to the Pit.

Just like she saw them do to the others.

The sound of gagging interrupted her thoughts as she entered the junction. She reached behind her ear to tap her little branch, reassuring herself the mask remained, and nestled her nose into her cowl. The dim light from the torch cast a shadow over the gag's culprit.

Brent. *Dammit.*

He convulsed a few times, then wilted onto the ground, gripping a flat book to his head. A part of Rho wanted to toss away the persona and show herself, but she kept her mask tight as she conjured up the ability to speak.

"Hey!"

Brent looked up.

"So, you came back, huh?"

"Oh, hi...uh, yeah," he croaked. "I guess so..."

"You guess?"

"I dunno..." His eyes darted along the junction before fixating on Rho.

She recoiled.

"You're—you're that Rho girl...from the room. The room with the vines and plants and shite...right?"

"Yeah, I kind of saved you from the invisible woman," Rho carped.

"Yeah, guess you did." Brent knitted his eyebrows together and flipped through the book on his lap. "So that—that means that you're not...you're not one of them?"

"One of who?"

"The people. The Council or whatever they call themselves...the Death mole people." He motioned to the empty wall. "They live in here."

"The wall?"

"No, behind the—the giant door!"

Rho squinted at the wall. *A door. Of course.*

"Don't you see it? It's right here!" Brent's voice cracked.

"I don't," Rho replied. "I'm sorry."

Brent rested his head against his knees and closed his eyes. Rho understood. She first discovered the tunnels at eight years old while playing a game of *Come Find Me* in the gardens. After, upon climbing out of the tunnels and rushing to her peers, all they saw was a patch of grass. They laughed in her face and said she was making up stories; they told her to be careful, or she'd end up with the black stamp. They left her panicking that her mind had gone awry. One person stayed with her.

And she'd stay with him now even if he didn't remember that day long, long ago.

"Hey..." She sat beside him. "Just because I can't see anything, it doesn't mean it's not real."

"But what if you're not real? What if...what if I'm crazy?"

"I am pretty sure I'm real." Rho waved her hand in front of his face. "See?"

"Could be in my head..."

"Trust me," she said, "I've been exploring these tunnels since I was a child, and I've been asking myself these same questions. There was no one else down here until now. What if you're part of *my* insanity? We have no clue! So, I'd say trust your eyes. If you see something, it's got to be real...somehow."

Brent's face softened. "So you're here alone?"

"I don't live down here if that's what you think." Rho scoffed. "But...I haven't seen anyone else in the tunnel...so...if you saw someone...that's big."

Brent grew quiet, but Rho wanted to scream. *Why does he get to see these people? I've been here for such a long time!*

Her anger subsided as Brent smiled crookedly and said in his usual mellow tone, "Thank you."

"For what?"

"I'm not sure. I feel a bit better though." He kept smiling, then flushed. "Oh, right! I'm Brent, by the way. Realized I never said..."

She sucked in her lips. Part of her wished to yell at him and tell him he was an idiot. Newbird's Arm wasn't that large. They had gone to school together...they had been friends! When she responded, though, she answered with, "Nice to meet you, Brent."

His grin grew wider, crooking to the left of his mouth, the same smile she'd seen over the years. The one that was real.

She smiled back beneath her cowl, then asked, "Can I show you something? Something you can tell is real?"

"Oh, uh...sure." He gathered his book into his arms, and they stood.

"Come on!" She motioned him through a tunnel. It climbed upwards, withering in and out of roots of the trees and the scrapping vines. A few of them reached stroked Rho's skin.

Rho slowed her pace as Brent hobbled behind her.

"You okay?" she called back.

"Yeah, I'm fine...just tired," Brent croaked. "You?"

"Why wouldn't I be?"

"I invaded your home, and you said..." He winced, still clutching that book to his chest. "You said you don't know anything. That must be...I mean, that must feel terrible. Alone down here. It's so dark and...depressing."

"They've always just been my tunnels."

"There has to be a reason, though."

"The world's not that complicated. Things just happen by chance, I think."

They approached a short rope ladder ascending towards the ceiling. Half of its rungs waited in tatters. With a wave of her hand, Rho commanded the roots to crawl from the land above and enshroud the ladder.

"Honestly," Rho muttered as she gripped the vines, "I'd be lying if I didn't say I was jealous of you."

"Why? I mean this—this is...it's amazing! You're a Magii! I mean, I've only ever heard rumors and hearsay, but...you have magic, and that's amazing!"

Rho flushed beneath her scarf. "It's nothing. I'm just a gardener."

"No...this is more than that!"

Rho shook her head. "Come on, there're more impressive things out there."

They climbed to the top and arrived at the peak of the Newbird foothills, coated in snow beneath the arms of hibernating trees. The sun painted the sky orange with wisps of clouds.

Rho brushed the snow from her knees and glanced back at Brent as he toppled to the ground. She watched as he gazed out at Newbird's Arm below, his eyes widening. Rho knew that expression: pure and utter disbelief. The way the dim lights outlined the town, trailing along the roads and around the Temple to the Senator's Gardens, made their town look enchanted.

The Pit hid in the firelight and trees, the grandest spectacle of all. From the top of the mountain, they saw inside that horrendous work camp. Small dilapidated homes gathered behind the walls, bordering up the foot of the mountain. Old Merchants gathered by the gate as the Black Market lit up along the fence, exchanging coins and food for morose deeds. Most, though, gathered around the bonfires to sing meaningless songs and tell tales to make the Order squirm, dreaming of a better day far from the mines and fields. Rho learned the ways of the vagrants by mere observation.

"That's my home!" Brent pointed to a house near the edge of town. It looks so small! Shite!" He put his hands behind his head and laughed. "I'm on a mountain! My ma would kill me!" Then, his face softened and he added, "It—it's all so—I mean, it looks so dead from here..."

"Most of the world is dead," Rho remarked.

Brent glanced at her. "Sorry?"

Rho wished she hadn't said anything. Over all the years she'd spent exploring the world, one thing had become obvious: while the Senator's Garden flourished in greenery, everything else sat in bole and fallow.

"What do you mean most of the world is dead?" Brent pressed.

"The tunnels, like the ones that took us here...I use them to see the world," Rho answered. "They're magic or something; they can take me everywhere. But everywhere I go, everything is just...dead. People exist, but they don't live. Trees don't bloom. Flowers wilt. Water runs dry. It's like...death has plagued the earth, except for Newbird's Arm. Which I guess is why I always return." Her gaze landed on the Year Glass. "I sometimes wonder if it's the Order's fault. They've made laws to rid us of magic and even take away our ability to believe. No one tells stories...not in public. Mostly. The Order is killing us."

"That's a bold statement." Brent followed her gaze. "True. But bold."

"It's not like they can hear me."

"And you trust me not to tell?"

With my life. She motioned to the book in his arms, "You're carrying a story around right now. I think you probably agree."

Brent glanced at the book as if he'd forgotten about it. "Oh, yeah. I grabbed it..."

"From the invisible people?"

"Yeah." He flipped open to the first page, filled with illustrations of a tiny woman with crystal blue hair. She rode on the back of snowflakes through the sky, fighting birds and drops of rain. It was a children's story, but it reminded Rho of the few stories whispered in the shadows. The most prominent, the story of Rhodana the Forest Queen, rang true across every walkway where storytellers spoke. The ending was never the same, but it always began with the same tune.

Rhodana, the Forest Queen.
She loves to laugh; she hates to scream.
She promised the world a reverie,
Rhodana.

Brent gazed at the picture book. He looked handsome, the moonlight highlighting the smudged dirt on his cheeks, his silver eyes glistening like stars. Rho reached for his hand but pulled back before touching him. *Stop, don't be ridiculous. It's better this way.*

Brent's stomach broke the silence, and he flushed. "Sorry."

"Have you eaten?"

"Um...no."

Rho reached into the pouch of seeds on her hip. She pulled out an apple seed and waved her hand. It blossomed into a small sapling, climbing towards the sky, then gave birth to the red fruit, before withering away.

Brent took the fruit and turned it in his hand. "This is...it's amazing."

As the night wore on, Rho produced more fruit for Brent to eat while flipping through the Snow Fairy book. It was a standard tale of a girl trying to save the world from an eternal winter. Rho would have liked it as a child. Now, it seemed pointless. No one girl could save all this; not when young men had black stamps and old women cried themselves to sleep at night.

Once Brent's stomach stopped talking, Rho scattered a few more seeds across the ground. With a flick of her hand, the seeds bloomed into an array of irises and violets. Shen then motioned them with her finger, and the stems of each flower braided into one long stream.

"Amazing." Brent's voice startled her.

"They're just plants..."

"Just plants!?!" Brent exclaimed. "You've brought them to life! You've—you've made something...something beautiful!"

"At least someone thinks so."

"I mean, if what you say is true, and the world is dying, couldn't you help? Couldn't you bring the world back? Or...something! It's—it's amazing!"

"Yeah, it's not that simple...as you're aware." Rho motioned to the black stamp on his wrist. He followed and repositioned his leather cuff, instantly uncomfortable.

"Yeah, I guess not." He removed a smoke from his pocket and lit it. He offered her a puff, but she shook her head. He sighed and murmured, "Wish it was more like those damn stories."

"We all do." Rho pulled a few more seeds from her bag as she continued. "It's not like I can do much with my magic as it is. I can't practice in the open. Even if the Order allowed it...it's not like anyone is born with magic like this anymore. Where magic is practiced, everything is parlor tricks. I'm just a girl with flowers hiding from the Order, just like you. Now that magic has disappeared, the Order has fixated on others...like children born with silver eyes, storytellers, and those who are different. They want the world cleansed into some picture-perfect ideal they believe in...so they're getting rid of everything that makes it spectacular."

"And that's why you say the world...that the world is dead?"

Rho frowned. "I mean, I think so at least. But there are still gems. I can show you one day if you trust me."

"I'd like that."

Rho wove together her flowers as they watched the town glow with the hidden lights of the Pit. Once Rho finished braiding the flowers, she positioned them on her head like a crown. Brent laughed, but their eyes never met.

Night overwhelmed the tops of the mountains, and at some point, Brent fell asleep, holding his jacket to his chin as a blanket. Despite the frost on the ground, the Effluvium exuded a quilt of warmth. Even with its comforting embrace, Rho never fell under fatigue's spell. She watched as the town descended into an early morning slumber, the Pit losing its bolster.

Dawn eventually made its way to them, as it always did, beginning with the Effluvium's lackadaisical descent from the mountains to the farmlands. The first chimes of the Temple rang, and only then did Rho realize morning would be upon them soon.

"Brent." She nudged him. "It's almost the morning."

He mumbled, "Five minutes."

"Brent..."

He cracked open an eye and then jolted up. His face went from confusion to frustration and then finally arrived at realization. "Shite!" he muttered. "Ma—Ma's gonna kill me! I haven't been home in two days! Shite! I promised her I would start getting better before Year Birth. Shite...shite shite!"

"It's okay. I can help you back home," Rho replied.

He pulled at his hair as he continued to panic. "It's not okay! My ma...she's been so worried...and...and...I turn twenty-one soon, and my betrothal might mean nothing if I don't get my act together and...shite!"

"Haven't you always—" Rho stopped herself. If she said anything that gave away her identity, they might both be at risk. She redirected her statement and asked, "Do you not spend nights away from your mother much?"

"No, no, I do...it's just that...she worried. My dad's in the Pit and if I end up there...I mean...it'll break her. Every day I'm not home she worries more that I ended up in the Pit, too. I'm a selfish prick and didn't think about her...shite."

Rho placed a hand on his shoulder. "A lot has happened. Don't blame yourself. Come on, I'll take you home."

Brent didn't say anything else as she guided him to the entrance to the tunnels between two aspen trees.

Brent placed a foot on the ladder before looking up at Rho with that dumb crooked smile again. "Thank you. You've been real kind."

"Why wouldn't I be?"

"I invaded your tunnels. And I've got a black stamp." The smile faded. "Most people aren't as nice. It means a lot and I wanna make it up to you..."

"You don't have to do that."

"I want to," he insisted, "So if I—if I learn anything about the tunnels or you or something...I'll tell you. You deserve to know."

"Thank you," Rho choked. "That means a lot to me."

CHAPTER EIGHT

YEAR BIRTH

Brent followed Rho back through the tunnels to the fields where no one would see him. Before he had a moment to thank her, the girl disappeared into the tunnel's abyss once again. There still was something familiar about her, although Brent couldn't put his finger on it.

He pondered it as he smoked by the cows. He couldn't have met her before, right? If she was from Newbird's Arm, surely she was in the Pit. But why did he feel so comfortable around her? All the potential explanations made no sense, so he tossed them aside and stared towards the mountains.

The sun climbed into the sky, creating shadow puppets from the foothill's peaks. Brent beamed when he looked up at them from below now. *I was there...right up there! Ma would've killed me!* He exhaled a puff of smoke and chuckled. A headache nestled in his head, and when he closed his eyes, his memories returned to the library and the woman in black.

No. She had a name.

Caroline.

I finally have a chance to live. Me, Brent Harley...the Apprentice to Death! He shook his head. It was a stupid thought; after all, it could have been a dream.

Although, if the book in his coat pocket indicated anything, it proved he saw *something*.

Brent finished his smoke. Already, the town had begun its hustle and bustle in preparation for Year Birth at the sun's apex. They opened the atrium around the Year Glass, so the glass itself cast a ruby shadow over the market square. Vendors lined the streets, selling miniature year glasses and other goods to commemorate the event. Steam puffed from the engine at the platform, mingling with the mist.

He walked along the perimeter, hands in his pocket. Guards gathered along the fence of the Pit where the vagrants gathered, hands outstretched, offering services and begging for food. Brent glanced once at his father, standing in the back of the crowd. His father sucked in his lips and waved once, wearing the same tired eyes

Brent saw in the mirror each morning. Brent quickly looked away. While he would have loved to wave back or speak to his father, every time he got closer to the vagrants, it was more likely they wouldn't let him return to his normal life. They belonged to two different worlds.

Brent did not stay long by the fence, his mind immediately fleeing to his mother. The Guard watched him, wearing their formal uniforms for Year Birth with the Order's hourglass-shaped symbol on their sleeve. One wrong move and he'd find a new home behind the fence with his father. He couldn't do that to his mother, not after everything.

Little do they know the truth. I probably do belong there now. Death's a demon, right? Guess the Order has a right to hate me.

He ducked into the market square, where a crowd had already begun gathering around the Temple's stairs. He began to search for his mother and sister, but his attention drifted instead to Bria. She stood towards the back of the crowd, her hand resting on her father's arm, their dog at their heels. She wore a dress the color of the sky, white flowers weaved into the braid resting on her shoulder.

"Bria!" He rushed over to her and grabbed her hands. "You look...I mean, you look...you're beautiful!"

"Brent! What are you doing?" Bria ushered him away from the crowd and behind a wide oak, "You shouldn't be—"

"I'm allowed to tell you that much, aren't I?" Brent placed a hand on her cheeks. "It's just that you—you look like...I mean, you're like spring."

Color filled her cheeks, but she pushed away his hands. "Are you feeling okay? You usually aren't so forward."

"I feel great!" Brent beamed. *If only I could explain without sounding crazy! I have an apprenticeship, Bria! I'm not useless after all!*

"But you're covered in dirt." Bria wiped his cheek with the edge of her shawl.

"I always am. I mean, it's not unusual."

She smiled, so her nose wrinkled.

"Life's gonna get better, Bri!" Brent leaned forward and whispered, "I have so much to tell you."

"It's only been two days since we last saw each other!"

"It feels like a lifetime! And I know you'll listen."

She turned over his hand, following his triangular betrothal mark with her finger. "We have a lot to talk about, and we need to do it soon before you marry."

"Fuck that, Bri. It's stupid!"

"Brent..."

"I wanna be with you, Bria. I want to—"

"HARLEY!" Someone grabbed Brent by the back of his shirt and tossed him on the ground.

"Christof! Leave him alone!" Bria shouted.

Brent squinted. Cadet Christof Carver stood over him, glaring at him with the same hardened stare as his father. A sneer ran rampant on his lips as he pressed his boot to Brent's neck.

"Chris—Christof..." Brent choked, "I'm not doing anything. I did nothing wrong."

"You best drift on outta here, Harley. You got Jemma; keep away from this one."

"Fuck off!" Bria sneered. "I can talk to who I want!"

"Doll, you better watch your tongue now, a'ight?" Christof retorted and loosened his grip on Brent, "People will start calling you a quiff like the rest of them ladies in the Pit. Ain't wanna end up there, right?"

Bria's nostrils flared.

"Cadet," Brent choked on his own laughter, "you're...I mean...I—I'm not really gonna—I don't really think anyone will—I mean, we don't respect someone trying to act like his father."

"Shut your mouth, Harley."

"You'd make a good villain in a story or something," Brent continued, croaking as he spoke. "The giant...mean...troll, Christof, came down from his mountain. He stole girls against their will to steer into wedlock. A hundred and five wives and none ever loved him. Poor troll. Sad troll who just wants his daddy to love—"

Clunk. Christof's shoe hit against Brent's forehead.

Then, his head hit a root, and he tumbled into darkness.

Brent landed in the tunnels, where a figure waited for him below.

"Rho?"

"No. Caroline." She moved out of the shadows, the glow of the torches adding a golden overtone to her pasty face. Something was different, though; dark circles rested around her eyes, her lips were no longer painted red, and her confidence had been replaced with nervous jitters.

"Caroline, right. You still exist..." Brent closed his eyes again. "How'd I end up here?"

"You fell through a root."

"I'll pretend that makes sense," he groaned. "No wonder everything hurts."

"Yes, no wonder," Caroline repeated. "Aelia can always fix you up if things get bad."

"Eh, I'm a'ight." Brent grunted as he sat up, rubbing the side of his neck. "Lucky I didn't end up in the Pit. That was...I was being stupid."

"Well, you do not have to worry about that anymore." Caroline fumbled with her fingers. Her voice no longer rang shrill as a crow but instead purred like a kitten beneath a blanket.

"I mean, not today...but probably I always will. I mean," Brent scratched his hand, "now that I'm your apprentice, it's more of a reason for them to throw me away!"

"No, no," Caroline replied. "I mean to say I made a mistake, and I am sorry but—"

"What? What are you talking about? I'm—I'm fine now. I mean, I'm almost sort of...I mean, it's exciting. Never thought I'd get an apprenticeship!"

"No, I should have never taken you into the library. It was not the time."

Brent's head started buzzing as he fumbled, pulling *The Snow Fairy* book out of his coat pocket. "If it's this, I can return it. I didn't mean—"

"No, no, the book is not the issue."

"Then...then what is it?" His throat tightened as he asked. Why was there always a caveat?

"Oh, this is difficult... Here, I'll try to explain..." Caroline grabbed a branch from the wall. She drew two circles overlapping and pointed to the one on the far left. "Think of this circle as life and this one," she moved to the one on the right, "as the afterlife. The afterlife is where we send the souls—a place where they can exist in peace, so to speak. But, there's a world between life and death," she moved to point to the overlap, "here. This is where the Mist Keepers reside."

Brent raised his eyebrows.

"It has many names, but you call it the Effluvium," Caroline continued. "It is the interim, the moment in-between, where spirits roam if unfulfilled. And it is where we—the Mist Keepers—perform our ultimate task of releasing souls of the dead. The living occasionally may get whiffs of the Effluvium, building religions and other philosophies around it, but generally, they just see the outer layer."

"But I can—"

Caroline cut him off. "Magic sometimes gives the living a form of sight. It used to be more common, but it is limited now to seers and some Magii. In your case, though, this is more than petty magic. Fate—or whatever you believe in—selected you to see *me*. But a Mist Keeper cannot thrive in this living world." She pointed her shoe back at the left circle. "A Mist Keeper must fulfill their quest, in the end, in the Effluvium."

"I'm confused..."

"You become a formal Mist Keeper by entering the Effluvium after escaping the gates of your mind." Caroline continued. "These are the gates of Perdition and

Hell, and you'll greet them in death like everyone else, but instead, you shall emerge in the Effluvium as a Mist Keeper once you leave."

"I...what?"

"Oh, my poor stupid child." Caroline closed her eyes and finally said, "To become a Mist Keeper, you must die."

Brent would never find the words to describe that moment. He pressed his head into his hands, pulling at his hair and mumbling over and over again to himself. "I...I..." Brent flinched. "No. I don't want to die...I don't want to be a Mist Keeper if I have to die."

"Usually, you would have a choice, but..." Caroline's voice fell, and she whispered, "I made a mistake."

"What? What did you do?"

"After you left yesterday, the others spoke with me. Very sternly at that. Typically, they informed me, when fate chooses an apprentice, we wait a few weeks to bring them to the library so they can understand the job of a Mist Keeper. I did not do that. I thought I was doing right..." She gritted her teeth and snapped, "They didn't tell me this would happen!"

"What would happen!?! What did you do to me?"

"You entering our realm does strange things to people deemed *normal*. Fundamentally, you are a normal boy—well, *were* a normal boy until you saw me. No magic. No sight. But I still brought you into our library. The tunnels do not grant any magic, they are much younger than the Council, but being surrounded by our history and our mist in the library...well, magic has a strange way of working on those unprepared. For lack of a better description, like the rest of us, you have been cursed."

"Cursed? Cursed to what?" Brent already anticipated the answer.

"To become a Mist Keeper, whether you wish to join us or not. Ultimately...you will die."

Brent shook his head. "What? When? I mean...yeah, I'll die someday but...when?"

"As I understand it, most of us do not last more than a year."

"A year?" Brent closed his eyes. His head was no longer buzzing but instead chimed like a gong. He gripped his hand, preventing himself from scratching at his wrist. The next words came out louder than he intended, "No...I can't! My ma...my family and I mean...no!"

"You no longer have a choice."

"You said you weren't here to kill me!"

"I said I messed—"

"You're as bad as the Order! They took away my freedom, my love, my everything...and you—you—" Brent's threw the book he carried at Caroline and screamed, "YOU KILLED ME!"

"I am so sorry," Caroline said one last time. Then, she vanished into the mist.

Brent gagged and collapsed in the spot where Caroline had stood. Did he still have legs? Or arms? He shivered into the dirt. *A dream. This is a dream. I'm going crazy. It's a dream.* Yet he could no longer convince himself of insanity. Caroline's voice rang in the front of his mind: "You will die."

"No...no no no no...no," Brent moaned into the darkness. He startled when another voice rang out, absorbed in his misery.

"What're you doing here?" Rho walked towards him, still hidden beneath her cowl and branch-made mask. He wanted to scream at her; how was she not dead? How come she saw the world and experienced magic, alive? He didn't yell, though; he couldn't.

"I thought I sent you home." Rho kneeled beside him. "Are you crying?"

"I—I'm..." Brent wiped his face, "I'm fine, just a little...I mean, I'm fine."

"Do you need help? Can I—"

"I'm fine." Brent rose and demanded, "Why would you want to help me, anyway? You don't even *know* me."

"Brent—"

"Fuck off!"

Before Rho could reply, Brent scrambled up the ladder and back out into the town square. The door slammed behind him, matching the thudding in his chest, the twisting in his neck, and the pounding in his ears.

He ducked behind a tree before anyone could see him, holding his chest tight. Christof stood with his father where Brent had initially vanished, pointing at the spot and flailing his arms in frustration. Captain Carver looked visibly bored by his son's antics.

You might as well come out of hiding and let them see you. You no longer have a choice.

Brent clenched his teeth.

You will die.

Brent waited until Captain Carver led his son away to duck out from his hiding spot. Not that it mattered anymore. If they saw him, Brent wouldn't put up a fight. Did it matter if he was in the Pit if he'd die within a year? All of this was for nothing.

He pushed through the patrons packing the market square. The Temple basked above in the sun's pinnacle light. The mist trickled through the crowd, muffling noise and bathing onlookers in a profuse and nauseating gas. Had the Effluvium always masked everything in such a disgusting way?

"Good Year Birth," a few townsfolk called out. They faked cordiality as if they hadn't shoved him out of their booths just the other day.

Brent didn't reply, trying to find his family—or someone—to hold. A hug, a touch, anything to tell him that yes, he was alive.

All else was a nightmare.

But why did the market feel so packed? Was it the Effluvium mingling in the air? Shadows formed within it, but it had to be in his head. *The Mist Keepers are messing with me. They're making me think I see things, but I can't. This is in my head. It must be in my head.*

There aren't monsters in the Effluvium!

But there are shadows.

Stop being stupid.

He found his mother and sister off to the side, each holding miniature year glasses. His mother's pointed expression greeted him as Alexandria embraced his legs. Brent half expected a lecture, but his mother said nothing, only placing a finger to his cheek and frowning.

He choked out, "Ma...I'm sorry. I should have been home yesterday."

"We'll talk later," she reassured him, placing a chipped year glass into his hand. "You're an adult...I can't lecture you about everything, a'ight?"

"Yeah, a'ight." Brent gulped and turned towards the stairs. Through the sea of people and mist, he couldn't *see* anyone; he searched for Jemma, for Madame Gonzo, for Captain Carver and Christof, and for Bria, but everyone wove together with the Effluvium.

A blur.

Elder Don Van exited from the Temple, with Brother Roy Al behind him. He raised both of his hands into the air.

The gong shattered the bustle.

But Effluvium did not part.

Nevertheless, the ceremony commenced.

The year has ended
As it must always do
Goodbye old son,
Goodbye old moon.

A new year is born
From our shattered sun,
Blessed is it
By the hands of the Effluvium.

The sky is dark,
Our fairy stars gaze through.
Blessings.

Voices.
Hello new moon.

The new sands count
The sun's new rays,
Whispering to the glass,
Tomorrow is another day.

So, turn my glass,
The new sun shall rise.
Turn my glass,
My life survives.

As with every year, the townsfolk echoed Elder Don Van's words. They raised their year glasses above their heads as the last of the dripping liquid slithered through the bottleneck of the ruby-coated Year Glass. As it fell, up in the Year Glass Atrium, two other brothers used the rotary dial on the fixture to turn it. In utter silence, except for one crying babe, the townsfolk turned their own year glasses in unison.

Yet Brent could not focus, the mist growing thicker with each passing moment. Was Caroline returning? It hurt to peer through it. Had the crowd always been this thick? At least two hundred more people had joined the fray in the last few minutes. But how? Where were they coming from? How did they get here? It appeared like two ceremonies took place at once. They choked him, enshrouded him, and sent him quivering to his knees.

"Brenton!" His mother sounded far away.

"Brent?"

"What's happening?"

"I—can't..." Brent croaked.

I'm going to die. This is it. The curse. I won't even be able to say goodbye. They'll shoot me dead.

A heartbeat, or maybe a drum, pounded against his ribs.

It almost popped out of his chest.

But no.

His skin started to itch, and he flailed his arms about, shaking away the sudden crawling feeling. As he fidgeted, a murky vapor expelled from his open palms, flooding his surroundings with a dense fog.

CHAPTER NINE

EARLY SPRING

Rho nested in a tree overlooking the Year Birth Festival, keeping her attention on Brent as he navigated the crowd. She could sense that something was wrong, but it wasn't until he dropped to his knees and a thick mist poured out of his fingers that she grasped the full gravity of what was happening.

Commotion erupted. The fog washed over them, and screams of the Effluvium's vengeance took over the ceremony. The guard rushed from their posts. Like shadows, they fought through the crowd, pushing people back and searching for the source of such magic. As they moved closer to Brent, the mist thickened around him, hiding him from everyone like the legendary dragons spoken in tales far away. They used the smoke as a cloak, never to seen again.

Screams and chants echoed from the Pit about how magic had returned and tainted the Effluvium. A guard hit the fence with his bat to send a few vagrants back into their slums, but many stayed, marveling at the chaos in the square.

Rho didn't want to believe it, but she couldn't avoid the truth: the mist was coming from Brent.

She reached Brent before the Guard and commanded the tree to lift him out of the square, away from capture. He didn't squirm, hanging in the tree's grip like a rag doll.

"Rho?" Brent grunted. "What are you—what are you doing?"

"I'm getting you out of here." Rho placed her finger to his lip. "Be quiet. The trees will protect us."

"I—"

"Please, we need to get out of here." Rho offered a hand. With her other one, she waved open a piece of the tree where the tunnels waited for them.

"I can't go back in there."

"Don't be stupid! Why couldn't you?"

"I'm dead because of those damn tunnels!"

"What? You'll be worse than dead if you stay up here!" She pushed him through the opening, and his body hit the floor below with a thud.

She ignored Brent protests and dragged him along the tunnel floor towards her hideaway. Mist continued to trickle from his body, creating a fog-like trail behind them. She may have laughed if the danger wasn't so great. *What a sight. I hardly reach his shoulder, and here I am, dragging him along. Stupid.*

They reached her hideaway, and she pushed him inside.

"Rho," he choked.

"Just rest."

"I need to—I need to tell you..."

"What? What is it?"

"The invisible people...you don't want to see them. You should—you should run far away," he sucked in his lips and murmured, "because they've killed me."

"You're delirious. Is this because you just discovered you have magic?"

"No, I will die, Rho. I'm going to..." He sobbed, pressing his forehead to the wall. "I'm gonna die..."

Rho pulled him into a hug, trying her best to comfort him with an out-of-tune song her grandmother used to sing. It did little to stop his trembling, but the storm raging on his face reduced to a light drizzle. The mist trickled away with his tears. Only a few clouds remained in the small enclosure, masking the light.

What am I going to do with you? She ran her hands through his sweat-riddled hair, and he cried himself to sleep, shivering on the ground, his head against Rho's leg. She draped one of her blankets across him. *Stay here. You'll be safe.*

Glancing back one more time at him, Rho climbed to the surface. Twilight trickled over Newbird's Arm, and with the night as her shield, she removed her head covering and let her little branch recede behind her ear.

She kept to the trees, watching the Guards as they marched while banging on the fence of the Pit to silence the vagrants. A few vagrants hung on the fence, forced back over with the barrel of pistols, while others laid bloody on the ground. Most homes sat dark, and while a single train whistled from the platform, it was the shouts of the Guards that sliced away at the silence. Obscenities, disgust, all of it roared, blaming the vagrants for their stories and tricks.

Captain Carver marched with vigor down the road, yelling at a despicable looking cadet who towered over a few young women with a smirk on his face to get back to the barracks. When the cadet objected, the captain hit him with the side of his club and shoved him down the road. Then he removed his whip from his hip and snapped the air, sending the couple young girls fleeing.

"Captain Carver!" Elder Don Van, draped in his evening blues, hurried towards the captain. "Have you discovered anything regarding the incident today?"

"Demons and magic, Elder, that much is certain," the captain replied. "An array of possibilities, but I believe one of the vagrants is dabbling again."

"Alas, the Effluvium has done well to protect us, but when our faith is tainted, we struggle." Elder Don Van gazed towards the Pit. "As the Senator has not returned from the Capitol, it is in my authority to request all vagrants undergo the Standard Levels of the Cleanse. We shall find magic at its source before it gets out of hand."

"Ay, sir. Shall I send a telegram to Knoll requesting additional Guards?"

Elder Don Van glanced at the train chugging back into the mountains. "Yes, that may be necessary."

"I shall send one this evening. They'll be here by the morrow."

The men headed towards the market, speaking in low whispers. Rho followed from the trees, picking up a few words about the destructive nature of magic and demons. Yet, to Rho's relief, they never mentioned Brent's name.

Maybe he's safe. A lot was going on; maybe no one saw him.

Her hopes shattered the moment they arrived in the market, where no one but Old Madame Gonzo loitered, sweeping away the glass around her home.

No one except for Cadet Christof Carver, squinting at the spot where Brent stood earlier.

"Cadet! I told you to go home!" Captain Carver snapped.

"Father!" Christof straightened his back. "I was waiting for you! I know who—"

"Christof! I said go home!"

"It was Harley! I saw—"

"I will have you reprimanded!"

"But Dad—"

"Now, Captain," Elder Don Van interjected, holding up his hand, "let's hear what your son has to say."

Christof puffed out his chest, goading, "A bit ago, I was putting Harley in his place. He was out of line was all, but after I hit him, he vanished, leaving mist like we saw earlier! Then, I saw him again in the square with mist surrounding his hands. He must've vanished again. The fucker..."

Rho gulped.

Elder Don Van nodded. "Ah, yes, the young storyteller."

"Harley has never shown any magic," Captain Carver replied. "A fuckin' storyteller and a menace, yes, but not a Magii. If it was not for my brother stepping in and finding him a partner, he would've been thrown in the Pit where he belongs."

"Captain Carver, whatever your qualms are with the boy, let's leave it in the past. We'll bring Mr. Harley in for a cleansing with the rest of the lot." Elder Don Van peered up to the Year Glass. "If his outburst continues and magic makes a home in his heart, then we shall look to extend the cleansing."

"Sir, if I may? With silver eyes and a penchant for stories...the magic won't be going away. It will latch onto him like the demons—"

"I shall consult with the One Scripture," Elder Don Van interjected. "Until tomorrow, let us get some sleep." He bowed, then walked back towards the Temple.

Captain Carver huffed and trailed behind him, glaring at Madame Gonzo as he marched past. His son remained for a moment, peering up at the trees before spitting on the ground and following as well.

Rho shook her head. *No. Brent isn't a monster. I can't let them treat him like one.*

I need them to forget.

She pulled a few seeds out of the pouch on her waist and rolled them in her hand. *When life gets a little petty, why not replace it with something pretty?* She tossed the seeds down to the cobblestones. As they hit the ground, saplings trailed through the dirt and across half of the market. When Rho snapped her fingers, the buds bloomed into whites, reds, purples, pinks, and blues.

Tulips, pansies, camellias, and wildflowers abound. Spring came early in Newbird's Arm that day.

Rho hopped down to admire her handiwork. When she landed, her knees buckled, and a sudden stinging shot through her spine. Dizziness overwhelmed her. She'd never birthed more than a couple flowers at a time; after giving life to a garden with one snap of her finger, someone might as well have hit her in the stomach.

Madame Gonzo paused on the far end of the market, gazing at the flowers and then in Rho's direction. "Ah! There you are! I knew it was you!"

Rho tried to stand, but her knees remained as planted in the ground.

"Are you okay?" Madame Gonzo rushed to her side. "You're pale, dear."

"Yeah, I'm fine," Rho assured her, straightening. "I'm always fine."

"You never were a good liar."

"Really, I'll be okay."

"Are you sure?"

"I promise, Grandmama, I promise."

CHAPTER TEN

TUNNELS, CITIES, AND TAVERNS

The whistling train woke Rho, where she lay on her grandmama's couch. The old woman stood by the window, grumbling and nursing a cup of tea, eyes narrow. From here, they watched droves of young cadets storming into town bearing the infamous stark gray uniforms with the Order's insignia on their sleeve.

"Knoll..." Her grandmama's nostrils flared. "They're really bringing in men from Knoll over this?"

Rho knew only two things about Knoll's Gully. For one, in its heart began the detrimental Smoke Riots that left a thousand people dead before her birth. Second, it remained the Order's stronghold, influencing domiciles like Newbird's Arm, all the way out to the Capitol Rosada, by electing Senators across the province.

Okay, there was a third thing she knew but hated considering.

The men of Knoll were barbarians, for lack of a better word, and their presence in Newbird's Arm would leave many quivering in the shadows.

"Dad won't be happy." Rho yawned. "Why would they come? It's not like anything really *happened*."

"There was magic, and if there's magic, the Order steps in." Madame Gonzo sipped her tea. "Poor Brenton. And his mother. They don't need this."

"Brent, right," Rho muttered.

"You should probably check on him, yes?"

Rho nodded. "Yeah, probably."

Madame Gonzo stumbled to her icebox and removed a parcel of fruits and vegetables, "Here. I'm sure he's hungry."

"Right," Rho filled her satchel and turned to the doorway. She picked at the trim, lowering her voice when she said, "I think I should tell him the truth."

"About what?"

"That it's me." Rho touched her own face, tracing her little branch behind her ear. "We've been through so much, and I kept this secret from him...even when—"

Her grandmama's eyes widened. "Don't! For both of your safety. There are too many watching."

"But—"

"Do *not* tell him."

Rho's head fell. "Yes, Grandmama."

She left her grandmama's home and grabbed a gazette before taking to the trees, avoiding the guards in the town square. Under the guise of Captain Carver, the guards lured droves of vagrants out of the Pit and towards the Temple. Some chanted a song of bitter return, while others trembled and begged for the Guard's mercy. Yet everyone stopped in awe at the newborn garden filling the town square, for like the Senator's immortal camellias, this patch of flowers would not wither.

As with the night before, the Senator's Gardens remained unscathed. There, she entered her hideaway beneath the earth, triple checking that her roots masked her face as she made her descent. Her grandmama was right, of course, but lying still made her uneasy.

Especially after everything she and Brent had been through.

Brent slept on the ground. His messy curls lay matted against one side of his face, while his mouth hung open. He tossed and turned, mumbling while a sweat broke out on his forehead. Tears stained his cheeks, and his hair stuck out in all directions. Rho went over to him and stroked back his matted hair. *You're okay, really, you're okay.* Part of her wanted to hold him close, baby him and make promises she couldn't keep. But she couldn't. Not if she wanted to continue hiding her face.

When he finally woke with a jolt, Rho backed away and tossed him her bag. "Eat."

Brent parsed through the produce, settling on a few citrus fruits and the newspaper. He flipped through the first few pages, mouthing words to himself and furrowing his thick eyebrows.

As he chewed on the edge of a lemon wedge, Brent broke the silence. "Are...I mean, did Knoll really send people?"

"They came this morning."

He winced. "Shite. This is my...it's my...I fucked up. It's my fault. I'm gonna...I mean the—there's *magic*."

"Brent—"

"I need to...this can't be. I can't..." He gazed at his hands. "I did that."

"Brent!"

"What's wrong with—"

"Alright, that's enough!" Rho yanked the newspaper from him. "We're going for a walk."

"What?"

"I'm not going to listen to you be a self-deprecating bastard. There're other things to see out there, Brent!

Sometimes life might get a little petty, but there's always something pretty!" She removed the lemon hanging from the corner of his mouth and tossed it on the ground. "Come on!"

"Something petty..." Brent repeated but said nothing else.

Rho yanked Brent into the tunnels. He tripped over his own legs as he followed. When they reached the junction, he paused at the blank wall, but Rho did not allow him to dwell long before she led him towards a tunnel in the south.

The tunnel ended in the mouth of a cypress tree opening on a freshwater spring. Tepid humidity dabbled in the air.

"Where are we?" Brent asked as he removed his jacket.

"Somewhere south of Rosada," Rho replied, guiding her fingers across the top of the water. Algae bubbled to the surface.

"So, we really did travel far?"

"Mhm."

"That's..." He glanced back at the cypress tree. "Magical."

"Yeah."

Brent kneeled by the water next to her. "I've never seen such clear water before."

Rho smiled and asked, "Can you swim?"

"What?" Brent's face turned red. "Yes. Why?"

"Because you stink. I'll be past the trees once you're done." Rho patted Brent's back, and she skipped away, only glancing back at Brent for a moment. He tilted his head to the side, but as his gaze followed, she put her wall up again. Hopefully, Brent didn't see through her disguise. After all, as much as Rho didn't want to believe it, her grandmama was right; for their safety, everything had to remain a secret. She hated lying to Brent, though.

Rho ventured into the forest to gather seeds, allowing the plants and trees to croon her. In moments like this, Rho became the Forest Queen. She created art out of the trees. The vines lifted her up and swung her between branches, and as she skipped, an endless array of flowers bloomed. Sapling roots twisted around her fingers with each seed, going to bed with a soft lullaby. With her hymns, the forest sang in harmony. And she danced.

Rho didn't hear Brent come back until his chuckle broke the silence. She spun around, pulling her cowl up to her lips. The roots on her face tightened. "Oh, you're already done—and you're not wearing pants!"

Brent glanced down at his waist and flushed, dashing off into the trees.

"How do you forget to put pants on!?!" Rho shouted after him, feeling her face redden.

"I just did." He hopped back toward her, buckling his pants and tucking in his shirt, "I'm not...I'm not all here. I don't know. My mind was going places and I..." He shook his head. "It's dumb."

"Well, no, *you're* dumb."

"Yeah, I know." Brent half-smiled. It was a smile that came with sadness, but in the clearing and the soft midday glow, Brent almost looked happy.

Rho blushed.

They didn't speak much as they traveled back to Rho's hideaway. Brent kept opening his mouth, but then hunching his shoulders over and staying silent. Rho saw him check his pants a few times, making sure he clipped his suspenders to his belt.

Once they returned, Brent sat on the floor with the newspaper spread in front of him. Everything seemed okay, with him back to chewing on a lemon wedge, tracing through the words. Yet, as Rho sat there munching on an apple and spitting blooming seeds from her mouth, Brent's silence broke with rippling sobs.

Rho gripped him by the shoulders. The urge to hold him returned, but she fought it back, replacing it with a single command. "Stop."

"I can't do this," he choked, "I can't...I can't die. I can't..."

"You're not going to die."

"No! No!" He clenched his hands over his head. "The woman, with the doors? Rho, she...the invisible people. They've killed me! I'm gonna die in a year! They're fucking mole people with giant fucking claws ripping me and—and...shite!"

"Mole people?"

"They've cursed me to die." Brent sobbed again.

She shook her head. He looked fine; sure, a little paler than usual, but otherwise fine. It had to be paranoia. He couldn't die, not now. Not when she finally shared the tunnels with someone.

"I won't let you," she whispered.

They didn't speak again for some time. Brent wiped his face and returned to his newspaper. He hiccoughed and commented on a few articles, mumbling about the senate elections coming after the summer, then trailing his finger across a photograph of a gorilla. The title above it read, "Juno's Den Welcomes Newest Resident." As he read, Brent's eyebrows scrunched together in an expression Rho knew all too well. She'd seen him focus like that right before telling the children stories in the alleyways. Beneath her cowl, she smiled and flushed to herself. Oh, how she loved that look!

He flipped to another page, read a few sentences, and then paused. "That's ridiculous."

"What?"

"The Capitol thinks they can build some sort of flying ship thing." He shook his head. "We're not meant to fly!"

"You haven't been to the Capitol, have you?" Rho smirked.

"No. It sounds like a load of shite."

"Well, it's true!"

"You're kidding..."

"No, really! The Capitol is years ahead of Newbird's Arm! They've pulled resources from Proveniro on the Southern Continent! Haven't you heard? Come, I'll show you!"

Before Brent could object, she yanked him back into the tunnels. Brent once again slowed when they crossed into the junction, glancing at the empty wall. Rho tried her hardest to see the doors he mentioned on the wall, but they never showed themselves to her. There was only mist. They did not dwell, though, heading west away from the junction.

At the end of the tunnel, a set of underground train tracks greeted them. The pungent smell of sewage trickled. A rat scurried by, highlighted by a set of headlights in the distance. *Chug, chug, chug*; the headlights pounded, shaking the walls.

Brent peered down the tunnel.

"Brent! You're going to get hurt!" Rho grabbed his shoulders and pulled him against the wall. An underground train rushed past them.

"The shite was that!?!" Brent shouted as the machine roared.

"I think they call it a subway." She loosened her grip on Brent's shirt. "An underground train."

"Shite! That—that didn't just...no way!"

"Of everything, that's what gets you freaked out the most?"

"It's underground!"

"Come on, there's more to see." Rho gripped his arm, and they left the subterranean tunnels via an occupied staircase that led them to a glistening city bustling with the dramatic noise of existence. Dead trees lined the dusty road while covered machines on wheels chugged down the path. In the sky, two balloon-like fixtures flew overhead, one a standard white while the other changed colors depending which way the light hit. Buildings, three times the size of the Temple, towered overhead, blocking out the midday sun. Buggies purred past them on the streets, their gears churning and buzzing as the tires hit the pavement.

Looming above it all stood three towers floating on the water, one decorated with an incandescent Year

Glass with a metallic red interior, almost identical to the one in Newbird's Arm, while the other two stood as stark gray beams, watchful eyes of the Guard.

Towers from Knoll. The towers never did make it to Newbird's Arm, but she'd seen them on multiple occasions in the Capitol and in the larger domiciles on the western plains, moving down the rivers and instituting the Order's firm beliefs.

No magic. No stories. Only obedience and order.

Newbird's Arm already had that.

They walked along the road while Brent pointed to the buggies and laughed at the airships. He mimicked the wind-up toys that the children played with and stumbled backward when he saw a photographer use a camera without a tripod. Rho loved watching him. He was clumsy in his amusement, his laughs didn't sound forced, and his smile lit up both sides of his face.

"This is amazing!" Brent exclaimed, rubbing his wrist.

Rho smiled back "The Capitol might have the Order watching, but they can't control thousands of people. They're looking for the troublemakers here...not just ever person with a black stamp or a few parlor tricks. But in a mountain town? Yeah. But here...no one notices the black stamp! Or your eyes! You're invisible!" She touched his wrist and added, "Just don't do anything that draws attention, and you'll be okay."

Brent twisted the leather bracelet on his wrist, and that stupid smile grew even wider. Then, almost without warning, he darted ahead into the streets, stopping at corners to stare at the unusual fixtures. Rho couldn't help laughing as he ran up one bridge and gazed at the road. He waved at her to come up, and once she got to the top, he grabbed her wrists and spun her around in excitement.

"I used to always think I'd run away to someplace like this." Brent stared out at the city. An odd seriousness washed over his face as he spoke, "Never did. I never could. Now I guess it doesn't matter, though."

"Because you're supposedly going to die?"

He nodded. "Yeah. It's not like I can run from death."

"Why don't you just try *living* then? If you're going to...die, then you should just enjoy life, right?" Rho's voice fell as she spoke, unable to believe what Brent told her. He wasn't allowed to die. She wouldn't let him.

"What would I do? I don't got a trade or money or anything." His eyes traced the street, and he muttered, "It's hard to sell stories in a place where stories are illegal. Like yeah, I can get some lemons or smokes and such with a few stories, but money to live? That doesn't happen. So what's the point in telling them, y'know?"

Rho's eyes flickered before grinning. "There are ways to sell stories for money in the Capitol."

"What do you mean?"

"Come on. I'll show you."

Rho led Brent down a road where less extravagant buildings decorated the land. The surrounding grass, frost-bitten, remained in a state of hibernation, unwilling to bloom even with spring knocking. The trees sat hallow and echoed no songs. Still, when Rho brushed her fingers against a gray trunk, it burst to life, only to suffocate in the musty smog in the air.

She ushered him into a small tavern at the end of the road. In the entranceway sat an old woman, knitting away at a blanket. She did not look up as Rho placed two silver coins onto her chair.

They proceeded down a tight stairwell into a speakeasy with a few tables gathered around a makeshift stage. Brent ducked in behind Rho and squinted. She watched his expression transform as he registered what was on the stage: a woman stood there, arms waving as she recited a tale about a dragon. It lacked the vibrancy Rho heard in Brent's stories, but it still filled the bar with a mythical tale of dragons shrouded in mist, defending two queens locked in a war.

Brent grinned as they sat before the storyteller, childish in his posture as he leaned forward. Rho ordered two glasses of scotch before joining him. They clinked their glasses as another storyteller proceeded onto the stage.

They listened to the stories as they drank. Brent stifled a few laughs, shifting in his seat as he mouthed a few words to himself, brow furrowed again.

"Why don't you go up there?" Rho urged.

"Huh? Nah. Couldn't." Brent finished off what must've been his fourth glass.

"You tell stories, don't you? This is where you sell them! This is your way out!"

"Nah." Brent gave her a sad smile. "I'm unfortunately gonna be a mole person and just...mole around. No point. 'Sides I need to go home with my ma and my sister and my—"

Rho cut him off, "Stop being ridiculous! Get up there!"

"But—"

"Go!"

Brent stumbled up and stared, sucking in his lips and hopping in place.

Come on Brent. You can do it.

"A'ight, so..." He straightened his back. "Listen here and gather closely, I have a story to tell! It's a tale about a man but covered with hair! He tried to hide it by wearing robes and keeping his head down. All he wanted was to live his life rather than fearing the people in his hometown. I bet you're wondering what to call him...let's call him Mr. G!" Brent puffed out his chest and deepened his voice, "'My name is Mr. G, and I work in the treasury, counting coins for you and for me!' But if you were to go to the treasury, you'd never see him. He hides in the back with his nose bent. He's extremely busy, making sure our wallets are fat.

"So, what's the story here you're wondering, right? Well, Mr. G is not like you and not like me. He's large and rarely speaks, and fur covers every part of his tremendous body. The "g," you see, in Mr. G's name, it stands for gorilla..." Brent chewed on his lip, face turning red. "It means gorilla, and he...he's a damn gorilla. And...and..." He burst out laughing, "Gorilla! He's a gorilla! That's it! That's all I can say...he's a..." He stepped forward and tripped off the stage, tumbling into Rho's arms. He guffawed, gripping her arm as he tried to find the seat. "He's a fucking gorilla, Rho, a fucking gorilla."

Rho situated him in the chair, "You shouldn't tell stories while you're drunk."

The patrons in the tavern laughed but most passed over the story without a thought. A shame, really, in Rho's opinion. Another, better day, a greater story, perhaps.

"Gorilla man..." Brent pressed his forehead to the table and produced a distressed monkey sound.

"Let's get—"

Bang. Bang. Bang.

The old woman banged two pots together at the top of the stairs. Rho jerked up in an instant.

"What is that!?!" Brent shouted as he covered his ears.

Rho pulled him up. "We need to get out of here. The Guard's coming."

"Thought no one cared here?"

"General populace, no, but the Order's still runs the government. Come on!"

They hurried up the stairs, past the old woman, and into the street. Darkness painted the sky. Lights shone down the road, casting a glow over the men marching towards them.

"This way!" Rho grabbed Brent and directed him to a crooked tree behind the tavern.

The tunnels greeted them as if nothing had happened. Brent tripped over his own feet as he walked, using the wall for support, continuing to mumble about the gorilla.

"You ever seen a gorilla?" he asked. "With all this magic traveling crud?"

"No, I haven't." Rho laughed and skipped a few paces back.

"Damn, that's too bad." Brent trailed behind her. He tilted his head to the side, then leaned forward on his knees. "You wanna know something, though?"

"Hm?"

"You remind me of someone."

Rho stopped in place.

"I mean, you can't be...but I have a friend who skips like that and—" He shook his head. "No. Sorry. I'm confused."

"Just drop it, Brent."

"But—"

"I said leave it alone, Brent!" she snapped. "Don't dig! It's better that way! For all you care, I live in these tunnels! Leave the rest alone!"

"But you're Madame Gonzo's granddaughter, aren't you?"

Rho stopped, a feeling of momentary paralysis washing over her. A knot formed in her throat. She responded in a "How do you—"

"Sometimes life gets petty, but there's always something pretty," Brent quoted. "That's one of Madame Gonzo's sayings. And the plants...the magic...I thought it was a rumor."

"I—"

"Who are you?"

"No one important," Rho sneered. "Leave it."

Brent went to say something else, but dropped his head, kicking the ground with one foot. Rho hoped he was too inebriated to remember the conversation later, but knew Brent was observant and far smarter than he let on, so he'd figure out the truth one day.

Not today, though.

Neither of them said a word until they reached the junction, where Brent stared again at that empty wall.

"You coming?" Rho called.

"I'll catch up," Brent whispered, "I've got things to do."

"With the invisible people? The Mist Keepers?"

"Yeah."

"Right, okay. Have fun then," Rho grumbled.

Brent glanced back at her. "I haven't forgotten my promise. I'm gonna find you answers, Rho."

"Oh...um...thank you." She hurried away before Brent dared to say another word.

CHAPTER ELEVEN

The Release

Brent kept confusing shadows with gorillas. So, it had to be the scotch playing games with his head when he thought Rho was someone else. *But it can't be. Don't be stupid.* Brent ignored those as he stared at the library's door. He touched the images of trees etched on its exterior. Carved figures danced around it, with mist dancing about their ankles.

At his touch, the door swung open, and the forest of books welcomed him home. Caroline stood by the stairway with her cloak draped over her arm as she spoke to a...*a gorilla?*

No.

Brent blinked a few times and his sight situated instead on a man as mountainous as the bookshelves. He wore his long raven hair loose down his back, while a thick beard masked his round face. At Brent's arrival, his eyes narrowed.

"Brent!" Caroline clapped her hands together, "You have returned!"

"I think...I mean...I...I want answers." He flinched. "I mean, if I'm dead anyway, I want answers. I want to learn about the mole people...or I mean...Mist Keepers. Yeah. The Mist Keepers."

"Really? Are you sure? You were quite angry the other day."

"I'm still furious," Brent stated, "but if I'm gonna die...I want answers. Like why the hell you all live in the tunnels! Like mole people."

"Is your apprentice always this inebriated?" the mountainous man asked Caroline. "Mole people?"

"Inebriated?" Caroline sniffed Brent's breath. "Ah, yes, he is."

"Shame."

"Who are you to judge, Jiang?"

The mountainous man snarled, before storming up one of the staircases and out of sight.

Caroline scoffed, "He is a child."

"He's huge," Brent gawked, "Like a—" *Gorilla. Stop. Enough.*

"Ah yes, he has giant's blood from the country of Yilk. I was on my way there today if you would like to join me."

"I want answers first."

"About what?"

"What's going on?" Brent flailed. "Like really...why me? I—I've just...I mean—I..." He gave up trying to form a sentence and looked away, before whispering, "Why do I have to die?"

Caroline pulled on her cloak. "I wish I had an answer, but I do not. I had no intention of being a teacher for at least another hundred years. But alas, fate has other plans. I have been this," she waved her arms in front of her body, "for 300 years. I hardly remember a time before it."

"Then why bother getting an apprentice? You're dead...it's not like you die again."

"I suppose, over time, doing this," Caroline motioned to her surroundings, "drains us. I feel fine. But like my master before me, and his master before him, and so forth, now I must train an apprentice. Frankly, I am not happy about it."

"But what is *this*?" Brent demanded. "I get you're Death, a gatekeeper, a god, or a Mist Keeper, or whatever...but what is *this*? What do you do?"

"Come with me to Yilk, and I will show you." Caroline guided him into the junction.

Brent half expected to see Rho watching from the shadows. But no, she was long gone. *Who is she? Why is she so familiar? She can't be...no.* As he watched Caroline stride ahead, his thoughts abandoned the girl with the root-stricken mask and fixated on his own future.

They walked in silence for a few prolonged minutes. Brent kept going to open his mouth but couldn't figure out what to say. He occupied himself by watching the shadows on the wall and bouncing questions through his head until finally, Caroline spoke. "I am sorry."

"Yeah?" Brent replied. "I don't think a simple apology is gonna cut it. You killed me."

"I am aware, but I will continue apologizing." Caroline clicked her tongue. "I am a Mist Keeper, not a teacher. You may think I am wise or attentive. No, I am impulsive and shrewd; you could say I am a child! The Council most certainly would. I do not understand things!" Caroline shook back her hair and laughed. "In fact, when you ended up in the tunnels, if I was still alive, I would have had a heart attack!"

"You hit *me!*"

"You might have been anything!"

"I'm a person!"

"With that hair? And those eyes! You could be a swamp monster!" Caroline laughed mid-sentence.

Brent shook his head and inhaled, stifling a knot in his throat, "Shite...that's not...don't—don't talk about my eyes. It's not my fault they're like this..."

Caroline paused, her face softening, "I am sorry. I did not mean to pinch a nerve."

Brent clutched the walls. The few moss-ridden roots lay dormant at his fingertips. "I—I...you can make fun of my hair, my stature, my face...anything about me. Just please, I'm—I'm sick of people judging me because I have silver eyes. Everyone who has them...and there aren't many of us...we all...the Order I mean...they take away everything. They think we've got demons on our back or some shite, and they never tell us why." He sighed. "They might've killed me long ago..."

"Well," Caroline said bluntly, "the Council is not here to judge you by your appearance. At least I am not. There is an understanding you gain from releasing the souls of millions. You see everyone as one, and all as the same."

Brent picked at his wrist. "Didn't stop you from killing me, though."

They walked a few more paces in that awkward silence. The pathway before them became thick with dust. Arid chanting from a desert replaced the frigid air from his home.

"How do the tunnels...how do they work?" Brent asked.

Caroline shrugged. "Magic. I believe it has something to do with the Mist. Alojzy built them some six-hundred years ago, but before then, the Mist Keepers traveled differently. You would have to ask the more senior members how."

"Alojzy..." Brent recalled the stout man in the library, "Was he your teacher then?"

"Yes, and Malaika was his, then Jiang, Julietta, Tomás, Aelia, and finally Ningursu," Caroline counted on her fingers, "Yes, that is correct."

"And are all eight of you...alone?" Brent used all his energy to stay focused, the drunken dizziness settling in the back of his head.

"No, of course not. There are those loitering in the Mist. The Dead, Ghosts, the Palaver, Seers, and Magii–they're all out there."

"Okay, I know all of those except for the Palaver. What's that?"

"Great, now I am digging myself a hole," Caroline grumbled. "They were a group of powerful Magii that had a way of seeing through the Mist as well as other powers. Personally, I know little about them as it is considered...taboo, I suppose. In Ningursu's mind, they are disregarding everything he stands for, so ever since the One War, we have considered many of the Magii our enemies."

"I'm sorry, One War?"

Caroline sighed. "Another thing I have little knowledge about. What I do understand is that it created the standing treaty between the Council and the Palaver of Magii." Before Brent inquired, Caroline held up her hand. "Back when the Council was of three and these powerful Magii had many more on their side, there was a dispute over power between the two groups. The treaty established minimal contact, and since then, we act as two separate, non-communicating entities."

"So...is that why there aren't many Magii left? Or—"

Caroline cut him off, "The disappearance of the Magii has nothing to do with the Council. That is the mortal world's prerogative."

"Oh...a'ight..." Brent pocketed what Caroline said in the back of his mind for Rho. It wasn't an answer for her, but at least it was something she might find valuable. He then asked, "So, we're not magic?"

"Not in the traditional sense." Caroline made a sharp turn towards another tunnel as the wind ruffled her hair. "We release souls from the body, as I mentioned. It is a connection with the surrounding Mist, and with humanity."

"And this—this releasing of souls...drains you? That's why you need an apprentice? Me?"

His questions disappeared as they passed under a glowing archway. The hustle and bustle of the crowds greeted them in an unfamiliar, arid marketplace. A city filled with buildings taller than the trees circled the marketplace, composed of dusty bricks, arches, and pillars. A tower watched in the distance, a blazing fire upon it.

The civilians all stood a head taller than Brent, while young children reached his shoulders. Despite his height, no one paid notice to him. Nor the black stamp on his wrist.

Caroline walked ahead, unalarmed by the transition. She caught Brent's questions lingering in the air.

"Imagine every day for three-hundred years, you have to enter the worst nightmares of hundreds of dying or dead individuals." Caroline ran her fingers across one building. "Every day, you walk into someone's personal hell, holding the keys to the doors that could let them out. You see people at their worst, and people at their best. You witness the most gruesome murders and the classiest saints. Even if you have heard their stories, you cannot skip anyone for this ultimate decision. Everyone must face us on their judgment day so they can join the Mist. That is what we, the gatekeepers of this death-filled Mist, do. We see everything."

"You play god," Brent mumbled as a man walked by with books the size of a medium-sized dog.

"We are not the ones who decide. It just happens," Caroline stated. "Fate, or whatever you call it, guides us."

"The Effluvium?"

"Sure, if that is what you call it."

"But...how?"

"It is hard to explain. I suppose it varies depending on the Mist Keeper."

"But how do I—"

"Come, you will see."

As they walked through the colorful garb and maze-like roads, Brent swore Caroline's face flickered, a mist-like quality washing over it to show the face of an elderly man with dark eyes. In an instant, it vanished again, leaving a familiar with her usual scowl.

"What the shite was that!?!"

"Hm?"

"Your face...it changed!"

"Ah, yes, my way of knowing where to go." Caroline shrugged. "I see the face of the dying or deceased and, I suppose, mimic it through the Mist."

"Magic then?"

"A type of magic, yes."

"Will that...will that happen to me?"

"Everyone has their own *magic.*" Caroline fixated on a tall archway at the far end of the city. Brent didn't understand the inscription written on top, but it was obvious they had entered a cemetery. Mist, which never really left his vision anymore, filled every angle of the cemetery. Yet, rather than the classic urns resting on the shelves in the Temple, or the empty plots out by the fields, this cemetery consisted of multicolored candelabras hovering above engraved plaques.

Two pyres burned in the center of the yard. Within each dosage of flames rested a body. Caroline approached the first one and stared at the body: a large elderly man identical to the mask she'd show before, lay in the fire's grasp.

"I shall show you what I do," Caroline spoke, "The fire will not burn me. I will reach in, and then I will see where he belongs."

"How?

"Watch." She stuck her hand into the fire, and the Mist encompassed Caroline, stroking over her body and replacing her with the image of the deceased man in the flames. Then she exhaled, and the surrounding miasma shot into the sky, comingling with the clouds before vanishing.

"What was that!?!"

Caroline shook back her hair, "I released his soul."

"Into the Effluvium?"

"As I do every day."

Brent blinked, then stared back at the clouds. "Do it again."

"Would you like to see what I am doing?"

"What do you mean?"

Caroline held out her hand, her face flickering into the image of the woman in the second pyre. "I can show you."

"Guess I gotta one day. If I have to die and be...this, I mean. So yeah, a'ight, I'll take a look." Brent took Caroline's hand. With her other one, Caroline reached into the fire. At first, nothing. Then heat shot through Brent's arm. The world spun, replaced with a sensation of falling as the ground disappeared beneath his feet.

A woman.
She ranted often,
Standing amongst droves.
She spoke of injustice.
She led a wealthy life.
But always outspoken.

She hated cats.

Her children stood by her side.
Despite her shrewd and angry words.
Her daughter got a cat.
For a while, no one spoke.
Except the woman continued shouting of
Injustice.
Glory.
For tall and short alike

And Death walked amongst these rants and shouts.
A key in hand.
Cats crossed the roads.
The woman sneered at them.
They clawed at her.
A wind blew.
The woman screamed.
Then Death took her key.
Opened a door.
And there was light.

Once again, Brent stood in the graveyard. Out of the smoke from the pyre, the woman's ghostly shadow overtook Caroline before fading into the Mist.

"What just..." He fell to his knees, his throat tight, his mouth hanging ajar as if he had awoken from a nightmare. The woman's essence surrounded him. He remembered the woman, the cats, her rants, but everything else faded...as dreams always do. Yet, her fiery personality eroded through his veins.

"Are you okay?" Caroline asked.

He gasped. "I don't know..."

"It will get better."

"But what I—I saw...what about—"

"Come, it is okay. Everything is as it should be." Caroline helped him off the ground.

A haze intoxicated Brent, who squinted at the cemetery gate as they exited. The words made sense now, woven together as a prayer:

Our sun shines with yellow rays. Join infinity with our sons and daughters.

For the first time, Brent understood the people walking about the road. Passing through the city, he slowed, reading the inscriptions on buildings and titles of newspapers. They were in a foreign language, but he read them like the common tongue.

"Brent?" Caroline called back, "Are you well?"

"I..." Brent furrowed his brow. "I understand the language now. Sort of at least." He paused at an inscription on the wall and read, "This is the Court House of Mariano." He stumbled over to a newspaper that lay jumbled on the ground and read, "And this something about a—a light festival?"

"You are experiencing residuals." Caroline yawned. "Language, memories, magic, the whole boatload; you get them from releasing souls."

"But I didn't perform the release! You did! How can I be—"

"I do not know," Caroline confessed. She pressed her finger to his chin and peered into his eyes. "Maybe there is more to you than I thought."

"I'm just a storyteller."

"But, you are also my apprentice." Caroline released him. "Magic has a funny way of working. Time will tell, I suppose, why the Mist chose you."

CHAPTER TWELVE

A Second Voice

Brent parted ways with Caroline and left the tunnels in a daze. She told him she was traveling to Mert, conducting more releases, and then going to fish out on the Red Sea if it interested him, but his head hurt more than when he was drunk. Sleep would be a better friend. As he traveled through the tunnels back towards Rho's hideaway, Caroline's words echoed within his head: *Time will tell why the mist chose you.*

He couldn't even imagine the answer.

Instead, the fiery personality of the old lady he'd helped release shuffled across his mind. He wanted to shout at her to be quiet, but like a mother nagging her child, the woman's persistence never vanished. On and on, she rambled about the injustice of tall stovetops and the wrongful sizing of shoes, and many other rudimentary concepts Brent figured bothered her as she aged. Or were these problems in Yilk? He'd been in that women's Hell for such a brief amount of time. Would this be every time? As the years go by, would he hear every single voice yelling at him?

He stopped outside of Rho's empty hideaway. The vines wove together, preventing him from entering. The ladder back towards the Senator's Garden mocked him: *It's time to go home.*

His gut told him it was risky, but his heartstrings pulled him forward, back up the ladder and into the Senator's Garden.

As Brent walked along the pathway, his gaze went towards the empty gardener's home. *Bria.* A smile would work wonders now, but the window's darkened stare told him to keep moving. To see her again would make this risk all worth it. She always listened to him; she'd be the rational one.

Brent paused at the edge of the market. Other than the odd foliage that bloomed out of the cracks in the sidewalks and the droves of men in gray uniforms bearing the Order's mark, everything appeared normal. No one flinched at his arrival. There weren't any posters with his name or image. The gardener, Mr. West, spoke with a vegetable merchant, while Madame Gonzo waltzed between vendors and shoppers, her long checklist in her hand. A group of travelers sat on the Temple steps. They wore tattered clothing and spoke in a butchered version of the common tongue. Then, of course, there was Jemma, reading the One Scripture beneath the Temple's fountain, looking as pure as a dove. *I wonder if she knows. Even if she doesn't...she's too pious. She doesn't deserve to be wrapped in this mess. It'd be best if we just ended this madness. It would be best if I ended it.*

Why don't you? a voice in his head asked.

It's my only way to freedom.

Freedom? What freedom? The voice belonged to that elderly woman; it was familiar when she was ranting. *You've already lost that.*

He pushed the woman's voice to the side when he saw Bria sitting on a bench with her father. They wove together wicker baskets, while their large box-head dog lay beside them, its head resting on a shovel. Her father's hand's trembled with the wicker, wincing every time he made a mistake. Bria smiled that soft smile that still made Brent's heart flutter, walking back the error and helping him reweave the basket. Mr. West joined them, placing his shovel down beside Bria and squeezing both of their shoulders, laughing.

They're so happy. Brent traced along the triangular mark on the back of his hand and then turned to the Temple.

And you're not. You're dying. Why not go to her? the elderly woman cooed.

Brent ignored the woman, focusing his attention elsewhere. On the other end of the market, a group of young cadets, led by none other than Christof Carver himself, sat around smoking. Their eyes locked.

"Harley!" Christof's voice echoed, causing a few to turn. Jemma looked up from her book and called out something, but Brent couldn't hear it.

Shite. Brent backed up. His mind raced. Why did Christof hate him so much? He never quite understood it. They used to be friendly as kids playing in the garden. Something changed. But what?

Christof shot up in an instant. Another cadet with broad shoulders and thin legs, as well as a forehead that could crack open nuts, followed.

Christof snatched Brent by the collar of his shirt, "Listen here you piece of shite; my father might not believe you got magic or demon shite going on, but I saw what you did. Go get cleansed like the rest of the fucking vagrants in this town, or ya gonna end up in the Pit with the lot. I don't care if you're betrothed to Miss Reds, magic is a felony."

Brent slid into his uncertainty, curling in on himself as he tried to avoid Christof's stare. Why did he always end up in this situation? "I don't know...I don't know what...what're you talking about?"

"Brent!" Jemma shouted from the fountain. "Please, go with him!"

The other cadet roared over Jemma's pleas. "If ya don't go, we can just end it all here, a'ight?" He took out a switchblade and held it to Brent's eyebrow. "Cut ya up. Slice your face to pieces."

"Cadet Lawry, let's hold back a little." Christof smirked.

"He's a fucking demon if ya ask me, Chris," the cadet snarled. "Where I come from, we woulda shot him dead."

"My father doesn't want that." Christof lifted Brent off the ground. "So let's go get you cleansed, eh?"

Spit on him, the elderly woman's voice cackled.

That's not a good idea.

What do you have to lose?

Nothing I guess.

Brent spat. Christof's face contorted, leaving Brent with a moment of satisfaction. A rare form of confidence boiled in his chest, only to be cut short as Christof cursed and pushed him over to Cadet Lawry.

"What the fuck is wrong with you?" Cadet Lawry twisted Brent's arm behind his back, "We're members of the guard!"

"Damn shitty ones if you ask me!" Brent almost laughed.

"I can throw you into the Pit with your father, Harley!" Christof lunged forward, slamming Brent into the nearby wall.

Brent winced. Already the rare bout of confidence he'd had slipped through his fingers, leaving him crumbling in Christof's grip. Christof was right; Brent was going to end up like his father.

No, that wasn't it.

He would be dead before then. Was that better? Brent didn't know. But it wasn't worth fighting the mountainous Christof over.

"What's gotten into you? Your mind was ripped from the Effluvium, right? You been hanging out with demons, sucking on their tits and drinking the darkness they spread, right?" He forced Brent to the ground and pulled his head back by the hair. "Look at 'em!" Christof continued. "This is why we lock up vagrants, and we give the black stamp! This one here, we let him run free! This one here has sucked the tits of demons, and he's drank 'em well and good. Now he's gone from the Effluvium!"

Murmurs moved through the tiny crowd. Brent bowed his head in shame.

"My father says," Christof boomed, "we should make an example of men like Brenton Harley. What do we do to men who have met demons?"

"We cleanse them!" the crowd cheered.

"I say we start it right here. Strip 'em, shave 'em, throw 'em in ice...EVERYONE will know the Guard and Newbird's Arm says NO to demons."

"CHRISTOF!" Bria yelled over him from the edge of the crowd. "What are you doing!?!"

"What we must." Christof then pushed Brent into the crowd. It couldn't have been more than ten people, but it felt like over one hundred hands tossed him like a rag doll. His head seared with the dead woman's memory. She wanted to be a martyr; Brent wanted to scream.

Or maybe he wanted to be a martyr?

He stumbled out of the mob and across the square. The Temple became a sigil of peace.

Jemma stared at him, tears streaming across her face, "Brent, just go...get cleansed and stop making a fool of yourself. You can change. I know you can. That's why I agreed to this—"

"Change!?!" Brent snapped. "You think I want to change?!?"

"You don't want to be like your father. And your poor ma."

"There's nothing wrong with my dad except that he's sick!" Brent huffed. "He's sick, and no one will help, so they toss him aside like trash! And my ma, yeah, I agreed to this for my ma...but you're miserable. I'm miserable. So, let's go our separate ways!"

"I'm doing this for the good of the Effluvium...and for you," Jemma whispered.

"You're sacrificing your own happiness!" Brent pleaded with her, "Just throw me into the Pit and go be happy! This isn't solving anything, Jem."

She turned. "Brent, you're delirious. We'll talk about this later."

The mob caught up with him. Someone yanked him back and ripped his sweater. Another person took a shaving knife to his right eyebrow, and a searing pain ripped through his face. Brent cursed out at them and tried to rip out of arms, but heaviness transcended his body, and even the woman's self-righteousness started to ebb.

No.

His head fell. A story washed over him. For a moment, Brent remembered the stupid drunken tale of a gorilla, but it commingled with the elderly woman's rants about cats. What if the gorilla had a cat? Or better yet, the cat had a gorilla? It made no sense; it need not make sense.

The mist told the story, too. It wrapped around his hands, and for a moment, an aura transcended out of his body. Across the market square, it masked sight, forming obscure blobs in the shapes of kittens and monkeys.

The mob's grip around him broke long enough for Brent to dart away, succumbing to murmurs and awe. Christof and his fellow cadets followed close behind, running after him and away from the thick cloud resting over the market square. Brent bolted into the woods, but the trees provided no saving grace. Fatigue came with a headache, causing him to trip over roots and fall onto the ground with a thud.

He rolled over to face Christof, once again towering over him. "Enough, Harley! Either go get cleansed or get in the Pit already!"

"I...no...don't..."

"Lawry grab him. I don't want to even touch him," Christof turned away.

Cadet Lawry lifted Brent up by his neck.

Clunk.

Brent watched as Christof stumbled backward, gripping a tree for support. A red, bloody welt formed on his forehead.

Bria stood there, both her hands wrapped around the shaft of a shovel, blood dripping from the blade.

Christof wiped the blood from the throbbing yellow cut on his head. His face turned red, his face sizzling before letting out another scream. "You fucking bitch."

"No!" Brent shouted as Christof lunged at Bria. His entire body froze, straining against Cadet Lawry's grip.

"Shut up," Cadet Lawry gripped Brent's neck tighter.

"No...Bri!" He coughed. Spots filled his vision. The world began to spin.

He sputtered, the world growing foggy. Even the elderly woman's voice had diminished.

"Bria!"

What was Christof doing? The spots in his vision had started to turn white. He couldn't see. The world spun. His throat continued to tighten; his head began to buzz. Each beat of his heart felt like thunder against his ribs. Where was Bria? Where was Christof? Where did the screams come from? Did he still see Cadet Lawry's face?

Or was it a gorilla?

Brent's head hurt like someone took a dagger and pried it under his eye. Everything was fuzzy, and the sunlight above blinded him. He covered his face with his arm to ignore it.

What happened? Fuck...Bria!

He shot up. "Bri—"

She sat on the ground beside him, her blue shawl wrapped around her neck, hiding her face with her hair.

"Bria," he breathed, "you're okay."

"Yeah...I'm fine," she squeaked.

"What happened?"

"Nothing, everything's fine." She glanced at him, her eyes puffy. "You caused a scene."

"Yeah, I know."

"You have magic." It wasn't a question.

"Yes, but—"

"And the Order knows, and you're in trouble, and I thought they were going to kill you..." She looked away, hiding her face. For a moment, it looked like she might cry, but then she swallowed hard and continued. "You were being...odd."

"I know," Brent admitted, sinking in on himself and picking at his hand, trying again to hide in his shoulders.

"Cadet Lawry was choking you...I thought they were going to...and I wasn't going...I can't...I..." She wheezed.

Brent took her hand, then used his free one to push back her hair. Red welts decorated her throat up to the bottom of her mouth.

"Bri..." He reached for her neck with a couple trembling fingers, then pulled back.

"It's nothing." She pulled the shawl up again. "I deserved it. I mean I hit Christof with a shovel...assaulted a guard. Got him away from you so..." She blinked away the tears again. "I did the only thing I could think of doing."

"What?"

"He was going to kill you...or me...or something. He was so close, so I...I..." She gulped and then blurted in a rush, "I agreed to marry him when I turn twenty-one. It was the only thing I could think of."

Brent sprung forward in a panic. "No! It's not worth it!"

"I know it's not!" she clenched her teeth together, "I know, okay? I'm not going to go through with it! I'm going to run away...but I want you to come with me!"

Brent gaped.

"You said you never wanted to run away," Bria's head fell, "and there's a lot we need to talk about, but...I can't do this without you by my side. I..." Each word arrived with care, "Brent...you're my best friend. I...I can't run alone from this bullshit. Please..."

"What about—"

"They'll be fine. It'll all be fine." She wiped her eyes.

"Bria...but...this...I..."

"Brent, I'm going no matter what. I just need a yes or no. We used to talk about this; we should've run like this years ago! But we didn't, and now things are a mess, and I need you and—"

She stopped when Brent brought his fingers to Bria's face and stroked back a strand of hair. Her dark eyes warmed his heart even to this day; from the memories of kissing her when they were but kids walking home, to having her place flowers in his hair as they strolled through the Senator's garden. *We could run away,* she whispered after he became betrothed to Jemma, after the Order shot down his choice to marry *her*. Why didn't he then? Fear? It felt like a lifetime ago. How could he break it to Bria that even if they ran, it would be but temporary?

But wouldn't that be enough? Some happiness until this curse washed over him; that's all he needed, right?

"Okay," he croaked.

Bria cupped his cheeks, resting her nose to his chin. Brent sank into her embrace, hugging her tight as she pulled him closer. The flood of tears brought a tsunami, trapping Brent in the undertow. He might have been drowning, but she kept him afloat.

She always did. But this time with a kiss.

The time they spent sitting in the woods, embraced with gentle pecks and hands entwined, might have lasted an eternity. Brent drifted back to a time when he didn't worry, when he was in love, and when everything made a bit of sense. Always Bria; she was there for him when he lost hope, when no one took him up as an apprentice and he was staring vagrancy in the eye. Even after the betrothal, there she stood.

"Listen," Bria whispered, "I need to go to the Temple. I told Christof I'd..." She gulped. "I'd meet him there to formalize this bullshit. But meet me in the Gardens tonight. I'll be there, okay? We have things to talk about."

"A'ight," Brent replied. *How do I tell you I'm gonna die?*

She kissed his forehead, gripping his fingers one last time and leaving a trace on his skin as she disappeared through the trees.

Brent watched her leave then reached for the last smoke in his pocket as he took the long way home. Ducking through the forest, he marched over roots, fallen leaves, and frost-bitten ground. There, the back wall of the Pit loomed over him with a less glorified structure composed of broken rubble and rotting wood. He followed along these walls, watching the vagrants as they marched up from the mines, while others meandered from the fields, wincing at the whip cracking and vulgar calls of the guard.

As he walked through the trees, a story inundated his psyche. It was darker and far more alive than usual, with images like nightmares scouring his brain. He saw a little girl wandering around the empty gates of the Pit. She traveled far and wide, only to collapse at the base of the wall, begging for water and food.

Did no one come?

Was she there now?

He ducked behind a tree as the gates to the Pit opened. The vagrants filed in one by one, accepting the brutality of the guard like cattle. Brent winced as a guard whipped his father and resisted the urge to bolt as they beat an old woman. But he was no hero; he'd stay in the shadows until this passed.

As it always did.

Once the guard left, Brent darted over to the gate. It wasn't as grand as the one near the market, locked with rusted bolts and barbed wire. A few vagrants called out to him.

The story in his head grew louder as he hurried forward.

A little girl.

Screaming.

Begging.

Where was she?

He reached the corner of the fence. The girl's story ripped through him, pounded in his ears. The mist situated at his feet in a thick paste. Ringing. Chanting.

She's here.

Brent dug, clawing past the woven roots. Beneath their twists and turns, he reached her. He was sure it was her; decomposed to but bone and tattered clothes, a skeleton stared at him with vacant eyes.

"Shite," he whispered, bringing his fingers against the skull's head. Her story tugged at him, reaching for his psych, and then pulled him straight into Hell.

Brent arrived in a shantytown. It wasn't the Pit, though; the trees were too tall, and everyone walked with frizzy and cropped hair. The girl sat in the center of the destroyed town, holding a burned dolly in her arms and hiding her face in her knees. In an instant came the fire. Her little dolly burst into flames, and the girl let out a cry. Commotion, incomprehensible commotion, filled this nightmare. Brent tried to keep his head wrapped around it as he approached the girl.

Maija...Maija...Maija... *the fire seemed to whisper. Brent's own voice mimicked its pattern, but it only echoed into the abyss.*

The girl rose and sprinted ahead of him to the water. A man waited there and offered her a hand. She took it, and in the man's boat, they rode out to sea...where no one could hear her screams. But Brent saw. The man and a girl, alone on a boat, and the young girl fearful as he removed her dress...and...and...

Brent didn't dare look.

A twelve-year-old girl.

A man who could have been her father.

A childhood stolen.

Maija...Maija...Maija...

The boat docked, but nothing changed. A new shanty-town, different trees. The girl limped away from the shore, her clothes torn, and eyes worn. The fires came again. Brent wanted to run to her, to tell her it would be okay. Instead, he stumbled over the root of a cypress tree, face-first into the muck of a swamp. The tree picked him up, opening its leaf-strewn hand.

A key dropped from its grasp and landed in Brent's palm. He gazed at it, then dashed ahead. "Maija!?!"

For the first time, she noticed him, "No! Leave me alone! Go away!"

"Maija, it's okay." He reached for her.

"No!"

She rushed along the river. Brent chased after her, pausing only to stare at his reflection. His face did not belong to him. Instead, the face of the man who took Maija out to sea rested upon his shoulders.

Brent hit his face, trying to reconstitute his own image.

It didn't change.

"Maija...I'm not him, a'ight?" he shouted

"No!"

To Brent's surprise, she sprinted past him and into the fire that had gobbled up the new shantytown. Her body went up in flames. Brent disregarded it and ran straight after her.

Maija screamed. She flailed. She buried herself in flames.

Brent pulled out the key and shoved it into Maija's hand.

A white light flashed around them...

He tumbled backward, gasping for air. With every breath, he swore his heart would collapse. The taste of iron coated his lips and seeped into his mouth, and he brought his own fingers to his lips. Blood painted his fingertips. At first, he didn't notice the weight in his other arm. But, once they loosened, thick smoke poured out from his grip. It mingled in the air, then took Maija's shape. A weak ghost, withering and unconscious, lay before him. Then, a blanket of the Effluvium washed over her, and she disappeared.

His mind raced, trying to reconcile his thoughts with the ones belonging to the girl. When he blinked, he saw that man on the boat. Just a man, reaching out, removing Maija's clothes...or were they his clothes? Which life belonged to him? Was he a girl sitting in fire now? Was he a man resting on the frigid ground? Who...who—

I don't know who I am.

"Brent!"

He squinted through the mist. The name sounded familiar.

"Brent!" the voice came again.

Is that me?

"Brent!"

Out of the mist emerged Caroline. Her blue eyes flared as she lifted him up by his shoulders, positioning him against the wall like a rag doll.

"Brent, what did you do? What is wrong with you?"

That must be me...Brent. What kind of name is Brent? He chuckled. His mouth tasted of blood.

Then the gong went off in his head. He quivered and shouted, wrapped in the mist's embrace. Where was the boat now? The fire? The girl?

Who was he?

Did he hate cats?

"I don't know who I am," he choked. "Help me...please."

CHAPTER THIRTEEN

CAROLINE

When Brent woke up, he lay in an infirmary with no recollection of how he got there. Caroline stood over him, placing a cool compress to his head, looking like a stain against the sterile walls. He shifted between the comfort of the bed and the fire in his head, belting out a scream before quivering like a child beneath the covers. When Caroline spoke, he heard only whispers; when he tried to reply, his throat produced words in a foreign tongue.

He couldn't count the faces as people spun around him, and when someone tried to draw blood, he screeched and backed up on the bed.

Don't touch me, don't touch me, please no one touch me.

Where's Bria? I want Bria.

Why can't I speak?

"Brenton," a man's voice spoke.

Brent squinted. Tomás, the man with the scarred eye and a lopsided smile, sat cross-legged on the bed across from him.

"There's fire...the boat...it's on fire..." Brent licked his lips. "I'm gonna drown."

"Listen to me," Tomás soothed, placing both of his hands upon Brent's shoulders. "I need you to focus. What is your name?"

"I'm...I...my name..." He winced. "Maija?"

"Try again."

"Uh...I'm...um...I'm..."

"I'll give you a hint. It starts with *brrr*."

"Oh, uh, Br-Br-Br..." He ran the noise over a few more times, letting the memory seep in. "Brent."

"What about your full name?"

"Brent...Brent...Brent—Brenton Rob Harley."

"Good." Tomás smiled. His body stabilized before Brent, and the room finally had stopped spinning. "Now, where are you from?"

"I'm from Newbird's Arm," Brent said, "in the Province Rosada."

"How old are you?"

"Almost twenty-one."

"Good. Now Brenton," Tomás continued, "I want you to focus. Find one thing in your life that centers you, that grounds you. It could be a person, an object, a memory...one thing. Your one constant."

Brent sucked in his lips, a knot forming in the back of his mouth as he spoke, "Bria..."

He lunged forward, and Tomás's gripped his shoulder. Once again, they ran through the exercises, repeating Brent's name, his age, his home, and his constant. Each time they went through it, serenity worked its way a little deeper into Brent's chest.

Tomás walked over to Caroline and whispered loud enough so Brent could hear, "Be careful. I do not want to do this again."

"You are not staying?" Caroline snapped back.

"I must inform Master Ningursu of this ordeal," Tomás exhaled. "Brenton is having a vivid connection with the dead, and it is concerning."

"He *is* learning."

"Too fast." Tomás left the infirmary.

Brent clenched the sheets, his knuckles turning white as he leaned back in the bed. "I've fucked up, haven't I? I did something stupid. I—I just...the story was so strong...and I had to...I couldn't...it was there!"

"You did...perfectly, to be frank," Caroline sat beside him. "The release, from all perspectives, was a success. You freed the girl from Hell."

"How long was she in there, though? I found her skeleton! She'd been dead for—for weeks, months even!" Brent wiped his eyes. "How did you let that happen!?!"

"I cannot save everyone moments after they die," Caroline snarled. "I am *one* person."

"There's eight of you! Nine, now...there's me. Nine, and we could...I mean, Hell is...good people are suffering. We have to...we need to—"

Caroline covered his mouth. "There might be eight current members of the Council, but only one is on the front line. The rest have retired, as I will soon."

Bullshit. Brent crossed his arms.

"I may not agree with it, but it is how it is," Caroline walked across the infirmary. It was a small room with a cluster of different needles and scalpels surrounded by vials of odd-colored fluids on the workbench. Caroline picked one up and peered through it, smirking at Brent, "Who is Bria?"

"What?" The blood rushed to Brent's ears. "I just...a...she's my friend!"

"You are as ripe as a tomato. Friend? Pah."

"I..." He raised his fingers to his lips. The kiss still lingered. "Just...someone."

"Well, make sure to kiss that someone plenty while you have a chance." Caroline kept smiling.

"I, uh...but I'm gonna end up breaking her heart if...*when* I die," Brent frowned. "There's no way to—"

"No."

"But there's that girl, Rho...she can see the tunnels. Why can't she see you?"

Caroline raised her eyebrows. "Rho? Oh, the plant girl. Yes, yes, right, I have seen her. She is an anomaly. Not many have Sight anymore—that vanished long before my time. But, even if the girl has Sight, though, or partial Sight or whatever it may be, the tunnels never open for someone outside the Council. They are our product."

"Wait...wait. Sight? Like able to see the dead sight?" Brent had heard rumors before, whispered deep in the heart of the Pit. "So people with Sight can see us? Then is there a way to get Sight to Bria? Or to my parents and sister? I don't...do I have to *die* die?" Brent swung his legs off the bed, ignoring how the room spun. "Is there a way, so I don't have to be alone?"

"It's not that simple, Brent. Sometimes the Sight makes people go crazy. Some just can't have it. And if they are not born with it, then it must be a Medii, or a seer, to grant the sight. Just like magic, Medii are rarities nowadays."

Brent rubbed his eyes. It stung as if he'd been crying. Maybe he had been, but what good were tears now? "Okay... so maybe Rho can still but...shite. I don't want to...I can't...I'm gonna break her heart."

"This has been hard for both of us, Brent," Caroline reassured him. ""My apprenticeship was much different from yours."

"Yeah, that doesn't help me! It's not like I know...I mean, I don't know anything about you, Caroline," Brent spat. "If this is you trying to make me feel better or give me something to connect with, it's not working."

Caroline's face fell, her brow knit together. "Well, what do you want from me?"

"The truth!"

"I am trying! I am not cut out for this *mentorship*, not like Alojzy was for me...or many of the others." Caroline stepped towards the exit and fidgeted with her cloak. From one of the large inner pockets, she removed a fishing net.

"Where are you going!?!" Brent sat up, but his head spun again, and he collapsed back on the bed.

"I am going fishing!"

"What? Why?"

"To relieve stress!"

"By fishing?"

"Yes! By fishing!" Caroline turned back, her eyes blazing, "You wanted to know about me? Well, let me tell you about my life as a child, growing up in a freezing coastal city in Heims Norte. I was the best female fisher in the whole city-state back when I was younger than you! Why? Because I had a motivation, a vendetta: a giant fish ate my mother when I was a girl, so consarn it I was determined to find it! I have yet to stop either. I will find my mother someday, and if it means I always smell like fish, then so be it!"

Brent's head fell to his chest. "I'm sorry...I didn't mean to insult you or—or something."

Caroline dropped her fishing rod and sat down on Brent's bed. She looked younger for a moment, but as she shook her head, she returned to her usual callousness. "No, I apologize. That was out of line. It may seem, Brent, that there are many ways you and I are similar. I suppose there must be a commonality between the Council members. Most of us were outcasts in society, which may be why fate latches onto us."

"So, you were marked..." Brent fidgeted with his leather bracelet, still not ready to make eye contact with her

"Not quite like you, but in theory, yes," Caroline replied. "Growing up, my interests in fishing, love, magic, and death put me at odds with our goddess, the Constable Gelida, who traveled on snowflakes in the winter and hid in the permafrost during the summer."

"It sounds like that book, *The Snow Fairy*."

"Ah yes, it inspired many children's stories. It fails to mention the more brutal aspects, though, where the preachers of Heims often made sacrifices in the summer to the Constable in our freezing waters. By *luck*, the Council offered me the apprenticeship during the summer."

"Offered," Brent repeated.

"Yes, *offered*," Caroline replied. "I accepted the apprenticeship without hesitation as I had nothing to lose. As I already mentioned, my mother was murdered by a giant fish. My father," she waved her hand over her face, which transformed into an elderly man for a moment, "died of venereal disease two years earlier."

Brent cringed.

Caroline once again changed her mask, half a man, half a woman. "I had a brother and sister, Victoria and William. They left long before then to travel to Sur with their partners. I was left alone." Her gaze fell to the wall. "I was chastised, as I always have been. By Heims, by the Council...in Heims that only involved the entire town ignoring me and calling me undesirable. They let me go on my way."

"Better than the Order," Brent mumbled.

"Most are better than the Order. They are a...temperamental group." Her face returned to normal "I do apologize that you must deal with them."

Brent shrugged.

Caroline looked away. "The preachers' hands-off approach certainly made my apprenticeship easier. But Alojzy was methodical in his approach to training...unlike me."

"You're chaotic."

"That is one way to put it, yes. Alojzy approached this much differently...with a Medii."

"A seer?"

"Ah, yes, good, you are somewhat intelligent, at least."

Brent grunted.

Caroline patted his hand before continuing. "Yes, with a beautiful woman and a local chef in Heims named Tilda, who claimed she could see the dead. She reached out to me first. It started as a normal kinship. She showed me how to cook my fish while telling me stories that only a dead man could tell about events from years prior, about dying, about ghosts and spirits, and," Caroline grinned, "about the Constable's embrace! As she told me these tales, she expanded my lessons to brews and spells...although I never saw them work."

"That sounds...witchy," Brent acknowledged, watching as Caroline's face shifted to a woman with broad lips and wide-set red eyes.

"Oh yes," Caroline grinned, "the people of Heims Norte hated Tilda! But she had harmed no one, so the Constable did not come to take her away. And I came to love her with every confine of my heart. A lovely woman with an array of talents. So, the longer we spent together, the more I saw of the Second World. At first, I thought she had cast a spell over me and that I was becoming just like her! And I loved it! I could see Father as clear as the sky, though not my mother; I have never found my mother..." Her voice cracked, and she cleared her throat. "But I was not to be the next Medii. It turns out Alojzy decided to communicate through Tilda...to ignite my powers and cover the basics. I must have run into him before our formal introduction, but I was never keen on details."

"What if he'd never shown up, though?" Brent asked, "Would you have kept...developing?"

"No," Caroline replied. "Mist Keepers keep their initials powers with the promise to die, and it does not fully develop until we enter the library and learn to conduct releases."

"Oh. A'ight."

"It was probably for the best, though. In Heims, no one cares until someone performs pernicious witchcraft. I was never in any danger...until some young girls saw me change my appearance to that of an old man. But I also happened to misplace one of my eyes. They screamed, accused me of witchery and defying the Constable, and through that, they sentenced me to death."

Brent pondered for a moment. "So, the Curse doesn't kill you...it brings death to you."

"Correct."

So I just have to avoid death, and I'll be able to live. He picked at his wrist again, not daring to look at Caroline. "How did you die then?"

"They took me to the far north in a rowboat and drowned me in the ice where the Constable hides during the summer." Caroline waved her hand over her face, and a gorged mask of her own face, gray and bloated, replaced her porcelain skin.

"Were you ready? You were young, weren't you?"

"I was twenty-eight," Caroline replied, "and to be candid, yes, I was ready. I had studied with Tilda for three months before Alojzy revealed himself, and for three months after that, he trained me! So yes...I was ready."

"Is everyone, though?"

"You would have to ask them."

Brent's heart sank. He was so sick of crying, sick of feeling like mere dust instead of a person. Puppet strings attached to his shoulders–and for what? To join some group of bizarre magic users that claim to be Death themselves?

Caroline nudged Brent's arm. "You like stories, yes? Well, everyone's story is different–open your eyes and ears, and you will learn their tales. Although you may have to prod some more than others to get the details."

Brent nodded, attention drifting to the blank wall. He had hoped Caroline's story would provide solace, a connection through a similar trial, but it left a tender ache in his mouth.

"You will learn, I promise," Caroline patted his arm. "Aelia will come to check on you soon. If she gives you the go-ahead, you may leave or do whatever it is you do in your free time."

"A'ight..."

"I am going to go fishing now." She gathered her fishing net, then paused. "I am sorry for lashing out before, Brent. Really. I did not mean to take my frustrations out on you. It has been a strange couple of weeks."

Brent couldn't disagree with that.

CHAPTER FOURTEEN

MONSTER IN THE LIBRARY

Brent struggled to recognize himself in the mirror. Stubble decorated his chin, and dark bags hung from his eyes. A yellow blemish surrounded one of his eyes, while above the other, a cut marked his brow. Black and blue blotches extended down his neck and against his visible rib cage. His knees shook as Aelia circled him, checking his pulse and reflexes while mumbling in some obscure language. The mist gathered around her fingertips as she examined him, and she sometimes paused to analyze it.

"Open your mouth," Aelia motioned.

Brent obeyed. She stuck a finger in and pressed against one of his molars. Brent bit down in pain, only to have Aelia prod his jaw open and mutter something. She continued to press her fingers to the top of his mouth and then yank at his tongue to peer down his throat.

"How are you feeling?" She released his jaw, running her fingers through the mist and making a note in the air.

"Shitty."

"And what does that imply? Have you eaten? Slept?"

"Sometimes."

Aelia grunted as she sat at a workbench to mix an array of liquids. She worked fast, her slim hands combining the ingredients with ease. Once finished, she passed a grotesque green vial to Brent. "Here. This should help."

Brent sniffed it. "Will it protect me from the curse?"

"Pardon?"

"I mean..." Brent gathered the words at his tongue. "How long do I have until I die, anyway? Will it protect me from death?"

"That is not a medical question," Aelia went about cleaning her workstation, "It could be tomorrow, next week, next month, or in a year. In my experience, it is usually not long. Death is attracted to the mist."

"Is it really, though? Or is it just bad luck? Can't it be broken?"

"We have all died because of the curse. There is no *breaking* it," Aelia stated. Her voice was like a knife, scraping through the air and carving on stone.

Brent took the hint to stop asking questions, instead sitting on the bed and exhaling. He couldn't cry anymore. The day, the week–or however long it had been–had taken a toll on him. What more did he expect? Caroline and the Council were the demons who latched onto his silver eyes. They rode his back and scratched at his skin, punched at his stomach, and picked hairs from his scalp.

He was dying. In his wake, he left a path of tears; his mother's tears, Maija's butchered release, Rho's frustration, Jemma's distrust, Christof's anger, Bria...

"Can I go home?"

Aelia shrugged. "If that is what you wish."

"Thank you."

"I hope you know the way out; I am meeting with Tomás in Mert, and I cannot stall any longer. I'm not a caretaker...why do they always assume..." She continued grumbling as she strode from the room.

Brent left the infirmary after dressing and stepped out onto the glass walkways that hung above the library.

The library was empty. No one else moved on the glass walkways nor on the stairs or on the shelves. Only his footsteps caused the glass to ripple with color

His attention fell to the walls of books that lined the glass walkway. Every few paces, he pulled a book from the shelves and flipped it open. Often, the text eluded him, foreign or ancient, or both. If he found a book he understood, the pages most often contained nothing but names. Stories, so many more stories than he ever imagined, towering above him like a city! Someday he'd understand them; he'd have an eternity to learn these tales.

At least that was something.

As he circled the second floor, he peeked into unlocked rooms. One looked like a tiny home. Another was an office with books piled to the ceilings. There was also a kitchen, a washroom, and even a room that overlooked a dazzling silver lake enshrouded in red flowers. *The Order doesn't know what they're missing!* If this was the work of the Effluvium, it was gorgeous. If it was the work of demons...well, maybe the demons weren't half bad either.

Brent recalled a hymn the Order often chanted, saying demons hid in dark pits of the Effluvium. They dragged away the innocent deep beneath the earth. The demons torment thee, the story went, in fire and water, until they rip away your blood and your soul no longer belongs to you. But the Mist Keepers as demons? Not here; not in the library.

Brent wandered downstairs, where the rivers of books flowed into an ocean. The bookshelves came as waves; books about warriors, history, romance, and the mundane surfed through the currents.

Brent followed the shelves. The back of the library came to life like a forest. The walls breathed with vines, masking the shelves with a wave of humidity. Furniture hobbled on crooked legs, seeming to watch as Brent continued pulling books from the shelves. Some large, some small, some old, some new, all begging for him to read. His pursuit led him to the border of a thin book. The binding dripped off the side. Like all the others, he removed it from the shelf. He couldn't read the title, but the picture on the front depicted a single glass jar.

The book itself didn't keep his interest long, though. As soon as it fell into his palms, he heard a click. The bookshelves rotated and revealed a door beneath them with a rusted bronze handle.

"Well, shite..."

He placed the book on the ground and walked to the door. It opened at his presence, revealing a rope ladder down into a pitch-black room beneath the ground

Brent's gut told him–no, begged him–to just step back and pretend he saw nothing. But whatever lurked in the darkness below compelled him. It was like freshly baked lemon cake or the open arms of a caring mother to her babe, impossible to resist. His legs and heart said yes, yanked forward by curiosity, and he climbed down the ladder.

The minute-long descent led Brent to a small, moist room. Jars, glowing with a yellow tint, rested on lopsided shelving. Brent grabbed one of the two the torches hanging on the wall and held it up to the shelves. One jar began to shake, rustling the shelf, so dust sprung into the air.

Brent jumped back and dropped the torch to the floor. The fire fizzled out.

All light came from the lone torch on the wall.

Did I climb that far?

The jar continued to shake, and around it, its brethren mimicked its movements. As their rumbling grew, the jars dove off the shelf and cracked open on the floor. The smell of rotten eggs and murky water poured outwards, replacing the lure of a mother's arms and lemon cakes with the fear brought by a storm and the taste of sour milk.

Out of them emerged an eerie, flaxen mist, merging to take on the form of a monstrous humanoid, climbing...

Climbing...

Climbing...

The creature towered over Brent. Its heartbeat visibly in its translucent chest and yellow eyes haunted its sharp face, with one hanging out of its socket. Its teeth were sharp and crooked. White hair cascaded from its head and down its back.

It shrieked once, shaking further jars along the wall.

Brent clamored for the ladder as the creature—no, the demon—still made sense of its own two feet. Every part of him wanted to give in to the monster as it breathed down his neck. With its breaths came flashes of perdition. He couldn't rationalize his thoughts, each weighed down by the unrelenting fear weaving through his body. One second his focus was on the small room, the next raving about cats, and then again, he returned to Maija's head, where a man much bigger than him held him and then...

Brent shook it off, choking down the memory while seizing the opportunity to race up the ladder. He climbed as fast as he could while the creature squealed after him.

It cries like a child. Brent regretted taking a second to look at the beast. The yellow mist had gathered around its feet and lifted it up into the air.

"Shite!" Brent scurried up, the creature's breath on his ankles. Once he climbed out, he slammed close the trapdoor. He grabbed the thin book and shoved it back into the case. The shelving pivoted over the door. It shook and trembled while the creature banged and screamed.

Brent darted away, cursing and crying out for Caroline or Aelia or Toma or anyone! Only his echoes responded. He rushed the stairwell. No one peered out of the shelves; no one hid behind the doors.

"HELLO!?! ANYONE!?! Please..." His voice clogged in his throat. "Why the fuck do eight people need a place this big!?!"

He peered into another door, open but a crack. To his relief, a woman not much older than him sat in a chair, staring at a blank canvas with glossy green eyes. She spun a strand of her ash-blond hair around her finger.

"Oh! Hello! Thank goodness, I...uh..." Brent winced. How could he explain this? It was like something out of one of his stories. "There's...I don't know if you know who I am, but I—uh...there's a monster."

The woman turned, smiling at Brent. "Oh ,Winston, I did not think you'd be back so soon."

"I...I'm sorry?"

"Come, Winston, sit. I'll help you with the piano." She glanced at her canvas. Brent squinted, seeing an image of a composer weaving its way across the canvas, a misty quality to its watercolored etching.

"I'm sorry, I'm not...I'm not Winston. My name is Brent. I need help."

"Of course, of course, I know." She smiled. "Winston, you'll be a great composer one day."

"I, um...listen, I'll go find Winston, okay? I'll be back."

"Take care now."

Brent closed the door. Back home, a woman like that would end up in the Pit, withering inside disillusioned life. He'd seen them take confused individuals away. When he was a child, Brent watched as they took his father away for rambling nonsense and washing his sorrows in alcohol. Was that woman any different? The way she ranted in befuddlement sent him back to those days in his childhood when he watched from the bushes as they dragged his father away. He ran home crying that day.

Brent wanted to wither into tears now as he glanced back once towards the door. Why did it hurt so much to see that woman now?

Because it affirms what you always knew. The Order is wrong. There's another way to live.

Brent checked a few more doors until he found Jiang lying unconscious with a bottle of wine in hand. When he tried waking the giant, the man rolled over and vomited onto the ground, shuddering only when a thud rang from beneath them.

"Shite." Brent kept moving.

He came upon another stairwell that led to an empty and dark hallway. Only a set of large double doors waited. No books or shelving marked the walk. Brent's was the only shadow among the flickering lights.

Brent cracked open the doors down the hallway and finally peeked into a dim room. Piles of scrolls and papers coated the floors, desks, and furniture. In the room's center sat a basin, pooling with a deep silver liquid and hints of red. Brent peered into it; a foggy image of a city filled its surface.

An orotund voice spoke and startled him. "Care to knock?"

Brent looked around the room before noticing a head–*a real head!* –on the bookshelf, with a petroglyph covered scroll pulled out beneath its chin. The head itself was bald with only one eye as white as parchment while the other socket sat empty. Thin lips formed a crease on its pale face, and where its nose should have been was but an empty, cracked hole.

"Who–"

It cut him off. "Ningursu."

"You mean–"

"The Head of the Council, the Original Keeper of the Mist, God of Death."

"But you're—you're a head," Brent breathed. He couldn't believe it! In fact, it was almost comical. Now wasn't the time to laugh over it, though, so he pocketed his amusement for later.

"Yes, I am aware."

"But—but how?"

"That is not important," Ningursu remarked. "I believe it is my turn: why did you intrude without knocking, Brenton Rob Harley?"

"I, uh..." Brent gulped. "I was—I was exploring the library. I was just curious. And, uh—a bookshelf opened, and there was a trap door. With jars. And they shook or something, and then they fell and cracked. And there was a monster or something...I don't know. I didn't mean to."

"I see." Ningursu made direct eye contact with Brent and said, "Take my head."

"What!?!"

"I said take my head."

"You mean...pick it up?"

"Do you not understand words, boy?" Ningursu sneered. "Show me where you saw the monster."

With his hands shaking, Brent picked Ningursu's head up and carried it back down the stairs. Everything was silent. For a moment, he was relieved, hoping the monster had quit.

Then Brent realized why.

Shelves lay on their sides.

The trap door hung open.

Books and debris cluttered the pathways.

And the library's entrance lay in shambles.

"Shite!" Brent shouted.

"Well," Ningursu declared, "we best organize a meeting to resolve this."

"But that—that thing! It's out there somewhere!"

"If it is only the Council in the tunnels, we can keep it contained. It only cares for Magii—"

"Magii..." Brent's entire body froze. His thoughts mingled together like a lattice of vines, like Rho's vines. *Oh no. She's in danger.* He ignored Ningursu's instructions, a numbness washing over his hands. Each finger loosened with his rising heart rate, and like the sudden realization that fell into his gut, Brent dropped Ningursu's head to the ground with a thud.

"Brenton!"

He gawked at Ningursu, "Rho..."

"What are you talking about!?!" Ningursu shouted, his voice muffled by the floor.

"Rho—I have to warn her!"

"Who? What? Elaborate, please."

"She's in danger! I need to help her!"

"BRENTON!"

"Sorry, sir! This is important!" he called back, before dashing into the tunnels.

CHAPTER FIFTEEN

SOILED

Rho wrapped her hand in a vine, watching as the flowers bloomed around her fingers and detailed the back of her hand. Her lips quivered, her head pounded, and it took all her energy not to cry. It would all be okay. She wasn't alone in the tunnels anymore; she could show it all to Brent now. This day would be a distant memory soon.

Yet, her nerves continued to pile into her stomach, and it didn't help that a strange shaking rumbled through the tunnels. She gripped the wall, letting a white flower dance about her fingers, and squinted towards the junction.

"Hello? Brent? Is that you?"

No response. The shaking continued. One by one, vines lost their grip on the wall and withered away at her feet.

A whiff of sulfur followed, galloping into her nostrils as a gust of wind-powered through the tunnels and nearly knocked her off her feet. It filled her head, dragging her back.

Choking.

Soiled.

Dead.

A profuse yellow fog gathered around her, tendrils locking down on her ankles like weights. Her head seared as fear crept over her. Not just normal fear, but a nightmarish sensation of dread weighing down on her. She struggled to fight against odd feeling, but with a determined grunt, she yanked one foot free and crawled backward beneath the torchlight. A high pitch screech ruptured from the...what even was this thing? A monster? A demon? Whatever it was, the light caused it to recoil, providing Rho just enough time to escape its grasp and dart down the tunnels.

The walls closed in around her, dizziness washing over her as she reached the ladder to the Senator's Garden. As her feet hit the ground, the roots from the oak tree latched the entrance closed. The yellow fog banged and ripped at the dirt before the door flung open.

Out it poured with the prowess of a storm.

It uprooted the old oak tree and flung the snow on the ground into the air with violence like a blizzard. Rho dashed ahead, avoiding the gardeners, the Guard, the civilians, and lovers in the garden's embrace. Yet, despite everyone else around, this strange yellow mist only fixated on Rho.

As it pummeled through, it ripped up bushes and trees, cracked open the walkway, and even caused the camellia bush near the Senator's home to wilt. Thunder and lightning rippled through its façade. Rho withered in its wake, her aches creaking, her heart pummeling her ribs, and her eyes searing. Her little branch dropped away.

She rushed through the gardens. Had the pathways always wound so much? Rho knew the facility like the back of her hand, but with the distorted mist surging after her, the gardens turned into an endless maze. The hedges seemed taller, and despite running, the gardener's house looked farther away than ever, and the Senator's mansion might have been a cloud in the sky. Her head seared, her eyes watered, but she couldn't stop running.

She ducked into the Senator's hedge maze. The high walls did not deter the monster. It launched itself over the hedges, causing all but the white camellias to wilt in its presence. Rho was small compared to this monster, and how could a glorified gardener ever take down a monster? Why would it even care about her?

Was she finally seeing the invisible people? Had they decided she was the intruder? The monster cared naught about the townsfolk or the Order or anything else.

Just her: the queen of weeds.

Rho came to a dead-end. *C'mon.* She waved her hand to open the branches, but her powers fizzled as the monster neared. Nightmares flurried through her head her grandpapa's bedroom the night of his death, the tales of her mother's murderous rage the day of her birth, the screams of her father when the Guard once came knocking. All of it rushed, twisted, and turned through her psyche. In an instant, she was lost, confused, and stranded in the dark.

Rho held her head, *No, stop, please stop!*

The monster towered over her, and another bellowing shriek rippled through it. Invisible fingers moved across Rho's face, tracing every indent of her nose and mouth. Its breath loitered through her hair. It reached behind her ear, and her little branch cried out in pain. She wanted to cry with it but kept back the tears.

No. She clenched her fists. Long ago, she pretended to be the Forest Queen. Who was to say she wasn't? She wouldn't let an invisible *thing* take away that choice.

Her pain turned into a strength, and she reached into her pouch of seeds and threw a fistful of beans into the air. They exploded outwards, latching onto the trees, bushes, and grounds. She then told the vine around her hand to expand out, towards the yellow monster, towards the sky, to take her far away. *Don't be afraid...please don't be afraid. Come to your mother...come on!*

And they did just that.

Almost.

As the roots, branches, and vines marched through the maze, the yellow force retreated. The foliage wrapped around it, personifying humanoid shape that towered towards the sky.

"Come on!" Rho seethed. After a few moments, a branch covered in camellias shot out of one of Rho's seeds. It flew right at the yellow force and through the center of its chest.

A shriek split through the beast, and it ripped away the vines before grabbing Rho. She felt its fingers–or nails or something–dig into her sides. She winced but didn't let up her command. Even as the monster lifted her up into the air, the trees followed and tried to tear her free. Up and up, the creature carried her towards the sky.

She screamed, and with her shouts, the trees grappled upwards, clinging to the vines about her wrist. The storm arriving with the beast filled the air.

Boom! Clap!

Thunder rolled. Flashes of lightning shot through the air. For a moment, it illuminated the monster, showing a lopsided and grayed face with fangs dripping in saliva.

Boom!

The monster bellowed with the rolling thunder, and it dropped Rho. She used the vines to hook onto a nearby tree, hitting hard before falling to the ground.

Already, the monster had vanished into the clouds, squealing as it departed. In its wake, it left behind a rotting garden and the endless stench of rotten eggs soiling the air.

Rho collapsed against the ground. Something moist coated her waist. She moved her hand to see a layer of blood staining her side.

Oh...

She closed her eyes. The root behind her ear extended across her neck and down her side, wrapping around her injuries and binding her to the ground.

And for the first time in years, Rho abandoned her greatest defense.

She cried.

CHAPTER SIXTEEN

WILTED

"Rho!?! RHO!?!" Brent darted through the tunnels. He hoped her absence meant she was safe, but if the wilted vines on the wall meant anything, the monster came and went with the power of a storm. It brought destruction all through the tunnels, tearing up Rho's hideaway under the ladder to Newbird's Arm. *Shite! Shite! Shite!* He wanted to collapse. This was all too much for one day. Yet now, the monster had climbed out of the tunnels...into the Gardens...and into Newbird's Arm, where his family lived.

Where Bria lived.

"Shite!"

It was too late when Brent arrived in the Gardens. The creature had laid waste to paradise. Trees lay across the ground. The pathway lay marked with cracked bricks and uneven flowers, with brown grass crunching beneath his feet. Even the camellia bushes wilted. Patrons rushed from the paths, holding their children close, shouting over one another as the storm raged onwards. It belonged to nightmares, and the looming haze of death even slowed the Guards as they rushed into the commotion.

Everyone paused as a thunderclap roared from the Senator's hedge maze, and the monster shot up towards the sky. In its grasp, a body traveled with it. Tree branches followed upwards, vines shooting from all angles. *Rho.*

The monster's screech pierced the air. It dropped the body mid-flight, sending it toppling to the ground. Brent froze, watching as the monster disappeared into the storm clouds.

"Rho!?!" he shouted again.

The hedge maze ate the body. With the monster gone, the commotion in the garden broke. Gardeners rushed about. Children cried. Mothers fled. The Guard arrived as a force as strong as the storm, ordering the citizens back home.

"Brent!" someone called out to him from the commotion.

He spun around. Caroline marched towards him, eyes blazing. She proceeded to remove a book from her cloak and whacked him with it. "What happened? What did you do?"

Brent winced. "What? I didn't—it just came out of the library! I didn't mean—" His eyes darted to the hedge maze again, "She's hurt...I gotta...I need to...Rho's hurt! And—and..." He glanced around, watching as the gardeners tried to clear the path. "Bria's not here either. I need to...where is she—"

Caroline smacked him with the book again. "Stop fumbling about and go! It's dangerous here!"

"But I—I mean—"

The book slammed against him once more. "We will talk later. Go."

"Stop using me as a punching bag!"

"I said *go*!"

Brent nodded, rubbing his forehead as he darted off. He passed by the head gardener, Mr. West, yelling for his junior gardeners to go home. The man called out to Brent, but whatever he said was suffocated in the shouts of the Guard gathering around the hedge maze.

"Rho?!" he cried out.

He pushed past a few of the guards, but to his dismay, he toppled face-to-face with Christof.

"Shite."

Christof grabbed Brent by the collar of his shirt and spat at him. "Why are you always here when things go wrong?"

"Please—Christof, I need...please..."

"C'mon," Christof dragged Brent away from the hedges. "A vag like you shouldn't be out and about. Time to go home."

"I'm not a vagrant!"

"Keep telling yourself that," Christof shoved him towards a few other cadets smoking just outside the garden. "Oi! Lawry! Jacobson! Get this one into the Pit. He ain't s'posed to be out an' about."

"Didn't we already beat this piece of shite up once today?" Cadet Lawry waltzed over and grabbed Brent by the neck, "Thought he'd learn his lesson. Guess we gotta repeat it."

Christof snarled. "I don't need more trouble with my father."

Cadet Lawry chuckled. "Fine."

Brent strained against their grip for a moment, but both Cadets proved too strong for him. Fighting them would likely only result in a broken jaw, and that was the last thing Brent needed right now. So he gave in, bowing his head, as Cadet Lawry and Cadet Jacobson dragged him away from the gardens and tossed him into the Pit. He landed on the ground with a thud.

The hard toe of Cadet Lawry's boot struck Brent's nose. He gasped, a sensation of whirling and spinning washing over him as he tried to sit up. Vertigo pulled down at him, and he pressed his forehead to the ground. "Please...stop..."

Cadet Lawry laughed, saying nothing else as he slammed the gates of the Pit closed.

Brent rolled over, wiping the blood from his face. The storm clouds cried above him. He might have sobbed with them, but the day's events weighed too heavily in his heart, suffocating even tears. He'd seen Rho soar through the sky. Was she hurt? He didn't know. But he couldn't muster the energy to get up, his head ringing like a gong, the vertigo replaced with a queasiness he couldn't shake. As he pictured her falling, his throat tightened. *What if she's dead? Then I need to release her soul...I can't let her stay in Hell!* He managed to his feet for a moment, then stumbled forward and vomited.

"Shite."

Brent fell again and clenched the dirt, hiding his face from anyone who might pay heed. Most of the vagrants hid away in their homes as the rain battered on the dilapidated and makeshift roofs. *Maybe, I'm finally where I belong.*

Were the gardens still burning? Was the Council going to come for him? Was this the place he would ultimately die? Brent didn't know. He wanted someone to comfort him, whether it was his mother, Bria...or even Rho. A pair of arms holding him like a child, stroking back his hair and telling him it would be okay, would certainly quell his fears now.

But the only a distant hum in the air wrapped around him. A song, a story, playing out from inside one of the shacks. Brent did not move to find its source, but as he shut his eyes, the tale became vivid–of warriors, of hope, and of dreams.

Ey oh
The sky is black
We shall come back
Ey oh
Our arms are tight
Swords cut to fight
Ey oh
Ey oh
We shall come back
We shall come back
Ey oh
We will be back

CHAPTER SEVENTEEN

THE PIT

It took Brent a few days to retreat from his deepening worries. While he meandered about the Pit, listening to the clumsy storytellers and drunken rages, he pondered his inevitable clash with the Council. What would they do to him? Would they kill him right there, like the curse intended? Or worse?

What could be worse? He didn't want to know.

At night, he slept on the dusty floor of his father's bunk, dreaming of Bria, his mother, his sister, and of Rho falling from the sky. He woke up from the nightmares in a cold sweat, climbing to his feet and sweating. Most night, his father sat on one of the broken chairs drinking and injecting his veins with a silver fluid. When Brent woke with a jolt, he offered Brent a hit or a drink. After the fourth night of waking, Brent took a swig of liquor, zoning out while his father went back to his dissociative mumbling and glazed stare.

Brent knew many of the vagrants, some he went to school with. They were, after all, the last group of children branded at a young age. Most had not been given the opportunity to marry out of the Pit as he'd acquired from the Order; instead, many lost their families, and others made decisions leading them into the fray.

In the droves, he watched his old schoolmate Micca dealing out smokes, playing with wind-up toys, and shouting obscenities. A few times, Brent sat smoking with Micca, recanting the old days, but he spent most of his time daydreaming about the Garden as they spoke.

My fault. Why did he have to pull *that* book off the shelf? And why did he go into that trap door? He should have minded his own business.

Of course, Caroline never came. He mulled over his own thoughts, of his family, of Rho, of his own sanity...and of Bria. Whenever he thought about any of them, he curled in on himself and hid his head in his hands. How could he return to them with a smile now? He was alone, washed away in the Pit like he'd been destined. Why didn't he expect this? He should've known this was how it'd all end up.

Forgotten. Abandoned. Alone.

As the week wore on, more vagrants recognized Brent as the lanky storyteller who came with tales to trade! They called for him to tell stories, offering bags of white powder and canisters of murky liquid in return. Some even went so far as to pull out the strips of paper he'd traded, begging for another in return for a smoke. A story for a taste of freedom, they called. As tempting as it was, he couldn't bring himself to form the tales. Hope vanished from anything he tried to concoct, leaving the stories in his head as dry as a desert. It was as if the monster stole his stories, filling his imagination with an empty pit of despondency.

So as with each passing day, Brent kept his head down and shoulders hunched, waiting in line with the rest to use the bathhouse.

"Ey, boyo," a man with three missing teeth and eyes as white as doves called out to him. "Ya the storyteller, eh? The one with the strips. Ya come to the market but never give me nothing. I gots some better stuff here y'know. Tell us a tale, and it's all yours." He waved the bag of powder in Brent's face.

"No—no, thank you..." Brent looked away, only to have his attention captured by a couple of scantily clad women leaving the bathhouse. They walked past each person in queue, dragging their fingertips over each person's chests, massaging shoulders, and leaning in for kisses. A few followed in their wake, but when they reached Brent, one of the women stopped.

"Oh, look at this young'un, Kimba!" the woman called, pursing her pink painted lips. "I ain't seen him before."

"Must be a newbie." The other woman pranced over and cupped Brent's cheek, "Oh, you're right, Maxi! He's so young 'n cute! Look at them eyes! I could sell 'em! They look like diamonds!"

"Don't he look like Rob too?"

"I...uh..." Blood rushed to Brent's cheeks. "I don't.... I want nothing...I don't..."

"Ay, Kimba!" Maxi cackled, revealing her golden teeth, "I don't think he done this before. I think he's a virgin!"

"A virgin? He's gotta be at least twenty!" Kimba stroked Brent's hair back. "We don't charge for the *first* time, young'un."

"Then only a couple of coins thereafter."

"I, uh...no—no, thank you." Brent stumbled out of line, "Really, I—I'm okay."

The woman didn't pursue him, returning to their business.

Brent collapsed by the fence and sniffled. The frisk air bombarded his back like stones, and he withered beneath the wind. Memories of the monster's attack returned like photographs in his mind: screams, heavy breathing, fires, and storms. He couldn't tell the difference between his memories, the Old Woman of Errat, Maija's hell, and reality itself. Which screams came from the vagrants a few shacks down from his father's dilapidated home, and what was in his head?

Yet as the sun rose, and the town's bustle picked up beyond the Pit, he stifled the energy to call out to one person beyond the fence.

"Ma?" He shouted as his mother hurried down the road, carrying her deliveries into town.

She paused, her tired eyes wide as she turned to the fence. "Brenton!"

"Ma!"

She darted over, reaching through the bars to stroke back his hair and kiss his forehead.

"I'm sorry I'm in...I'm here. I'm sorry..."

She soothed him. "It's not your fault, it's not your fault."

He unraveled into tears at his mother's touch. He blubbered and pressed his head to the fence. "I'm sorry...I didn't want to. I didn't mean to..."

"You're not supposed to be in here," she murmured, "You're betrothed...they said you'd be fine until you're twenty-one. They promised."

"Ma, I..." How could he tell her he tried to break it off? Or about his feelings for Bria? Or that he planned to run away? "I want a normal life."

"You will have one, you will," his mother whispered, pressing her fingers against his cheek. "You'll marry Jemma once you're both of age, and you'll be a fantastic husband. You have kindness...like your father."

"But Dad's still in the Pit...it's pointless."

"Your father has other issues. We've tried many things with him." His mother peered past the fence. "War does that, I suppose. We did everything. I thought our marriage would keep him out, but it did not. I bought his freedom, but he came back. And then they tried cleansing him, but the Demons of War continue to haunt him. But now there's no Smoke Riots to speak of, so you don't have to worry about those demons. You can be free."

"Ma, I didn't know." He wiped away one of her tears. "You never told me. But that doesn't...I mean...I'm sorry."

"Of course not; it is not something for you to worry about." She wiped her face. "After I make my deliveries, I'll talk with Brother Roy Al. He can pull some strings with his brother."

"Ma, you don't have—"

"Promise me you'll come home though."

"Ma—"

"Brenton, please."

"I'll try." It hurt to lie to his mother, but it pained him more to see her cry

His mother squeezed his hand once. Brent didn't want to let it go, but eventually, he gave in, letting his mother depart towards town.

Brent leaned his head against the fence. It didn't matter anymore, did it? If he was cursed to die, why bother trying to escape a life in the Pit? *Because Rho might be hurt. Or Bria might be worried. And because I'm still a Mist Keeper. Or will be.*

As the vagrants returned to the mines and fields, the Pit became a ghost town. Brent checked every tree for a tunnel entrance, but nothing budged. Everything was devoid of life, absent of magic. Dead.

He kicked another one with his foot. *Rho would know a way out. She could fix this.*

Rho might be dead, the voice of the old woman in Errat spoke. *Dead and gone.*

She's not dead.

You don't even know who she is, boy.

She's my friend.

Brent sat on the ground and lit a smoke. With each puff, the mist of the dead roared. It never seemed to leave his field of vision, dully aching between his eyes.

Brent watched it, scouring for stories in its movements. Sometimes, he envisioned vagrants moving throughout time, riots by the fire and songs leaving tongues cut out. In others, he saw lovers, adventures, and skilled wanders, all in search for a new day.

He might have stayed lost in them, but footsteps caught his attention. As if walking out of the mist himself, Micca stumbled towards him.

"Brenty-boy!" Micca collapsed next to him and pulled his long hair back. "You lookin' mighty pathetic sitting here all lonely and shite."

"Yeah, and you look like a skid rogue if you ask me." Brent puffed on his smoke. "Up to no good, are you?"

"Nothing no better than the rest of these rubes. 'Sides, I think I might get a way out of here in a few. Take a looky here." He pulled a wind-up toy from his pocket and started it up, "Call this lil' man Fredrick."

"Fredrick?" Brent laughed. "A'ight, I'll bite. Why's he called that?"

"Why you called Brent? 'Cause your mama named ya that! I'm Fredrick's mama!" Micca poked the center of Brent's head. "C'mon, use that noggin of yours. Thought you was a storyteller or somethin'."

"Okay, okay, I get it." Brent watched as the wind-up toy fizzled out, falling to the side. "Why do you think Fredrick is your way out then?"

"Been selling 'em to the lot, with my smokes and all. Got myself a good grand or so saved up from selling all that. Think I can buy my freedom with that much." Micca winked. "Then I'll get outta this damn town. Shite, man, I'll get outta this damn country! Maybe I'll head to Proveniro. Ever heard of that? Everyone owns a buggy down there, and they got these Glass Cities and moving pictures and all. Or—or maybe I'll go over to the City of Mert. They seem pretty cool too—lots of magic..."

Brent's attention faded as Micca continued rambling, his hands in the air and hope evident on his face. He was glad to see someone optimistic about the future, but Micca always had been, ever since they were kids.

He watched as the vagrants returned from the fields and the mines, passing smokes back and forth with Micca and commenting about their general days. Micca mentioned Bria once, causing Brent to turn red, then proceeded to ramble about the latest man he'd met one night in the Black Market.

After Micca left, off to the market to deal his wares, Brent moved towards one of the many bonfires where the vagrants danced and sang. Men and women gathered around. He noticed his father sitting a few paces down, flinching and mumbling about the cackles from the bonfire and the 'noise of the war drums.' His gray eyes stared with a haunted embrace.

Brent absorbed the songs—stories and tales of a happier time. A time of magic, A time of faith, but more importantly, a time when people were free. Brent wondered if a better life existed somewhere beyond the Province Rosada, as Micca said. A place where storytellers spoke, magic touched the skies, and those in need of help received it.

Rho had shown him some of it, but could there be more?

Would he be able to see it all if he ran away with Bria? Or was that dream gone like all the others?

Like the stories, the song came to an end when the real world entered the Pit. As the main gates opened, the vagrants fled to the shadows.

Yet this time, the Guard did not enter the Pit alone.

Instead, in a blue dress and with her hair pinned in a glowing orange bun stood Jemma. A sadness washed over her face.

"Brent!"

"Jem..." He walked towards her with his legs heavy. Would she belittle him? Shame him? He never could get a good reading on her.

She gripped his hands. "Brother Roy Al talked with Captain Carver. You're free to go...but only if you are cleansed first."

He glanced in the direction of his father. "I'm not sure."

"What are you not sure about?"

"That they'll take away who I am!" Brent shook his head. "I told you, Jem, I'm calling this off."

"Brent, please!" Jemma continued gripping his hands. "We can save you. Let us try. Only Levels One and Two—it will save you!"

"I don't need to be saved!"

"Then you'll end up here! Do you really want to spend your life here?"

"No, but I can always leave!" Brent clenched his teeth. "Leave this town, I mean. Just...I can go. Then you don't have to worry about me! You can have whatever life you want!"

"Brent..." Jemma bowed her head, "Please, go get cleansed."

"Why does it matter?"

"Because I need you to!" She snapped back. "Please, I need you to, so I might still have a chance to become a Sister of the Order. That's what Sisters of the Order do; they save people! Let me try to save you! Please. Just the first two levels. If you care at all...it's all I ask."

There, Brent finally saw her: a girl longing to be more than her destiny. Her heart belonged to the Order, and for it to love her back, she'd agreed to this nightmare.

How had he missed it before? *Because you're a selfish fool,* the woman chimed in his head. *All about your suffering, never others. Don't you see what you've dragged this girl into?*

I can fix this.

Pah.

"Okay, fine," Brent whispered. "If you insist...I'll go."

CHAPTER EIGHTEEN

Three Lanterns

Hun — are you okay? Oh no..."

"Wake up dear, you're safe now."

"Do you think my belle is going to die?"

"She can't. She's fine. See, look, blossoming as she did like a babe."

"The camellias still bloom."

"But all else is dead."

"Please wake up, dear."

"Please."

Rho woke up gasping. Pain seared through her stomach and up her back, and as soon as light trickled into her eyes, she began to sob. Her little branch had retreated behind her ear, leaving a coat of bandages to heal the wound on her side.

After blinking away her tears, the room filled her vision. Her room, her home. She had one of her grandmama's knit blankets wrapped around her. A lemon cake with a cup of tea sat on her end table. When she tried reaching for it, the cup of tea clattered to the floor.

Her grandmama rushed up the ladder into the bedroom and cried out, causing Rho to bawl all over again. Had the room grown humid? She choked on the thick air as her grandmother lulled her, rocking her back and forth, stroking away her unkempt hair.

"How long have I been—"

"On and off a couple days." Her grandmama stroked her face and whispered, "You were wilting."

Rho reached for her little branch, tracing it down the side of her neck, "What about the gardens?"

Her grandmama looked towards the closed curtains.

"Grandmama?"

"They will bloom again." Her grandmama redirected her attention to the lemon cake, thrusting the delicacy into Rho's hands. "Eat."

Rho pushed it away and opened the curtains. Her bedroom window overlooked the gardens, but if she hadn't known any better, she would have thought she slept amid a warzone. Like the world she'd seen beyond Newbird's Arm, the gardens sat charred and dead, fueling a strange emptiness in her own soul. Trees lay toppled against the paths, vines lay strewn like snake skins, and the grass a beige coat matching the Guard marching through the paths. It was everything she never wanted Newbird's Arm to become; it reminded Rho of the cities she'd visited in the north. Even though white camellias bloomed, Rho withered beneath her quiet tears.

"Let me go...let me save it." Rho choked. She rose from her bed, but after a single step, her legs gave out, and she held herself against the floor. "Let me save it..."

Her grandmama helped her up. "Come back to bed now. You're too weak."

"I'm fine!"

"No, no, come...relax."

"How can I relax?" Rho barked. "The gardens are destroyed! That monster thing is still out there, and—"

"And you used your powers more than you ever had before, dear." Her grandmama forced her to sit on the bed. Despite the old woman's shaky stature, her strength might have belonged to the strongest guard right then. "You've never fought with them. You've always—"

"Gardened? Well..." Rho stared at her hands. "Maybe it's time to do more."

"Do not put this on yourself. You've hidden in the shadows since you were a girl - no one has seen you. Now is not the time—"

"But when is the time!?! A monster was released from those tunnels! I don't know what it is! It might be a part of the Effluvium or some other demon entirely, but it went after *me.*" She clenched her fists. "And now there's another like me in town. Brent is struggling, and he needs help."

"Do not tell him the truth."

"He's going to figure it out! He's smarter than he lets on and...and..." Rho looked away, "I don't know how much longer I can hide it."

"You care for him."

"It's more than that."

Her grandmama took her hand. "Stay rational, dear. You know I worry, but I cannot stop you. You've blossomed into a young woman...but I worry I'll lose you like I did your mother."

"I'm not my *mother,*" Rho lashed out, clenching her fists and wiggling away from her. "You know that!"

"I know, I know," her grandmama sighed, "but finding you in the gardens, wrapped in roots like when you were a babe, I worry that the Order will find you."

Rho sighed, giving into her grandmama's worries. "I know. I'll be fine. I promise."

Her grandmama continued brushing back her hair, trying to distract Rho with updates on the town. She reaffirmed that Rho's father was okay; she managed to get him into town that day, despite his frequent requests to stay by his daughter's side. The Senator would not be happy about this, not at all. Already Captain Carver had been terrorizing most of the population with questions, his cadets brewing up a storm in the market.

"Captain Carver's always been a Reuben," her grandmama rambled, shoving the lemon cake back into Rho's hands. "His son's gotten a bit of a stick up his ass since his mother went missing, though. I think she's dead, of course—bet Carver killed her. She was a sweet lass, too..."

Her grandmama rambled about Captain Carver's family as Rho zoned out. Everyone whispered in the shadows about how the Captain probably killed his wife in a fit of rage. Their fights often descended from their home and into town, leaving a veil as thick as the Effluvium over the townsfolk. Rho didn't want to think about it. She didn't want to think about anything.

Once her grandmama bumbled back downstairs, Rho curled up on the bed while picking at her lemon cake and watching the gardeners work to bring the garden back to life. The Senator would return in the coming days; how could they let her home go to waste? Rho's heart sunk. *Why did I flee back home? I should have run to the plains or a desert...somewhere the monster couldn't harm everyone else.*

She tried closing her eyes again, but the moment darkness filled her vision, another flash of realization washed over her. *Brent...*

She shot up. Was he safe? Had he been in the gardens or the tunnels? Something in her gut said that he wasn't okay, that something was wrong.

She hurried out of bed, pulling on a white day dress and a shawl to cover her wounds. It hurt to climb down the ladder, but it did not deter her, despite wobbling on her feet as she landed.

"Ah, there she is!"

Rho turned. Captain Carver stood in the foyer, towering over her grandmama.

"Oh, um..." Rho straightened her back. "Hello Captain Carver. How can I help you?"

"Eyewitness accounts place you in the Senator's Garden the Night of the Yellow Storm," Captain Carver remarked. "Standard procedure requires us to bring you in for questioning."

"She's still recovering!" Rho's grandmama protested. "Give her a few days. A small tree fell on her during the commotion."

Captain Carver held up a hand. "Madame Gonzo, I can assure you that she isn't in trouble. Procedural talks at best."

"Then why didn't you send one of your cadets to come get her?"

"My cadets have been causing enough problems. I decided to handle this personally." He held his hand out to Rho and said, "Come with me, girl. Just for a few hours. I have questions."

"Any questions you can ask in front of me," Madame Gonzo snarled. "She's a girl—"

"She is a young woman," Captain Carver spat. "Why do you care so much for her? Trying to replace your dead granddaughter?"

Madame Gonzo's lip quivered. Captain Carver's towering presence made even Rho's grandmama look small. Rho hated seeing her grandmama weak like this; she was used to seeing her as the mallet of the town, swinging and taking hits. But Captain Carver backed the old woman into the corner, and Rho knew only she could protect her grandmama from further questioning.

"I'll go!" Rho spoke up. "I'll answer your questions."

"I knew you were a smart one." Captain Carver placed his hand on Rho's shoulder. Then he narrowed his eyes at Madame Gonzo. "You should go back to counting your apples, Madame Gonzo. The Market ain't gonna run itself

Rho's grandmama huffed but did not reply. The facade best remained, for now. For the protection of Newbird's Arm, for magic, and for Rho's true face.

The barracks sat on the west side of town, just past the river and beyond the railroad tracks. Captain Carver said nothing, but once out of sight from her grandmama, his grip around Rho's arm grew firm. She hid her face, not making eye contact with any of the guards passing. A couple cadets from Knoll hollered at her, but with a single glare, Captain Carver silenced them.

He left her in a windowless room with the only light coming from three lanterns rocking on the ceiling. Time passed as told by the persistent rumbling of hunger and scratching soreness in her throat. Rho listened to the shouts in the hallway, the banging of doors, and the marching of steel-toed boots. When Captain Carver returned, light created a halo around his body as he sat down at the chair in front of her.

The captain removed a notepad from his pocket and peered at her with beady eyes. "Well, I never thought I'd see you here. Must admit, I'm disappointed."

"Isn't this a routine questioning, sir?" Rho asked.

"Ah, a shame it isn't. Mighta flubbed a little there to get the old hag off my back." He popped his lips. "A few eyewitnesses saw you fleeing the area during the Night of Yellow Smoke. I am not saying it is your fault, of course, I would hate to make a...*false* accusation. But it did appear to follow you."

"I didn't—why would you—-"

"Please, let me ask the questions. A proper young lady like yourself, getting ready to marry at that, should know when to speak. If you want this to go smoothly, I recommend you cooperate."

"Yes—yes, sir."

Captain Carver flipped open his notebook, "Well, m'dear, tell me. How many lanterns are in the room?"

"I'm sorry?" Rho winced at the three lanterns.

"Oh, you aren't bright, are you? I asked how many lanterns there are in the room."

Rho looked back at her fingers. "Three."

"Oh silly, silly gal." He glanced at the ceiling. "Can't you see there are four?"

"Four? No, there's...it's three," Rho whispered. "What does that have to do with anything?"

"If I can't trust you to say there are four, then how can I trust anything else you say?"

Rho shook her head. "Why would I lie and say there's four?"

"It's not a lie." Captain Carver slammed his hands onto the table. Like a gong, the noise shattered the room. "If the Order says there are four lanterns, what shall you say?"

"There's three."

Rho thought the Captain might hit her. Instead, he eased back into the seat and turned to the next page in his notebook. "Fine. If you insist there are three, let's say there are three. I won't make you wrack your brain much further, a'ight?"

"Yes, sir."

"So, let's try something easier. What were you doing in the gardens on the Night of Yellow Smoke?"

"I was..." Rho's gaze locked on the wall. "I was helping Mr. West."

"Can he confirm that?"

"Of course."

"Hm." Captain Carver rose, pacing across the room to stare at the first lantern. "Well, unfortunately, Mr.

West has a habit of lying for those he cares about, so I do hope you have another alibi."

"I—"

Captain Carver pivoted. "Who is your mother?"

"What?" Rho blinked. "My mother?"

"I swear, do you not listen? Are you inept? Stupid? Useless? Why would anyone think you'd make a good wife?" The captain snarled to himself, then removed the whip he always carried on his hip.

Rho cringed and looked away. The whip carried an essence around it, reminiscent of blood and fear. She'd heard that whip often in the town square. It haunted her nightmares.

Someday she knew it would come for her.

Today was that day.

Captain Carver had none of it, forcing Rho to face him again. "Who is your mother?"

"I—I don't...I've never met her," Rho croaked.

"But do you know of her?"

"I—I don't...I..." Rho tried to find the best way to answer. To tell the truth would place her freedom from the Order in limbo, but not telling it meant—

The whip cracked in the air. Rho buried her shoulders against her ears.

"Answer the question."

"All I know is she tried to kill me!" Rho barked. "I've never met her! She's not important. I'm not important."

Captain Carver raised the whip again, but instead of hitting Rho, he hit one of the lanterns on the ceiling, and it shattered on the floor. He straightened his back, proceeding to replace the whip onto his belt. "Now, girl, I told you not to lie to me. So, answer simply yes or no. Is your mother Angelana Gonzo?"

Rho's heart sank. Of course, the Captain already knew everything. She'd been foolish to dart through the gardens; the destruction no doubt belonged to her, and all the captain wanted was verbal confirmation.

But there were only three lanterns in the room.

No. Two.

One lay broken on the floor.

She replied, "I never met her."

"Well," the captain maintained his composure, "you are her daughter. The little girl born with a flower sprouting from her head. You've done well to hide under the Order's purview."

"I don't know what you're talking about."

"I asked you to stop lying to me."

"I'm not lying—"

Smack.

Captain Carver's hand left a pain rippling through her jaw. She gripped the table.

"Who is your mother?" the captain demanded.

"I said never met her!"

Rho expected him to hit her again and braced.

Instead, the captain exhaled and marched across the room once more, "You worthless piece of shite. Learn to speak the truth and the truth alone. These foolish lies do nothing to help your case."

Rho didn't reply, restraining every desire to give into him. If she stayed standing, if she stayed quiet, they would have nothing against her.

"We saw what you did to the gardens. The Yellow Demon that you guided into the Hedge Maze, the way the monster towered above all else. You sent it to the mountains, and now it will join the Effluvium!" He reached up to another lantern and tapered out the flame. Only the one above the door remained.

Three lamps. One broken. One turned dark. One lit.

"Magic is a crime, my girl. But you know that, yes? That's why you've kept it hidden."

"I'm just a gardener," Rho reaffirmed.

"So, you say. But you're lying." He walked over to the last lamp, "So tell me, how many lanterns?"

"Three. But one is broken, one is out, and one is lit."

The captain shook his head. "It's a shame you cannot see the truth. So be it."

The last light fizzled out. With the opening and closing of the door, darkness became Rho's only companion.

CHAPTER NINETEEN

ICE

Stares, slurs, and slanders followed Brent as he walked to the Temple. Jemma kept him in her clutches, walking him a step at a time up to the Temple. The train chugged to a stop at the platform, the smoke decorating the station with smoke. Elder Don Van waited on the platform as a train arrived, and as the doors opened, a woman with a wide smile punctuated with dimples stepped out.

The Senator is back! The revelation sent relief through Brent's chest. Perhaps with Senator Heartz's arrival, the tension in the air would cease.

His attention fell away from the train and back into the square. The pressure in town haunted him, only made easier by the kindness of a few. Mr. Smidt wove baskets, humming to himself, while Mr. West talked with vigor to a vegetable merchant. A few smiling merchants glanced in his direction, but except for a woman with wide eyes and feet too large, no smile appeared sincere.

Wait.

The woman vanished in an instant, replaced with Caroline's glower disappearing into the morning fog. "Brent, are you coming?" Jemma called, slowing her brisk walk.

"Uh, yeah, of course." He stared down at Jemma, her hair caught by the wind, her eyes hinting a twinge of sadness. He sucked in his lip before speaking again. "Can I ask you something?"

"Yes, what is it?"

"Why are you agreeing to this? The betrothal, I mean. It's not the only way for you to become a sister of the Order or anything.

Jemma turned from him, taking a few steps forward, her head high on her shoulders as she spoke, "My mother and father didn't approve of me joining the Order. Sisters are celibate, and they desire grandchildren. Ridiculous, I know, especially with my younger brother, but I was the oldest and so intended to pave the way for the family."

Brent understood, of course; he felt the same with Alexandria.

"Torn between my desire to be loyal to my family and to join the Order, I asked Brother Roy Al for a solution and...the betrothal was just that. Save a soul through marriage and be honored by the Order." She glanced back at him. "Granted, I don't think your soul is all that tarnished."

They reached the bottom of the Temple's stairs, and Jemma walked up with a slight bounce in her step. Before reaching the top, though, Brent grabbed her hand. "Wait."

"Brent, please...go get cleansed!"

"No, it's not that. It's..." He sighed. "We can't keep up with this façade anymore. Living for our families and all, I mean. It's...I mean...it's stupid. You should just join the Order...do whatever it is that you want. And I—I'm going to...I want to—"

"Is this about you and Bria?"

"How do you—"

"I am not stupid. You fawn after her like a lovesick puppy...and she loves you, I can tell."

"Then, let's stop this."

"You can't change something if you've gone and run away from it."

"You don't have to run...I will. And I mean...then is it really your fault?"

Jemma didn't reply as they reached the top of the stairway, where Brother Roy Al greeted them in the atrium. Brent always liked the young brother, with steel eyes that seemed to glisten when he smiled.

"Ah, Brenton," Brother Roy Al bowed his head, "I am glad you've come. Your mother will indeed be happy. As well as your lovely fiancée."

Jemma bowed her head in return before turning to Brent and squeezing his hands. "Levels One and Two. That is all."

"I know."

"Miss Reds has been vital to securing your freedom, Brenton," Brother Roy Al added. "The cleansing takes a couple days, pending how you react. I think you'll do well, though. You're a good lad."

"Yes sir," Brent glanced one last time at Jemma, then followed Brother Roy Al down the stairs into the prayer crevasses below.

The Brother said little, leading Brent into a prayer crevasse with a mirror. He handed Brent a razor and a white robe. "Clean yourself. I hope you ate; you shan't for a few days."

"Level One is fasting, right?"

"Ay, but you'll feel rejuvenated after–clears away the toxins, frees you of unnecessary weight. A great tradition to practice in your life, if I do say so myself." Brother Roy Al beckoned him into the prayer crevasse. "I shall return soon."

Brent took the time to shave and change, cutting his face in the process. He tried combing his hair with his fingers, but the curls continued to knot together in a mangy mess.

An elderly sister with short-cropped hair and a white robe came to retrieve him, chanting scripture in the ancient tongue. Brother Roy Al waited in a washroom at the end of the hallway. A large steamy tub filled the room, a chill rising from blocks of ice on its surface and twisting into the air.

"Level Two," Brother Roy Al whispered as he helped Brent remove the robe, "is the washing of sin. You will feel a slight twinge as you step into the ice bath–that is the demons fleeing. Then there will be peace. After which, you will have time to recant in one of the prayer crevasses and welcome a sin-free life."

The ice burned as Brent climbed into the tub. His toes and fingers grew numb.

He lowered his head into the water.

Ma...

He gasped, shooting out of the water. A set of hands pressed him back down into a fuzzy memory.

Ice. Drowning. A screaming child.

No. He screamed. He was the child.

"Ma...Mama..." he sobbed out.

He was small, a child just learning of the world, and a man with bright blue eyes carried him into the room. Soothing voices, singing songs...but then they dunked him into the water.

Brent screamed both then and now. Or did they belong to his demons? Or the woman in his head?

Who am I? Where am I? What am I?

I'm Brent Harley. I'm alive. My one constant is Bria Smidt. I'm alive.

Look at you, the woman cackled in his head. He'd have to find a name for her if this kept up. *Alive. What about that friend of yours? Rho?*

I can't do anything now.

You can run out of this tub stark naked to find her.

Don't be ridiculous.

He gasped, swallowing a mouthful of water before sputtering for air. He closed his eyes and shook his head.

"No more...no more..."

"A bit longer, Brenton." Brother Roy Al's voice sounded distant. "The first time always stings. Eventually, it will be tranquil. You are doing great."

"I don't want...I don't want...I don't—" Into the water again, this time with no warning. Was he drowning? Was he swimming? Was he somewhere else entirely?

My name is Brent Harley. I'm not a monster.

My name is Brent Harley. I'm not a monster.

My name is Brent Harley —

His senses returned as he stumbled down the hallway, a towel draped over his shoulders, dripping wet and shivering. Brother Roy Al guided him back to a prayer crevasse.

"I was...I was...that happened to me before," Brent gasped. "When I was a babe."

"We don't cleanse children, Brenton," Brother Roy Al replied. "The cleansings are frightening to all, no matter the type of person."

"You also don't stamp children, but I've had this thing on me my whole life." Brent picked at the black stamp on his wrist. "I remember now, and...I...and I want—"

What? To go? His mother? Jemma? Bria? Rho?

"Go take time to breathe," Brother Roy Al soothed, concern painted on his face. "We shall resume in the morning. Rest now, son."

Brent huddled in the corner of the crevasse, tightening his robe and bringing his knees to his chest. The One Scripture decorated the wall. He couldn't understand it. His hunger gnawed at him and twisted with the shivers vibrating through his body.

When was the last time he slept in a bed? Weeks now, it felt; and even before Caroline, Rho, and the library, he rarely made his way home. Would he ever sleep in his bed again? How many nights did he leave his mother waiting by the window?

Anything could kill me now, and if I'm cursed to die, I should go back to her—

The door opened, cutting off his thoughts.

Caroline stood in the doorway to the crevasse, arms crossed as she examined the room. "Come along, we have much to do."

"You...I—I was locked in the Pit for days and—and you come...you're here now?!?" Brent snarled through his teeth. His chest tightened watching her lean against the entranceway as if everything was normal.

As normal as it could be when talking face-to-face with Death.

"Well, it looks as if I am rescuing you. They tried drowning you."

"I'm here by choice," Brent didn't sound sure of himself. *Or perhaps it's validation.*

"You look horrendous."

"I said I was in the Pit!"

"I do not know what that is."

"It's like a jail...but for the scum of the earth...like—like me."

"You, scum? Pah!" Caroline crossed her arms. "You look miserable and have a cut through your cheek, but scum? That is going a little far."

"The Order would think it."

"Well, the Council does not. So, come along!" Caroline tugged a handful of his hair.

"Fuck! Stop!" Brent pushed her back. "I'm so damn sick of people grabbing me by my hair!"

"Then cut it!"

Brent huffed.

"Come, there's a tunnel entrance in the back of this hallway. Yes, you shall come with me," Caroline ordered while ushering him. "We shall talk. You shall listen. You shall learn."

The tunnels progressed naturally from the basement of the Temple. Caroline didn't say anything for a time, waltzing ahead as the last remnants of the Temple's basement disappeared to be replaced with the usual cavernous walls.

"Where have you been?" Brent asked at last, scratching as the stamp on his wrist. "It's been almost a week.

Thought you all would...I thought I would be in trouble."

Caroline shook her head. "It wasn't your fault. That...*thing* should not have been in the library."

"What is it, though?"

"I do not know."

Brent halted, staring past Caroline and at the junction. "You don't know?!? How do you not know? That—that thing might've killed my friend! You—you're hundreds of years old—"

"Three-hundred and seventy-nine to be exact," Caroline muttered.

"Exactly!" Brent clenched his fists.

"The Council is not always open about its past, even with its members. It does not help that I was a vagabond of sorts for a time," Caroline replied. "But we are meeting now for answers which they have failed to provide even me. The senior members are quite elusive."

"They've kept it hidden for this long?"

"I never took time to explore in depth, nor did such monstrosities ever make their presence known. It is not my forte to explore." She shrugged. "Malaika may have, but who knows where she has wandered off to these days."

"Great..."

Silence returned as they entered the junction. Vines still lay scattered on the floor, only a few torches remaining. The putrid scent of the monster still lingered. As much as he tried, Brent couldn't shake it. With it, the scent added invisible weights to Brent's ankles, slowing his pace.

"Brent, come." Caroline ushered as she reached the door.

"Are you sure they're not mad at me?" Brent asked.

"Ningursu is not mad, and Ningursu is the only person who matters."

"But..." Brent gulped. "I, uh, dropped his head."

"You *what*?"

"Ningursu's head. I, uh...I dropped it."

Caroline gawked at him, then slid to the ground and gripped her knees as she guffawed. "You dropped his head!?!"

Brent nodded.

"Oh sards!" She wiped her eyes, choking on her words. "Consarn it, you have no clue how many times I have wanted to punt his head across the room. Oh, oh this is glorious! Golden! I am sure he is bitter...but consarn it, it is worth it!"

"I was...I mean...I didn't mean to!"

"Does not matter! This is fantastic!" Caroline rose, still gasping between chuckles. "Come. We should join them."

Caroline led Brent into the library. The destruction laid waste by the monster had vanished, replaced with upright bookshelves. A few ghosts-like figures wandered between the shelves, books in their arms. Brent watched them, human in form but with their stories following them. One male ghost with a long red beard walked past. Brent saw the man's life pass by, a tale of men on a ship, sailing the seas from the Region Delilah and around the border of the Nation of Yilk. As soon as the vision arrived, it vanished, replaced with the echoing footsteps from up the stairway.

Aelia and Tomás joined them at the foot of the stairs.

"Caroline," Aelia sighed, "what is he wearing?"

Brent looked down at the white robe wrapped around his body. Blood rushed to his ears.

"What? He is wearing clothes. That is all that matters." Caroline crossed her arms. "At least it is not like Malaika. She showed up naked last time."

Aelia exchanged a glance with Tomás. "Well, I think he would do best looking presentable."

Tomás left, returning moments later with a pair of trousers that reached above Brent's ankles, a loose-fitting shirt, and shoes that caused his foot to curve up at an odd angle. If it wasn't for the urgency in getting him dressed, Brent might have complained, but once he changed, they ushered him into the gathering hall at the back of the library.

A long table dominated the room. An empty pedestal headed the table, while eight additional seats lined the perimeter. Members of the Council appeared to gather in seniority. Aelia and Tomás sat closest to the pedestal, and Caroline took a seat towards the back, motioning for Brent to sit across from her. The giant man, Jiang, walked into the room, guiding the woman with blonde hair into her seat next to Aelia. Her green eyes remained glossed over, but upon noticing Caroline, her face lit up.

"Caroline! Did you catch the fish? The one who swallowed your mother?" she asked.

"I am still searching, Julietta dear." Caroline reached for the woman's hand. "But I have someone else I'd like you to meet. This is my apprentice, Brent."

She turned to Brent, with that same empty expression as the other day. A delicate smile bloomed on her lips. "Yes, yes, Harold and I met."

"It was nice meeting you the other day." Brent held out his hand. Julietta took his fingers with care, and for a moment, Brent succumbed to a wave of emptiness. It filled him, like a forgotten story hidden in the walls of the library, before vanishing in his shallow chest. Julietta appeared unphased, her gaze returning to the wall, humming an offbeat tune.

Caroline sighed. Was that sadness in her face? It didn't last long enough for Brent to tell, replaced with attentiveness as Alojzy joined them at the table and took a seat beside Brent.

The stout man, with his beady black eyes, greeted each person with a nod, before turning to Brent and smiling, "Ah, Brenton! It is nice to see you!"

"Yeah, a'ight...I suppose." Brent grimaced.

"Listen, boy," Alojzy continued, "I would like to offer you some additional tutoring if you wish."

"Oh, uh, I—"

Caroline snarled. "Al...do not do this."

"Caroline, I can offer him guidance is all," Alojzy replied. "I am not trying to steal him from you. I only want him to be successful—just as you were!"

"That being said," Jiang spoke up as he circled the table, nursing a glass of wine, "if Brenton here thinks you're being ineffective, we'd be happy to take over your job. Let you focus on more *crucial* issues at hand."

"Keep your trap shut!" Caroline snapped.

"I..." Brent hunched his shoulders and mumbled, "I think Caroline is doing an a'ight job." *All things considered.*

"You hear that? Brent thinks I am doing fine!" Caroline gloated.

Before Alojzy or Jiang could respond, the door opened. Ningursu graced them with his presence, carried upon a velvet pillow by what looked like a ghost with a full black beard. Around him, a story merged in and out of the mist, overlapping and leaving traces in the air. Brent's head spun, trying to watch it.

The ghost placed Ningursu's head on the pedestal.

"Thank you, Nedo. You may go."

The ghost hunched his shoulders and left.

Ningursu proceeded to scan the meeting hall with his one eye. He stopped at the empty chair beside Caroline, then turned to Jiang, "Where is your disciple?"

"I have not seen Malaika in at least a fortnight, sire," Jiang replied while twisting his black hair into a braid.

"She is off hunting *dragons* again," Alojzy muttered.

"Noted." Ningursu turned his gaze onto Brent. "So, I would officially like to welcome the new bane of my existence to the Council of Mist Keepers: Brenton Rob Harley."

Brent shrunk into his chair.

"Sire!" Alojzy interjected. "You do understand he is the reason for this gathering, yes?"

"I am aware, Alojzy!" Ningursu spat.

"Sorry, sire."

Brent fidgeted again, staring at his hands as he spoke. "I'm sorry...for everything..."

To his surprise, Ningursu smiled, revealing his remaining few teeth. "My child, do not fret. I do not blame you."

Murmurs erupted around the table, but Jiang's voice stood out from the rest. "Well, of course it's not *his fault*. Caroline should keep a closer eye on *her* apprentice!"

Caroline jumped up. "CONSARN IT, JIANG! I have another job!"

"WE ALL DID!" Jiang slammed his fists against the table, shaking his glass of wine.

"But you were at least prepared for...for this *shite!*"

Brent smirked.

"SILENCE!" Ningursu boomed.

Jiang collapsed back into his chair and kicked his feet onto the table. Caroline looked away and twiddled her thumbs.

"What happened has happened," Ningursu stated. "Brenton exhibited the natural traits of a Mist Keeper...which many of you have forgotten. Intuition, curiosity, truthfulness, exploration, and humbleness. Before Brenton came, I had not seen all of these in one person in a while. It may be because he is young, innocent, unjaded by the brutalities of Hell. Nevertheless, because of these traits I *value*, a Diabolo is loose."

More murmurs. No explanations.

Brent managed to choke out, "I'm sorry...a Diabolo?"

"The monster." Jiang's nostrils flared.

"Yes, but...what...I'm sorry, I don't... what is a Diabolo?"

"Hell on legs," Tomás spoke, his attention unyielding from his notebook. "We designed them during the One War."

"The war with the powerful Magii, right?"

Tomás nodded. "Yes."

"So, it was a war against magic...with people like Rho." Brent frowned, his heart sinking. *Is she okay?* He picked at his stamp, and he spoke through his teeth, unable to keep back the next statement. "Because you hate Magii...my friend might be dead."

A few more whispers crossed the table, but Ningursu silenced them with a flick of his brow. He then addressed Brent. "This Rho you speak of is fine. We have monitored her."

Brent straightened his back. "Is she hurt?"

"I said she is fine, Brenton."

"But how do I know you're not lying? You obviously hate Magii, or you wouldn't have created this...this monster or...or whatever it is."

Alojzy cut in. "She's not powerful enough for us to care about."

"I don't trust you!" Brent's stomach tightened again. Nausea of over what happened in the gardens crept into his stomach. "Why do you hate them?"

"It's a long story for another time." Ningursu yawned. "Just know that Magii pose a threat to the safety of the world. They kill, they destroy, and often they attempt to beat death. That is not how this world works. They're abominations."

"I disagree!" Brent recalled Rho dancing in the forest. She was at peace there, creating the foliage...not destroying. Never destroying.

Ningursu appeared unphased by Brent's objections, "Well, if you do, then you must agree that we must find the Diabolo before it wreaks any more havoc."

"Sir, if I may," Tomás interjected. "We owe the Palaver—"

"NO!" Ningursu's voice boomed. "We will not get them involved!"

Brent stared at Caroline, but she shrugged.

Ningursu recomposed himself. "We shall find the Diabolo in haste, yes? It ravaged Newbird's Arm, and

I imagine it has its eyes set on this...*Rho*. So, if my inference is correct, it will stay near as it regains its strength."

Alojzy offered, "We could use her as bait, sire."

"NO!" Brent rose, clinging to the table, so his knuckles turned white. "She's my friend! You—you can't!"

"*Friend*? Pah." Jiang snarled. "We're talking the future of the World, boy. What's one life?"

"Do not be ridiculous," Caroline added. "She's innocent!"

"Why do you care?" Jiang barked.

Caroline barked back in a different language. Jiang lunged at her, but before he hit her, a rope with a mist-like quality wrapped around his ankles and suspended him in midair. Brent followed it to where the mist jutted out of Ningursu's mouth and latched onto Jiang like a marionette. It repositioned Jiang back in his seat before disappearing.

Ningursu growled at both Jiang and Caroline, but words again arrived in a foreign tongue.

"Brenton, it is fine," Tomás said firmly. "We shall not use *Rho*. It would violate the agreement we made with the Palaver anyway."

"Besides, if what Caroline reported is true," Aelia chimed in, "then it fled into the mountains and shan't have gone far."

"It will need to feed," Jiang mentioned.

"And what does it feed on?" Brent croaked.

"Magic."

The knot in Brent's throat tightened, and he closed his eyes. *I'm so sorry Rho. This is my fault.*

"It is a terrible thing," Julietta said in a sing-song voice. "A terrible-terrible thing. Why would such a thing exist? We should let it be."

"Julietta?" Tomás touched her hand.

"Oh, Tom!" Julietta beamed, "You look well today!"

"If it has weakened, we must act fast," Ningursu interjected. "Brent and Caroline will be our eyes in Newbird's Arm. Alojzy shall take the west, Jiang shall take the east." Ningursu then motioned to Aelia and Tomás and said, "You two, come with me. We have...things to discuss. This meeting is adjourned."

"Wait!" Caroline protested. "How do we capture it?"

Jiang snickered, but Ningursu replied to the innocent question with little ado. "Tomás will review that with you presently."

"But—"

"Later, Caroline." Tomás rose.

With that, the meeting came to its swift conclusion. Aelia picked Ningursu's head off the podium, and Tomás helped Julietta from the room, while Alojzy and Jiang followed, leaving Brent alone again with Caroline.

Brent gripped his face. "I killed her—I killed Rho!" He exhaled. "She's in danger, isn't she?"

"Brent, she is fine. We shall not use her as bait."

"But the Diabolo—"

"I checked on her; she is fine. You are the one who needs rest," Caroline pressured. "Go home now, rest—"

Brent stopped her. "How can I go home now? I left the Cleansing! I was...I'm supposed to be in the Pit!"

"You did not seem to have a problem going home after multiple outbursts in town. It seems there are a few guards who have it out for you. People as a whole do not typically care." Caroline guided him towards the door. "So, go home. Rest in a bed. Then we can search for the monster in the morning. Find it before it harms your *friend* again."

Brent shook his head.

"Once your head is clear, you can protect her, yes?"

"Why do you care?" Brent asked, picking again at his wrist. "I'm a screw up...I'm a...I'm getting you in trouble."

"Sometimes, just sometimes, I can be sympathetic." Caroline squeezed his shoulder. "I've been in a million-million Hells. I have seen boys like you with broken hearts and broken dreams. I do not want you to be one of them."

"Guess you aren't the demon I thought you were..." Brent hiccoughed.

Caroline smiled, so it lit up her eyes.

"I should go home..." He fumbled, rising to his feet. "Thanks...I guess."

"Wait."

"Please...I just want to go home."

"I know, but..." Caroline patted his hand. "You know that girl, the one that made you blush the other day?"

"Bria?"

"Yes. That is the one. Kiss her a million times if she makes you happy, yes? Live for a bit longer."

"Oh, uh..." Brent flushed. "Yeah, a'ight, I'll do that."

"Go on then, get moving."

Brent nodded one last time, then stumbled from the library and into the tunnels.

CHAPTER TWENTY

ALMOST WITHERED

How long?

Minutes? Hours? Days?

Not days. Rho wasn't hungry enough for it to have been days.

A crack under the door provided the only slither of light.

Is that the fourth lantern? The crack? Is that what he wants me to see? She clenched her teeth. *No. Don't fall for it. There are three lanterns. One is broken. Two others are out. Only three. No more.*

By counting the lanterns, she kept herself grounded. She wore her identity close to her chest, and if Captain Carver ever returned, she would not budge.

There are three lanterns.

Captain Carver marched back in after a time, a scowl on his lips. He lit one lantern, before collapsing in the chair, arms crossed.

"So, are you ready to talk?" he snapped.

Rho looked up.

"How many lanterns?"

"Three. One lit. One out. One on the ground in shambles."

Captain Carver sneered. "Are you sure?"

"Positive."

"Then tell me," Captain Carver leaned forward, "what did you summon in the garden?"

"What do you mean?"

"Don't be coy, gal." He snarled, his knuckles turning white as he gripped the table, eyes flickering like that of a beast. "You destroyed the gardens. What did you summon to destroy them?"

"I don't know."

The captain banged his hands against the table. "Everyone saw it following you. What did you summon?"

"I don't know!" Rho repeated frantically. "It followed me, but I don't know why! It was just some sort of yellow mist—"

"Mist..." Captain Carver curled his lip. "Yes, a *mist*."

He paced across the room. Rho held her breath. Part of her expected him to strike, but it concerned her even more why he fixated on that word. *Mist.* Rho bit her lip. *Brent.*

"He's not a part of this!" Rho shouted.

Captain Carver smirked. "You mean Brenton Harley, yes? I am sure you, like all the rest of us, saw his outburst a few days ago."

"But he wouldn't do this!" *Please, he's going through enough. We all are.*

"Why do you care so much about a vagrant like him?"

"He's a...he's a friend." Rho shook her head. "This wasn't his fault."

Captain Carver leaned forward. "Is that a confession?" Are you accepting this as your fault?"

"I—I...no. I don't know...I didn't do anything!"

"Then it won't hurt to question Mr. Harley, now will it?"

"No...don't—"

Captain Carver slammed the door as he left, leaving the single lantern burning in the room.

Time moved slower with light. She counted each shadow, but every thought fled to Brent, to her grandmama, to her family. Once Captain Carver returned, she'd tell him the truth. She'd tell him that there were four lanterns, just to protect everyone else. Besides, who cared about a little gardener? In the grand scheme of things, she'd be better off in the Pit, or under the Order's watchful stare. Or she could run into the tunnels.

She quivered. At the mere thought of the tunnels, her head seared like nails on the chalkboard, and she gathered her knees against her chest. The atrocious mist with the Yellow Monster pummeling towards her replaced the images of her home. It destroyed everything she'd claimed since childhood.

You're stronger than this. Rho clenched her ankles as she leaned forward. *Remember, there are three lanterns.*

The door opened, and the captain returned sooner than Rho expected. He slammed his hands on the table. "Where is he!?!"

Rho gulped. "What are you talking about?"

"Harley! Where is he?"

"I—I don't...I'm sorry, I don't know."

Captain Carver raised his hand. "Of course you don't. You're nothing. It's not like you've got *magic*! Right!?! All you got is your mother's legacy. Otherwise nothing. Nada. Nothing. Except..." He lowered his hand, "You do know where Mr. Harley spends his time. So, tell me, where is he?"

Rho shook her head. "I haven't seen him in—"

Smack.

Her face burned.

"He was at the Temple an hour ago! Where has he run off to now?"

"Hopefully far from here!" Rho restrained her tears. "I don't know where he would've gone. Please stop...I don't know...please."

"Have you not learned!?" The captain rose and demanded, "How dare you defy the Law?"

"The law? No, you're—you're under the Order, not the Law."

Captain Carver shoved Rho into the wall. The left side of her face continued to burn, and every bit of pain shivering through her body pulled at her heart, demanding she cry. She wouldn't let her emotions get the best of her. *Stay in control. You're in control. Don't let your emotions get the best of you. Stay in control.*

"A broad should stay in her place." The Captain reached for his whip. "Obedience. Chastity. Loyalty. I should brand you for such obscene behavior, girl."

Rho shook her head, holding back another sob. "I've done nothing wrong!"

"I don't care," he spat, raising his whip. "If I say you did wrong, you did wrong. So, tell me, how many lights are there?"

Rho glanced between the whip and the lanterns. *Give him the answer he wants. He'll stop.* She closed her eyes.

She couldn't grow numb to this. Not yet. *Maintain your sense of identity. Stay in control. There are three.*

Captain Carver gripped her tighter and shouted, "HOW MANY LANTERNS?"

Rho felt the Captain's desired answer slipping from her tongue. "There—there are—"

The door opened, "Captain!"

Captain Carver spun around, "Ah! Cadet Lawry! Good! It's time to show our little prisoner what we can do."

"Sir." Cadet Lawry stepped into the room. "The Senator is here."

The Captain cursed and released Rho. "What is she doing back already?"

"She wants to speak with you. That was all she said."

"Fine! Watch this one! I'll be back soon." The Captain stormed out.

Cadet Lawry's presence decorated the room with a heavy void reminiscent of a humid summer day. He sauntered over to Rho and lifted her off the ground, holding her up by her jaw. When he smiled, a set of crooked, gold-plated teeth spread across his face. His breath stunk of smoke.

"A shame," the cadet breathed, "a pretty gal like you, misbehaving. Y'know, back where I come from, dames like you stay in their place. Ya'll are livestock, product...nothing more. If ya good enough, you get a nice home. But you're nothing." He ran his free hand to her shoulder and pushed down her sleeve, fingers digging into her collarbone. "By now, you'd be carrying *at least* your first babe."

"Let go of me!" Rho tore away from his hand and begged, "Please."

He grabbed her wrist, pulling her towards him. His breath wreaked of smoke. "I can make a woman of ya. All ya gotta do is ask."

She cringed. It felt like hands were grabbing her feet, pulling her towards the floor. "I'm already the type of woman I want to be."

"Nah, not yet." He reached for her skirt.

Rho reacted in an instant, her heart rate rising in her chest, and lurched backward. Then, just as her grand-mama showed her as a child, she shot her knee into Cadet Lawry's groin, sending him to the floor. No magic. She couldn't use magic. Not here. Not if she wanted to protect herself.

"Ya fucker—"

She darted at the door.

To her relief, the captain left it unlocked.

To her dismay, he stood right outside.

Yet, beside him stood Senator Heartz. Decked out in an array of silvers and golds from the Capital, her frizzy hair curled to cup her face, she was more than garnished with authority. She may as well have been a queen.

"And you are not to act without—" The senator turned as Rho exited. Her face lacked its usual wide smile. "This! This is what I'm talking about! What proof do you have that she caused the destruction?"

"Witnesses," the captain hissed.

"It is no excuse to hold a young woman for hours!" The senator reached out for Rho, "Dear, are you okay? Madame Gonzo told me of your predicament, I took the first train home from the Capitol."

"I'm fine...thank you." The room spun as Rho caught her breath, hugging herself. She wanted to embrace the senator, hug her tight, but knew that would not be appropriate.

"You should go home and rest, love."

Captain Carver interjected, "We're not done—"

"Yes, you are," the Senator snapped. "I am going to take the girl back home, and then you have some explaining to do. Is that understood Captain Carver?"

The Captain grumbled but didn't stop Rho from leaving with the Senator.

Still, even under the Senator's guise, Rho sensed the Guard watching. She refused to meet their stares as they left. The haunting walls, the echoing footsteps, they all belonged to nightmares.

Even the early evening sky belonged to dreams.

At each step away from the stone fortress, her heart grew more and more numb. Her throat tightened, her face seared in pain, and shivers assaulted the corners of her soul.

Only when she crossed the river and entered the garden did her emotions take hold. Charred and dead, the garden reminded Rho of the destitute fortress, of the empty lands beyond Newbird's Arm, and of her soul.

The senator stopped and placed a hand on Rho's shoulder. "Dear, it's a'ight now, yes? The Guard isn't gonna touch you, understood?"

Rho shook her head.

"It's okay there, look, here's your grandmama coming down the path now."

Madame Gonzo walked towards them, bursting into a run when she saw them and pulling Rho close to her. "What happened?"

"It seems in my absence, Captain Carver has taken the law into his own hands," the Senator remarked.

"Perhaps if you didn't spend all your time in the Capitol, then he wouldn't!" Madame Gonzo barked. "If you want to be reelected, then you should start caring for

Newbird's Arm instead of the razzle-dazzle of city lights!"

"Beatriz, I don't—"

"We'll discuss this later, Helga."

"Yes, of course." The Senator left them, marching towards her mansion in the center of the garden.

Madame Gonzo ushered Rho into the house.

"What happened to my belle!?" Rho's father waited for them inside the parlor. He pulled Rho into a hug, stroking back her matted hair, while his dog joined at their feet and nuzzled against them. "You're bloody, —like war, oh war...it's coming—it's gonna—it's gonna beat you silly—you're gonna—this can't happen—my belle!"

"Noah," Madame Gonzo soothed him, "Why don't you go prepare some tea? Let her rest, yes? Ric will be home soon."

"A'ight..." Rho's father sniffled before venturing into the kitchen.

Rho climbed onto the sofa. Everything hurt, and she only desired sleep. When she closed her eyes, Captain Carver's snarls, Cadet Lawry's smirks, and the three lights painted the back of her eyelids.

"Can't believe they're at it again...infiltrating the Guard...beating women...thought the Smoke Riots took care of them..." Madame Gonzo grumbled as she brought Rho a cup of tea. "It's going cause your father to spiral...and so many others. I swear never thought I'd deal with this again."

"Again?" Rho asked.

Her grandmama took Rho's hands, "It is nothing to worry about, dear. Just bad men—"

"I'm not a child anymore, Grandmama, I just dealt with *bad* men an hour ago."

"I know—"

"So, *tell* me."

Her grandmama didn't make eye contact, staring past Rho and at the wall. "You heard of the Smoke Riots, yes?"

"The war in Knoll before I was born, yes," Rho replied. "I've learned of it. A lot of the vagrants...they're messed up because of it. Like Brent's father, Mr. Harley. But I don't know what happened or why or anything, really."

"That's how they want it," Madame Gonzo sighed. "They're back...because no one talks about it. People forget."

"What happened, though?"

"A couple years before you were born," her grandmama started braiding Rho's hair, "there were rumors about young women and children being abducted. No one knew why. Some said it was to eliminate the last semblance of magic, others claimed it was for experiments, and even more claimed it was for constructing the towers out in Knoll. Some said that a group in Knoll had learned of some new ways from the northern men in the country of Kainan. No one knows why to this day. At first, it was all rumor and hearsay, but then one day, a group of Guards reciting old scripture from the Order arrived in town. They took a group of young women and children; your mother was one of them. They left Captain Carver—Lieutenant at the time—here in charge, as well as placed a more radical leader in the Temple."

"Elder Don Van?" Rho asked.

"Brother Don Van back then, yes." Her grandmama frowned at the memory and continued, "After taking the group of children and women away, the Brother instigated new rules: magic was dead, as we all were aware, but a demon had taken its place. There were children with silver eyes that attracted monsters, men and women with outbursts that tried to bring back magic, and stories that turned everyone against each other. Under his leadership, and that of those like him across the province, general sentiment turned against those like—"

"Like Brent." Rho gulped. "He was one of the first."

"Ah, yes, poor Brenton. His mother has tried so hard to keep him safe."

"It's not fair, though. For any of them."

"I won't argue with that, dear, but with magic gone, they needed a new scapegoat." Madame Gonzo finished one of Rho's braids and sighed. "Not all was lost though as there were members of the Order who split off from the new group out in Knoll. They teamed up with the Senate of Rosada to end the Order's short reign. This was the Smoke Riots. Civilians marched with their own pistols, but civilians aren't ready for war, so when they returned, they came back with nightmares that overwhelmed them of war and blood."

Rho interjected, "And most are sent to the Pit, so no one hears them."

"Because that is what the Order wants. There was never an end to the war, an armistice perhaps, but never an end. People don't want to believe that; people want to go about their lives, thinking everything is okay. But it puts people like you and Brenton at risk. Sure, most of the children returned, but where are they now? The Pit. My daughter came back, but what was she? Pregnant, aloof, and insane; she was lucky your father was kind enough to bring her home—a good man of war, but still with his own terrors. We've done a lot to keep him out of the Pit."

"But what happened to my mother?" Rho begged. "Why did she try to...*kill me?*"

Tears dotted the old woman's face. "I don't know. They took away her curiosity and innocence and replaced her with a woman jaded and full of hatred. She once loved the idea of magic. Her heart desired stories. But when she returned, I didn't recognize her. When she gave birth to you, I hoped it would change, but then she planted you in the ground because you were born with a flower on your head."

Rho reached behind her own ear, letting her little branch curl around her fingers. A white camellia bloomed from it. Its pedals hung soft on her fingertips. So delicate. Just like she'd been as a babe. No wonder she tried so hard not to cry.

Her grandmama tucked a strand of Rho's hair back to give the flower light. "We've done a lot to hide you. Few know...your father, Mr. West, the Senator. But you've evaded all others. I worry if they find out, and then I'll lose you like I did your mother."

Rho gripped her grandmother's fingers with one hand and wiping the tears away with the other. "I won't wither away. I promise."

CHAPTER TWENTY-ONE

Cows, Kisses, and Monsters

His mother's tears welcomed Brent home after he snuck back into town through the woods behind the Pit. He sank into her embrace, overwhelmed with fatigue as beef stew bubbled on the stove. His younger sister bolted to him and hugged him around the legs. It felt like an eternity since he last came through the door, and in its own way, the entire house belonged to someone else.

After being lectured about abandoning his cleansing and then forced to eat and wash, he sat on the edge of Alexandria's bed and wove her a story about mice living in the Pit. He worried that the mist he saw around his sister's head would take the shape of little mice, and with each word, it moved closer to becoming true. So, he left the passion in his pocket, and while Alexandria did not notice, the emptiness remained.

He managed a few hours of sleep, basking in a nightmare. It was a terror of yellow mist, chasing after a small woman in the tunnels; when she turned, Brent thought it would be Rho, but instead, he saw Bria. The monster grabbed her and ripped off her face, leaving her withering like a flower on the ground.

"Bria!" Brent woke up sweating. "Just a dream...just a dream...shite!"

He dressed and snuck out of his home, following the fence of Pit out towards the fields and naming each cow as he passed. He found a smoke in his pocket, and at the first whiff, his shoulders relaxed, and his headache vanished. The fog traveling down the mountain looked inviting, showing a group of travelers venturing across the world. They would ride up into the clouds and see the world. Relaxed, calm, tranquil...it wouldn't be a bad life, right?

It disappeared as he rounded the bend where the fields met the edge of the river and looked out at the garden. By a fallen tree, like where they met as kids, Bria sat, holding a flask, her head down with hair hiding her face.

"Bri," he cooed.

She looked over and dropped the flask, "Brent!"

"Listen, I know I was...I didn't show up the other day, but I was...with the destruction and the Pit, I..." He gulped. "Please don't be angry with me."

Bria bolted over to him, squeezing him around the waist and pulling him close.

"You're okay," she sniffled into his shirt. "There was the...the gardens...they're dead. And some monster thing...but you're okay."

"Yeah, was in the Pit for a bit, but..." He trailed off, stroking her hair back. A yellow bruise dotted her face. "What happened?"

"What?" Bria touched beneath her eye, "Nothing. I'm fine."

"Bri..."

"It's nothing, I promise." She brushed her hair back in front of her face. "I'm fine."

Brent scowled. He recognized Bria's lie, but if he pried further, she'd shut down. Immediately, his mind fled to Christof. In his stomach, the anger of the woman of Yilk flared, but he scarfed it down.

Bria grabbed her flask off the ground, downing it, before passing it to Brent. He took a swig.

"I'm so...I'm sorry I didn't show up. With the gardens and the monster thing...and they threw me in the Pit..."

Brent sighed, his gaze darting to the cows. "Then they tried cleansing me, and I didn't want to go, but I...Bria, I'm sorry."

She shook her head. "A lot happened."

It was a pointed statement, with nothing additional to guide it; why talk when the garden loitered behind them, its wilted exterior and charred paths telling the story in plain sight. Brent could have pressed her about it, but he didn't have the energy. He was sure Bria didn't either, by the looks of it.

"Remember when we used to come out here and name the cows?" Bria took the flask from Brent and finished it off. "That one there." She pointed at a bull with a crooked ear. "We named it Pig."

"It's still a stupid name," Brent teased.

She grinned. "Nah, it's a good one. I'm good at naming things. Better than you."

"Hate to see what you'll name our kids." Brent bit his tongue, his stomach performing somersaults as he looked away.

"Our kids?" Bria laughed. "Have you been smoking too much?"

Brent stammered but couldn't form words. Warmth rushed to his cheeks, and he hid his face in his hands.

"You're silly," she hiccoughed, "Little soon to be planning a family."

"I—uh—it was a slip of words. It doesn't matter...I mean...yeah, it doesn't matter." He frowned and repeated the statement to himself. "It doesn't matter..."

"What's wrong?"

Brent didn't meet her gaze. After his betrothal, he spent nights dreaming of Bria, mourning the loss of their love to the Order. Now, he could have Bria again...but not for long. He carried the burden of a curse on his shoulders, and however it took him, the end result would be the same. "Bria, I need to tell you something...and you probably won't believe it. But...I've been cursed to die. I'm...I'm gonna die."

Bria furrowed her brow. "You look fine to me."

"I don't know what's supposed to happen, but I feel like something is on my back, and it's not going away." Brent picked at the brown grass. "Like a nagging sensation that means I—I don't think I have a choice. I'm gonna die. It's just this weird feeling."

"Stop being paranoid. We all die in the end."

"It's more than paranoia, though. I just...know."

"No, you think something is going to happen. That's not set in stone."

Bria paced forward and leaned against the fence. The wind caught her hair. Why didn't she seem shocked? Her confident aura had returned, despite the tears still on her face. Death did not cause the flood gates to reopen.

Brent joined her by the fence. "Soon, though. If we run, I can't promise...I may not be around—"

"No. You're not allowed. I won't let you."

Was that a smile?

Bria hopped up onto the fence and stared out at the cows, fingers around Brent's hand. "Well, Mr. Good-at-Names, what would you name that cow, right there? The baby calf?"

"What? Uh...Eem...I, uh..."

"Em-ay-uh?" Bria laughed. "Great name."

"No! Um...Emi! I'd name it Emi...like Emilie or Emilia...or something." Brent flushed again. "Don't put me on the spot like that!"

"Eh, Pig's better."

That smile came again with a kiss.

They remained by the fence, snuggling and kissing, watching as the early morning mixed with the storm clouds above the mountains. Brent told Bria about his time in the Pit. Upon mentioning the two harlots selling their services, Bria broke out laughing, forcing a flush to rise in Brent's face. He hid it with his sleeve, pivoting to another story about a shrewd talking skull. All of Brent's cares wilted like the garden as he spoke.

Once the sun painted his aura yellow, Brent walked with Bria back to her home

"My Dad and Ric are still asleep," Bria whispered, taking Brent's hand and pushing her fingers between his knuckles.

"It's early yet," Brent noted.

"Do you want to come inside?"

"What?" Brent turned red and rubbed his neck nervously, "I, um...if it's okay, I..."

Yes. The word you're looking for is yes. Just say it, boy. Don't be foolish, the woman in his head goaded.

Brent nodded, focusing on the mist behind Bria. He swore he saw Caroline there.

He followed Bria up to her small attic bedroom. They sat beside each other on her cot. Bria looked smaller than normal, picking at the new betrothal mark burned onto her hand.

"Does it hurt?" he asked.

"It's fine." Bria beamed at him and said, "Christof won't win."

"You don't have to lie to me."

"I know. It's just that...I need to tell you something."

Brent tucked a strand of hair behind her ear. "What is it? What's wrong?"

"Promise you won't be mad?"

"What is—ow!" Something firm yanked at Brent's arm and pulled him forwards to the floor.

Caroline stared down at him. "Come, I've sighted the Diabolo. We must act fast."

Brent flared his nostrils.

"You'll have time later, lover boy."

"Brent?" Bria gathered at his side.

"Shite!" He got to his feet. "Listen, I need to go. I'm sorry...I don't mean to...I—I'm sorry. I understand if you—"

"Is it because of the Invisible People?"

"What? Yeah...how did you...did I tell you about them?"

"Um yeah. You told me earlier. Just go. We'll talk about it later." She straightened out his shirt and pecked his cheek, seeming a tad distracted. "Be safe."

Brent raised both his eyebrows. "Bri, what's wrong?"

"I said we'll talk about it later, okay?"

Brent sighed and nodded. How he longed to stay by her side, gripping her fingers for a few seconds longer. But he didn't have a chance to ask anything else as Caroline yanked him away by the back of his shirt.

Once they got outside, Brent snapped, "What the shite, Caroline? Couldn't you tell I was...I was busy!"

Caroline stomped on the leaves, guiding Brent towards the foothills, "Oh, for sard's sake, you will have time. There are more important matters—"

"You told me to kiss her!"

"You will have time later."

"But I was...she...it's rude!"

"Oh, it is not anything I have not seen before." Caroline waved her hand, "Kissing, touching, naked bums—when you see as much as I do, you are generally not phased."

"And that means not being polite?"

"Polite? What a waste of time! Reports speak of a Diabolo nearby only an hour ago. We must act fast. Besides..." Caroline glanced back. "The sooner we catch it, the sooner she will be safe."

Brent glanced back as well and huffed. The garden glowed behind him in the dull sunrise, masked by the storm cloud waltzing over the mountains. When he squinted, the shape of a monster rallied in its grasp, sending droves of mist – or were they people – dashing down the mountains.

Caroline led him through the tunnels to the top of the foothills. The wind bellowed, and with each obnoxious gust, Brent tasted the stories of a hundred pernicious men and women, shrieking, clawing, cursing, and murdering.

"Brent! Listen closely," Caroline shouted over the storm. "We must wrangle the creature. I brought some jars to force it into." Caroline opened her cloak and handed him two jars. "Use the mist and our magic to usher it, understand? The mist is your weapon."

"How do I..." Brent squinted. "I can't see. How do I do this? I can't—"

"Just focus. The mist is a tool, remember that," Caroline recited. She was farther ahead now, stepping into the fog and becoming one with the storm.

Brent tried to follow, but the rain masked his sight. *Was* it raining, though? The wind tackled him, and with each drop pounding on his face, he heard a different tale: a woman making a poisonous stew, a man on a murderous rampage, and children crying.

So many children crying.

Upon stepping through the fog, Brent locked onto the monster's glowing yellow eyes. The rest of its body blended into the storm wreaking of sulfur and brimstone.

Caroline's outline beckoned Brent to encircle the creature, waving her arm through the mist as if creating a barrier. The monster avoided the jar, roaring and shrieking, dismantling the mountain with thunder and lightning. Brent navigated around the perimeter and held out his jar as Caroline ordered.

"Beckon the mist!" Caroline called.

"How?" Brent choked. He imagined the mist moving around the monster, but the stories of the worst people ever battled for attention. Each tale appeared vivid, the screams of children struck him. They spoke. Even more, they showed: a man of golden hair slashing a woman's breast; a woman with green eyes biting into a pig's heart; two people plotting to assassinate a kind king. Brent saw it all, and the more he saw, the less he could fight.

The Diabolo cackled.

"Brent!?" Caroline shouted. "What are you doing? What—"

A thump, and Caroline's body flew past Brent.

The Diabolo peered down at Brent with a smile so wide it cracked the monster's face in two.

Brent fell to his knees. The images turned the mist red. Brent saw nothing else. Children cried. Mother's wept. The world burned.

"No...no...I can't..." Brent clenched his teeth. "My name is Brent Harley...I'm turning twenty-one...I was born in Newbird's Arm to Janette and Robert Harley. My name is Brent Harley...and my one...I can't...she...the town...I can't..."

He gasped, sinking his head to his knees, the creature's breath inches from his skin. *Is this it? Is this the curse? Am I gonna die?*

"Oy, ugly!" Was that Caroline's voice? It must have been. She darted past him, her black cloak swarming about her. Her face transformed to the match the monster's countenance, and as she yelled, her jaw unhinged. The mask mimicked the Diabolo's every move. One moment, the monster snarled, but a game of imitation meant Caroline did the same. When the Diabolo swiped, Caroline responded with the same dexterity. A slash, a cut, then blood, smog, and more children singing.

Brent backed into a tree. The thunder boomed, the storm sobbed, and each strike left blood like a river on the ground. Did it belong to Caroline or the monster? Brent lost track of his mentor in the fray.

What can I do to help? Shite. I must do something. Brent licked his lips. *Find a different story.*

He shut his eyes, recalling what Tomás said about the Diabolo. *It feeds off magic.*

Brent loosened his fingers. "Let me tell you a story..."

Neither the Diabolo nor Caroline turned.

Brent imagined a tale about a sorcerer who lived on a mountain, conjuring spells and setting the world ablaze. Not the most creative story, but, nonetheless, the mist obeyed. On top of a taller mountain in the distance, Brent envisioned the sorcerer building a castle lit aflame, with dragons soaring in the sky, sending fireballs flailing towards the Diabolo in the foothills.

The Diabolo stopped to stare at the fireball. A roaring blaze shot through the sky like lightning. It darted to the side as the mythical lightning struck, shrieking as the mist showed a tale of fire rippling through the forest.

Go away...go away... Brent clenched his teeth, *Please.*

Another fireball shot from the top of the mountain.

The monster howled.

Then, with a blast of smoke, it climbed into the sky and towards the story of the sorcerer.

Brent exhaled.

Around him, the storm passed. He finally had his mind again, and while the fake fire disappeared with the storm. It would take time for the tale of the Fire Emblazed Sorcerer to become a distant memory.

"Brent!" Caroline darted over to him. Her face had shifted back to normal. Blood soaked her nose and lips, but other than that, she looked unharmed.

"I'm sorry I couldn't...I didn't catch it. I fucked up again." Brent collapsed against the tree, wincing. Everything spun around him, and for a moment, he confused the shadows with a sorcerer's flames and the wind with the monster's screams, before being able to speak. "It's still out there."

Caroline gripped his cheeks. "You did fantastic. We fought a beast. If the Council looks at you with distaste for acting human, then they will have to answer to me. You did amazing, Brent. You really did."

"It hurts..." Brent swallowed. "I wanna go...I need to...I wanna sleep."

Caroline hoisted Brent up by his waist. "Let's go to the library, yes? Aelia can look you over. You can rest and eat, and we shall recuperate."

"But we didn't catch it. I wanna...I wanna go home."

"Of course, of course, you're tired." Caroline beamed, and her face changed tone, becoming the mask of a man with long blond hair. She touched her cheek. "Oh, consarn it, someone is dead close by. Is it alright if we take a detour? Might be a tad bit of a walk, but it is another learning experience. I do understand if you are too exhausted, though."

"I'm fine," Brent grunted. "Duty calls."

"Yes, yes, good boy, thinking smart." Caroline patted his shoulders. "Come, it is not far. About a five-minute walk."

Brent trudged behind Caroline down the foothill for a time. The storm left trees upturned, with the mist–or ghosts, or something–fleeing in all directions. Sometimes he heard their screams, but beneath the weight of his headache and the fatigue nestled between his eyes, he couldn't put it together.

He nearly tripped over the body of the man, lying face down, skin eaten away by maggots. A fly landed in the man's eye socket.

"Shite!" Brent gagged.

"The smell?" Caroline asked. "You will get used to it."

"It's all...it's horrendous."

"Then imagine your favorite essence. Keep it right in your mind and let it fill every corner of your body. Focus. That will be your incense of death."

Brent inhaled, pushing aside the stories and keeping only his own tale at bay. He smelled the rain, a crackling fire, lemons, and parchment. Memories of times in the garden after a light rain, kissing Bria as she tasted and smelled of the earth.

At an exhale, the stench of the dead man vanished, "I—I think it worked."

"I am over three-hundred years old! Of course, it worked!"

Brent grimaced.

Caroline leaned over the body. Once more, her face resembled the man in life, then her own face returned.

"Do you...you want me to try to release him, don't you?"

Caroline grinned. "Smart boy, you are. Smart indeed. But only if you are able, of course. We did fight a monster, but the world does not end. Our duty is, after all, to humanity."

"I...I can try." Brent reached towards the body and touched its forehead.

Then came darkness.

Screams.

A child dead.

A man with a pistol.

Unphased.

A woman in the woods.

Terror.

Rape.

Hostility.

Thump.

Thump.

Thump.

Nothing at once.

Everything together.

A vicious laugh.

No sight.

But smoke.

A gate closed.

Locked.

"Agh!" Brent flailed back into the world, "I can't do it! There was too much noise!"

"Brent! Brent! Calm down!" Caroline was beside him, hands on his shoulders, "Relax! It is okay."

"What? No, I was...there was darkness and a pistol. Thumps...like a heartbeat. I can't..." He scratched his wrist.

Caroline placed her own hand on the dead man's head. "Brent, you're fine. You did perfect. He belongs in Hell."

"I—I did...it?" He winced. "I don't feel...it. I mean—"

"Yes, you did it." Caroline hoisted him from the ground. "Come. It has been quite a long morning. Let us get you cleaned up."

CHAPTER TWENTY-TWO

THE MIST OF THE WORLD

Brent took refuge on a couch in the back of the library by a fire, wrapped in a woolen blanket. Caroline vanished a couple hours earlier with Aelia and Tomás, and while he was free to leave, life on the sofa was more appealing than wandering alone in the tunnels.

I should be looking for Rho. Or I should go back to Bria. Or go home. His legs wouldn't budge. Stories kept flashing before him, the thumping in his head rang, and more than ever, he wanted to be with Bria.

"Ingrid!"

Brent looked up.

Julietta bumbled over to him, her lilac dress wrapped around her curves, a cup of tea in her hands. "You look not well, dear Ingrid! Here, here," she handed him the cup of tea, "drink."

"Oh...um, thanks," Brent took the cup and grimaced.

The woman smiled absently. "You always loved your tea. But dear, you should get a haircut so we can see your diamond eyes."

"I will consider it."

"Good, good, I am sure Aelia could help or—" Her green eyes flashed past him, "Oh! Tom!"

Tomás emerged from the bookshelves behind them. "Good day, Julietta. You up and about, I see?"

"I do enjoy a stroll." Julietta peered at the ceiling and asked, "Can we go outside soon?"

"Yes, soon." Tomás placed a hand on her shoulder. "I would love to see you finish your painting. The one of the meadows? You remember?"

"It's almost done. I should finish it now. Then we'll go walking in them, yes?"

"Yes, yes, I look forward to it."

Julietta grinned. "Oh, Tom, it will be glorious! And Ingrid," she turned to Brent, "I shall show it to you, too!"

"I'd like that," Brent assured her.

"I will be with you in a bit. I cannot wait to see your artwork." Tomás guided her towards the stairs, and Julietta skipped away. "Poor Julietta. She was my apprentice and a sweetheart. She started to lose her mind the moment she entered Hell, though, and when she emerged months later as a Mist Keeper, her past was but a ghost. She has struggled her entire tenure; she tried to train over twenty apprentices before Jiang succeeded. Ingrid, the name she called you, was one of them. Her memory has gotten worse over the last few decades. Even with her magic to paint them, she does not remember well. Quite a shame..."

"There wasn't anything you could do?" Brent prodded. "Don't you all have magic?"

"Yes, but when the mist claims your mind, there is not much anyone can do."

"Claims your mind," Brent repeated. "As in...go crazy?"

"Yes, yes, that is correct. Some fail."

"How many fail?"

Tomás didn't answer.

"Tomás? Am I...is there a chance that I'll...will I fail?"

"Many do fail, but it does not mean you will," Tomás replied. "I think you are stronger than you look. Although, the way your magic has manifested is worrisome. Others have struggled through reading the mist as you do, but if you harness it correctly, I think you could be fantastic."

"I don't even understand it...like, how it works or anything. From what I can tell, it's not normal magic, right?" Brent watched the mist as it gathered around Tomás, telling a story of two young lovers.

When Tomás moved, it disappeared.

"Mist magic, yes," Tomás motioned Brent along. "That's an interesting subject. Come, we can discuss over drinks."

Brent trudged behind Tomás, keeping the blanket around his shoulders and the cup of tea in his free hand. They ended up by a fire in a corner of the library, where Jiang lounged on the couch, and Alojzy sat stiffly in a chair, reading. A bottle of whiskey rested on the table with a few glasses.

Jiang rolled over. "What's he doing here? He up fucked enough today."

"I didn't mean to," Brent mumbled.

"He did fine." Tomás ushered Brent into a chair. "It was not wise on our part to send our youngest into the fray like that."

"His powers are erratic," Alojzy noted without looking up.

Jiang yawned. "Always knew magic was dangerous. The boy is going to prove it."

"I agree. He is bound to fail."

"Oi!" Brent snapped, sitting up taller in the seat to make sure they saw him and didn't look over him like a child. "I'm right here!"

"Now, now," Tomás interjected, passing a glass of whiskey to Brent, "no need to get in a fuss. Brent, you have much to learn still, but it is not our place to determine your failures."

"Yes, it is Caroline's," Jiang added, much to Tomás's disapproving glare.

Brent sniffed the whiskey. A lemon scent trickled over the edge. "I just don't understand—the magic or any of it. I mean, I—I see stories; I create them, and I can read them. All with the mist. They're all in my head. I don't...it doesn't make sense..." Brent gulped, "Caroline makes it look easy with the masks. Aelia with her healing. Julietta with her—her painting, right?"

"So, you've already noticed," Tomás remarked.

"Guess he's not a total idiot." Jiang rolled onto his back again, weaving his hair into a braid.

"You all have...you have magic of some sort, right?" Brent asked.

Tomás grinned. "Yes. We each treat the mist as our own. I have what I call *mental examination*; I can read minds via the Mist of Soul. It's a connection to the living and the dead, as I understand it."

"And what about the rest?" Brent glanced between Alojzy and Jiang.

"Well—"

"I've got nothing!" Jiang interrupted. "Don't hide it, Tomás. You know how I feel. Magic is an abomination."

"You sound like the Order," Brent murmured, "and now magic's gone because of it."

"Good. 'Bout time they—"

"Enough." Alojzy refilled Jiang's glass and shoved it in his hands. That shut him up for the moment. "I apologize for our comrade. He is *sober.*"

Jiang sneered and rolled onto his stomach.

"Tomás," Alojzy continued, "it does not do well to beat around the bush. I think Brenton should know why we are concerned."

"Concerned isn't the right word." Tomás scratched at the scar cutting through his eye, "Perplexed may be better."

"About what?" Brent fidgeted with his glass. What was so different about him? Why couldn't anything ever be simple?

"You've been exposed to all three types of Mist Magic in a matter of weeks," Tomás explained. "I mentioned the Mist of the Soul, but there are two others: The Mist of Surrounding and the Mist of Distortion."

"I don't understand."

Alojzy hijacked the conversation. "It's simple really: The Mist of the Soul is magic relating to people, the Mist of the Surrounding has to do with the world around you, and the Mist of Distortion is creativity. It all starts with the Mist, or Effluvium, or whatever you call it. Tomás has Mist of the Soul as he can connect with others, Caroline has Mist of Distortion as she creates faces, and Ningursu has the Mist of the Surrounding with his *all-knowing sight.* It's the way our magic manifests under three guises." Alojzy exhaled, "You are touching all three fast, and in ways most do not."

Brent shook his head. "So wait...that's a lot. I...you mean...my magic, or this Mist Keeper life thing I'm dealing with...I'm learning too much too soon? And that it might cause me to, I dunno, implode or something drastic like that?

"We do not know," Tomás answered, "but you are able to see stories, and you seem to latch onto the stories of people. You also create them. It is...fascinating, really. But we worry for your mind."

"I'm fine." While he firmly punctuated the statement, he didn't believe it himself. Would there be a day when he would close his eyes and not wake up himself? Even after he died and became one of the Mist Keepers, would he continue to struggle beneath the weight of this confusion? Often when he opened his mouth, the personalities of the others came out dancing with his speech. Sure, the woman from Yilk hated cats...but did Brent Harley hate cats? He couldn't remember anymore.

Tomás expression fell, his good eye staring at the bookshelves. "There have been many apprentices who had their powers come to fruition like this."

"And they all failed," Alojzy finished.

"I won't fail." Brent took a swig of his whiskey at last. "I mean...I don't want to."

Jiang cackled. "Pah. No one wants to, but most aren't able to handle the voyage out of Hell when they die. Plus, if your minds a mess, it ain't going to be easy."

"My mind isn't a—"

"We see you, boy. We know what's been going on."

"I'm okay. I'll be okay." Brent's head fell, trying to shake off the stares. Did they think his outbursts were getting worse? Or did they blame his state of mind on the Diabolo? He couldn't even figure out why they looked at him with such dismay. Sure, he'd gotten sick more than once from releasing souls...but he was new? So what?

"All we can ask, for now, Brenton, is for you to be careful," Tomás requested. "Your magic is volatile and unpredictable. I would hate to see you in the wrong hands."

"Or manipulated by the wrong people," Jiang sat up. "Like the little enchantress in the tunnels."

"Rho won't hurt anyone," Brent murmured.

"Pah! You don't know. You're as lovestruck as a man in a whorehouse."

"What? What does that have to do with anything?"

"Caroline has told us how you've been with your little Magii." Jiang puckered his lips and teased, "*Kissy kissy*."

"No, that's not with Rho—that's with—that's with Bri—" Brent shook his head, realizing what Jiang inferred. "No...she can't have...how do you know?"

"How do you not?"

"He is quite dense," Alojzy added.

"We've watched her for a while now," Tomás explained, squeezing into Brent's shoulders, "Relax. Deep breaths."

"But she would have told me...she should have told me. She...no..." Brent's temples pounded and even downing another glass of whiskey didn't keep the tremors away. "It can't be..."

"Brenton?"

Tomás's voice faded. Brent recalled through the times he spent with Rho. He pictured her hiding her face in the darkness, laughing on the mountain, dancing in the forest, and squeezing his hands. It felt natural, it felt normal...how didn't he realize?

Perhaps he didn't want to know.

Brent poured himself another glass and guzzled it.

CHAPTER TWENTY-THREE

REVEALED

Rho hadn't slept. Long after the sun rose and her home grew silent, closing her eyes sent her back to the barracks, the words of her grandmama about the Order echoing around her head. Vulnerability and loneliness followed her, and even as she headed into town with a basket in hand, her blue shawl wrapped around her shoulders, the feeling did not cease.

The townsfolk greeted her with smiles on their faces. If they knew the truth, if they saw what she could do, wouldn't they send her to the Pit with the rest?

Despite everything, she kept her head up, returning each smile with one of her own, basking in the sun rays peeking through the clouds. After helping her father set up his wicker baskets, she dallied over to the edge of the town square and leaned against the fence. Invisible, unnoticed, she watched the sky. Dark clouds gathered over the foothills. It beat like a heart, and in tune, a yellow tinge pulsated around it.

As Rho took a step forward, the storm exploded. Clouds shattered in every direction, and an offshoot of chartreuse yellow spiraled into the sky. For a moment, she swore she saw a ball of fire rocket towards it.

Then nothing.

Brent...

"Odd storm, eh?"

Rho spun. Cadet Chet Lawry stood at her side, towering over her with a smirk.

"The Effluvium must not be happy," the Cadet continued. "Must be all the magic fucking about."

"I'm sorry, Cadet, I don't know what you're talking about." Rho refused to meet his stare.

He grabbed her face with one hand. "Well, my captain still thinks you do. He woulda sent his son along, but y'know, he's all hard on you. Doesn't know you're a little quiff though, does he?"

"What?" Rho furrowed her brow, trying to pull away. "I don't know—"

"One of my mates saw ya with that Harley boy this morning. You were neckin' like a succubus, weren't ya?"

"I don't know what you're talking about." Rho shoved his hand away. Her pulse rose in her ears, her stomach twisting in knots and climbing into her throat. How did he know?

"If you're so willing to kiss scum like 'im, you'd probably fuck anyone, wouldn't ya?" Cadet Lawry took a step forward.

Rho dropped her basket, letting it roll towards the road.

"C'mon, the captain ain't got all day." Another step forward.

"The Senator said I was free to go."

"That was yesterday, this is today. We ain't done with ya yet."

"I don't want to—" Rho stumbled, gripping her fingers around a nearby branch. "Please don't make me—"

Cadet Lawry snagged Rho's shawl. She spun out of it, and without looking back, darted into the trees. The pain in her abdomen stabbed as she ran.

She cursed herself for not wearing pants when a part of her white dress tore on the thickets deeper into the forest. While she could use her magic to make the path clear, it was bound to land in her more trouble. *I got to get out of here. They really think I destroyed the gardens...*

Perhaps she did. The monster was chasing *her*, nothing else, and she brought it home.

If I ran somewhere else, this wouldn't be happening.

Rho tripped over a root, clunking her chin against the ground and biting her tongue. Cadet Lawry grabbed her feet and pulled her towards him, then pressed one hand onto her stomach. A scream formed in her throat. With a gulp, she thrust it down, tears dotting the corner of her eyes.

"Running to the forest ain't a good idea, doll." Chet's pulled her up by her braid. His hands slithered down her waist and twisted around the fabric of her skirt, "Ain't nobody gonna hear you scream."

"Stop!" Rho begged, sending one of the thicket branches flying towards the Cadet's face. The thorns dug into his cheek.

He cursed, pushing harder on Rho's body. "I've been kind so far, doll. Knew you had that damn magic. Now stay still."

"No! Go away!" Another wave of thickets attacked. They ripped him off her, carrying him up and away into the canopy. His shouts filled the leaves.

The desire to stay on the ground was strong; Rho's body seared, her face trembled, and her legs wobbled. She closed her eyes, keeping her command around the branches until Chet's screams were but a whisper with the wind. Beneath the ground, the echoing of the tunnels entered her fingertips. *I can't go home.*

The mere thought of the tunnels tightened her throat. The monster, as far she could tell, was in the mountains, though.

Besides, wasn't the Order a monster itself?

She exhaled and sank into the dirt. The roots gripped her, passing her beneath the surface and to the cold floor of the tunnels. For some time after, she lay there, counting the roots on the ceiling until her breaths returned to a normal rhythm.

A small tunnel took her back to her hideaway. There, a pair of pants, a cowl, and a long sweater waited for her, as well as a jacket Brent left a week ago. She pulled it around her body and inhaled its stench. *Gross.* She grimaced but kept it.

She ventured back into the tunnels, surprised to find them almost untouched from the monster's rage. A few vines withered on the floor, but the lanterns remained, and any overturned stones rolled back into their place easily enough. Even the junction looked the same, with the thick mist shrouding the northern walls and the tunnels echoing the same tunes.

Rho sat against the wall and stared into the mist. She squinted, trying to see past it, but it didn't budge. Once again, she had no answers. Just empty tunnels, a withering heart, and a mouth full of lies.

She wiped her face and wrapped Brent's jacket tight around her shoulders. *I won't beat around the bush next time. I'll tell him.*

Rho stayed there, huddled against the wall for hours, hugging the jacket against her chest, and trying to shake off the feeling that someone watched her.

Thud.

It sounded like a door. Or were those footsteps? She climbed to her feet and peered into the mist, reaching for the vines on the wall. A shadow moved towards her.

"Brent? Is that you?" she called out. "It's me. It's—"

"Yeah, I know who you are." Brent walked out of the mist. "What the shite, Bria?"

CHAPTER TWENTY-FOUR

A Drunk and a Fool

For the first time, Bria stood in the tunnels as herself rather than Rho. Vulnerable, she wanted to hide into the darkness, to have never come out of her hideaway when he first invaded her tunnels. Now, everything she had worked on hiding was out in the open. But it wasn't fear over having been discovered; it was the worry of how he would react next that paralyzed her. Yet, despite it all, a glimmer of contentment wove its way between her fears.

He finally knew. No more secrets. He knew.

Bria stared at Brent, watching him stumble towards her with a blanket wrapped around his body and a bottle of liquor in his hand.

"Brent," she squeaked, "I was...I tried—"

"No! This is stupid!" Brent slurred. "Why didn't you tell me? I keep secrets—lots of secrets! You don't need to hide from me! You're my best friend...and you lied!"

"I tried telling you but—"

"But you didn't. You just said your name was Rho. What kind of name is Rho? A damn stupid one!" He chugged from the bottle. "Rho, Rho, Rho—like rowing a boat! What type of name is Rho?"

"If you thought it was a stupid name, you should've—"

"Asked? Tried that. You just were like," he swung his voice up midsentence, *"don't ask things Brent. It's for your safety*. Bullshite!"

He sent the bottle flying into the wall behind him. It shattered, and he startled.

"It was for your safety," Bria whispered. "And mine."

"Well fat load of good it did! You've got that thing on your face," he pointed to the bruise, "and then we got this monster-thingy that I released because I'm a piece of shite."

"You released it!?" She straightened her back. "It tried to kill me! Captain Carver thinks it's my fault!"

"Not on purpose! I just am a dumbass who does things and—and you didn't tell me! Don't try to change the subject."

"I tried to tell you! Things kept happening, and I was...I tried!"

"Well I don't know shite!"

Bria covered her face with her hands and exhaled, shaking her head. Why did it have to be Brent Harley? She still wondered that; things were okay until he came into her tunnels. Now her heart ached, her head spun, and her life crumbled.

Brent cursed to himself, tripping as he took a few steps forward.

"Let's talk about this when you're sober, please," Bria whispered. "You're drunk."

"You're drunk!"

"What?"

"I don't wanna talk about this. I'm—I'm—" He pivoted in a few circles, stopping before a northeastern tunnel. "I'm gonna go this way!"

"You don't know where that leads."

"It's an adventure! I like those. I'll figure it out."

"Brent, wait!"

Before she could stop him, he darted down the tunnel, dragging the blanket with him.

Bria gawked after him, choking down the tears in her eyes. Her name said out loud dialed up her vulnerability; alone now, she worried the monster would come pummeling towards her.

Even worse, she didn't remember where that tunnel went.

"Dammit." She bolted after him.

The tunnel he'd gone down diverged in three directions, and at the fork, Bria's paced slowed. She called his name out again, getting no response. The roots and vines slithered past her. *Are you showing me where he went?*

Step by step, she followed the roots to the north. A frigid wind bombarded her face, and she used the sleeve of Brent's jacket to protect her face. Even the roots grew sparse, leaving evergreen taproots to guide her towards the surface.

She emerged to speckles of fairy-like lights in the sky, creating an ethereal glow from the frost-covered ground around the city in the distance. Towers filled the skyline. Steam speckled their peaks, with workers banging away against beams and toiling in the factories. Against their backdrops, Bria saw hundreds–or maybe thousands–of young men marching. A train chugged up the tracks, its whistle drowned out by another noise. It reminded Bria of an elephant, or the scrapping of a chalkboard, or a horn on a steamboat.

Bwaaamp. Bwaaamp.

The honking ceased. On the last note, the skyline changed. The towers moved, marching off down the stream towards the South.

Shit. We're in Knoll. Those are their moving towers!

She darted up the dirt road, coming to a barb-wired fence. A few vagrants leaned against it—one busy eating dirt, while another sat enthralled with their own finger. The guards patrolled the edge of the fence, hitting each vagrant on the head. Bria ducked behind a tree to avoid their gaze.

At least we're already in their Pit. She wrapped her cowl around her hair and hurried into the droves of tents and shacks on her side of the fence.

The Pit of Knoll had to be at least the size of Newbird's Arm, maybe larger, with hundreds of vagrants huddled around fires. Black stamp lined their skins – not only the wrists, but upon their arms, on their faces, and their breasts. No hiding it; the mark of vagrancy sat pure on their skins.

This was where the worst came to rot under the Order's guise. They hid the suffering, pretended it was for the best. Instead, people rotted away with flies on their mouths and crusted mucus on their faces.

Bria continued calling for Brent. The worst scenarios ran through her head. What if the guard found him and stamped his face? What if he hurt himself? What if he was dead?

She shook the thought away and called out again, "Brent!? Where are you? You don't belong here!"

She started to hyperventilate and collapsed behind a derelict home. Her heart vented in her chest, and she closed her eyes, listening to the drumbeats in the tent city. Men and women danced around the fire, singing songs and telling stories. She stood again and let them carry her forward; after all, where else would a drunken Brent head towards?

She ignored the hoots of men as she walked past, her cowl tight around her face, checking the faces of those who danced, playing with smokes and gaspers, painting the air with colors. In each tent, she called Brent's name, begging he return, pleading he survived.

A sob responded from one of the tents.

"Brent?"

She peeked into a few of the campsites. Behind the curtains, sleeping men, women, and children gathered. No familiar faces. No Brent.

Another sob came out of a nearby tent, masking a muffled voice. "She's gonna hate me..."

"Brent?" Bria peeked inside.

Brent sat in the middle of the tent, bundled up in his blanket, tears staining his face. Three women sat around him, stroking his hair and wiping his face.

"There there boyo," one woman in a bright red dress and even brighter lipstick cooed. "She ain't gonna hate ya. Just a lil' argument was all."

"Sober up, why dontcha?" another woman with strange purple hair reassured him. "Will help ya think this all through."

The last woman, older than the others with dark eyes and equally warm cheeks, noticed Bria. A black stamp marked her right cheek. "What're you doing here, girl?"

"I, um...he—"

"Bri!" Brent perked up. His eyes still looked like glass, but a smile replaced the scowl he wore in the tunnels. "You came! And so tall...I've shrunk...you're so tall..." He crawled over to her feet. "You're the tall one now."

"You're drunk." She helped him sit upright, then glanced at the three women. "Thank you."

"Found him fumbling about by the bonfire. Thought he was gonna walk into it." The woman with the mark on her face scowled.

"He's been sobbing 'bout a girl for 'while now," the red-clad woman added. "Must be ya, yeah?"

"I was so mean and angry." Brent pressed his head against Bria's shins. "I'm sorry."

"We'll talk in the morning," Bria whispered.

"We can let ya stay 'ere tonight," the purple-haired woman added. "Usually reserved for clients, but this boy ain't going nowhere by the looks of it."

The woman with the mark on her face objected, but the red woman cut her off, "It's not like we getting no more clients tonight. Mighta well let this boyo rest up a 'lil."

"This ain't ya operation, Tiff! I'm in charge—"

"Yeah, well, then take it from our pay. The boyo needs some rest."

The marked woman huffed and stormed from the tent. The two others followed, leaving Bria alone with Brent.

"Lie down." Bria guided Brent onto the straw mat and tucked the blanket around him. "Sleep it off. We'll talk in the morning."

Half-awake, Brent gripped her wrist. "Is it you?"

"Yeah, it's me. Go to sleep."

He obliged. But his fingers remained within inches of her wrist through the night.

CHAPTER TWENTY-FIVE

Breakfast in the Swamp

Brent's head throbbed when he woke up. Light seared and his ears popped. It took him a few minutes to orient to his surroundings. Canvas...a tent. No floor. Where was he?

Tunnels. The tunnels took me to...I was in a Pit or something.

"Knoll!" He shot up, heart racing. Bria slept in the dirt a few paces away, using a jacket as a blanket. *It really is her...* He gulped. He couldn't remember what he said to her, but it could not have been good. Not with the way his head felt.

He draped the blanket over Bria and stepped outside. Women walked down the road with children, black stamps garnishing their skin, heads down. A light frost munched on the ground, and whiffs of fresh bread scrambled over the gates of the Pit. Brent's stomach grumbled.

"Shut up," he muttered to himself. "You can wait. Let her sleep."

Bria mumbled behind him.

"Bri..." he spun around to face her.

"Hi."

"I...last night...I mean I—"

Bria rubbed her eyes. "You have every right to be mad. Don't apologize."

"I was...I mean..." He sighed, unsure of what to say.

"We can talk about it, but first, let's get out of here. Are you hungry?"

"I—" His stomach cut him off to rumble again.

"Let's go get something to eat." Bria rose and folded the blanket. "We have a lot to talk about."

"Yeah...a'ight."

Bria gave Brent the blanket, and they walked out into the sunlight. He dared to look at the towers in the distance, those infamous towers with windows as dark as the black stamp. They stared at him with judgment. He stared back with fear.

All-knowing sight.

Did they see him as he moved? Did they watch his every step?

Did they see the stories he saw, too? The thousands of stories in the streets, nagging at his head. They sent him into spirals of confusing personalities. Was he a child in the Pit? A man on the run? A boy, lost and confused? A hundred stories at once threatening his reality.

Vagrants lay about, and children ran through the streets. Seeing children in a Pit made Brent's heart hurt; at least back home, they kept the young out of the Pit. Were these children born here? Was this all they ever experienced?

He slowed as they passed a mother nursing her child. She sniffled in the chilled air, lips chapped and hair cut in uneven layers. The child suckled at the woman's breast but wailed as a wave of wind battered the two of them. No matter how the woman tried to lull the babe, nothing stopped the child's tears.

Brent paused, and Bria stopped beside him. "Brent? What is it?"

He turned to the woman and offered his blanket, wrapping it around the babe. The child stopped fidgeting, finally relaxing into a restful state of nursing.

The woman thanked Brent by kissing both of his cheeks.

"Oh, uh..." Brent flushed. "You're welcome."

Bria tugged at his sleeve, and they continued into the tunnels. The tension in his neck subsided and his breathing returned to normal. Chilled air vanished with each step away from Knoll, replaced with sticky humidity as they turned south.

Bria said nothing.

They arrived in a swamp and trudged to an old shack hidden in the cypress trees. Fresh bread mingled with the stench of mud. Brent's grumbling stomach blended in with the croaking of alligators in the distance.

Inside, the café reminded Brent of the one near home. No one noticed him as he sat down across from Bria. She removed her coat and rolled up her sleeves before ordering a round of biscuits, sausage, eggs, and cold sweet tea from the waitress.

Bria spoke once the food arrived. "Discovered this place when I was about thirteen. Always loved the swamp and, I don't know, I feel safe here." She picked at the biscuit. "It's somewhere south of Rosada."

"No one notices me..."

"Mmhmm." Bria put the biscuit down and glanced at him.

Brent's heart sank. She was just as beautiful now as ever. Even with the crumbs on her cheeks, the dirt smudged into her forehead, and the bags beneath her eyes, Brent could not ignore his heart. *Why are you so damn beautiful? I want to be angry at you...but I can't.*

"Why didn't you tell me?" Brent whispered. "I wouldn't have told anyone it was you."

"I know, but..." Bria sniffled. "My entire life, my grandmama told me to hide my truth. She told me not to talk about my birth and that I was just a motherless girl. She was Madame Gonzo in public, never my grandmama."

"So, you are—"

"I am Madame Gonzo's granddaughter like that same story you tell the kids in town. She named me Rhodana like that song sung in the night, but my mother buried me alive soon after my birth." Bria wiped her eyes. "If the Order knew I was alive, I would have been stamped or—or worse. Eradicated, maybe? I shouldn't exist..." She glanced at Brent's wrist, "It's not fair that you have that and haven't done anything wrong. I have magic, and I've had a normal life. Well, I did...I don't think I can ever go back now."

"Bria—" He reached for her hand then pulled back. Now wasn't the time.

She shook her head, "Captain Carver thinks I caused the Yellow Smoke. Then there's Cadet Lawry...he keeps..." She trailed off, blinking a few times. "It doesn't matter. I—I used my magic near him. I'm sure they're looking for me."

"But...the Yellow Smoke...that's not your fault." Brent croaked. "It's mine."

"Stop saying that."

"No, Bria listen, what I said when I was drunk is true! I set the monster free! Me. It was an accident. I was exploring the library, and I found it, and it escaped, and it's my fault."

"It almost killed me."

"I didn't mean to...I..." He squirmed, looking over the bruises on her face. Which ones came from the monster? Which from the Guard? His bones rattled with guilt as he brought his head down, speaking in a whisper. "Can I explain what happened?"

She nodded.

Brent recounted the events from that night over a week ago. Bria's face paled as he spoke, eyes darting past him as he detailed how the Council had created the monster to attack the Magii. He wanted to reach out to her, squeeze her palm, and tell her it was okay, but something held him back, diverting his gaze to his wrist and scratching at his black stamp.

"If I had known it was you," Brent finished, "I would have...I mean...I don't know what I would have done. I was so worried about Rho...about you...but if I had known it was you...I don't know. It might have made a difference. I mean, I would have...I might have known where to look. I would've been more willing to run. I mean, I guess...I guess I should have known. It's—it's so obvious now."

"It was for your safety...and mine." Bria picked at her biscuit.

"It didn't work."

"I know that!" She turned away. "I know it didn't work! Captain Carver interrogated me for hours because it *didn't work*! He almost broke me! He kept asking about lights and things and...whatever, forget it!"

"Bri—"

She threw some coins on the table and slammed the door on her way out.

Brent stared at his plate for a moment, the tintinnabulation of the bell echoing about the restaurant. One ring, two rings, three; he counted each one, worried that the longer he sat, the more people would stare. It already seemed like everyone watched him, blaming him for Bria's outburst. But even as the bell's chimes fizzled, only the waitress acknowledged him when she picked up the coins.

"Shite." Brent grabbed the biscuits and rushed outside, praying Bria hadn't gone far.

He found Bria sitting on the patio, knees against her chest, hair covering her face. The humidity danced in the air, thickening as he neared her. She didn't meet his eyes when he sat beside her and offered a biscuit. She took it and sobbed into the dough. Brent had seen her like this only a few times, but now he saw it all. Her pure tears, her lost expression...all of it belonged naught to a single flower in the garden, but to a forest shifting across the world.

"I'm not mad at you, Bria," Brent finally said. "I'm frustrated and upset, yeah, but at myself. I should've known, and now you're right here and...and I'm sorry for last night."

"You shouldn't apologize."

"Doesn't mean I feel a'ight about this. Besides," Brent glanced at her, "I still love you."

Bria snapped, "Do you love *me* or the idea of me?"

"What?"

"Are you in love with the idea of the sweet girl in the gardens or with *me,* because there's a difference! I'm not the mask I wear back home."

Brent furrowed his brow, mouthing to himself before finding the right words. "I'm in love with *you.* I still see *you.* It's always been *you.* I never saw you as some sweet girl. I saw you as someone who—who could...I mean...who could set the world ablaze with a smile, or—

or cursed because she saw things that're unfair. You might have this magic shite, but...it's still a part of you. I love *you.*"

Bria looked away from him again and shuddered. Brent sat on his hands, holding back on his instinct to touch her, to lull her, and to hold her tight. *Not yet. Wait for her to let you back in.*

They remained staring out at the swamp. The grunting of alligators, the croaks of frogs, the buzzing of cicadas, and the chirps of birds orchestrated a song around them. Even Bria's tears ceased, replaced with a lucid smile. *She's at home here.* The lack of stories and mist allowed his head to clear, and while the occasional tale of a visitor coming to the swampy café graced his presence, most of the time, he separated reality from fiction while they sat.

The canopy above shook as a flock of wise woodstorks descended from the sky and perched themselves on the cypress roots.

"I don't think I can go home," Bria breathed after a while. "The Guard probably wants my head. I assaulted Cadet Lawry, and they think I'm a monster. They'll give me to the Order and then I don't know what will happen. I need to run. Stay hidden."

"Well then," Brent glanced at her, "where are we gonna run to? I mean...we were talking about it and I...I mean if you don't want me to."

"I didn't think you'd—"

"It might not be smart...we're kids and dumb and all but..." Brent looked away. "I'm cursed to die, so what do I got to lose?"

"I told you already, I'm not going to let you die."

Brent shrugged.

"But you would still run with me? Even now?"

"You're the one thing constantly in my life. I couldn't not run with you." He reached out to stroke her hair but drew back, clenching his hand into a fist. "As I said...it should have been obvious."

Bria pulled his hand forward and rested it against her cheek. "Yeah, you're dumb. But I love you."

They embraced as if they hadn't seen each other in years until their sweat stung their eyes, and their tears soaked their cheeks. Their breaths sank into a rhythm while they watched the wood-storks make their perches, masquerading through the swamp with wise reptilian eyes. A story caught Brent's attention, one about a dragon made of mist following the wood-storks to their homes, and granting them a choice: immortality or wisdom, in exchange for their loyalty. The birds, to the dragon's disappointment, chose the aging look of wisdom since immortality was a burden no wise man would carry. The dragon screeched, outsmarted by the birds who needed no dragon to teach them the correct path.

He told this story to Bria, watching from the corner of his eye as her face lit up. She pressed her head against his shoulder, clutching his arm, asking questions about the imaginary fable like a child in a class.

"Well," she topped off her last question, "can you tell me why those storks look like you?"

"What?" Brent laughed. "What're you talking about?"

"Big beak, tired eyes...they're you!"

"Oi! You're mean!"

She beamed. It was that smile Brent loved, that lit up her face, highlighting her mild overbite and punctuating her dimples. She may have hidden the truth from him, but all the same, every time he saw that smile, his heart fluttered like a butterfly.

"You think you're funny, don't you?" He crinkled his nose and asked? "Well, you wanna know what I think?"

"Yeah? What is it?"

"You look like that!" He pointed to a round-faced frog perched on the patio. It croaked once.

She whacked him in the head with a cypress branch.

CHAPTER TWENTY-SIX

THE STORYTELLER IN THE TAVERN

Bria didn't expect Brent to follow her, but he never left her side, staying with her as she guided him away from the Swamps of the South and out towards Opal Canyon. They basked in the crystalized rainbows of stone, dancing in shadows and descending into the stalagmites. She led him through the caves to the Glass City of Proveniro, filled with buggies and picturesque cinematography reflected upon the ocean's surface. From there, Brent took her to Yilk, explaining the architecture of Errat, before leaving the city and heading across the Midnight Plains, where baobab trees towered across the landscape.

They didn't keep track of time as they traveled. Home became a moot point; they couldn't go back when the Order waited to toss Brent into the Pit. Together, they had freedom.

"Come on!" Bria ushered him through the tunnels as they abandoned the Volcanic Caverns of a western island.

"Where are we going now?" Brent yawned mid-sentence, though a smile–that stupid half-smile that always crooked to the right–remained on his face.

"Thought I'd find someplace for us to rest. A proper night's sleep and all." Bria spun to face him and teased, "Can't have you getting sick now."

Brent slowed a few paces behind her, "Bri..."

"Yeah?"

He chewed his lip for a moment. "I'm cursed to die... getting sick...not a big deal, I guess."

"You keep saying that, but do you want to know what I think?"

Brent raised his eyebrows.

"Curses are meant to be broken." Bria gripped his hand. "Now, let's get you some rest, so you don't die of fatigue. We have so much more to see!"

He leaned in to kiss her, but Bria responded by placing a finger to his lips and shaking her head before skipping down the tunnel. His voice echoed after her, and they did not reunite until they reached a ladder at the far end of the tunnel. Bria clapped her hands, and a vine lifted her up towards the door above, while Brent wheezed and huffed up the ladder after her.

They arrived in the center of a tree on the outskirts of the Capitol, as they once did weeks before. The old home with the porch swing glistened in a pale light. Bria slowed as she walked along the road. Even with spring blossoming in Newbird's Arm, here the ground remained brown. A few evergreens kept their immortal green hair, but other than those, the world slept.

They entered the home where the old woman slept in her rocking chair. A few men and women in flamboyant clothes ran past her and into one of the rooms, dropping coins in her lap. Bria placed a coin of her own on the rocking chair, before luring Brent down the staircase and into the speakeasy.

A storyteller sat towards the back of the room, telling some obtuse tale about an ugly goose. Bria ordered two drinks and brought them over to where Brent sat, gazing at the storyteller with the bewilderment of a child and the excitement of a puppy. Like before, it never left. While the stories changed every few minutes, Bria couldn't take her eyes from Brent. At one point, he reached under the table and squeezed her hand before pulling her close, so his arm rested around her shoulders. For once, they didn't need to hide; how many of those around them wore black stamps?

Stories of princesses, heroes, knights, and valleys passed through the lips of each storyteller. One caught her attention about a magician in a city called Mert in the East. With each story, the candles dripped, waning away with the night. Bria tried to get Brent to go up and tell a story of his own, but he sunk down in his chair and nursed his whiskey instead, perking up once the next storyteller took the stage. Yet, as each story came and went, his confidence bolstered. Either that or the alcohol painted his eyes with the golden liquid of false aplomb.

After downing a second glass of whiskey and listening to a disheartening tale about a horse named Arnie, Brent rose.

He glanced at Bria. "You—you want a story?"

"Only if you're comfortable, but..." She touched his fingers. "This has always been what you wanted, right? To tell stories. Last time you flubbed, but you had fun."

"I think Mr. G was a fantastic story," Brent laughed. "But yeah, I can try something a bit less lame."

He climbed onto the stool in the center of the makeshift stage. He looked small up there, despite his tall stature, resting his feet on one of the bars and curling in on his shoulders. For a moment, he fidgeted with the cuff on his wrist, then turned his attention to Bria and grinned.

"I'm going to tell you a story," he recited, not turning from Bria's gaze, "about the Queen of Summer and the Pauper of Winter."

Off he went, weaving a tale about how the Queen of Summer sat on her throne in the sun, watching the Pauper of Winter play with children in the moon's rays. He described it in detail, throwing his voice as the Queen of Summer descended to Earth, and deepening it as the Pauper of Winter bowed in her presence. The story enshrouded Bria, to the point she didn't even realize Brent's voice faded away, replaced by the visuals of the tale. Summer and Winter merged together in the room, fingers laced, and gave birth to children named Spring and Autumn.

He finished the story, and once again, Bria sat in the tavern. An ephemeral mist drizzled around the room, leaving behind the residual images of falling leaves and blooming flowers. She held her hand out to one of them, but as snowflakes break upon landing, so did the mist.

No one moved as Brent retreated from the stage, back hunched and eyes forward. The mist trailed after him as he rushed by the table.

Bria grabbed his wrist. "Where are you going?"

"I used...the magic...it happened, and now I'll..." He closed his eyes and whispered, "We need to run, don't we?"

"No, stupid." Bria nudged him. "Look around."

She followed his gaze to where men and women with stamped wrists and cocky grins continued to tell tales. A few performed parlor tricks - a disappearing coin, a floating candle, a transformed piece of paper - while others gathered around Brent. Yet, the attention caused Brent to retreat on himself again, staring at his fingers, then at Bria.

"You're safe here, son," one man promised.

"This is where we come to hide."

"Ole Miss Doris above, she's from Mert. We all free here because of her, y'know."

"The Order thinks they ran us out, but they didn't."

"It's okay," Bria added. "You're okay. That was amazing."

"I don't know..." Brent gulped. The crowd grew.

"They want another one."

"I don't...I mean...I'm not sure..."

Bria pushed him back to the stool. "Go!"

He hesitated at first, but when Bria smiled at him, it got him to climb back up and launch into another tale, while Bria got comfortable at the table again. Brent told tales of far and wide - of the Zeppelin Warriors of

Proveniro, Nine Giants who walked the plain of Yilk, and of a scientist who attached wings to a woman. At each story, the mist joined the tale, painting miniature images across the bar. A hawkish woman joined by playing piano at the edge of the room. People danced with the tales. Bria joined by dumping an array of seeds on the table, weaving the flowers and vines into crowns to disperse amongst the patrons.

"I have one more story...if that's a'ight?" Brent said as he finished the story of the flying woman, "There's a legend back home where I'm from...about a child born with a camellia growing from her head," his voice grew softer as he spoke. "The story says she was planted in the Earth. But...that's false, I think. She grew like trees and flowers do, to become the Forest Queen we all know and love. Rhodana...right, you've heard the tale? How does that song go?"

The hawkish woman began a tune on the piano.

"That's right...that's right." Brent smirked and teased, "I don't sing, don't worry. But I don't...I'm not sure where I'm going with this but...I..."

The patrons saved him. A soft tune hummed turned into a full song.

Rhodana...
... the Forest Queen

She loves to laugh...
... she hates to scream
She promised the world a reverie...... Rhodana

She planted the trees...
... stopped the black
Dust and soot...
... It vanished like ash
She cried the rivers...
... to existence they may
A queen of life, some might say...
... Rhodana...

They kept singing, but Bria shrunk. A story, that's all it was. Not her—never her. Yet, as Brent approached her, she couldn't help but feel like a queen herself.

A story changes, so it must...
... Never the same, like a wind gust
Let us sing, let us dance...
... The queen will bless us a second chance...
Rhodana...

Bria climbed onto the table, standing at Brent's level and placed the last flower crown on his head. He cupped her cheeks. "Is it okay if I...am I...can I kiss you?"

She nodded. "You don't ever need to ask."

"I always will."

Bria pulled him forward. She never wanted to release him. Not ever again.

A musk of smoke and liquor filled the tavern room. Bria pulled the woolen blanket up to her chin and glanced at Brent. He lay next to her, running his hand through the air, a misty aura dripping over his fingers. Their eyes locked. Another smile, another kiss. Bria nuzzled beneath his arm, their sweat sticking, breaths rampant, and heartbeats ringing.

"You a'ight?" Brent asked, his fingers digging into her hair.

"Yes, of course. You?"

"Yeah." He rolled over to face her and pushed a strand of hair from her face. His eyes fell to her stomach. The bruises from the Diabolo–as Brent called it–over a week ago had left a yellowing tinge on her skin. "I'm so sorry..."

Bria cupped his cheek. "I'm fine. And I don't blame you."

He didn't respond, staring beyond her while playing with her hair. His free hand ran again through the mist, commanding it almost, while he whispered a story to himself. It was something about a woman ranting about kitchen counters, and as he mumbled it, the mist took the shape of the same woman, ranting and raving next to the bed.

"It's strange," Brent murmured. "It's like I can see stories in the mist...true or not. They told me there were different types of mist magic, but I don't know what that even means."

"The Mist Keepers you mean?"

"Uh-huh." He clenched his hand shut.

Bria reopened it, "Don't be ashamed of your magic, okay?"

"I...I'm not."

"Good. Because I was ashamed when I discovered mine."

Brent gaped at her. "What? Why? It's amazing!"

"Don't worry, I'm not anymore." Bria grabbed the flower crown from the end table and placed it back on Brent's head. "But I was...when I was younger."

"Why, though?"

"Imagine finding out your mother tried to kill you because of your magic. That story, the rumor you've heard? It's true. I was born with a camellia on my head. My mother panicked and buried me alive. I survived, but I grew up not just without a mother but knowing what she did. My grandmama didn't hide it from me."

Bria blinked and wiped her eyes. "She tried to keep me away from all that. My father and I lived in Hutch's Creek for about eight years, but we came back; we couldn't let my grandmama be alone after my grandpapa died. And he liked Mr. West, who offered us hospitality. All of them hoped my magic would never manifest again, but then one day, I spit a hundred full bloom poppies from my mouth. It terrified me. What if my mother came back and buried me again? Or worse?" She glanced at Brent. "The tunnels provided me some sort of safety net. Let me bolster...but it was lonely. Until you had to show your ugly face."

Brent wiped away her tears. "Well, the Order's a load of idiots if you ask me. Why would they want to...I mean, why do they want to get rid of something so wonderful?"

"Because they're scared of what we can do." She weaved a few new flowers into Brent's hair. "We can give them Hell."

"Yeah, you can do that." Brent rolled over and murmured, "I wanna sleep."

They lay there, using their giggles and smiles to talk until Brent left for the lavatory. Bria dressed and threw Brent's jacket on over her shoulders, then turned to the window. One of the evergreen trees on the dirt path below greeted her. She went to wave back, but stopped, noticing a trail of guards in navy suits marching towards the tavern.

"Shit!" She banged on the lavatory door. "Brent! Get your pants on! We need to leave!"

The water stopped, and he peeked out. "What is it? What's going on?"

"Guard's here." She tossed him pants and his shirt.

"What? Was it...did my...did I attract...I mean...was it my fault?"

"Probably not, but let's not stick around to find out."

Bria helped him button his shirt, then proceeded to hook on one of his suspenders and drag him out of the room.

"Shoes."

"Forget them!" Bria dragged him down the stairs, past the old lady rocking in her chair, and knocked the pile of coins off her lap.

The woman woke, blinking twice. "Guards?"

"Yes."

The woman jolted, kicked her coins under the rug, and rushed into the kitchen. She came out moments later with a pot which she proceeded to hit while screaming up the staircase.

Bria dragged Brent out of the tavern. They ducked into the bushes as the guard marched past in their stark gray uniforms. The distant drumming and shouts made the hair on the back of Bria's neck stand up straight. Goosebumps dotted her arms. Yet, they managed to make it back to the crooked tree and sneak back into the tunnels as a gunshot powered through the sky.

They collapsed together on the dirt ground. Bria glanced at their bare feet and snorted. Brent fell into the same trap, resting his head against the wall to laugh, reaching forward to wipe the dirt from the top of his foot.

Bria offered Brent a hand off the ground, but he pulled her forward as he climbed to his knees, brushing her hair back with his free hand. "So are we gonna run away? Like we...I mean, we talked about it..." He shook his head and asked, "It's not being too brash?"

Bria gazed at him, trying to form words. How many times had he pushed the idea away? Was this happening after so long? She lowered her voice. "We've been talking about this since we were kids."

"We're still kids."

"Kids can't grow facial hair." She poked the stubble above his lip.

"The Mist Keepers will know...and the Guard...they're everywhere..."

"Not if we leave Rosada." Bria pulled at one of the curls on his head. It sprung back in place. She then dug her fingers in deeper and brought him close, forehead-to-forehead. "What do you have here? Really? The black stamp is going to ride on you for your whole life. And you still have that damn binding betrothal..." The last words cut into her tongue like knives.

"I'm gonna call it off."

Bria narrowed her eyes. "When?"

"I mean, I've tried!"

"Have you?"

"Yes! I keep telling Jemma I wanna end this shite and...and it hasn't worked. I've tried. She sees it as her only opportunity, just like my ma saw it as mine...I guess. I dunno. I tried."

Bria relaxed, watching Brent fidget again in place. "So, it won't ever work that way then, right?"

"Yeah."

"And Christof won't agree to calling off mine." Bria glanced between the triangle on her hand and the one on Brent's hand. Her triangle still felt tender. The marks on Brent's skin always seemed like a part of him. Why did hers feel so alien? "So, I'm running whether you come or not."

"You haven't run yet."

"Because I didn't want to go alone." Bria coiled in on herself. Admitting that made her feel small and vulnerable. "And after the monster attacked, I was scared. I didn't know what to do."

"But before the monster?"

"I held onto hope that life in Newbird's Arm would get better. It didn't. It's gotten worse. But now we're here, together, and we could go anywhere."

"But where will we go?" Brent asked with uncertainty. "It's not like magic is welcome anywhere."

"Except Mert," Bria noted.

"That was just a city in a story."

"No, it's not." Bria motioned him down the tunnels. "Come on. It shouldn't take too long to get there!"

CHAPTER TWENTY-SEVEN

THE CITY OF MERT

The City of Mert sat on a cliff overseeing the Blood Sea with bustling pathways untouched by the Order's hand. Magicians raved in the winding streets, creating illusions in their palms, performing slights of hand, and creating dazzling presentations on the walls. Brent marveled at the sight. A man summoned birds from his hat, while another rode a bicycle with stars in its wake. Men in suits handed out silver vials, exchanged for coins, while elderly men and women sat against the flyer covered alley. Even the stories hidden in the alleys of towering skyscrapers sang a different tune; tales of hope, fantastical desires, and children chasing miniature dragons. Papers advertising the *Seer of Red Eyes, Tattoos of the Dragon,* and *Storytellers of Gorge* lined the walls.

He grinned at Bria. *This isn't Rosada, that's for sure.*

Bria led Brent by the hand through the market between a panoramic palace and multicolored shops on the waterfront. She stopped by a seamstress with an array of colorful clothes and pulled a blue, white, and green sweater out of the pile and held it up to Brent's chest.

Brent wrinkled his nose. "It's hideous."

"But it doesn't smell," Bria laughed. "We've been traveling for days."

"I bathed!"

"Your clothes still stink!"

Brent grumbled as Bria purchased the sweater and trousers for him and a bright dress for herself. Like the magic in the alleyway, the clothes glistened, radiating color across Bria's cheeks. He stopped her as they walked over the bridge into the heart of the city, pointing out the bright koi swimming through the ponds, and over to the children kicking about a rainbow-colored ball.

"Why wouldn't you just come here? Live here I mean?" Brent asked, gawking at everything. "You could be...here you could be amazing, I mean."

"I've only been here a few times." Bria fidgeted. "I think I was last here a year ago? There's so much else to see in the world. Plus, I'd be here alone..." She picked at the wood banister.

"But, I mean, I'm here now."

"Yeah, I know."

Bria found them a room for the night in a small tavern that overlooked the rocky beach. They gathered into each other's arms, watching the sunset capture the blood sea, before succumbing to their emotions. They lay in an embrace until a slither of moon winked in the sky.

As Bria showered and changed, Brent watched the sea thrash about on the rocks. Children ran about with sticks, while mothers danced with the waves. The leader of the group sent offshoots of water into the air, sculpting an image of a dolphin above their heads. He scratched his wrist. *I'm finally free. My stamp means shite here.*

He didn't hear Bria return and jumped when she stroked his back with her fingers. "We could stay here."

"In Mert?"

"They speak the common tongue. Magic is legal. They love a good story." She gripped his hand. "We'd be safe...like you said. And if anyone can stop your curse, it would be someone in Mert. I was thinking we could ask that Red Eyed Seer, the one on the flyer. She might—"

Brent turned to her. "Bri...I know you think—"

"There must be a way to break the curse! It's not like curses are permanent. How did it happen? Did they just say some spell or...or something?" She shrunk and looked away. "I don't want you to leave."

He took her hand. "I'm not gonna anywhere for now. We can try but...I mean...I don't know. If we're gonna stay here and figure it out, though, we're gonna need money. We're...I don't...we're running out."

"We'll have to sneak back home and get our stuff. I have some money until we find jobs." Bria's face fell, and she added, "At least we'll be able to say goodbye."

They huddled on the bed, counting and naming each of the stars. Yet sleep came for neither of them, so they ventured out into the streets.

The City of Mert contained a livelihood Brent hadn't seen anywhere else. Magic may have brought it back, but in its essence, life reverberated through the city. Those without homes still found a way to smile, and flowers bloomed in the small gardens lining the streets and in the boxes hanging out the windows. Even the night sky winked with songs and stories.

Yet despite the flowers blooming and the sky's psychedelic sky, the air tasted dry, and weeds often stroked the cracks in the cobblestone.

Brent's grumbling stomach led them to a small quiet restaurant between the Blood Sea and the Dark Plains. A meal consisting of a well-rounded steak and spinach coated with a lemon glaze satisfied Brent's hunger.

Certainly, though, dessert was the best part: a cold delicacy, coated with flakes of chocolate.

"What is this?" he asked, mouth full.

"Ice cream," Bria laughed. "You've never had ice cream?"

"Sorry, I didn't get a chance to explore and shite! Damn! This is amazing!"

Bria giggled, her eyes lighting up, face absorbing the multicolored dress wrapped around her body. She still wore his jacket over it, and as ridiculous as she looked, Brent couldn't keep his eyes off her.

"You've got some on your face," Bria pointed.

"Where?"

She came over with her handkerchief and wiped it away. "You're a mess."

"It's worth it for ice cream."

Bria captured his happiness with a kiss.

"And that," Brent croaked. "Constantly that..."

They finished eating. Outside, from the edge of the restaurant, the Blood Sea crashed, riding the winds of a storm far in the South. The Plains in the north blossomed into something more spectacular. Splats of white, checkered as far as Brent could see, filled his vision.

"What is that?"

"Just another natural wonder...the locals call it the Chessboard Plains." Bria gripped his hand. "You want to check it out?"

"Chessboard Plains..." Brent grinned. "A'ight, yeah. Let's play."

They followed a tunnel out to the plains. Droves of tulips, white and black in color, capsuled the land as far as Brent could see. Bria walked in front of him, her fingers drifting over the blossoms, a skip in her step as they moved with her. He followed her, but with each step, his throat tightened. A drumbeat, pounding, called in his head, the fog of war embellishing the surrounding mist.

"Bria..." He reached out for her.

Like the mist, she vanished before him.

Thump.

Thump.

Thump.

It couldn't be his heartbeat. No. Men marched across the plains. Magic blazed across their fingers as lights and darkness mingled. Screams, blood, and shrieks rang out; a monster rose within them. A man lost his head, a woman slaughtered a leader, and a thousand warriors died without knowing their cause.

He saw it all, a flash of lightning striking his mind, followed by a gasp.

"Brent! Calm down! Relax!"

Bria's voice faded away. This time, the mask of a storm surrounded the Chess Field. A dragon soared through the sky, masquerading in ashes and smoke. A hundred miniature dragons offered their backs to the army, and into the sky they flew. Those left behind withered, dying, like a parched tree in the middle of a desert.

Screams.

Shouts.

Thump.

Thump.

Thump.

"Bria!" He reached out. There were too many stories filling the area in front of him. Was that actually a woman walking past him with a knife? Or a soldier with a head slung over his shoulder? Where was Bria? Had she always been in his head?

His psyche started to slip. Where did he fall? He didn't know. Could he ever return now?

But this time, Bria's hands on his shoulders brought him home. Brent collapsed into her embrace, sobbing against her as she cradled his head. The war ended. Blood gathered at his bottom lip.

"What happened? What's wrong?" Bria sat next to him, holding his hand, "Are you okay?"

"I don't know."

"It was like you were having a seizure. I thought that it was the curse." She shook her head. "I was scared I was about to lose you..."

"No...I just...I saw it all. There was a war...and—and—and—" He bit down on his lip. *I can't speak. I can't do anything. Words. Say words!*

Bria cupped his cheeks. "I'm right here, I'm right here, it's okay. "

"I see it all...the world...the history of it, I guess," he cried, "It's in my head...it's there...all of it. This was...it was a battlefield. So many died...they're dead and I—I see them all."

"I didn't think this would cause you to go on the fritz." Bria cradled him against her chest. "I'm sorry. We can leave."

"No, I gotta learn to deal with this, I think." Brent closed his eyes. "The world wants to tell me a story; I gotta figure out how to listen."

"What's the story then?"

He shook his head.

"Try to explain. It'll help you make sense of it all."

Brent quivered. "It was...this was...it was..." He clenched his eyes shut. "A war happened here. I don't know what is real or fake or—or—or—"

Bria touched his arm and asked no more, kneading his back with her knuckles and humming a soft tune into his shoulder. He still heard the stories, the war cries, the shouts, but Bria kept him in the present. After a few moments, he could speak.

"A war happened her, a long time ago. With dragons, and magic...and in its place, a chessboard field emerged. And—and...it was terrible, I mean, I think it was terrible. It looked like it. I see it..." He picked one of the flowers and traced along the petals. "These tulips basked in blood..."

"But it's gone now." Bria took the flower from him and wove it into his hair. "It's just us."

"Stories remain. They leave a...they leave something in the air. It has to do with the mist or something." Brent glanced out onto the field, watching the fabled warriors march away from their war. "And I can't stop seeing it...it's always there if I look hard enough. I—I'm gonna lose my...what if I lose myself in the stories?"

"Then I'll lead you back," Bria assured him. "You're a storyteller. These are just a bunch of new stories for you to learn, and a bunch more to tell. You might see blood in the tulips, and you think you're dying, but if I know one thing, Brent, is that you're going to be fantastic. Truthfully, honestly, fantastic."

"You really believe that, don't you?"

"I know it."

He smiled.

Bria continued decorating his hair with tulips, telling him how she came upon this place once as a child. She didn't see the blood or the war but created her own tale.

"What was it?" Brent asked.

"It was stupid," Bria wove the tulips together into a misshapen rod. "I'm not a storyteller."

"Tell me anyway."

"It was...there were two giants in my story who planted a garden to play chess. They left it here so their great-great-great grandchildren could play. See, stupid story."

"I think it's great," Brent chimed in, watching as she finished tangling the tulips together. "What're you doing?"

"Well," Bria rose, "you say this is a battlefield, yeah?"

"Uh-huh."

"Well," she said, a half smile on her face, "then a battlefield must have a queen."

"What?"

"En garde!" Bria pointed the tulip rod at him like a saber.

"You're joking, right?"

"En garde!"

He laughed. "This is stupid! I don't have a weapon!"

"Hold on." She tossed him her tulip rod and pulled a few seeds out of her satchel. She threw them up into the air, and when they returned to her, they arrived as a stiffly wrapped vine covered in ripe tomatoes.

"Touché."

They dueled, the stiff plant-made rods bashing into each other. The tomato juice drenched the white tulips. Bria laughed like a child, tossing her troubles away while slipping on the tomato. Brent gained a bounce back in his step as he wielded his tulips, matching her laughter with his own. It was a battlefield of farmers, not with blood but produce scattered out on the board. For a long time, there was no winner. Bria had a clear advantage, though. After her tomato vine withered away, she took another bundle of seeds out, and within moments she had an ivy wrapped weapon as her new tool.

A wind circle caught the tulip covered rod from Brent's hand and sent it soaring into the air. Bria leaped, catching it and twirling around to face him. She crossed the weapons to his neck. "Surrender?"

"Guess so. Am I your prisoner?" he asked with a smirk.

"Yes! And as my prisoner, you have to do as I say."

"Like what?"

She dropped her weapons and pulled him down to her level. Yet, as their lips touched, something else pulled on his ears. His first thought went to Caroline, but no, it was different this time.

It felt like a whisper, a child even, telling secret tales under the Order's nose.

Bria read him like a book. "What is it?"

"Something's calling me...a different type of story..." He bit his lip and whispered, "Someone died."

"How do you know that?"

Brent chewed on his bottom lip. "The Mist Keepers are death-like gods or something. I guess my ultimate job is to release their souls."

"So, you save them?"

"That's one way to put it..." Brent trailed off. The story of a woman and her son walking in the field, a drizzle of bliss about them, entered his vision. "I feel like I need to...I should go and...I mean, if I'm a Mist Keeper..."

"You have a job to do; I get it."

"If you wanna meet me back at the—"

"No, I'm coming with you!" Bria clenched his arm. "I want to see what you can do."

"It's not anything special."

"Don't undersell yourself. You're Mr. Death. Not many people can say that! And I want to know everything about you."

"And I guess we can find answers for you, too," Brent reminded her. "I haven't forgotten promising *Rho* that. I mean...they told me they'd been watching you."

"Why?"

"Because you're in the tunnels. And they watch powerful Magii. I don't know why. They don't give me answers." He stared out at the tulips and counted down as the wind skipped through the pedals. "It has something to do with a war long ago...with powerful magic users who kinda messed with the Council. I mean...I don't know the full story or anything. It's why they created that monster. But since then they watch people with magic...I guess maybe they know why you are the only person other than them in the tunnels. Like why you can see them or...or something. And I know it's not likely but...yeah."

"Just the fact you remember means everything to me."

"I wouldn't forget."

Bria hugged him around the waist. Together they walked through the tulips as the story shrouded Brent, transforming him into an elderly woman laying her adult son to rest.

CHAPTER TWENTY-EIGHT

PAST THE MIST

Bria watched Brent kneel beside a rotten corpse in the middle of the tulips. She gagged, stepping back, and Brent turned to her with a smile that still, after these days together, made her heart flutter.

"Imagine your favorite smell," he insisted. "Just kind of leave it there in your mind. It will make it seem better. That's what Caroline told me."

Bria recanted the scent of lemon cakes baking in her grandmama's kitchen. The warmth of the home filled her. She could still smell the rotting flesh, but a whiff of lemon kept her stomach together.

"Better?"

"A bit," Bria replied.

Brent's face fell. "Good. Just, um, stay back, a'ight? A few paces. I don't want...I mean, I don't think I'll hurt you, but...I don't know."

"I can probably take you on. I'm not harmless."

"I know, I know." Brent clenched his eyes shut. "I still don't want to hurt anyone and if I hurt you I—"

"You won't. Now go release that poor fool from his Hell."

Brent reached down, then stopped. "Bria, what I mean is...every time I've done this, I get like residuals of the story stuck in my head. I sometimes don't know who I am. I get confused...and scared...and I don't know what you'll see after I finish this release. I might not be myself for a bit."

"You're stronger than you think," Bria assured him. "You'll be fine. And if not, then I'll be right here."

Brent sucked in his lips and returned to the body. He placed his hand on its decomposed skull and closed his eyes.

Bria expected to see something extraordinary. Yet, like Death itself, the process was mundane—a blink, a heartbeat, and a spin of mist. Brent was the needle leading the thread of mist into the sky. Like another heartbeat, it thudded, then dissipated.

Bria's heart skipped watching as Brent stumbled back, holding his head and cursing, "Mama...Mama...Mama, I'm sorry...I should have tried harder, Mama...I'm sorry I'm sick, Mama..."

"Brent! Stop! Calm down!" Bria rushed over, stopping short of touching him, fearful that one simple touch would break him. "It's over! You're okay."

Brent curled on the ground. "My name... what is... my name is Gregorich... no... Arabella... no... Maija... no, no," he snarled. "Brent. My name is Brent. I was in Newbird's Arm. My parents are Janette and Robert Harley. And my one constant is..." His eyes rose to meet Bria's. "Help me, please."

He looked small and frightened, like a child. Part of Bria wanted to cradle him, the other wanted to cry for him. But she had to stay strong. He couldn't see how much this broke her heart.

Bria grabbed his wrists, "I'm right here."

"I can't...I don't know..."

"Your name is Brent Harley," Bria massaged his knuckles and stifled back her own tears, "You were born in Newbird's Arm. Your parents are Janette and Robert Harley. And I'm right here with you. Just fixate on who you are, okay? The stories are just that, stories. You're Brent."

"Yeah, okay, yeah," he closed his eyes again, "but who will I be when I have ten thousand lives in my head?"

"Brent Harley with ten thousand new stories."

He didn't argue. The way he held himself made him look small. He continued to bounce between stories for a time, mumbling and cursing under his breath. No wonder he was so frightened. Bria didn't know how to help except by keeping him close, reminding him of his identity, and telling him he'd be okay.

So, she hoped.

"Maybe...maybe Mert is a good place to stay," Brent whispered. "Maybe they got resources or some shite like that to help with my fucked-up head..."

"I'm sure they do," she cooed. "We'll figure this out. I promise."

"Don't make promises you can't keep."

"But I intend to keep it. I swear."

The walk home left Brent in a futz, mumbling to himself about cats and crying that a 'big mean man' was coming for him again. Once back at the tavern, he passed out in the bed. Bria didn't sleep, waiting until the sun rose to venture out into the market square.

Her journey into the city left her locked in a haze. Worry seeped through her about Brent, and while the merchants greeted her with smiles and small talk, she replied with an empty grin and "good day to you."

Before the sun fully rose, Bria returned to the room with a parcel of food and a couple tunics and pants.

Brent still slept in the small cot, a pillow over his face, fingers twitching as he slept. She organized a plate of peas, carrots, and potatoes for him and left it on the end table. Her own plate was sparse, a fullness in her stomach. She let the peas dance around her fingers, saplings piercing from their skins as she ate away at them. A few took refuge in her satchel.

Brent stirred, and she put her plate down.

"Brent? You there?"

"Mm-hmm." He squeezed his eyes tighter. "Sleeping..."

"I brought you food. Some vegetables and all. You need to eat."

He opened one eye, "Bria. You're here."

"I'm not going anywhere," she helped him sit up, "Drink. Eat. Please."

Brent fumbled to lift the cup of water to his mouth, spilling half of it across his chest. He shook his head, putting the glass on the floor and picking up the plate. At first, he stared at it, then took the fork and pushed each pea to the side in an even row, while separating the carrots onto the other side. He used the side of the fork to push the potatoes into the center of the plate, more intent on making them sit in a perfect circle than eating them.

"Brent?"

"Oh, um..." Brent stopped, "Sorry I...no...the man, Gregorich, he was intent on keeping things organized and I—I—I..." he cursed to himself. "Dammit! The story...I just...I want this to be organized, and I—no, not me, it's not me. It's Greg...he's...it's not in order and—and—and—"

The plate clattered to the floor.

"I'm sorry..." Brent scratched at his wrist.

Bria pulled his fingers back. "What can I do to help right now?"

"Just..." he gulped, "Stay. Here. Please."

She held him until tears became whispers with the beach winds outside. He kept mumbling a mantra to himself: his name, his home, his parents, and his constants in life.

"Do you think," Bria asked as his breathing returned to normal, "that the Mist Keepers can help you? They know things...maybe this has happened before?"

"Caroline knows shite, and everyone else is elusive," Brent replied. "I think some others had similar reactions, but I don't know if they succeeded. But it's worth asking, I guess."

"We can head there, get you fixed up, then stop by my grandmama's place to get enough coin to rent a little apartment here in Mert," she helped him button his shirt as she spoke, "We're going to be okay."

Brent nodded, though she knew he barely believed it. She wasn't sure if she believed it either.

Bria helped Brent down the stairs, where he hit his head on a wooden beam before stumbling into the alleyway. The walls closed in, and once again, the tunnels reigned.

They walked in silence. The junction came into view with a heavy smog suffocating the light on the far wall, mingling with the shadows of roots and vines.

"I guess," Bria glanced up at Brent, "You'll go talk to the Council, and I'll go see my grandmama?"

"I..." Brent sighed, "I don't want to leave you."

"We'll see each other soon." It hurt to admit that they needed to part for just a little while. He still twitched every now and again, mumbling about the disorganization of his surroundings and the need to clean before returning to being Brent...not one of his stories.

"It's just, I don't know who to trust in the Council," Brent flexed his neck, "What if they—I don't know what they think—I've disappeared on them for days. What if they hold me hostage or—or something?"

"They have to want you to succeed."

"Yeah, Caroline does, at least."

"You'll be fine."

Brent gulped and placed a hand on the barren wall. "You really don't see it?"

"Just a wall..." Bria reached out to the vines. A white trumpet flower bloomed. Second later, it wilted, and the mist wrapped around it. "Every time I try, my magic dies..."

Brent ran his fingers over the mist and shivered, "I wish I could show you. It's... amazing... really, it's amazing."

"It's okay. Really. It is."

"I'll find a way," Brent mumbled, "I promise. I really do...I mean it...I promise. It's—you're so close, you should be able to see it. I guess the Council doesn't want you to..."

"You make all these stupid promises, but you'll get frustrated if you can't keep them. So, no need to promise..." Bria frowned, "It's not your job."

"I feel like it is. Besides, I *want* you to see it," Brent's nose crinkled. "If I'm a Mist Keeper, I should be able to show you. I mean, you already have some sight or something..."

"Brent, it's no big deal."

He stroked the air. This time the mist shifted at his touch. Bria tried to see into Brent's head, but his expression left an aura of confusion that often rested on his face. Then it relaxed like he was telling a story, and he opened the web of his hand to let the mist seep through his fingers.

Bria blinked. The mist rose beyond their heads, and in its place stood a gold-laced door engraved with stories. It showed thousands of tales, from lovers to fighters, to kisses and blood. She stumbled backward in awe. "Wait...you...how..." She licked her lip. "What did you do?"

"The mist is more than vapor..." Brent squinted. "I don't understand it...it gives me a headache. But, since I'm a Mist Keeper, I guess it listens to me." He turned back to her. "I want you to see something pretty."

"Because the world is petty?"

A half smile. "Guess so."

"You're spectacular, you know. Don't let anyone tell you otherwise...cause they're wrong!" Bria kissed him, then glanced behind her at the door, "This is more than I imagined..."

"Oi," Brent tugged at her arm, "It's more than a wall. C'mon...let me show you around, a'ight?"

CHAPTER TWENTY-NINE

LOVERS IN THE LIBRARY

Brent always loved Bria, but the moment her face lit up as they entered the library only deepened his admiration. *She may as well be a queen.* She turned back to him, tears staining her eyes.

"What is it?" Brent asked, "What's wrong?"

"It's beautiful." her voice broke, "It's a tree."

"A tree?"

She rested her hand on the wall. Bark swarmed across it. It etched up her arm, mingling to the side of her neck and with the little branch across her ear. She turned into a forest queen.

Then, with a mere flick of her wrist, the bark rescinded, and there Bria stood again.

"Wow," he gawked, then smiled wider, "C'mon! There's more to see."

He took her by the hands through the shelves, letting her marvel at the towers of books and gaze at the glass ceiling overhead. It must have been what Brent looked like when he first entered, only fear masked his discovery.

"This is like paradise for you..." Bria said, removing one of the books from the shelves. Some obscure language scrolled over its cover. "There must be a million stories in here..."

"And answers for you," Brent replied. "I'm sure one of these books has an explanation of *why* you were the only one in these tunnels for so long."

"I hope so."

Brent took the book from her hand and flipped it open. Hundreds of names scrawled across the pages.

"Names in this one...nothing important."

Though, as he closed the book, it was like a whiff of a thousand stories floated through one ear and out the next. He winced for a second, *my name is Brent Harley. I am not some little girl named Helen. My name is Brent Harley, and Bria Smidt is with me right now...*he closed his eyes and reached out for Bria's fingers. *I am here.*

"Brent?"

"I'm okay."

He put the book down and continued walking along, resting his arm around Bria's shoulders and pointing towards the different areas of the library. Rehashing the events with the Diabolo made her shiver, but as he told her about the way the glass glistened overhead and opened different doors filled of miracles, her body relaxed.

With each door, they discovered new worlds: one door opened to a miniature swamp, another with a field of red flowers, and one where the mist drifted through an array of colors.

Let me tell you a story... Brent waved his fingers through the mist. A miniature horse galloped through the variegated smoke, leading refugees draped in gray into a realm of color and light. He couldn't figure out how the stories worked; some of them he saw without thinking, but others came from his mind. The mist chose to act at his will, but never to the full imagination; it stopped at the thought of blood, or steam or sweat. It was but a mere tale...a parlor trick.

After checking a few more rooms, Brent stole a plate of dried meats from the galley, disregarding the uncaring stares of the few ghosts who loitered amongst the iceboxes and sat beneath one of the shelves. He listened as Bria told him how she'd been exploring the tunnels since she was a little girl, but not once did she imagine something so spectacular lying in plain sight.

"It's so empty, though. Must be lonely..."

"Only eight—err, nine—of us really," Brent lined the pieces of jerky along the side of the plate, fidgeting with the final piece until it was straight, "Feels like I'm alone whenever I'm here though."

"And this is where you would live if you become a Mist Keeper?"

"I think so," Brent picked at the jerky, "I don't know. I still haven't met one of the Mist Keepers. Don't know if she even lives here or not."

"Then do you think if you *do* become a Mist Keeper—like if we can't break this curse or whatever..." Bria's face paled, "Do you think it won't matter? That we will still be able to see each other? I mean, I can see the library now with you..."

"I—I hope so." Brent's heart thudded. "More than anything. I mean, Caroline mentioned something about people with sight. So maybe that's you? I mean, I hope it's you. But even if you can, it doesn't mean I want to die. I want to..." he shook his head. *Don't be stupid. That's a stupid thing to say.*

"I know," Bria's voice cracked, pulling her knees to her chest.

"Bria," he took her hand, "I promise...I'm here. I won't leave you alone."

"Don't make promises you can't keep." She smiled and wiped her eyes.

Dew nestled in the air, tainting the carpet and Brent's skin as they continued eating. He organized the jerky for a bit longer until Bria snatched one of the pieces and shoved it into his mouth.

Footsteps rocked the silence through the bookshelves. Bria straightened and glanced behind her, "What's that?"

"Probably one of the Mist Keepers," Brent rose, "Stay here..."

"What? Why?"

"I didn't even think of what they would do if they saw you..." Brent whispered, "You've got magic protecting you...which I didn't when I came. So, I know you're safe from the curse and shite but..." he frowned, "They have mist magic too and—"

"I'll stay a few paces back." Bria clenched his hands, "Remember, we came to see if they can help you. I'm fine."

Brent agreed and helped her off the ground. They rounded a bend and ducked behind a shelf as the voices grew louder.

"I read the report," the first voice said, "We all have. It's quite concerning."

Alojzy entered the aisle. "The boy is probably lost and experiencing massive psychosis. We won't find him alive."

Tomás joined Alojzy in the light, shaking his head, his good eye shut closed.

"Even if he is alive, under such stress, he shan't succeed."

"I have faith in him and in Caroline," Tomás reiterated. "We would know if he were dead."

"He had drunk much of Jiang's special brew," Alojzy hissed. "He probably walked right into a sword—"

"Swords are not common weaponry nowadays. Perhaps you should get outside more."

"That is beside the point," Alojzy scoffed. "Caroline should start seeking out a new apprentice immediately. Even if he is still alive, I give Brenton no more than three weeks once death sets in. And that does no good for Caroline."

"Do not be rash," Tomás grunted. "The boy is sharp."

"Yet being sharp does little to train the mind. You should know after what happened with Julietta."

Brent's heart landed in his stomach. *They think I'm going to fail. Typical.*

"I want to have hope," Tomás replied, matter of fact. "We have to have hope."

"Ningursu has not been able to find him in all his searching. He must be dead; how could he avoid our watch? And without Malaika here we cannot track him as well," Alojzy spat. "You and Caroline need to give up."

Brent turned back to Bria and ushered her away from the shelves. They tiptoed past the two Mist Keepers.

Their steps caused Alojzy and Tomás's voices to cease.

Shite.

Tomás peered around the bookshelf. "Brenton!"

"Oh, Tomás, hi." Brent pushed Bria behind him. "Hi...I'm—I'm alive."

"We were quite concerned." Tomás stepped forward. "How long have you been here?"

Brent paced backward. "Oh...a bit..."

"Come, we should inform the rest of the Council." Tomás gripped Brent's shoulder.

"I'm fine—" Brent stumbled.

Bria kept him steady, hand on his back, her breaths heavy.

"What is that?" Alojzy sneered. As if at his command, a chair skidded from up the aisle and captured Bria in its seat. "What is she doing here?"

Tomás turned his head, so his good eye faced Bria. It dilated at the sight of her. "Brenton, this is a tremendous violation. We need to—"

"Violation of what?" Brent spat.

"Magii aren't allowed in the library!" Alojzy continued glaring, "First the Diabolo...now this! This is a violation of everything we have constructed."

"What are you...I haven't done anything wrong..."

"The library is for Mist Keepers only!" Alojzy waved his hand, and the books fell from the shelves and disintegrated before them.

Beside him, Tomás stepped forward, his good eye locked on Bria. A humming mist filled the space around her head.

She shrunk into the seat. "Stop..."

"What are you doing to her?!?" Brent snapped.

"She's not allowed to see this, Brenton," Tomás replied. "It's best that it's a dream..."

"You're erasing her memory?"

"I'm confusing her. Memory is not my forte."

"No...this is...stop! This is ridiculous..." Brent snatched a remaining book from the ground. The walls around him closed in, claustrophobia replacing the endless ceilings and weaving shelves. Bria moaned beside him.

"Brenton, please. Let's behave like adults."

"Not if you're going to do...no!" He threw the book at Tomás.

Tomás toppled backward, disappearing into the mist. Alojzy jumped out of the way, taking refuge behind a shelf, and giving Brent the chance to pick Bria up and dart back through the library. As he ran, the surrounding shelves vanished, the books scattering across the floor. Everything grew tighter; breaths became less potent. It never ended, replaced with a weaving library of books taller than his body and candles dangling an eternity away.

"Brent..." Bria grunted.

"We're gonna get out of here, a'ight?"

"Please put me down. I can walk."

"No, no, relax...your head..." Brent slowed to a stop.

"Just a headache." She climbed out of Brent's arms. "What happened?"

"Tomás has mind powers or something. Alojzy..." Brent sucked in his lips. "I don't know what that was. It's like he can control the library or something with the mist. I'm sorry...I didn't—"

They reached the wall to escape, both sides barricaded with books.

"Shite!"

"I have an idea..." Bria laced her fingers into the odd bark-like coating of the wall. Then, the veins in her neck bulged, her eyes closed, and their surroundings rumbled.

The wall broke open into the tunnels. Bria tugged Brent forward, then with a wave of her hand, the wall closed.

And they were alone.

Bria barricaded them in a narrow tunnel. She exhaled, then slid down against the wall, hugging her knees and staring ahead with trepidation.

"Bria..." Brent reached for her arm.

She shoved it back. "Please don't touch me."

Brent sank to the ground across from her. Shadows danced on the walls, and for a moment, he let the stories take him away.

"Are they all like that?" Bria squeaked.

"Like what?" Brent scratched his wrist.

"Terrible."

"No, I mean—I don't think so." Brent looked down the tunnel. "Caroline, she's supportive in her own way. It's just, they haven't told me things..."

"Like how no one except the Mist Keepers are allowed in the library!?!"

"Exactly!"

Bria wiped her eyes. "No wonder they hid this from me. They hate me. And you..." She turned to him. "They think you're going to fail, with the Diabolo and your magic and everything! They're ready for you to fail. But they don't see what I see. You're not...you can't."

"Oh, well, maybe, I guess. I...I don't know." Brent shoved his hands in his pockets. He wasn't sure if he agreed with Bria. His head constantly hurt, and his mind wandered. According to Tomás, they'd seen this before. What would make him any different?

He blinked a few times, and watched as the mist down the tunnel masked them from the torchlight. "It doesn't matter, a'ight? Let's do what you said. We'll run away...go to Mert...open a little shop or something and explore the world. And what was it that you said...about curses?"

"They're meant to be broken," Bria whispered.

"Then we'll break this death curse on me or whatever shite it is...a'ight? Because I don't wanna be a part of any group that treats...I mean, if they're gonna be like this then...I don't want to be a Mist Keeper."

CHAPTER THIRTY

THE FORGOTTEN WOMAN

They made a home for themselves in the small offshoot tunnel, away from the torchlight, masked only by the roots. Brent rested across from Bria, watching as she curled in on herself, hugging her knees and tracing her fingers through the roots.

"Bri..." He frowned. It'd been hours since she said anything.

"I'm so sorry, Brent. I destroyed your chance of getting help," Bria croaked. "I was being stupid, sticking my nose where I shouldn't have. I should've just stayed hidden in the tunnels—"

"No, the Council is..." Brent sucked his lips in and searched for the words, "Backwards and old. Everything they say is about *tradition.* Let's break that shite, okay? I think, maybe, we'll be stronger together. I think the Mist Keepers don't remember what it's like to have magic in their lives or something. I don't know. I don't know anything about them..." He dug his fingers into the dirt. "They want me to follow them blindly...but how can I follow them if I don't know who I am? For all I know, I'm a rebel living in a skinny body of a twenty-one-year-old! I could be that woman from Yilk leading a revolution against giant stovetops. But all they see is some fucking boy who makes mistakes and..." Brent shook his head. "Sorry, that was dumb; I'm being dumb."

Bria glanced at him. "That's the most confident I've heard you in a long time. I like it."

"I mean, I—"

"A brave storyteller who never shut his mouth in the eyes of the Order, turning around to face an ancient organization and tell them they're wrong." She crawled over to him. "That's something I can get behind."

"And there's you, the Queen of the Forest, who could take them down with a flick of her wrist, I'm sure," Brent responded. "I'll follow you to the end of the world."

"Let's not die for each other now. That's not a good way to build a relationship." Her smile returned. "We have a lot of work to do."

"Like answers for you."

"I don't need them."

"But you *do*," Brent assured her. "The Council has them. I know they do. And they have no fucking right to—to..." He winced. *Why am I so angry?* He couldn't pinpoint the voice. It didn't belong to him...or did it? He gulped down his fury and continued speaking in a hushed tone, "You deserve answers, is what I mean."

"The Council hates me for whatever reason. I don't have a way to get answers—I can't make them trust me." Bria pulled a seed out of her satchel, rolling it around her palms as a sapling entwined with her fingers. "Just like the Order says–magic belongs to demons."

"Demons..." Brent peered down the tunnel. The mist swayed, a yellow tinge from the torchlight haunting him. "What if—and this is terrifying and stupid—but what if we find that monster...the Diabolo?"

"What?"

"If we find it, together, and contain it...with these jar things they have...then we can—I mean—we can show the Council that we're on their side. Then I can get help, and you can get answers, and then hopefully, we can be together or something and—and—" he closed his eyes. "Sorry, it's dangerous and stupid."

"It *is* dangerous and stupid, but..." She nodded. "It's worth a shot. After we get settled in Mert, though, right? Unless you don't want to anymore—"

"No, of course." Brent leaned forward. "I want to do exactly what we talked about. We need money anyway. We gotta eat."

Bria beamed, finally letting him pull her into a hug. They remained embraced as the candles waned, sleep waxing over them. Brent never found rest, despite the dreariness in his eyes. He cradled Bria against his chest, whispering a story to the darkness about a candelabra fairy and a fire dancer.

Once she locked herself into sleep, Brent's own mind wandered, back to the mountains where the Diabolo snarled down at him, back to where it certainly still loitered, waiting for him to make its next move.

When Bria woke, they developed a plan. Bria would head back to Newbird's Arm to gather supplies, while Brent would sneak once more into the library to find something—anything—that could help.

"So, we meet back here in three hours, right?" She fiddled with her jacket, staring down the small tunnel's offshoot. "You're not going to do anything stupid?"

"I promise." Brent pushed back her braid. "I'll be right here in two hours and fifty-nine minutes."

"Okay...just stay safe."

"You, too."

She kissed his cheek before venturing off into the side tunnel. Brent watched her and, once gone, headed towards the junction.

He expected to find the entire Council waiting there, but there stood no one. The mist left a shroud, tarnished and withering, before the door. *You think you're so tall and mighty,* Brent thought. *You stare down the tunnels, thinking you own them. There's more to this world than just you! The living, dead, magic, no magic...we're all here!* He stuck his tongue out at the door.

His courage vanished as he entered, the cool air catching wind of the candelabras flickering overhead. His shadow grew a hundred feet taller upon arrival. It climbed over the shelves and matched the cracks in the walls.

Still, no one came.

A hollowness made a home in Brent's stomach. He had no clue where to begin. The shelves went on farther than the eye could see, and he doubted the Council left books about their deepest secrets in the front rows.

There must be some form of organization, though. Brent squinted. Sometimes, glancing at one of the shelves sent a hundred stories tiptoeing through the top layer of his thoughts. Opening a book revealed thousands of names, scribbled in a font so small it might have been a paper cut. Some books were more vivid than the next, leaving a haze of befuddled stories clear before Brent.

So, the names are kept over here. Brent backtracked. *So that means over here —*

Along the far eastern wall, historical tales of far and wide waited: stories of massacres and genocides, kings and queens, and rebellions and solace. Any other day, he might have delved into the past, learned what the Order hid, and understand the world at last. But he had not the time to spare.

Brent skimmed over the hundreds of titles, detailing wars and battle regiments. One title, simply written in golden trim, grabbed his attention. *I.* The dialect scribbled through the pages only echoed the Common Tongue. Yet the surrounding stories, harboring tales of war and sorrow, magic and death, and life and death, lured him. Brent pocketed it.

The remainder of the aisle provided no additional clarity. One book detailed the ongoing dismay between the Dueling Nations of Kainan and Evylain, another of the tenuous history between the Cities of Tencauri and Errat in Yilk, and one about the Order's Purge of Magic on the Rosadian continent. Brent skimmed through each, keeping only the last one.

"Marlo, dear!"

Brent turned. Julietta waltzed towards him, a smile on her round face, her long blonde hair flowing. Her green eyes still glazed past him. Brent's heart sank looking at the woman; looking at her left him in a befuddled maze, masked by rain and erosion.

"Oh, hi, Julietta." Brent bowed his head. "I'm sorry. I know I'm not supposed to be here—"

"Why would you say that, dear?" Julietta crossed her arms, picking at one of the patches on her sleeve. "You are always allowed to be here."

"Oh...good."

"But I must ask, why do you choose to be here? These are boring and sad books. There are much more interesting books yonder." Julietta pointed towards the galley. "A nice cup of tea, a crumpet or two, and a wonderful tale of a romance and betrayal. Wouldn't you rather read that?"

"I would, but um," Brent shook his head and tethered a lie together, "Master Ningursu asked me to do research for him about a monster. Do you know where I would find any books on that?"

"A monster?" Julietta paced a few steps forward and peered at Brent. "A real monster?" He nodded.

Her face illuminated. "Yes, yes, we have books on monsters! Come! This way!"

Brent followed her through the shelves. Truth-be-told, lying to Julietta left a gnawing feeling in his gut. The time for honesty had passed, though; where had honesty gotten him the past few weeks?

Dead, the woman's voice from Yilk squeaked in his head.

He pushed her back, replaced with a loudmouthed man, *Got ya killed and dead.*

"Shut it," he hissed to himself.

Julietta didn't hear him, directing him towards a corner by a fireplace where blocks reminiscent of a children's play area towered. Droves of picture books sat in a basket off to the side, with *The Snow Fairy* positioned on top of them.

"Here we are." Julietta turned to him. "Monsters galore!"

"The children's section?" Brent sank. "Here?"

"Monsters are the purest in a child's heart, only amplified by the painter's mind."

"Um, okay."

While ignoring Julietta's gaze, Brent browsed the books, his heart full and ready to burst. Poetry sang across the pages, dancing with images of gods, goddesses, giants, and dragons. No monsters. No fear. No

Hell. He should have known better. Answers would not come falling before him like rain. Answers required searching and —

Thump.

Julietta dropped a thin sienna covered book in front of him.

How to Build a Monster

Beneath the words, a picturesque creature with horns and sharp teeth stared at him. Another children's book, for sure, but Brent still opened it, enchanted by the title if nothing else. In its pages, poetic prose knitting together the pages, intermingling with childish diagrams.

Julietta beamed. "I hope that helps. But maybe Alojzy knows where your real answers lie if it does not."

"No, no, this is fantastic." Brent grinned back. "Thank you, Julietta."

"I shall go see if Alojzy has an idea—"

"No, no, it's okay! Really!"

"No problem at all, Marlo. Please, wait here, we'll be back shortly."

She disappeared into the sea of books. Panic settled, the voices of the stories in his head joining in with shouts of dismantled anxiety. He hid the book in his coat. The sooner he left the library, the better; he'd hide until Bria returned from Newbird's Arm, then they'd run. Right?

Why did the trek out of the library feel so long? Winding through the books rocked him with nausea, and each footstep sounded like a gong against the hard floors. His breath belonged to a storm, and his thoughts no longer belonged in a private vault.

They already know I'm here; he slowed his pace. "Hello? I know you see me...don't—don't hide. Can we—can we talk?"

Julietta emerged from around the corner. "Marlo! I found Alojzy! Come, he's right here!"

"Brent!" Caroline walked out behind Julietta. Her eyes sat in dark pits, lips smudged and hair wiry. She poked his face once before smiling, "It is you! Alojzy said you were going crazy...that you were talking to yourself...saying *Bria* was with you."

"She was! She is!" Brent tongue twisted. "I'm not imagining—"

"I know," Caroline's voice fell. "I have seen you with her in the tunnels. I am not foolish. I do not know what he is trying to do."

"Ah, Julietta, thank you!" Alojzy joined them. "We've been concerned about him for a while. Talking to himself, believing he has a *lover*, a *savior* even. Shame, such a shame. He has potential."

"I haven't done anything wrong!" Brent stepped back into a bookcase. *Was that there before?*

"You know what you did," Alojzy continued.

"What did he do?" Caroline spat. "You told me he was gone! He seems fine!"

"I brought Bria here," Brent mumbled.

Alojzy boomed over him, "He freed the Diabolo and has caused dishonor to the Council. Ningursu agreed this best be done."

"What must be done?" Caroline barked back.

Alojzy turned from her and faced Julietta, taking her hands in his own. "Julietta, love, you remember your dear Verity, yes? Remember her, long ago, lost her mind?"

"Oh yes, my dear Verity. She walked through Hell for far too long and learned of horrors and monsters..." She languished over to Brent. "Oh, dear Marlo. Is this why you've been researching monsters?"

"No, I'm just...curious." Brent glanced at Caroline. "Really."

"Marlo, spending time dwelling on monsters does little good for the soul," she brushed away Brent's hair, "It does well for you to forget."

Fog seared through Brent's vision at Julietta's touch. It masked his vision and lulled his memories to the back of his mind.

My name is Brent Harley.

My name is Brent Harley.

I was born in Newbird's Arm.

He gritted his teeth.

My name is Brent.

Brent what?

"Stop," he begged. "Please."

My name is—

My name is—

Who am I?

Then it came back, all at once. Brent flew backward into Caroline's arms.

Julietta backed away. "He's not yet ready."

"Julietta..." Alojzy pushed.

"His mind is well, and his memories are strong." Her eyes flickered, more alive than Brent had ever seen them. "Brent Harley does not need his memory erased."

"Julietta, you are not well. This is not Brent. It is Verity; she's lost her mind."

"Verity is dead, she's dead and dead and dead...and gone..." She trembled, sinking to her knees. Caroline, upon making sure Brent could stand, went to her side and consoled her.

"Go, Alojzy," she snarled. "Tell Ningursu or whoever made this decision that Brent is *fine* and under *my* guise."

Alojzy straightened his back in protest, but rather than arguing, he returned into the sea of books.

Julietta turned to Brent, her glossy gaze passing over him again. "Are you together, Marlo?"

"Yeah, I'm a'ight," Brent shivered. "Why do they—they hate me? Why do they...what is...why?"

Caroline stroked Julietta's hair as she spoke. "I do not know. They have been lying to me as well. Ever since we fought the Diabolo...something about your magic..."

"And that I brought Bria here..." Brent gulped. "They tried messing with her head, too."

"Is she okay?"

"Yeah, a bit out of it, but she was fine..." He shoved his hands into his coat pockets, trailing along the spines of his books. "I should get back to her—we're meeting, I mean, we need to go..."

"Go then," Caroline insisted. "I will come find you when the time is right. For now, go. Stay safe. We still have much work to do."

Brent nodded and started to leave, only to turn back after a few paces. "Caroline?"

"Yes?"

"I—I don't want to be a Mist Keeper." His head hung. "Not if this is what it's like."

"Brent—"

"I know. I don't have a damn choice." Brent left, not bothering to wait for a reply.

CHAPTER THIRTY-ONE

A GOODBYE

Bria returned to Newbird's Arm amid droves of Guards marching through the garden, loitering about on the roads and in the town square. Mothers and children stayed in their houses, while moans echoed from over the Pit. She hid in the trees, hopping through town back to her home. It did her well to stay invisible, like the wind pushing through the clouds; if the Guard saw her, certainly they'd take her into custody.

Or worse.

She climbed in through the small window of her attic bedroom. The floorboards creaked as she walked, no matter how light she tiptoed, causing her father's dog to bark beneath her room.

Bria cursed.

"Gato! Shush!" her father shouted.

The barking continued.

"There's nothing up here." Footsteps climbed up the ladder, and her father, with a scruffy beard and blood-stained eyes, entered her room. "See, noth—Beebelle!"

She choked, "Daddy...hi..."

He embraced her, squeezing her against his chest and stroking back her mangled braid. "Oh, my Beebelle...I was so worried! But you're back—you're back!"

"Noah? What is it?" Mr. West joined them upstairs.

"It's Beebelle, Ric! Beebelle's back!"

Ric rushed over and embraced Bria.

"I'm sorry," she whispered, squeezing them back with as much force as her little body could handle.

"I was so worried," her father insisted. "So so so worried. The Guard, they said you ran into the forest. But there's been rumors that the Harley boy kidnapped you or killed you."

"A load of hogwash, if you ask me," Ric scoffed.

"We ran away together..." Bria frowned. "I should have told you I was leaving. I'm so sorry. It happened so fast..."

"Was it his idea?"

"No! No! We've been talking about it for a while...but then the Guard came for me and I—I—"

"It's a'ight. You're home now. It's a'ight, it's a'ight." Her father wouldn't release her despite Bria's squirms. "We'll make poppy chicken. Your grandmama can make lemon cakes and tea. We'll tell the Guard you're back and—"

"Daddy, no," Bria stopped him. "I'm in trouble. The Guard can't know I'm back," she looked away, "I have to leave again in a couple hours."

"Beebelle!"

Bria gripped his hands. "I told you once that I was going to go explore the world. That's what is happening. Now's the time."

"With Brenton Harley?" Ric asked.

"Yes."

"No! No!" Her father clenched his fists and brought them to his head. "You can't leave me, Beebelle! I need you to stay! You're too young...you're a good girl. Please stay, Beebelle! Please!"

"Noah! Noah!" Ric grabbed his arm. "Calm down. She's safe. She's nearly twenty."

"Nearly!"

"Some gals have kids by now. She's allowed to leave." Ric pressed a hand on her dad's back. "Come, go lie down. It's okay. She's fine."

"No..."

"Come." Ric helped her father down the ladder, then called back to her, "I'll get your grandmother. At least see her."

"Of course."

Alone again for a time, she gathered some of her clothes and her pouch of coins she hid under her bed. Over the years, from helping her father with his baskets and her grandmama in the market square, she'd amassed a small fortune under the guise she always knew she'd leave Newbird's Arm someday.

It wasn't much, but it would get her and Brent through the month without asking for help. By then, they'd be able to find jobs, a home, and a new future. Bria shook her head in disbelief. It had been a fairy tale, but now she saw a future outside the browned mountains, deserts, and fields of Rosada.

Her grandmama arrived within the hour, not speaking as she climbed into Bria's bedroom and pulled her close.

"Oh, Briannabella." Her grandmama stroked back her hair. "I thought I told you to tell me before you ran."

"I meant to, I did..." She sniffed. "It's just...I hurt a cadet...again."

"Lawry?"

"Yes."

"I thought so. He was ranting in the market the other day about vines." Her grandmama scowled. "Captain Carver has been bothering me relentlessly. He thinks I know where you are and that it is prudent for questioning. Of course, I didn't, but he is fixated on you."

"I am betrothed to his son." Bria rubbed her hand, "In theory."

"Ah, yes, that could be it. But he goes on that you've done wrong—assaulting guards, rumored magic, and so forth. He would not elaborate. Then, yesterday when they were rounding up the vagrants, I saw Cadet Lawry with a welt on his head. Had a feeling it was you—and then with Christof before that! Briannabella, you shouldn't be bringing attention to yourself!"

"That's why I ran!" Bria released her grandmother, returning to her suitcase. "It's why I'm still running. I'm going to—"

"Don't tell me," her grandmama cut her off. "The more I know, the more danger you'll be in, do you understand?"

Her grandmama helped her put together another bag of blankets, seeds, and mementos of home. They didn't say anything, sharing the mutual silence and understanding. After they tied up the bag, Bria helped her grandmama downstairs.

Gato, the dog, greeted her with his big boxed head banging into her legs. She stroked back his ears before turning to her father at the kitchen table. He stared past her, picking at the newspaper on the table.

Bria paused to glance at the date. *Brent turned twenty-one three days ago. He must have lost track*—she stopped at the title beneath it.

Elder Don Van's Call to Action

After the attacks on Newbird's Arm by demons summoned by young adults in the recent weeks, Elder Don Van is reinstating the black stamp for all age groups. The rule declares that anyone, young or old, who has colorless eyes, displays signs of magic, or disregards the Effluvium by spreading lies and stories, must be stamped.

All those with the black stamp, it is hereby decreed, will undergo Level 1 to 3 cleansings on a monthly basis.

Until the worst demons are sent back to the Pit in which they came.

"Children?" Bria whispered.

"Janette is a mess," her grandmama replied. "She's been keeping her daughter close now—but she worries that the Order will come for her, too. Two children stamped! I can't imagine the burden."

"If Brent finds out, he'll rush back."

"I think it'd be wise to not tell Brenton."

"I can't keep lying to him." Bria folded up the newspaper and put it in her satchel. "I'm giving this to him. He's smart enough to figure it out on his own."

Ric came out of his bedroom, carrying another bag. "I put together some clothes for Brenton. He is a bit taller than me and not as round in the belly," he chuckled, "but thought he might need some."

"He'll appreciate it," Bria replied. "Um, can you let his family know he's okay? He misses them."

"Of course."

"Thank you." Bria embraced Ric. She then returned to her father and kissed his forehead. The man didn't budge, still mumbling. Her voice couldn't find words, and when she turned to face her grandmama instead, she sank into another puddle of tears.

"You're so strong," her grandmama whispered as she coddled Bria's cheeks. "Promise me you will stay safe."

"I will. I'll come back. I promise."

"I know you will."

After a couple more goodbyes and many more tears, Bria patted Gato once more on his head, then ascended the ladder, and climbed out the window into the trees.

She hopped through the branches, letting them carry her bags, and back to the tunnels. In her hideaway beneath the surface, she gathered the remainder of her belongings. Then, with a mere flick of her wrist, and the lattice of vines rolled back, returning to their homes on the walls. Yet they followed her still as she traveled through the tunnels to the rendezvous point.

To her relief and surprise, Brent waited exactly where they agreed. He sat with his knees against his chest, a thin book in hand, his gaze directed at the far wall. Despite his smile, sadness rested in his eyes.

She wondered if he saw her trepidation as well.

"How'd it go?" she asked.

"Shitty."

"Same." She sat next to him. "But at least we're here now."

CHAPTER THIRTY-TWO

Collecting Hope in Jars

Bria found them a small apartment in the bustling heart of Mert, not far from an alley leading back into the tunnels. The rent was cheap, the furniture cheaper, and the faucet in the bathroom never stopped dripping. But no one noticed them, and that's all Bria ever wanted.

Brent often spent the days sitting on the floor, pouring over the books he'd taken from the library and mumbling to himself. After Bria shared with him what she learned about Elder Don Van's decree, he almost bolted back home, but she managed to talk him back. No good running home and causing a scene; his sister would be safer without him there. If he dared return, Bria reminded him, she would become a new target for the Order. So instead, Brent used the newspaper to bookmark pages in his book, while reading articles to himself about the upcoming elections in Rosada and scribbling notes on the pages in his illegible handwriting. He never spoke of what he read, but in the hours when the candle dwindled, his face often paled. Bria forced him to eat, and on some nights, even had to drag him to bed.

It was much harder to find a job than Bria imagined and proved more difficult when her monthly bleeding left her withering on the bed for three days. Brent took the reins then, buying her a box of chocolates, cottons, and warm tea. He told her stories to pass the time, knitting together tales of far and wide while helping with housework, not once complaining.

After it passed, Bria continued her job hunt. She found most shops belonged to families, and an outsider from Rosada raised more questions than she felt comfortable answering. Odd jobs, such as helping an old woman in her garden using a subtle hint of magic, provided extra cash, but as the days progressed, so did Bria's frustration.

With another day of lackluster job hunting, Bria arrived home to Brent decked out in one of Ric's suits.

With a smile on his face, he held out a glistening knee-high dress.

"I helped Mr. Brody downstairs with some housework," Brent grinned midsentence, "so he gave me some cash, and I thought you...I mean you've been working so hard, I thought you needed a nice evening."

Bria kissed him. As he leaned in for another, she pranced away to change.

She looked like a stranger in the mirror, her hair done up and dress shaping her shoulders and waist. The skirt spun about her thighs as a twirled into Brent's arms.

Dancing, drinking, and eating decorated the evening. They spun together in the dance hall and laughed over drinks. Brent's shoulders loosened through the night, and after his second drink, he climbed up on a chair and weaved a story about three farmers who grew up on the backs of giant sea turtles. They came to the mainland after years of sailing, but as they dueled over to whom it belonged, the turtles climbed ashore and claimed it for themselves. It was a drunken tale, with little to do about anything, but the people in the Dance Hall gathered around Brent in awe.

The people of Mert sure did love a good story.

After dinner and further kisses, Bria sat in the sand with Brent, eating ice cream and pointing out images in the stars. Brent named each one with a story.

They collapsed in their bed, conversing in hushed tones and touches until sleep washed over them.

A vacancy beside her woke Bria later that night.

"Brent?" She squinted around the room. The apartment was empty, with only the streetlamp providing a glimmer of light. Brent's shoes remained in the doorway.

She rushed into the street. The mist of dawn stroked the alleyways and streets, an orange tinge worn by the sky. No one occupied the early morning. An ominous silence paraded through the building, except for a single automobile trudging down the main road near the shore.

I'm sure he just went out to get a smoke or something. Everything is fine. I'm sure everything is fine. Bria collapsed on the stoop to her building and hugged herself. A few blades of grass gathered at her toes.

She waited outside for over an hour until Brent returned. He wore only his undershirt and a pair of pants, blood covering his hands and dripping from his nose. It stained his shirt, and with each step, he winced, muttering to himself and holding what appeared to be a pineapple in his arms.

"Brent!" Bria rushed to him, "What happened? Where have you been?"

"Please don't hurt me, Mister," he spoke in a soft, sing-song voice. "I've only done as you asked, Mister. Please don't hurt me."

"Brent, look at me," she directed his face down to her.

He gazed past her, hugging the pineapple tighter to his chest. "And my babe, don't hurt my babe."

"Look at me," she reiterated, managing to capture his attention. She repeated his mantra aloud. "What is your name?"

"Miss Gina—"

"Try again."

Brent extended his neck and blinked twice. "Brent."

"Where are we?"

"The City of Mert..."

"Who am I?"

His eyes narrowed as he stared at her.

"Brent, who am I?"

"You're Bria..." He sank to her level. "Bria..."

She helped Brent home and into the tub, forcing him to leave the pineapple on the table despite his incessant demands. They said nothing for a time as Bria scrubbed the dried blood from his hands, washing his face and hair.

"I woke up with a weird migraine," Brent muttered as he sank into the water. "Like...I kept hearing a story...and screams...and I decided to go out for a smoke."

"That's what I first thought."

"The stories didn't go away...so I followed them. I mean, I went where they were the loudest." He shook his head. "Found a girl a bit younger than us...brutally beaten. Released her. But the stories were still there, and they took me to an elderly woman who tended to a baby doll...thought it was her grandchild. Miss Gina was her name. I must've taken the pineapple from her apartment or something..." Brent pushed back his hair. "Last was a man. Don't remember much about him. Nothing remarkable...except he was a chef or something. I don't know. It's all jumbled and I—I—I—"

"Shush, relax." She squeezed his hands. "You were doing your job."

"Well I don't like it. Sometimes, I don't know who I am because of it!"

"But right now, you do."

"I guess so."

Bria squeezed his shoulder and returned to bed.

She didn't realize she fell asleep until the sizzling of eggs on the stove woke her. Brent's books once again lay open on the table across the room. He stood over the counter, cutting away at the pineapple. Upon tasting a piece, his face scrunched up, and he chucked the remainder of the fruit in the trash.

"Disgusting. It burns," he grumbled.

"You threw out a perfectly good pineapple." Bria stretched and went over to him.

"Never had it before." He wiped his mouth. "It's like licking carpet or something."

"You've licked carpet before?"

"No! Um, let me try a better analogy: you know when you have a burning cup of tea? You drink it too fast and suddenly the top of your mouth is scorching? That's what pineapple does! Why would you subject yourself to that!" He flipped one of the eggs in his pan. "On top of that, what is a pineapple even? It's not citrus, it's not an apple...shite it's not even pine! And now I have strands stuck in my teeth, and it's just...it's vile!"

"Okay, goofy," she laughed and watched him sizzle a piece of sausage. "You cook?"

Brent blinked. "Guess so. Must've picked it up from a story. Maybe they're not all bad."

They ate a meal of eggs and sausage before Brent returned to his droves of books, proceeding to mark the page and scratch the stubble on his chin. Bria picked at her food and watched him. She'd tried to read with him, help him find context, but one book was completely foreign to her, while the other two wrapped themselves in riddles and enigmas that, without context, left her head hurting.

"This is terrible," Brent said as he read one of the pages. "I think...I think I figured out how they made the monster."

"Isn't that a children's book?" Bria motioned to the thin book.

"Yes, but from what I've experienced, it makes sense." He flipped back a page and bit down on a sausage, speaking as he chewed, "Here, listen..."

Let's build a monster
For fun and lust
A game of pleasure, yay?
Let's build a monster
Of yellow mist
To keep the sorcerers at bay

We start with a peck of evil
The men who walked to Hell
Gather them in jars and shake 'em
And scream in 'em as well

Then take your nightmares
Dunk them in
And swirl them well

You are like a monster too
Men, children, and women of Hell

Finally, a body empty as slate,
Must be used to make permanent place
They're kept beneath in crypts
Yearning in detriment space

Swish
Swirl
Screams and shouts
The monster's coming
It's coming about

Last but not least
Add yourself
A child is the monster's feast
And hand in hand
With you it does not cease
You've done it now
A monster, a beast

Bria put her fork down. "But what does that all mean? It's a poem...riddles..."

"I think..." Brent rubbed his wrist, picking again at his stamp. "I mean, back when I last saw it. There were...so many stories; terrible stories, about people who just, I mean, should be in Hell. So, I think—somehow—the monster is created out of people who belong in Hell. Like, in the poem, it says 'gather them in jars and shake 'em.' I think that's exactly what they did...with magic, or something. I don't...I mean most of the poem still doesn't make sense. Children's screams, an empty body..." Brent shook his head. "I did hear children when I was last with it, but I thought it was part of the story."

"So, it's created of the worst people ever is what you're saying?"

"At least at the time of its creation," he huffed. "I don't even know why I care anymore! We're safe and happy here! The monster isn't gonna find us any time soon. And even if it does...it doesn't have a body, so it will probably vanish, right?"

"Brent..."

"And besides, it's not like I even want to return to the Council anymore! What does it matter? The Diabolo isn't my *problem!*" He carried the empty plates to the faucet. The water squealed as it exited. "I don't want to be part of the Council. I don't but...but it's my fucking fault and if...if I ever want to be better or be left alone or something..." His face fell. "I've gotta clean up this mess."

Bria grabbed his hand. "If it does come though, we should be ready at least. You said that Caroline told you how to capture it...by harnessing the mist, right?"

Brent nodded.

"Then let's get some jars and be ready. Capture this thing if it comes for us." She turned off the faucet and hopped onto the counter, sitting at eye level to him. "So, let's go shopping, okay? Get those jars. There's this little shop a few blocks down. They sell a bunch of odd items. I'm sure they have some magical jars or something."

"A'ight," Brent clutched her fingers. "Yeah, you're right. Let's do it."

The shop sat on the corner of Myrtle and Celosia, two narrow roads in the heart of the city where merchants gathered in reds and yellows. Brent stuck out like a sore thumb in the colorful roads, insisting on wearing a beige tunic that hung a little too loose around his waist. Bria loved the array, decking herself out in a blue, yellow, and red dress, with a wreath of flowers woven through her hair.

The bell rang as they entered the shop. Rows of jars, old books, and ingredients lined the shelves. At their arrival, a little boy darted out of the backroom, stark red eyes haunting his face.

His father hurried out and ushered the child back into the room, “Garrett! Get back inside. Don’t bother the customers.”

Brent and Bria exchanged a smirk.

“Sorry ‘bout that,” the shop keeper grumbled. “Curious bugger.”

“It’s a’ight,” Brent replied. “Cute kid.”

The shopkeeper’s face softened. “Ah, you’re Rosadian ain’t ya? Not many of you folk make it here.”

“How d'you—”

“Accent. Been a long time since I heard one...” He shook his head. “What can I get ya then? Here for a tattoo, perhaps? Or for my wife’s services?”

Bria glanced elaborate dragon tattoo decorating his arms. Beneath it, she swore two of its teeth looked like the black stamp. She smiled. “We’re browsing. Shopping and all. That’s it.”

“*Browsing*. Got it. Here if ya need me then.” The shopkeeper collapsed on his stool and snatched up the newspaper.

Bria followed Brent over to a row of books. He picked through them, his face hardening at each title, before exchanging a brief smile telling her it was okay. She kissed his shoulder, then wandered over to an aisle of vials and jars. Every few minutes, she peeked around, watching Brent collect a few books in his arms, and then proceed to try on some colorful boater hats.

Bria snagged a few jars and headed to the counter to pay for the books in Brent's arm, the hat, and her lot. The shop keeper counted the coins with his eyes, nodded, then turned back to his newspaper with a scowl on his face.

She tugged Brent away from the books, stealing his new green hat in the process.

"Oi, that's mine!"

"Not anymore."

"You're so—" He stopped as they exited the shop, attention drawn to an elderly woman approaching them. She wore all black but for the red trim laced about sleeves. As she drew closer, the mist passed over her face, and in its place stared two bright blue eyes against the smooth face of a pale-faced woman.

"Caroline," Brent gawked.

Bria dropped one of her jars, catching the other two before they hit the ground.

"Caroline?" Bria glanced at him, "You mean...but I can see her!"

The woman spoke more poignantly than Bria imagined. "I believe entering the library strengthened your sight, Miss Smidt."

"You know me?"

"Of course, it is hard not to. Brent is enthralled with—"

"Okay, yeah, we get it." Brent's face turned red. "What's going on? What's happening?"

"The Diabolo is moving." Caroline didn't blink. "It's headed east."

"That's good, isn't it? It's going away from home?"

"No." Caroline glanced to the sky. "It is coming here."

"What? Why?"

"Is it because of me?" Bria whispered.

"Something is drawing its attention." Caroline glanced behind her. "The magic is strong in this city. Perhaps it is that."

"But weren't they created to chase the powerful Magii?" Brent shook his head. "This is just...it's just people with their parlor tricks."

"It doesn't matter; it feeds on magic."

"If it comes here, no one is safe," Bria interjected. "It will destroy the city."

"It will be unstoppable," Brent fidgeted. "But if the Council knows this...why aren't you doing anything?"

The expression on Caroline's face told it all, her mouth quivering and eyes looking away. Brent turned from her and threw one of the books against the wall in frustration. As soon as it hit, spine up, he picked it up and coddled it like a babe.

"Brent, calm down." Bria placed a hand on his back. "It's okay. We're going to be okay."

"This is all my fucking fault!" he spat, crouching on the ground and bringing the books to his forehead. "I should've just minded my own business, stayed to myself, and this wouldn't have happened! Everyone hates me!"

"Well I don't!"

"Does that even matter if they want us *dead*!?! I've killed you, too!"

"Don't you say that!"

"It's true!"

"Brenton Harley! Get out of your head and *listen.* We'll catch it!" Bria brought the book away from his face. "We'll stop the monster before it leaves the Newbird Mountains. We know how to catch it. We've got your magic and mine. And we've got Carol—"

She turned towards the woman. Only a passing cloud of fog remained.

CHAPTER THIRTY-THREE

How to Fight a Nightmare

Brent stayed up long past the candlelight waned, using the lantern outside to help him navigate the books in front of him. He'd purchased two books to help translate the *I.* book into the common tongue, but it proved more difficult than he'd anticipated. For hours, long after Bria fell asleep with the blanket up to her chin, he scribbled across the book. But even the sentences he managed to translate sounded confusing when read out loud.

"'So, he says the world is ablaze," Brent murmured. "A fight of woman and man, life and death, magic and mist; neither can survive in the fire world. Who burns first? The one not victor on the Plains of Cypress.'" He groaned. "What the fuck does that mean?"

His head throbbed. It'd been enough of a headache to understand the children's book, but at least he knew that the stories he heard in the Diabolo were more than just stories.

Yet, even now, Brent struggled to ignore them. Another tale sent a whiff through his head, the odor of a rotting corpse in the morgue of the hospital to the west. Per Bria's request, and his own sanity, he fought the urge to go, no matter how much it screamed.

He cursed again, throwing the book across the room. It hit the ground with a loud clunk.

"Brent?" Bria glanced at him from the bed.

"Go back to bed." Brent went over to her. "You need rest if we're going to do this."

"You do too," Bria sat up. "What's wrong?"

"It's noth—" he stopped, watching her gaze soften. "You'll say I'm being self-righteous."

"Probably but say it, anyway."

"I want to protect Mert...and you...but I can't help feeling it is my fault," Brent sighed. "If I kept my hands to my sides, it wouldn't have escaped. I might have—I mean, everyone would be safe. Worst yet, I don't understand this thing! Like I get it's a monster made of nightmares—that it is created of past Hells. But what does it mean?" He snatched the children's book. "'Finally, a body must be used to take its form. They're kept beneath in crypts yearning for a purpose more.' The only thing that I can think of is..."

"You're worried the stories will take you over, right?" Bria interjected. "They won't."

"We don't know that." Brent slammed the book shut. "You've seen what happens. What if I...what if I *become* the Diabolo? What if I'm the empty body in the poem? The blank slate?" He clenched his eyes shut and scratched again at his wrist. The stories circled around him for a moment, but after whispering his name to himself a few times, he managed to stay together.

What if he wouldn't remember his name next time? What if the Diabolo tore into him and replaced him with actual demons. Wouldn't that be something worse than death?

"You've come back from the stories every time. The Diabolo is no different." She turned his face towards her. "We're going to find it and shove it back into those jars. Then the Council will see we're on their side; we can get answers finally."

"I just...I don't want it to hurt you again."

"You never have," she cooed. "Come back to bed."

He did. But even huddled beneath the covers together, Brent never found sleep.

As dawn trickled into the room, they prepared for the battle to come. Brent hooked a couple jars up to his belt and pulled on a pair of hiking boots. Meanwhile, Bria reassembled her Rho-facade, cowl and all.

"How did I not recognize you?" Brent chuckled as he hooked the last jar to his belt.

"It's because you're an idiot," Bria finished braiding her hair, then helped him button his tunic. "A klutzy, ridiculous, handsome idiot."

Brent's face grew warm.

"So, what's the plan then?"

"I thought you said I'm an idiot."

"Yeah, but with how obsessed you've been, I would think you'd have a plan."

"We, uh, find the, um..." He scratched his wrist. "I don't know. I mean—I don't know where it is. Caroline didn't...she left us hanging and um..." He winced. "I'm sorry...I'm—I don't—"

Bria took his hand, "It's okay. It comes and goes."

"I've been getting better," he gritted his teeth.

Yes, but you've still got the mouth of a bumbling buffoon, the voice of a man in the mountains snarled. *Learn to speak properly, boy.*

Shut it.

Bria squeezed his fingers, "Listen then. You last saw it in the mountains, right?"

Brent nodded.

"Then why don't we go to the tallest mountain in Newbird. You can use your magic to see if you can track it, right? The Diabolo is bound to have a strong story...and even a whiff of it will send us in the right direction."

"And if it's heading here," Brent added, "it's probably heading northeast. So at least we have a direction."

"See? It's not all lost." She smiled, and as her dimples appeared, a camellia flower blossomed behind her ear.

"It might take a few days to catch up to it."

"Just another adventure."

From atop the highest peak in the Newbird Mountain range, the story of the Diabolo struck the landscape like lightning. It shouted, it screamed, it knocked Brent to his knees. He held his head, trying to shake off the images. The worst men marching to war, the cutting of skin, and the screams...every time he saw one tale in the trees, the next assaulted him with a bang. He collapsed to his knees, trying to recollect himself.

But with Bria's touch, he managed to return to reality.

"It's loud," he whispered. "I can't—it definitely went north though."

"Then we'll head north." She hoisted him to his feet. "You'll be okay, right?"

"For now, yeah. That was a visual story. I mean, it didn't get in my head."

"I know. I saw some of it, too."

"I made it visible, you mean?"

"Yes, a bit." She nudged him. "Come on. We'll head down the mountains. See if we find anything. If not, Hutch's Creek isn't far. We can make camp there for the night."

They followed the whiffs of stories through the forest. In their wake, trees lay toppled on the ground, leaves strewn about, and the foliage that remained turned black. Bria ran her fingers across the dying trees, blessing them with green and casting away the dead. She smiled while doing it, an aura of tranquility around her face, focus shooting through her eyes. Brent yearned to kiss her in excitement.

Now wasn't the time.

Some spots along their path eroded like a rotting corpse; other times, the mist seemed to dissipate, leaving a hollowness in its wake. In his toes and fingers, Brent sensed the Diabolo. Was it watching them? Did it laugh when they made the wrong turn?

As the moon and sun exchanged places in the sky, they arrived in Hutch's Creek. The town was a miniature version of Newbird's Arm, with a town square bustling beneath the watchful eye of a small temple. It guarded over their Pit, makeshift at best, with the guard standing watch by the gate.

"Oi, boy, what are you doin' outta the Pit?" a guard called at Brent.

"I..." Brent gulped. The leather cusp had slipped, and like a target, his black stamp lay visible.

The guard approached them. "Ain't a free-day. Get back in there, or we'll force ya, a'ight?"

"He's with me." Bria stepped forward.

"That don't matter, doll. Best you be off and away from demon-fuckers like him."

"He's not—"

He grabbed her by the chin. "Listen 'ere doll. I don't wanna find ya in contempt. But my domicile captain's got rules, ya hear me? So, go on your merry way—"

She shoved him. Much to Brent's surprise, the hit sent the man tripping over roots and landing with a thud on the ground and a bloody nose.

"Come on!" Bria snatched Brent's hand and dragged him back towards the tunnels before the guard climbed from the ground.

Bria collapsed against the wall once the tunnel closed. "I'm so sorry."

"What? No, that's not your fault."

"I forgot about your stamp...and Hutch's Creek doesn't know you...and you're twenty-one now, so they actually care, and I've gotten so used to you being okay to live in Mert that it didn't occur to me—"

"It's not your fault." Brent sat next to her and scratched his wrist. "I'm used to it anyhow."

"It's not fair, though! You've been dealing with this for too long."

"We'll...I mean, we've got a way out now. Maybe we can fix it someday."

They gripped hands in the darkness. It was that reassurance as Bria sat beside him, keeping him sane; his one constant, always there, always with him.

Replaying the stories of the Diabolo in his mind, Brent finally said, "It is probably turning west from what I last saw. Needs to get across the sea to Mert..."

"You think it will really cross water?"

"It *can* fly."

Bria's face lost color. Once their breathing settled, they left their spot in the tunnels and headed west towards the villages on the coast. The tunnels grew musky, a chilled spring rain dripping through the soil overhead.

They emerged on a foothill at the edge of a village. At first, Brent thought a story surged through him, but as he peered through the mist, he knew it was more.

It was too vivid, too alive.

The terror on Bria's face confirmed his suspicions.

The monster loitered in the mist, thunderclaps following its footsteps, with incomplete strikes of lightning ripping through its body. Since Brent last saw it, the Diabolo had tripled in size. Elongated toenails on its misshaped feet scraped the ground, its naked body coated in blood-smeared cuts that hid any semblance of sexuality. Mustard eyes glowered, one that looked through a slit in its face while the other hung against its cheek. Its jaw gawked unhinged, flaunting its sharpened teeth. Upon its head, long white hairs avalanched like snow.

It continued oozing nightmares from its skin. Brent shielded his mind with a few stories around him, letting them become but a dull ache in his mind. Beside him, Bria whimpered and held her head.

"Bri...Bria listen." He kneeled to her level. "We're gonna get it and these nightmares...they'll stop, a'ight? We need to...we need to contain it."

"I have an idea," she mumbled. "Stand back."

Bria dug her fingers into the ground. Trees grew, up and out, surrounding the beast on the outskirts of town. At their peak, the trees curved in, forming a dome around them and the Diabolo. It screeched, leaving a buzzing noise bouncing through Brent's ear, and into his sinuses. The screams did little to stop Bria, though her arms palpitated more with each passing second, letting the canopies weave together.

It wouldn't last long. The Diabolo would break through any moment.

He rushed forward, focusing on the stories in the mist. *Use it as a lure, pull it forward like a whip*. He wove each story in his head, connecting them as humanity does while unclasping the jar on his hip.

The creature spun forward, towering over Brent and breathing down his neck.

A bit closer. He held out his hand, "Come on...come on..."

The creature sniffed it and let out another screech. It sent Brent flying backward, and a few trees uprooted. He managed to dodge one as it fell, but another large branch snapped against his shoulder.

"Brent!" Bria screamed.

The Diabolo snatched Brent, digging its elongated nails into his arms and backs. Pain ripped through his body, and up his feet went, away from the ground, into the air.

With his fleeting consciousness, he focused on the Diabolo and its stories. Hundreds of stories fought for dominance in the creature, each woven in a confusing rope. Separate, they were individuals, trying to tell their stories.

And were those children crying?

He pulled one story away from the rest of the Diabolo's confusion, of a man leading an army to take down a magic-bustling city. The man's name emerged from it all, a name Brent couldn't pronounce or hear, but it sat at the forefront of his mind.

The story freed itself. The Diabolo shrieked.

Brent tumbled from the sky.

And the Diabolo vanished into the clouds.

CHAPTER THIRTY-FOUR

THE GIANT AND THE QUEEN

BRENT!" Bria rushed forward, watching as Brent spiraled into the sky. For a moment, she swore that would be it, but then the monster shrieked and released Brent, flying into the clouds. With it, her head roared, oscillating between darkness and light, but she reclaimed herself as Brent fell. A nearby tree lowered him to the ground.

As soon as Bria was positive the monster had left, she joined Brent's side. Blood seeped from the wounds in his arm and back. His head drooped into his chest, and every gasp shook his body.

"Please be okay...please be okay," Bria cupped his face, "You're okay. Please...look at me...please..."

He grumbled, "Bri..."

"You're okay," she stroked back his hair, "I'm right here."

He managed to open an eye, and a smile trickled on his lips, "Hey."

"We need to clean your wounds...stop the blood..." she removed her sweater and used it to dab the cuts in his arm, "You're going to be okay."

"Bri...it's a'ight...just...it's a'ight..." he coughed.

"No, we need to stop the blood..." she restrained the tears. "I can go to the village below...they can help—"

"I'm sure they saw the monster. And me, with my black stamp...these small towns aren't gonna be...I mean, they're gonna see me for what I am."

"Don't talk like that!" she tore a strip from his tunic and wrapped it around his wrist, "I'll find someone to help. I won't let you die."

"Bria—"

"I won't let you!"

"A'ight," Brent leaned into a tree, "I'll try not to."

"Just keep putting pressure on it. I'll be right back," she kissed his forehead, "And stay awake, please."

"A'ight," he winced, "Be safe."

"I'll be fine," she took a few steps forward, "I love you."

He managed to smile.

Bria didn't like leaving Brent behind, but there was no way she'd be able to carry him down to the tunnels. *He'll be okay,* Bria hugged herself, shivering as the tunnels led her back towards the junction. Had they always been this cold? So dark? She didn't know where to go either. Brent was right; no one in Rosada cared for a boy with a black stamp. To die in the woods would rid them of him, another demon wiped from this earth.

She wiped her eyes, *Caroline will help. I'll see if I can find her.*

A long shot, she knew, but what else could she do? Who else could she trust?

The journey to the junction took longer than Bria remembered. Her heart raced as she approached the mist-covered wall. *No door. Fuck.* She gripped her hands tighter. *Focus. Focus. It's there. You saw it. It's there.*

She closed her eyes, trying to view life through Brent's gaze. A story, perhaps? A view behind the veil, past the mist, and it would be there, right?

Brent and Caroline both confirmed she had sight of some sort, at least. The door was there. She saw it once, climbing up the wall, etchings of the past inscribed upon it. If only she could stare past the mist and *see it* again.

"Please!" she banged her fist against the wall, "Please! He's going to die! Please! Let me in!"

Nothing.

Bria sank to her knees, clawing into the dirt. A few saplings spun about, extending from the ground and against the wall. They formed their own barriers, sticking against the cavern wall as moss or fungus growing on a tree.

A tree.

Taking a deep breath, she stepped back, then ran into the wall. She braced for impact.

But instead of hitting it, the roots pulled her through, and she tumbled into the library and into a case of books.

She recollected herself, then darted into the shelves. She needed to find Caroline or someone who would help; not Alojzy, not Tomás. Anyone else would be fine, right? They'd come running to help their own. Surely. Right?

Bria struggled to believe it.

The aisles her to the stairwell. When she first saw the multicolored glass above, her heart skipped. As she slammed her boots on the glass, it shot out veins of red, yellow, and orange, like streaks of lightning.

Hold on, Brent. I'm going to find you help. Just hold on!

She skidded to a halt upon hearing footsteps and darted behind a door. The steps rocked the path, sending shivers of reds and greens across the glass floor. Bria waited as the shadow passed, then peeked out.

A towering man with long black hair walked past, swinging a flask at his side.

Bria gulped and stepped out of the shadows, "Excuse me!"

He spun and narrowed his eyes, "You!"

"Please help! Brent's in trouble. He's going to—he's going to die. I got in here...but we need to...the monster, the Diabolo I mean, it cut into him. He's bleeding..." Bria looked away from the man's hardening face. "Please."

"*You,*" the man growled, approaching her with a snarl on his lips. "You reek of magic and taint this library. You are not supposed to be here."

"Please..." Bria backed up, curling in on herself beneath the giant's gaze. "Brent—"

"Brenton is not my responsibility. If he dies, so be it." He tossed the flask to the side and took another step forward. "*You* should not be here."

"I—I'll leave then," Bria never felt so small. Even Captain Carver, Christof, or Cadet Lawry never made her feel this tiny. This man was more than them. "I'll find another way to help him if you all won't."

"You've seen too much, Magii," the giant stood only a step away now.

She backed into the metallic banister, "I said I'll leave!"

The giant snarled and pushed her over the balcony to the sea of books below.

CHAPTER THIRTY-FIVE

THE MYSTICAL CHEER

Brent drifted off to sleep as he forgot the whereabouts of his arms, each breath more harrowing than the last. Nightmares rocked his brain, recanting the tales boiling within the Diabolo. Monstrous men and women traveled through each of its thoughts, blanketed with the songs of children. In the moments he spent awake, sometimes he woke with the identity of a murderer, or a brutalist, or an animal slayer. The Diabolo's mind mingled with Brent's, and while he tried to ground himself in his past, sometimes the monster screamed louder.

When he managed to wake as himself, a purple twinge highlighted the sky, and leaves took refuge against his skin. He craned his neck and called for Bria, but the hooting owls and the empty shadows only verified what he feared: she had not returned.

He used what energy he could salvage to hoist himself up, limping from tree to tree, and applying pressure to the wound on his side. I should be dead. Every step sent bolts through his nerves, and after five minutes, he curled back onto the ground, choking on blood and spit.

How long had he been walking? He saw the sky again in a tinge of orange and only managed to crawl forward a few paces before succumbing to light-headedness. It couldn't be that long, right? Parched, hungry, and alone, he clung to his identity with both hands and cried for help with all the energy he could muster.

As time passed, consciousness came in spurts. At one point, he recalled as someone dragged him across the ground. He grunted a plea, hoping for a response, but when his head hit something firm, he slipped away. Another time, he awoke to a warm cloth on his head and a whirring noise beneath a white canopy. And a third time, he spun awake to a scorching liquid as it trickled down his throat.

Consciousness returned to him like a war-time march. Soft, followed by a bang. It rocked him awake, and as soon as his mind turned, his body screamed out with a sharp pang in his side. He gasped and tried to sit up. Another sharp pang attacked his side, and with an anguished groan, he fell back onto the cot.

"Ey, slow now," a woman's voice spoke. "I'll get ya an extra pillow."

A small hand propped his head against another pillow. Squinting, Brent absorbed his surroundings. A heavy woolen blanket lay over his bandaged, naked body. Wooden walls climbed around him with a step ladder leading through the ceiling. A whirring noise putted beneath the floor, shaking the cauldron that boiled beside him. Brent turned to his savior, a small woman wearing a loose-fitting white blouse and tight trousers. Her black curly hair puffed out around her smiling face.

"Atta boy."

"Where—what—how—" Brent gritted his teeth. "Who—who are you?"

"I'm Malaika." She grinned, showing her yellow overbite.

"Ma—Malaika." He leaned back. "Oh, right, of course."

"I know who you are, of course. Brenton Harley...the new bane of the Council." She picked up the bowl at her side and stirred it.

"How—how am I alive?"

"I've no damn clue if you want my opinion. Those injuries should have killed ya, but here you are, still beating along. Must got something to hold on too, I reckon. Got ya bandaged up best I could, though."

"How long—"

"Couple nights, I think. Dragged ya to my ship about a day ago. You looked like you'd been out and about at least another two nights, I think." Malaika shoved the bowl into his hands. "Eat. You'll feel better."

He stared at his reflection in the murky liquid. Hallowed cheeks, empty stare; he almost didn't recognize himself. Malaika pressed the spoon to his lips, rupturing the reflection and sending a burning fire down his throat.

Brent spit it out.

"It hurts, yes?" Malaika cooed. "We shall take it slow..."

Brent tried to down the soup, but each spoonful made his entire body shrivel, and he pushed it aside.

Malaika didn't press him, returning to her makeshift chair across the room where she continued knitting a blanket.

He managed to speak, "Bria...where—where is she?"

"Ah, yes, you kept screaming her name occasionally...ahem." Malaika shook back her hair. "Breee-uhhh, Breeee-uhhhhh."

Brent's ears turned red.

"Who is she?" Malaika cursed under her breath as she continued knitting. "Dropped a damn stitch..."

"She's my—my best—she's my girlfriend." He gulped, letting the word hang before continuing. "We were traveling together...looking for the Diabolo...and I got hurt. She was going to get help. She—she said she would be right back. I don't know—I don't know what happened to her."

Malaika put down her needles and squinted. With a mere wave of her hand, the mist solidified before her in the shape of a globe.

Brent stared.

"What is her name again? Full name."

"Bri—Briannabella Smidt."

She spun the globe about, zooming in upon one of the locations. "Hmph...great. Must be malfunctioning..."

"What? What is it?"

"It says she is in the library..." Malaika furrowed her brow. "That's got to be wrong...unless she can get in there?"

"What? Still?" Brent shot up, but the pain sent him withering back onto the bed. "If she hasn't left...why would she...I mean she's—she's in trouble if...she's gonna get...she could be hurt. They hate her and I...this is my—"

"Relax, boy."

"We gotta help her!"

"Well, we're currently hundreds of feet above the sea. Don't think we'll make land for another day or so. Gotta ask Jun where we are—"

"What? What're you..." Brent used his elbow to hoist himself up. "Where are we?"

"In my airship, the Mystical Cheer, sailing leagues to the west." Malaika spun her map around. "I think, at least. Dee is sailing her above. I don't know where I'm going half the time."

"Wait—wait." He shook his head. "You mean we're in an airship? We're flying?"

"Dense, ain't ya? Yes, we're flying."

His insides twisted. "We're not meant to fly..."

"Excuse me?"

"Flying...we're not birds." He gulped. "We're really in the air?"

Malaika helped him over to the small porthole window. Far below, islands-like-dots mingled with the thrashing waves.

He stumbled back onto the bed again. "But—but how—I mean, I guess..." Brent gulped again. "How d'you find me? I—I was in the forest. I mean, there were trees..."

"And a fuckin' monster blew through a ton of trees, so it wasn't that hard," Malaika waved her finger through the globe, causing it to disperse. "Had been tracking for you a bit. Saw you spent a lot of time in Mert, but always out and about. Noticed you change over to the Newbird Mountains...then stopped moving. Figured I wasn't too far, so best check it out. And look at you now, alive at least."

Brent took a moment to let what Malaika said sink in. So, he hadn't been as under the radar as he thought. No matter where he went, someone watched. It made his head hurt again, but it might have been from the whirring of the airship. The idea of being in the sky made him squirm. People weren't meant to fly.

"We're gonna rendezvous with Caroline soon. Honestly thought we'd be dragging her corpse," Malaika continued. "She just doesn't know it yet."

"But how are you gonna...I mean, can't she just go into the tunnels?"

"Caroline is a creature of habit. I know exactly where she'll be when we make landfall in, err..." She glanced up the stepladder. "Oi! How long 'til landfall?"

"For goodness's sake, I told ya twelve hours an hour ago!" A woman called back, shaking the ladder as she came down. A misty exterior trailed along her body, clad in thick leather armor. Her short graying hair created waves along her eyebrows. Despite the sternness in her voice, her face lit up upon seeing Brent. "Ah, the young man is awake! Looking well too!"

"Brent, I'd like to introduce you to my comrade Lady Dobroslawa Goryl."

"You can call me Dee," the woman added. "I know, my name's a mouthful."

"A'ight, yeah." Brent nodded. "Nice to meet you, Dee."

"We've heard a lot of rumors about you, Mr. Harley. The Bane of the Council, Discoverer of Secrets, Collector of Stories, yes?" Dee smirked. "But, we can talk about that later. You need rest."

Brent grunted. "I don't think I'm that special."

"Oh, we do—"

"Dee!" Malaika spat. "The boy needs rest. We can talk 'bout all this later, yes? Once he's, I dunno, not dying?"

"Fine," Dee huffed and started up the ladder. She paused and added, "Better get him clothed though before we make landfall. Sure, we got something that fit him. Nobody wants to see his naked bum."

Malaika provided Brent with a pair of trousers that stopped at his ankles and a frilly blouse that was too wide at the hip. He wore them without arguing, happy to be in clean clothes.

Walking hurt more than he would admit, welcoming the wooden chair they placed him in by the window. Outside, the orange glow of the sky turned the water below red. The days in Mert, kissing by the blood sea, already belonged to another man; his story now sailed through the clouds.

Several women tended to the deck where a tall woman with long black hair spouted orders. She never regarded Brent, only dropping some bread on the table before him, then grumbling and heading off towards the helm.

Brent wrapped himself within the stories of the ship, listening to the purring of the engine and watching as the ground grew closer with the passing hours. His thoughts, when clear, stayed with Bria. Why was she in the library? What was she doing? Why didn't she return?

And was the Diabolo still heading towards Mert? Or had it detoured back to the mountains? Was it heading back to Newbird's Arm?

And why did he keep screwing everything up?

The airship struck the ground with a clatter, skidding about on the surface, causing plates and forks to clatter to the floor. Brent shot up, knuckles white as he gripped his seat, choking down the nausea in his throat.

He rocked back and forth as he stepped off the ship, resisting the urge to upchuck his meal as he reached hard ground. Malaika skidded off the railing after Brent, landing on both of her feet.

They arrived in a land of brimstone and smoke. Creatures scurried before them, disappearing as shadows, some walking on four legs and other soaring on wings. Were they mammal, birds, reptilian, or something else? It was like a dream–a story even.

"Oi boy." Malaika handed him a crooked stick. "Might help ya walk a bit."

"Thought Caroline was here..." Brent leaned on the stick and winced. "I need to...if Bria is still in the library, I gotta get to her. This is bullshite. Why didn't you just...I mean, you could've brought me to the tunnels?"

"Caroline is not far." Malaika reopened her map. "Just beyond the gaslight there, in the town of Graycott. She must've gone a bit fishing in their lake then went into town or something. That's her usual routine, at least."

"Graycott—that's not in Rosada. Where are we?" Brent limped after Malaika, coughing as they passed through a plume of smoke.

"Spinoza," Malaika jeered. "Land of Dragons and Smoke! Love comin' here to find dracones."

"Dracones...you mean, like dragons?"

"Ay!"

"They're not...those are stories, aren't they?"

"Nah, I grew up with 'em."

"You're lying."

"What does the mist tell ya, boy?"

Brent squinted. Another shadow, with a wingspan as wide as his arms, flew past. Another critter scurried past his heals. With it, he saw a story of two sisters flying on dragons, dueling with fire and blazing the sky with ash. Another creature roared; or was it again the mist trying to tell a tale?

"I...I don't know." Brent grunted and rubbed his forehead. "All of this it's...I don't know what's real anymore. Sometimes it's...I mean, I see you, I see shadows...but I see stories. It's confusing."

Malaika stopped walking, her shoulders falling. The jovial tone in her voice ceased as she spoke, "You mean you are seeing everything?"

"I guess—feeling it, seeing it..." He closed his eyes. "It hasn't stopped really since I first entered the library."

"That is...perplexing." Malaika scratched her bushy hair, pulling a knitting needle out of her curls. "Oops."

They continued into the smoke, where the town of Graycott hid. It almost looked like a ghost town, but as they strolled through, life shone out of the men, women, and children in the streets. They wore bejeweled cloth, dancing in the streets and painting the drab landscape in a prism. At the focal point of the town loitered a building in the shape of a dragon.

Malaika led him inside its mouth.

Brent's head seared as they entered. A thousand stories called out to him from the boxes and plaques on the wall. Names screeching, reaching, crying. Tales of men and women, old and young, and happy and sad. They mingled together into one giant stew.

"Brent! Brent! What's wrong?"

Brent blinked. Caroline stood before him, gripping both his shoulders. A whiff of fish and the sea permeated from her body.

"Caroline! It's you!"

"Yes, it is, but what is wrong with you? Where have you been? You are pale..."

"There are just...so many stories..." He squinted past her. Malaika sat on a smaller statue of a ruby eyed dragon. "Where are we?"

"A mausoleum," Caroline remarked. "I do have work beyond spying on the Council for you. It really is not my forte; I have enjoyed the quiet life these past hundreds of years."

"You're good at it, though," Malaika chimed in.

Caroline grumbled.

"Right. Work. Death work..." Brent leaned against the wall and clenched his side.

"What happened to you?" Caroline clenched his wrists after throwing another glare at Malaika.

Brent sucked in his lips and looked away, before recanting the tale with the Diabolo in the mountains. His head roared at the thought of its story, and his throat tightened as he worried over Bria.

"Bria...I need to go to her...if she's still in the library, I mean. She could be...what if she's—"

"If she is in the library, she is fine. They will not kill her," Caroline insisted.

"But what if they do something worse?"

"They will not. I trust them."

"*Do you*? You saw what they tried to do to me!" Brent's lip quivered. "They would've erased my memories if Julietta didn't pull back."

"Tomás explained to me what happened in depth." Caroline stroked Brent's hair out of his eyes. "They are worried for you."

"Yeah, they think I'm gonna fail." Brent leaned on his walking stick. "Tried to erase my memory."

"They thought it would make it go away."

"Make what go away?"

"Tomás told me that there have been others like you." Caroline fiddled with her thumbs. "Ones who see and feel everything. None of them have been successful..." She trailed off, turning to one of the plaques on the wall. "They went crazy. Confused. They became blank slates."

"They thought erasing my memories would stop that?"

"Yes."

"But I'm still cursed to die!"

"But at least your mind would be whole!" Caroline wiped her eyes.

"I'd rather die knowing what the fuck is happening than—than a shell!"

Brent's mind raced to the children's story he read. *A body...an empty body; the Diabolo needs something to latch onto...shite!* He gritted his teeth and glared at Caroline. "If they erased my memories...I'd be...they would have used me for the Diabolo."

"What? What are you inferring?"

"The Diabolo needs a body! They wanted to use me!"

"No! The Council would never!"

Malaika chuckled. "Keep telling yourself that."

"Well, it does not matter anymore! Julietta stopped. She said you were whole still, whatever that means. Either way, the Council stopped!"

"It means I know who I am. I mean, I don't...but I am able to get back here. I—I'm not going to lose myself." Brent had a hard time believing it, though. He still felt the Diabolo's stories brushing his skin. The stories in the mausoleum only grew louder. "And if I do," Brent continued, "if I do lose myself, then we can look at forgetting. But give me a chance. I'm—I'm a storyteller. That's always what I been. And—and if someone believes in me...then I don't have to fight this shite alone. Please—"

Caroline touched his arm. "Brent. I do believe in you. I am only telling you what Tomás told me."

"But if that's their rationale behind hurting me, why wouldn't they hurt Bria?"

"Because that'd be stupid," Malaika spat. "They don't need a war over a girl like her. The Palaver is watching."

"She doesn't want to be watched. She just wants to live."

"The Palaver watches all Magii, always looking to fledge out their ranks, the damn bastards."

"Well...then why didn't she come back?"

"I do not know. But you need to breathe," Caroline urged. "You are growing pale."

Brent leaned forward, dizziness sweeping over him as he inhaled. "I'm...scared."

"It is understandable." Caroline helped him sit. "Let me finish these releases, and we shall head to the library. Malaika, would you like to help? Or are you off hunting dragons again?"

"I'm heading off with Dee soon, but I can help a few." She cracked her knuckles, the smile returning again to her lips. "Been a while since I've done one of these."

"I can—I can help." Brent pressed his fingers against one of the plaques. "There's one right here."

"Are you strong enough? I do not want to drag you through the tunnels by your feet."

"I can do it. I've been doing it the past couple weeks," Brent reassured her. "The stuff you did teach me worked out in the end."

Caroline allowed it, turning towards one of the other spots on the wall. The wind blew up in her hair, and the mist masked her face. Malaika, meanwhile, trailed her fingers against the wall, a mist-made compass in her hand.

Brent listened, hearing the tale of an elderly man teaching his son how to harvest eggs and tend to the poultry. It mingled with another tale from across the mausoleum, of a dancer skipping through the fog, until an offshoot of smoke encased her with a masquerade of fire. One last story came bombarding from the other end, this time about a man who learned to juggle axes while hopping on one leg. The tales danced, and each one pulled a part of Brent's mind down into their Hells.

Fires.

Cuts.

Blades.

Forgotten.

Alone.

Screams.

Shouts.

Shrieks.

Silence.

Brent came to again, and three souls stood vivid in the mist. They motioned to each other, then back to him, before dissipating into the land of the dead.

He sank into the ground. His hand hurt, his mind bouncing between three voices.

I'm dancing, I'm spinning, on one leg...look at me go.

Look at me go.

He chuckled.

"Brent." Caroline crawled over to him, her face reverting back from that of an elderly man with a bushy beard to her usual blue eyes. "You released three at once. Perfectly."

"Their stories danced together...dancing...dance! All the same tale." He stumbled into Caroline, laughing. "Don't you see? It's just one big tale—one big story. We're all a part of it. We all are."

CHAPTER THIRTY-SIX

THE ARCHITECT

Darkness dripped.

Bria curled up on the ground, a sharpness digging behind her right ear and a thudding pain in her hip.

It was too bright to open her eyes.

Drip.

Drip.

Drip.

When the silence quit buzzing, then came the screams. Distant, beyond the darkness, echoing. Shouting.

Inhuman.

Food and water arrived in sporadic intervals, with faceless ghost dropping the dishes just in reach of her cell. The few times she tried to call her magic, it fizzled out.

Alone. Powerless. Wilting.

The pang behind her ear didn't stop. She caressed her little branch behind it, but as she traced the offshoots, her fingers softened upon congealed blood.

"Oh no..." she gagged before upchucking her dinner.

A piece of her branch had gone missing.

She didn't know how much time passed. Her eyes struggled to adjust to the light. *There are no lights. I won't say there are four.*

Restless hours sent her bouncing between her time with Captain Carver and the present. Perhaps she'd never left the barracks; did she only wake up after hours of interrogation? Did she dream of an adventure by Brent's side?

No. That happened. It had to have happened.

But Brent was probably dead now. There was nothing she could do now, except curl up and sob. Everything that made her Bria had withered with her little branch. Helplessness paralyzed her. In her chest, her heart thumped loud enough to deafen her, eventually sending her into a restless sleep.

When a slither of light cut through the darkness, at last, she fed on it, inching closer and closer until the darkness vanished. In its place, she discovered there were no bars holding her back, but an endless hallway with candles lit in the distance. Here the screams chanted, guiding her forward. Cells lined the walls. Mist masked what lay within, but as Bria squinted past it, she saw a skeletal creature lurked behind the bars.

Its empty silver gaze washed over her, whispering nonsense into the emptiness. Food laid scattered about its cage, torn to bits, while a discarded cup of water leaked under the bars. Blood dripped from the creature's lips.

"You're not a Diabolo," Bria stated, her voice trembling.

The creature growled.

"What are you?" Bria begged.

The creature waved its hands, exasperated and scared. Its hallowed face and silver eyes reminded her too much of Brent.

"No..." Bria shook her head and darted down the hall. Each cell contained a similar creature, some more human than the next, some more feminine than others, but all with desolate silver eyes.

"This isn't real. It can't be real." Bria hurried, hugging herself tighter as she restrained more tears. She swore the pathway would never end. Stuck, wandering forever, alone, she would never escape.

She stopped at a dead-end. A basin sat beneath the single torchlight, bubbling and wreaking of rotting corpses. In its silver-coated surface, she saw glimpses of nightmares, of prisons, and of vagrancy. She squirmed as it reached for her, reminding her of the Diabolo when it touched her those weeks ago in the tunnels. Stroking...pulling...scratching...

"Please...I want to go home." She buried her head into her hands.

When she lifted it again, a cloaked figure walked her back in the darkness. She couldn't see his face, but the prisoners in each cage they passed hissed in his direction.

"What's happening?" Bria sobbed.

"You are not a canvas, my dear," the figure remarked. "The Pool is not for you."

"What about...what about the others?"

"Their screams and nightmares are powerful. Yours are too," he motioned her back into the cell. "Go back to sleep."

The darkness grew heavier around her, and sleep became her companion. But not a good one. It sent shivers of terrors through her psych.

Was the Council planting these dreams? Dreams of her grandmama dying, of her father finally losing tangible speech, of Brent bleeding in the snow. They battled for her attention, each worse than the last.

None could drown out the screams. She swore they grew louder with each passing moment.

The darkness deepened.

Dripping.

Whistling.

Dripping.

The light came again as a tsunami, washing Bria against the wall. Footsteps followed, and a shadow towered over her through the bars of her cell. Her jailor used the brightness as a shield, but his height told her who he was. The giant man from before, this time with his hair wove into pigtails, unlocked the door.

"Get up," he commanded.

Bria trembled as she rose.

"Come," the man ushered. "Don't try running."

Even if she wanted to run, she had no energy to spare. Her head buzzed, her sides seared, and her eyes itched. The giant led her back up into the library. The towers of books reaffirmed just how small Bria felt; in fact, the entire library appeared to have tripled in size from the last time she saw it. Mazes of shelves, ceilings of identical glass, and chandeliers repeated every few steps; each turn looked identical to the last.

This isn't how it was. But with the dense fog in her mind, she couldn't be certain.

The giant led her through an archway, and back towards a corner of the library where an intricate mahogany desk sat. In the velvet chair waited the stout man who'd turned the bookshelves into a weapon. Alojzy, if Bria's memory served correct. He didn't look at her, instead pouring two glasses of wine and placing them on each end of the desk.

"Thank you, Jiang." Alojzy handed the giant man the bottle of wine. "I will inform you if we need anything else."

Jiang left, taking a long swig of the bottle as he disappeared through the shelves.

"Please, Briannabella." Alojzy glanced up, his eyes scurrying about like beetles on his face, "Take a seat."

The chair moved, catching her legs and forcing her into it.

"Have a drink."

The wine glass slid into her hands. She stared at her own reflection in the liquid. Her hair was matted to her forehead, her eyes worn, and her lips chapped. How long had she been below ground? Days? Weeks? Months?

No. Not that long. It couldn't have been that long.

"You can control things in the library," Bria whispered.

"Well, you're definitely smarter than Mr. Harley, aren't you?"

"Brent," she gasped. "Where is he? Is he okay?"

"He has not resurfaced," Alojzy shrugged, "but that is not important."

"Not important? He's one of you!"

"As were the others. But they failed, and we moved on." Alojzy leaned forward. "We're here to talk about you, Briannabella."

With a mere flick of his chin, the doors behind Bria slammed shut.

She glanced back to her glass of wine. "I want to go home."

"Where? To the tunnels? You don't have a home there," Alojzy spat. "You've been trespassing for years. They were never yours, my dear. I'm their architect. I created all of this. Your tunnels, the library...the entire infrastructure of this world!" He slammed his fists on the table. "You are lucky I did not stop you long ago, Briannabella."

"I haven't done any—"

Alojzy slammed his fists on the table, cutting her off. "You are a monster. Magic like you has been responsible for destruction across this world. Petty. Destructive. Mortals don't know how to use it."

"You're magic, too, though."

"We are the keepers of the mist. It's bigger than you. Bigger than all of us, so we do need the magic. But mortals? All you cause is destruction." He motioned at her cup and ordered, "Drink."

She brought the cup to her lips. It was bitter, not in the typical way of wine but instead like an unripe orange mingling in a bowl of fruit. Bria scowled and lowered the glass. "What is this?"

Alojzy ignored her, standing up from his desk and pacing about the room as he continued his rant. "Fortunately for you, Master Ningursu has decided that holding you here would cause further uproar. We don't need another war over a hostage—no matter how powerful."

"I'm a gardener...that's all."

Alojzy ignored her. "Whatever you are, Master Ningursu instructed me to let you go. We had hoped to lure Brenton back here, but seeing as he never came, he is either dead or never actually loved you."

"No..." Bria shook her head.

"Whatever the reason, you are not worth our efforts. Finish your drink, and you are free to go." Alojzy reopened the doors with a wave of his hand. "I cannot promise you'll find your way home, though. You're in my world now."

Bria rose, but the drink flew into her hands. Alojzy shifted his head to the side, and the glass raised, brushing her lips until the remaining liquid poured out of the glass and down her throat. Its bitterness slid down her tongue and into her throat.

She choked and dropped the glass, letting it shatter shattered on the floor.

"Now, you may go."

Bria stared at Alojzy, thinking it was a joke, but the man moved back to the desk and didn't regard her again. Her heart pounded, racing, pouring through her ears.

She ran out the door.

And ran.

And ran.

Through the shelves, she moved. Towers of books hid the exit.

Bria kept searching for freedom, no matter how long.

Minutes.

Hours.

Tick.

Tock.

At every turn, at every twist, the same towers of books greeted her. Her head spun, turning in circles, through the same arches and past the same titles. Or was it the walls that moved? The wine couldn't have been that strong.

If it *was* wine.

Her legs grew heavy, and she collapsed onto the ground, sobbing. All her thoughts raced to Brent, home, and her grandmother. Why couldn't everything be quiet? Why couldn't she live a normal life?

Because you were born with a flower growing from your head. And your mother planted you in the Senator's Garden, and you lived. Why did you live? What was the point if you're just going to die here in this—

She stared up towards the ceiling.

In this tree.

Shaking, she rose. Around her, the tree breathed. It buried stories in the growth rings beneath her feet. Thousands of years of history beneath her feet. Memories, stories, left unseen. *This doesn't belong to anyone.* She touched the floor with the tip of her fingers. *Alojzy may have constructed this library...but it's not his.*

She straightened her back. The tree whispered to her.

That's right. You belong to everyone.

And me. You belong to me.

Upon flattening her palm on the ground, the library trembled. Shelves fell over, the chandeliers shook, and embers danced from the candles. They scorched the floor, so Bria could see at last.

Another rumble shook the ground, and the maze fell. At last, the bark and vine-covered walls were within reach.

But the roaring did not hide the footsteps nearing her.

Bria turned to face Jiang and a birdlike woman with beady eyes. Alojzy walked a few paces behind them. Was he carrying something in his hands? From where Bria stood, it looked like a skull. The pounding in her head blurred her vision, so it could have just been a book.

Right?

"Come lie down," the woman beckoned with a thin finger.

Bria stepped back.

"Come here, girl," Jiang snapped.

"She's disoriented," a voice spoke from Alojzy's direction. It didn't belong to him, though.

"Good," Alojzy spoke next.

"Come," the woman said again. "You need rest."

"No," Bria whimpered. "You said I could go."

"You won't be able to like this. You're tired, you're dying—"

"No, I'm not!" Bria flung her arms back. The vines obeyed her as her fingers stretched out. They pounced, slithering through the books and knocking over tables chairs. At her feet, they lurched at the Mist Keepers and snagged them up by their legs.

Before they had a chance to react, the vines yanked the woman, Jiang, and Alojzy up by their feet. The object in Alojzy's hands fell into the aisle with a thud and rolled away.

Bria gripped the last remaining vine and let it carry her to the closest wall. When she arrived, she dropped. The wall collapsed before her. A few loose roots remained embedded in the dirt, and as soon as she passed through, they laced together as if she'd never been there.

She arrived in the tunnels, empty but for the cooing wind.

But Bria knew this tunnel like no other.

It was the one that would take her home.

CHAPTER THIRTY-SEVEN

THE GOD'S MEAL

Brent's mind wandered as he and Caroline strolled through the tunnels, but the library brought him back to the present. He gawked at the sight. Vines, roots, and dismembered bookshelves lay before him. Aelia, Alojzy, and Jiang dangled from the ceiling above by their ankles, while a muffled shout called from beneath a few books. Tomás had joined them at the edge of the stairs with the ghost with a long black beard. What was his name? Ned? Nedo? Brent's mind spun too much to remember. Both Tomás and the ghost yanked at Aelia's wrists to help her down. Yet with each tug, the vines around their ankles grew tighter.

"Bria..." Brent leaned against a table and gripped his side. "What happened?"

Caroline went to assist Tomás in helping their comrades down, but it was for naught. Whatever Bria did, wherever she ran off to, the vines weren't budging. Brent sensed her rage pulsating through the room. Her story lingered still. She'd been wandering in circles in the library, a glossed look on her face as if trapped in an endless maze. Circles and circles, around she went. A less vivid tale depicted Jiang pushing her off the second story and then carrying her away into the mist. She returned later, following Jiang, her head turned to the floor. Back into the haze, she loitered, only to use her anger to break free.

"Bri..." He stepped backward and glared up at Jiang. "What did you do to her?!"

"Nothing!" Jiang spat. "She's the one who did this to *us*."

"She came for help! You pushed her..."

"Well, she's gone now!"

"Where?!"

"Enough!"

Brent glanced towards the sound of the new voice. Ningursu's head rolled out from beneath one of the shelves, using his partial nose to push him into the center of the group. His one white eye darted about, before resting on Brent.

"Shouting does us little good," Ningursu spoke, chewing on his words. "Caroline, Tomás, please get the others down. We shall reconvene in the conference room."

"The vines aren't letting us, sir," Tomás replied.

"We have blades." Ningursu's stare did not waver. "Brenton, please take my head and join me. We shall talk."

Brent looked to Caroline for approval. A steady nod granted him permission, and he scooped Ningursu's head into his arms. Part of him wanted to punt the head across the room and return to his anger. He managed to pocket the rage for now and instead took Ningursu's head back towards the conference room.

Ningursu kept on munching on something in his mouth. He stopped for a moment as Brent placed the head on the pedestal at the forefront of the room.

"Have a seat, Brenton. We have yet to have a talk like this." Ningursu smiled. It was a weird smile where the lips he still had crooked upwards, while the other half formed an eerie line of rotting teeth.

"I don't have time, sir. Please—"

"Yes, you do."

Something coerced Brent into consent. "Okay, a'ight, a few minutes."

Ningursu chewed aloud again, not speaking. Brent fidgeted with his hand, picking at his wrist, as the odd silence lingered between them.

That didn't mean it was silent, though.

Mist drizzled through the room, passing over Ningursu's head and washing through Brent's vision. It reminded him of what the Order said: The Effluvium always watched; it was always there. Did they know a thousand stories lived in one small corner of the world? Could they see the past like Brent did?

Why didn't it stop?

"I know we have not been as welcoming as we should have been these last few weeks," Ningursu stated. "I promise it has all been with good reason."

"You tried wiping my memory, you...where did you take Bria? What did you...I want...what's happening?"

"There have been other apprentices like you who developed this sort of sensitivity."

"Caroline already told me that! She said they failed." He didn't like that word after saying it. Failure meant there was a chance at succeeding. What they'd been saying though...there was no chance. He was going to succumb to the stories and forget his identity.

"To be frank, they went insane before the curse even took them. We hoped to save you that fate and make your death less painful."

Brent clenched his teeth. "But maybe I want a chance." For a moment, the story of the juggler invaded his thoughts. He reached for Ningursu's head, but before throwing it, he managed to return to his own mind. "I know who I am. My name is Brent Harley. Give me a chance."

"You honestly believe you can control the stories? That you can keep them at bay?"

"I can try." Why wouldn't they give him a chance? There had to be a way. Every member of the Council seemed all too willing to concede. Perhaps they were even too willing to surrender to death. Curses were meant to be broken. Failures were supposed to become successes.

Bria would tell him that, at least.

"Why do you think your experience will be different from the others?"

"I don't think that," Brent admitted, fidgeting again beneath Ningurus's judgmental gaze. "But if...I mean, someone's gotta be able to understand this power. I think...I think I gotta try at least. I don't wanna lie down and die or something."

"I see. If that is what you want."

"Does that mean you'll let me? That you won't...I mean, you won't erase my mind?"

"For now, if that is what you want. But you must follow the *rules*."

"How can I if no one tells me them?" Brent's nostrils flared. "Why isn't Bria allowed here? What do you have against Magii like her? She's All she wants is answers! That's—that's all."

"She has sight, and she's powerful...very powerful. And that is enough for us to worry." Ningursu ground his teeth. "We will teach you all you need to learn, my child. But you must be patient with us."

"No! I tried that! Where is she? You've been holding me back. Where is she?" Brent rose, tension rising in his chest like an army marching upon a city. "If you hurt her—"

"She's fine, she's safe. She's not here, so she must be, right?" Ningursu choked on whatever was in his mouth, then cleared his throat. "She's fine."

Brent furrowed his brow. "I'm sorry, sir, but I didn't think you ate anything?"

Ningursu stopped. "It is a habit. I enjoy tasting things."

"But you haven't got a tongue."

"I still have remnants of taste." He hacked again.

"Do you want me to help? You're choking."

"It is fine."

"Are you sure?" Brent peered through the hole in Ningursu's jaw. Something thin and white sat between the skeleton's teeth. "It looks like...paper."

"Yes, I enjoy the taste of paper."

"You're lying."

"Do not pry into my affairs, boy."

"Open up," Brent demanded.

Ningursu shook his head.

"What is it?"

"That is not your business, Brenton."

"Open your damn mouth," Brent grabbed Ningursu's jawbone and pulled. Despite continued objections, a sudden stiffness in Brent's shoulders, and Ningursu's attempt to bite, Brent unclenched the mouth and reached inside.

Stop! Stop! Stop! This isn't right! You must listen and stop!

No, keep going, boy!

Grab the skull! Dismember it!

Stop!

Brent wrapped his fingers around the white item, removed it from his skull, and clutched it to his chest. His hand shook as he unraveled his grip, revealing a single white camellia, unscathed.

"Shite...Bria." Brent looked at Ningursu and demanded, "What are you doing to her?"

"Have you considered I enjoy chewing on flowers?" Ningursu scoffed. "Do not read into it, Brenton, it does you no good."

"This," he held up the flower, "is one of *her* camellias."

"Brenton—"

"I'm not stupid! What have you done?"

As he shouted, Aelia, Tomás, Jiang, and Alojzy joined them in the conference room. Brent spun around, wide-eyed, and backed away from them.

"Brenton, relax." Tomás reached out.

"No!"

"You are ill," Aelia insisted. "Come lie down. I shall mix you a sleeping tonic."

Brent pushed back from them. "No, I don't...I can't trust any of you!"

"Brenton!"

Dizziness tightened around his head as he fled from the room. He ignored the Council's shouts.

He toppled over Caroline just outside the door.

"What is it?" She gripped his shoulders and shook him. "What is wrong?"

He showed her the camellia. "It's weird. Ningursu was chewing on this..."

Caroline's face colored, blotches of gray and purple highlighting the terror on her face. Offering no explanation, she shoved Brent forward. "Oh for sards sake..."

"What's happening?"

"Ninguru's primary magic circles around controlling and omniscient sight,"

"So, he's controlling her?"

"Possibly. Just go! Find her!"

"I don't...I don't know where."

"Use the mist."

"Right...the mist," Brent gulped. "Use the mist..."

He trailed along the rows of books, searching once again for Bria's story. It ruptured the library as a bursting heart. The vines twisting and turning, Bria screaming for freedom, and then her escape through the wall. Clear as day to Brent, he darted out of the library.

"Bria?!?" he shouted down the tunnels.

Nothing.

He glanced down the paths to Mert and Hutch's Creek, but no recent story highlighted the shadows. The tunnels from the Capitol reflected his nights with Bria, laughing and kissing, sending heavy waves through his chest. It'd be so easy to get lost in the happy stories, abandon the fray and live in a dream.

Brent turned to the Newbird's Arm tunnel. There, the story returned: Bria toppled out of the wall and ran. In her wake, the vines and roots moved, following her as she headed home. As did everything else. The ground shook, the stalagmites trembled, and the fire skipped off the wall. Even the mist grew thicker.

Or was it the story?

When Brent blinked, the story vanished, except for the garden now making a home in the passage.

CHAPTER THIRTY-EIGHT

Trepidation

Bria was everything at once. She was the wind as it fluttered through the trees, skipping through song notes and surfing across the river running through town. At every step, the trees breathed, the flowers cooed, and ground beat. It brought her back to her childhood, of fantastical dreams and few nightmares, where stories and magic thrived.

A distant nagging in her mind brought her home to Newbird's Arm. The colors of the Senator's Garden nearly blinded her, shimmering in the daylight sun. She commanded the trees to provide shade, straightening her back to the sun as she walked, her bare feet digging into the ground.

Why did I come back? It made more sense to return to the mountains and find Brent. Newbird's Arm provided no refuge or hope; her father's home sat dark, the roads belonged to the guards, and the Temple still watched with its red eye. To venture into the market would put a bullseye on her back.

The nagging continued in her head. *Keep going,* it urged. *Go. Exist. Be.*

She clutched a tree. Bark created a varnish around her wrist. More roots, branches, and saplings bore life at her ankles. As she walked, they followed. Everything vivid, everything alive, spun through her as if she still stood in the library.

Where am I going? Why am I here?

Nature followed her from the Senator's Gardens. Did someone call her name? A buzzing clogged her ears. Stones overturned as she moved. A gentle dew formed in the air, mingling with the clouds strolling from the top of the mountains.

When did she start crying? Tears dripped from her cheeks and onto her neck. Sweat and salt stung her skin.

The market square already swarmed with patrons. Even with the light, the entire situation appeared dark. The Guard controlled everything. Children clung to their parents. Bria swore one wrong outburst, and the market would go up in flames.

In her own daze, Bria witnessed Janette Harley kneeling at the foot of the Temple with a group of other women, all gazing towards the Year Glass and humming prayers. Elder Don Van, as he often did, peered from his perch above the atrium. Cadets marched about, led by Cadet Carver and Cadet Lawry, dragging the vagrants to and from the Pit. Shouts rang. Curses screamed. Everything spun.

"Stop," Bria whispered.

At her voice, the small garden she once planted in the market exploded. She ordered the flowers and trees to grab those who did harm: a cadet beating an elderly vagrant, a merchant denying another with the black stamp a purchase, and another woman who dared to spit on those smaller than her.

Had the square always been so dismal? It used to be a spot of life, of prosperity. Was all of this because the monster ravaged the down?

Perhaps it really is my fault.

The foliage continued blooming. She heard it all growing. It didn't stop.

It couldn't stop.

It wouldn't stop.

The storm clouds thickened over the edge of the mountains, taking all color from the sky except for a tinge of yellow.

"Bria."

She flinched at her name.

"Briannabella!" Her grandmama hobbled over to her. "What are you doing? Briannabella! Can you hear me? What are you doing?"

Bria curled in on herself. "I don't know."

"Do you recognize me?"

"Yes."

"Then you need to stop!"

"I can't."

"Briannabella!"

"Everything's alive," Bria choked out. "I feel all of it."

Her grandmama held her. "Let go. It's okay. Let go."

"I can't," she sobbed and curled up on the ground. When she closed her eyes, she saw four lights illuminating the twisting paths of books and shelves. Her mind became the maze again: locked, starved, and decayed.

I'm so confused. I don't understand what's happening. Bria wiped her eyes. What was that Brent always recited? His mantra: his name, his birth, his permanence. *I'm Briannabella Smidt. Sometimes I call myself Rho. I am in control.*

I'm Bria Smidt.

I'm Rhodana, the Forest Queen.

I am in control.

She reached for her grandmama, committing to her mantra. As if the lock in her head unsnapped, she found a way to breathe again. The trees retreated, the vines withered, and the flowers rescinded. While the clouds remained and the mist thickened, Bria, at last, returned to herself.

Whatever had locked her into the mania fell. She glanced to her grandmama, then towards townsfolk. Everyone saw her as she was: her name would paint newspapers for weeks.

Captain Carver broke the inaction. He stood at the stairs of the Temple. Behind him, a figure in a red robe loitered in the doorway, but the Effluvium rolling off the mountains captured the tower, masking him. It reminded her of—

No, don't be stupid, that's Elder Don Van. Bria rose, her hands trembling.

"Oi! Where the fuck ya been, doll?" Christof scolded. "Get over 'ere. We got some shite to talk about."

"Christof, be quiet!" Captain Carver barked.

"But Dad! I should decide. I'm betrothed to—"

"We can discuss your poor judgment later." The Captain stepped forward. "Miss Smidt, what do you have to say for yourself?"

Before Bria could answer, thunder rumbled through the sky. The putrid clouds had grown closer, reeking of sewage and gas. A few of the townsfolk gagged. Bria couldn't move; the stench had left an imprint in her mind. It still haunted her, a memory of a beast with crooked eyes and dismembered skin.

A memory of Brent lying in a pool of his own blood.

"Miss Smidt!" Captain Carver yelled over the thunder as he took another step forward, "how do you explain all of this?"

"I can't!" Bria snapped.

Her grandmama stepped in front of Bria. "Captain Carver! She needs rest! Let's not interrogate her now! Let me take her home, please. Her father must be worried."

"Be quiet, you old hag," Captain Carver snarled. "This isn't an interrogation. Miss Smidt is under arrest on counts of witchcraft and terrorism."

"She's done nothing wrong!"

"We all saw." Captain Carver ordered his cadets, "Grab her."

Bria skidded back and stomped once. Roots overturned the bricks beneath the cadet's feet, sending them backward. As they regained their footing, she unhitched from her grandmama's side and darted out of the market.

Her energy fled as soon as she ran. Calling upon the trees took the effort of lifting two fully grown men and running placed two more on her ankles.

Just need to sit for a few minutes... The grass caught her as she toppled forward.

Footsteps neared.

She hoisted herself onto her elbows and crawled forward, using each blade of grass as an anchor.

They came closer. Someone called her name.

"Go away!" she shouted. She didn't look back, but she told the nearest tree to reach for whoever came, snag them up by their ankles, toss them—

"Bri! It's me!"

She glanced behind her. "Brent..."

He hung by one foot from the tree, wearing a puffy blouse and pants too short for him. His hair stuck out at all angles, eyes tired and cheeks hallow. But, of all things, he was *alive*.

The tree dropped him, and Brent gimped to her side. Bria bawled as he gathered her into his arms.

"Hey, hey, it's okay, a'ight? You're okay," he whispered. "It's okay."

"You're alive."

"Yeah. Yeah, I don't know how, but I am. Let's get outta here, a'ight?"

"I don't know what's happening; I couldn't control it. I'm a...I'm a monster."

"No, no, it's okay. Relax." Brent started towards the garden, holding her tight against his chest.

She touched his cheek. "I thought you were dead."

"A few fortunate circumstances saved me."

They turned into the gardens. Hearing Brent heave for each breath, she climbed out of his arms. Something felt different, though. The Gardens had retreated to their normal selves, but the silence they slept in murmured of fear. The yellow tinge in the sky hadn't set.

Something, or someone, watched them.

Pow!

A pistol sounded off behind her.

"Harley!"

Bria recognized the voice. "Christof!"

Brent turned. "Ah, Cadet Carver. Fancy seeing you out and about. Thought you'd be brooding."

Bria stomped on Brent's foot.

"Get away from her, Harley," Christof spat. "It don't do ya well to be with her as it is."

"Why? Because you want to arrest her?" Brent furrowed her brow. "She's not a monster. You should know that."

"She wasn't...until you kidnapped her! You've messed with her head."

"No, he hasn't!" Bria shouted.

"Be quiet, Briannabella. If you're gonna be my bride, you better learn to keep your lips sealed."

"I'll never marry you!"

"What? We have already been marked for each other, Briannabella. Who do you think would marry you?

Him?" Christof scoffed. "He broke the heart of beautiful, pious Jemma. She would have *saved* him. Well, perhaps. He may have corrupted her just as he has done to you."

"Jemma..." Brent stiffened. "I tried to call it off."

"Well, she's been in the Temple for over almost a fortnight now, cleansing her soul of yer fuckin' despicable ass." Christof's eyes lit up, obviously relishing all of this. "She gave everything. Now, she'll be nothing but a prude cause ya had to go drilling down in that thing, didn't you?" Christof sneered at Bria. "Fuckin' whore, am I right?"

"Enough Christof!" Bria begged. "You've been spending too much time with Cadet Lawry. If you're so disgusted by me, then call off this bullshit. Let us go in peace."

"Ya can get back, y'know." Christof stepped closer. He smelled of tobacco on his breath and liquor on his tongue. "Cleanse yourself, free yourself of this damn demon."

"He's not a demon!" She glanced at Brent. He hadn't moved since Christof mentioned Jemma. "You used to be at least sort of nice, Christof. I don't know what happened."

"I grew up."

"No," Brent retorted. "You became a daddy's boy is what happened. Was it after your ma disappeared that you clung to him? Your father's not a good man, he..." Brent looked up, a mist gathering at his feet. "You know that he killed her, right?"

"What did you say!?"

"He beat her...carried her body right over there." Brent pointed into the forest. "It's still there."

"Liar!" Christof rushed at Brent, shoving Bria to the side. She fell back, caught by the roots, but Brent's body thudded to the ground behind her. Punches and curses, grunts and shouts began, Bria couldn't bring herself to look. Was Brent even fighting back? Had he given up?

No, he can't handle that...he'll die. No, please... She shook her head and dug her fingers into the roots. *No. I won't let him. He can't.*

"CHRISTOFER CARVER!"

Bria had never been so relieved to hear Captain Carver's voice.

"CADET! LET GO OF HIM!"

Christof retreated. To Bria's relief, Brent sat up, his face bloodied.

"Grab the girl. I'll deal with Mr. Harley," the Captain demanded. A few other cadets gathered behind him.

"Dad! Miss Smidt hasn't done anything—it's Harley! He's manipulating her."

"You're lovestruck, son. Grab her and take her to the barracks, a'ight?"

"But Dad!"

"Cadet Carver, I am ordering you to take Miss Smidt. She is under arrest for use of witchcraft and terrorism. Harley is a vagrant and nothing more."

"Dad, Bria wouldn't hurt—"

"He's right!" Brent grunted as he rose. "It isn't her fault. It's...it's mine."

"You might be a damn vagrant, but you haven't caused much of a problem since Year Birth. She has!" Captain Carver spat. "Don't try to protect the girl."

"None of this has anything to do with her!"

"It's sweet you want to protect your little friend, but what do you have any proof?

"You want proof?" Brent glanced at Bria. "I'll give you proof. My whole fucking life, every single one of you decided that I was a demon and a vagrant because I had gray eyes. You kept saying I was susceptible or whatever! I tried to ignore it and be a model citizen, but no...it didn't matter. No one hired me; I couldn't even leave. So, I told stories, because it made people smile. But then you took that away and told me to grow up.

"You told me they were *lies*! No one...*no one* gave me a chance because you stamped me when I was a child." He lifted his wrist. "And now you're stamping children again! You stopped, but now...no...you didn't learn. So, you know what? Fuck it. At least the demons let me be...me. You think that's wrong? Fine. Let me show you what I can do."

He threw his arms back. The mist exploded out of his body, seeping through the surrounding trees. A hundred stories took over the garden at once: of the Senator's gardeners trimming hedges, of past galas and weddings and parades, and of Bria's childhood, learning flowers with her grandpapa in the summer haze.

Brent emerged from the mist and joined Bria. The stories twirled around him while he gripped her hands. "Run, a'ight? Get outta here and run. Please."

"I don't want to leave you. Let me help," she pleaded.

"No! Go! Please. It will do us no good if we're both arrested. I'm not gonna last long; they're gonna grab me."

Bria understood, but it didn't stop her from crying. "You're not allowed to die. I'll come get you. You'll...we'll be okay."

"I hope so."

"Brent—"

"Go, please. This is your territory. Own it." Brent squeezed her hand one last time, then let her go, falling backward into the mist.

She didn't look back, scampering into the trees. Shouts raved, and men goaded. Another pistol sounded off. Bria ducked against a trunk, holding her ears. She could not see Brent through the smog coating the gardens. Sleep pulled at her eyelids, but she had to keep going. Find an entrance to the tunnels, and she'd be safe.

Unless the Council waited below.

Her magic continued to be unreliable. It caught her from falling before, but now it fizzled as her head seared. The flowers sang out of tune songs while the trees gasped. She wanted to bury herself away in the ground, let the foliage heal her wounds, and let her dreams bring her to a simpler time. But she had lost control. She couldn't leave. Things fell apart. Everywhere screamed.

"Lawry! Arnolds! Cooper!" Captain Carver barked. "Go after her! Now!"

Bria darted further into the forest, ducking into the foliage and grappling at the roots. Still, the trees didn't obey. Alone and powerless, she ran.

It proved fruitless.

The Cadets trampled through the bushes, crunched on leaves, and rushed towards her. Cadet Lawry led the pack, barreling towards her on his skinny legs. He reminded her of the Diabolo. No mercy, no kindness; he could slash her open without flinching, she was sure of it.

"C'mere little flower," Cadet Lawry beckoned. "It's time to play."

Bria tripped back, clunking her head against the root. Despite her pleas, the trees did not come to rescue her as the two other cadets circled her.

"You disgusting lil' bitch," Cadet Lawry snarled, revealing his crooked, gold-speckled teeth. "Back where I come from, sleeping with vagrants meant you're a harlot...a whore. An upskirt. It's a shame too, 'cause you're such a pretty little thing." He gripped Bria's cheeks. "You woulda made a fine wife to Chris or someone of the like. Shame ya gonna end up in the Pit. Or dead. A fucking whore and a fucking demon-infested cretin."

"Please let me go," Bria begged.

"Let you go? Why? So, you can spread more magic?" Cadet Lawry's breath hit her face. "So you can fuck another twelve vagrants? I don't think so."

"Fuck you," Bria spat.

Cadet Lawry backed away, feigning disbelief and fumbling with something on his belt. Another smirk. He removed his switchblade and brought it to Bria's chin. "If you insist."

Bria squirmed, but the other two cadets tightened their grip around her. Cadet Lawry cut open her blouse. Belts fell. Hands reached. Pushed. Tore. Dismantled.

A scream.

With the scream, the forest spoke. Bria's powers flooded back at just the right moment, protecting her from all else but a violating touch. The roots launched themselves at the cadets. A small tree landed on one cadet's legs, and the roots tossed the other into the bushes.

Bria ran, not daring to look back at Cadet Lawry. Not wanting to look back at any of them.

"Oi!" Cadet Lawry shouted.

Trees toppled behind her. *Thud, thud, thud;* each fallen tree shook the ground. Cadet Lawry kept at her, though. The one time she looked back, his eyes flared like a monster. He might as well have been the Diabolo.

Another tree fell. Roots grappled to the sky.

And another.

And another.

They kept collapsing. A barricade formed.

Thud.

Thud.

Thud.

Cadet Lawry kept shouting after her, "GET BACK HE—"

A large oak fell. Dirt flew into the air.

As did Cadet Lawry's body.

It hit the ground like a rag doll. His neck cracked as it hit a root. Cadet Lawry's eyes bugged out of his head, gasping for breath, but remaining locked on Bria as his face turned purple.

"No...oh no," Bria gulped. "Please, no..."

He stopped squirming. A smirk inched across his lips in those final moments, before unhinging, leaving his mouth ajar.

"No. I didn't mean to...no, please!" Bria cried out. "Please you can't be dead, please!"

She fell to her knees, holding onto the shreds of her blouse. The roots stiffened around Cadet Lawry's body. The wind bellowed and cast leaves across his body. Mist followed.

From it emerged a figure, but she could not make out its face. Bria scrambled backward. "No...no, please, I'm not...please don't take me back!"

"Bria! Calm yourself!"

As the figure emerged from the mist, Bria screamed, burrowing deeper into the ground. Cadet Lawry's face stared back from a woman's body.

The face blinked, and in its place, the mist took away one identity and replaced it with Caroline's haunted stare.

"Go away, please go away." Bria shook her head. "Please."

Caroline stooped to look her in the eye. "You are okay. I am here to help."

Bria glanced between Caroline and Cadet Lawry's body. He still did not move.

"No...I don't trust any of you." Bria glanced around nervously. "Brent needs—"

"*You* need help," Caroline offered Bria her hand. "You are tired and distraught. Let us help you."

"I don't want to go back."

"I shall not take you back to the library. There is a small house where an old woman died just beyond the clearing," Caroline assured her. "It is empty. You can stay there until you are well. Do you understand?"

Bria shook her head, not daring to look Caroline in the eyes. "Leave me—leave me alone."

"You will not be able to keep fighting if you do not rest."

Bria resisted. She attempted to scurry backward, only to hit her head against the tree. Like her powers, she sunk to the ground. Her mind kept circling back to Brent. She had to go...she couldn't let him fight alone!

"I shall not put up with stubbornness. Up. Now." Caroline beckoned. "I will carry you if you refuse."

Resistance proved to be useless. Bria grew limp as Caroline picked her up, carrying her away from the destruction.

As Caroline had promised, a small cabin resided deep in the woods, nestled between the river and a series of oak trees. It smelled of mothballs and old vegetables. A few flies buzzed about the rotting fruit on the table, and cobwebs decorated the ceiling. The couch Caroline lay her upon reminded Bria of the one in her grandmama's home.

After changing into a blouse too large for her and a pair of men's pants kept up by a thick belt, Bria ate the mediocre potpie Caroline cooked and gathered herself onto the couch. The tears, at last, stopped, replaced with humidity in the air, and dabs of sweat on her forehead. Closing her eyes brought nothing but nightmares, of Cadet Lawry's hallowed face, of Brent's pleas, and of the emptiness in her home.

But sleep never cared about nightmares. Eyelids fell, and consciousness waned.

Bria let it come with a blanket full of horrors and trepidation.

CHAPTER THIRTY-NINE

THE CLEANSE

How am I not dead?

Brent asked it after Christof bloodied his face, after the mist told a hundred stories at once, and after Captain Carver dragged him to the Temple and down into the prayer crevasses.

Still, Brent didn't die.

Was it Bria's pleas that kept him alive? Did she whisk him away under her magic spell? Or had his own desire to prove the Council wrong kept his heart beating?

He didn't know, lost again in voices shouting. Hundreds of voices, young and old. Children cried, vagrants hollered. The crevasses overflowed into the hallway. What belonged to the past? What belonged to the present?

The Captain locked Brent into a private crevasse on charges of collusion and terrorism, without food or water. Not that Brent wanted to move, or eat, or drink; even blinking sent pain through his skull. Dizziness settled in, and in his dysphoria, he traveled the personalities of the dead. The only thing that kept him sane was the thought of Bria's face, her smiles as they walked along the shores in Mert and the flowers in her hair. Then he remembered her wails from the forest and, in frustration, threw his body against the wall to demand freedom.

The door didn't budge. Brent collapsed, gasping for air, holding the wounds on his sides.

He may have slept, but it came in whispers. His hunger argued with his thirst. Weak. Dying.

But not dead.

When able, Brent paced around the crevasse, reading the Scripture to occupy his thoughts. It spoke of the welcoming arms of the Effluvium, of finding peace and tranquility, and warding away all that taints the pure sole: magic, stories, and imperfections.

Stupid. Brent dug his nail into one of the carvings. *They've never seen the Effluvium.*

The door opened at last when Brent finished reading the Scripture for the fourth time.

"The bath is ready, Brenton," Brother Roy Al did not make eye contact as he entered the room.

"Right...Level Two," Brent bowed his head, stumbling forward.

Brother Roy Al stripped Brent down and guided him out of the crevasse. Vulnerability mocked him as he joined the line waiting outside of the washroom. They spared the women and children the humiliation, garnished in robes to protect such crucial innocence.

Someone called out to Brent as he took his position in line. A woman's voice, distant over the crowd of vagrants. It came past his father, who stood with a glazed look in his eye, and Micca, who bolstered at the front of the line. *This must be most of the vagrant population, but why are there children here? Did Elder Don Van go through with it?*

"Brent!" the voice called again.

Jemma pushed through the line back to him. He raised his hand to wave, but then his heart sunk. At Jemma's side stood his younger sister, her dark gray eyes forming tired pits in her face, a fresh brand on her wrist.

"No..." Brent gulped. "No...Alexandria!"

"Brent!" His sister darted to him, wrapping her arms around his legs.

"I'm so sorry, Alexandria. I should've come back sooner. I'm so sorry." He picked her up, glancing at the brand on her wrist.

"Is this because I told a story to my friend?" Alexandria asked. "I wanted to be like you..."

"No, it's because there are evil people." He traced his own stamp. "It'll be a'ight. I promise."

"Brother Roy Al has voiced his opinion on the matter," Jemma interjected. "It's absolutely appalling! This wasn't supposed to ever happen again, not after the Smoke Riots, but no one wants to listen. We'll make sure your sister isn't treated the way you were. It isn't right."

"Thank you." He sighed. "Jem, listen, I'm sorry. I—I ran away with...I mean, I ran, you know? We should've called it off before...and now you're...I'm sorry."

Jemma placed a finger to his lips. "I'm here on my own terms."

"Christof said—"

"Christof is a fool."

"You used to say that he was—"

"It doesn't matter. I was a fool." Jemma straightened her back. "We never should have agreed to something that made us both miserable. I thought I was doing right by the Order, but the Order needs a good talking to if you ask me."

"So, you don't want to join anymore?"

Jemma beamed. "After this last round of cleansing, I will join the Order as Brother Roy Al's protégé. The Order might be wrong—cleansing children, treating people like scum—but how else can I change it if I run away?" Jemma's smile radiated across her face, a slice of joy in the sterile hallway mourning the day. Perhaps in another life, another time, the betrothal may have worked—or at least they may not have had the tenacious discord that governed their betrothal. No, they may have at least been friends.

But Brent saw his life hanging by a thread. One snip and it would most certainly be over.

"Brent?"

He glanced at Alexandria. "Hey, it's a'ight. We're just gonna have a quick bath, okay?"

"I'm not scared."

"You're brave then...because I'm scared."

"It's because I've been telling myself stories...you should tell a story to make yourself less scared," Alexandria pled. "One about a man who fights evil ice mermaids! Or maybe the mermaids are good, and the man is evil!"

"Oh, uh, I dunno..." Brent placed Alexandria on the ground and peered around the corridor. Already a hundred more tales mingled in the mist, swerving in and out of the living. He saw a story of a man who for hours rang a bell, day after day, and another of two lovers making their home in one of the crevasses. Most stories stayed dry, fundamentally the same tale told of brothers and sisters preaching, men and women witnessing the cleanse, and of children screaming.

Including his own childhood, if he looked deep enough.

"Please, Brent!" Alexandria begged again. "Tell me a story!"

A few others in line glanced at him. Micca called out from his spot. His father turned. Even Jemma, for once, glanced in his direction.

"Oh, uh, a'ight." Brent flushed and picked at his wrist. "I guess I can tell you one...about the mermaids of ice..."

Off he went, constructing what he could about a pirate sailing off to sea in an obscure flying machine. Past the Lands of Mert and Spinoza the pirate flew until a storm knocked the pirate's ship into the Eastern Sea. Crash! The pirate fell, awoken on a bed of rainbow ice to meet a mermaid with white hair and snow for eyelashes, and a song as vivid as waves crashing to shore.

Any other time, he would have pulled back from the story as his powers took hold. But as Alexandria suggested, his fears vanished, and he wrapped himself in the mist. By the time the story ended, everyone watched him, and the mist presented the mermaid of ice freezing the pirate upon a glacier to look upon the world forevermore.

"So, um, yeah," Brent exhaled, letting the mist dissipate. "That's the story."

Applause erupted and captured whispers about magic returning. But the conversations stopped moments after they began, halted by a crack of a whip.

Captain Carver and Elder Don Van stood in the front of the corridor.

"Mr. Harley, I should have known you'd cause trouble again," the Captain snarled. "Should've left ya in confinement."

"Now Glenndal," Elder Don Van remarked, "it is crucial to cleanse the boy, correct? With all the others, we shall rid him of demons...even if it takes a few additional levels."

"Additional levels," Jemma muttered beside Brent, then she flexed her back and called, "Sirs, pardon, my name's Jemma Reds, and I'm joining the Order in a couple days. If my studies are correct, no one has performed a cleanse beyond Level Three in decades. Is this really—"

Captain Carver cracked his whip again. "Shut it!"

“Ah Miss Reds.” Elder Don Van approached her. “It is a rarity for you to speak out. You have been taught what the Order stands for.”

“Peace and Prosperity,” Jemma replied.

“Peace, Prosperity, and Obedience, as you have forgotten.” Elder Don Van glanced at Brent. “We have been fortunate not to need to cleanse anyone in a long time beyond Level Three, as Humility seems to wash away most people’s self-righteousness. But can Humility wash away demons? I think not. So, we must do our best to cleanse the Effluvium, even if it means more extreme measures.”

Brent looked away.

Hold your tongue. Don’t speak.

But he’s wrong.

Shush.

After the Elder and Captain abandoned the crevasses, the other Brothers and Sisters of the Order led each person into the bath one by one. Unlike the time before, the cleansing took mere seconds, leaving Brent with a dull stinging on his skin.

They then led Brent and the others into the atrium above, where patrons watched as they filed along to the stage, where Elder Don Van and Brother Roy Al preached. Captain Carver leaned against the far wall, chewing tobacco and combing the side of his whip with his fingers. More than half of the patrons watched in horror as they entered, while the others spat in their direction and threw obscene gestures.

Brent held his sister back as they passed their mother. His heart stung, watching her, thinner and more exhausted than he'd ever seen her. She wiped her eyes with an old kerchief and refused to meet his gaze. He understood; he'd left her without a word. She'd done everything to keep him and Alexandria safe. Nothing mattered, though.

This had to be Level Three: Humility and Honesty in front of the entire town. Would anyone ever turn away from the Order with all eyes on them?

Each time Elder Don Van called a name, the line moved.

"Mr. Robert Abe Harley."

Brent watched as his father walked forward. He hardly recognized him. They had shaved his father's hair down, his gray eyes had turned white, and face as was smooth as a babe's bottom.

"Do you promise to give your mind, body, and soul to the Order of the Effluvium?" Elder Don Van asked.

"Ay," Brent's father croaked.

"Our arms are open and welcoming. You have cooperated with pleasure, and we are happy to send you home." Elder Don Van kissed Robert's cheeks. "Be well, my child."

Brent gawked as his father walked to the back of the atrium, slouching and unmoved, not daring to look at his children or his wife.

Brother Roy Al called out this time. "Miss Alexandria Jan Harley."

Alexandria glanced at Brent.

"It's a'ight," Brent mumbled.

She tiptoed to the stage.

The Brother kneeled to Alexandria's level. "Do you promise to be a good girl and avoid evil?"

"Yes." Her voice rang with the confidence Brent lacked.

"Good girl." Brother Roy Al then guided Alexandria to her mother. Brent watched them reunite, but even then, his mother refused to meet his gaze.

Elder Don Van spoke next. "Mr. Brenton Rob Harley."

Brent stepped forward. Murmurs followed his name; this time, they were real.

"Do you promise to give your mind, body, and soul to the Order of the Effluvium? Do you agree to denounce all sins and turn over all evidence of demons and magic? Do you promise to help us cleanse the world?"

Brent glanced behind him. Jemma mouthed the word, "yes" at him. Others with gray eyes, others who told stories, others who had demons on their back...they all would say yes. But nothing would change, would it?

Besides, the world needed magic and stories.

"No. I don't think the world needs cleansing. And if you...if you believed in the Effluvium, you would agree."

Elder Don Van's eyes narrowed. "Is that really your answer?"

"Yes."

"So be it. Brenton Rob Harley, we hereby sentence you to the five levels of cleansing by the Order of the Effluvium on counts of magic usage, terrorism, rape, and collusion. This is non-negotiable and outside the jurisdiction of the Senate of Rosada."

Brent bowed his head, accepting the defeat. At this point, despite the pleas of his mother and even Jemma's objections, he believed this to be right. If he turned himself into this madness, his sister wouldn't be harmed anymore. Perhaps Bria would be able to run.

So, when Captain Carver left his dragged Brent back into the empty crevasses below, Brent did not struggle or fight, but merely yield to the man's strength.

Brent lay on the floor of the crevasse for hours, recalling Bria's face, and reciting his mantra to keep his head in place. Despite giving in, he wouldn't let himself become nothing. If he was to become the Order's victim now, he'd go as himself.

His name. His birth. His constant.

My name is Brent Harley.

I am not a demon.

My name is Brent Harley.

I am a Mist Keeper.

My name is Brent Harley.

You won't change me.

The door opened sometime later.

"Harley!" Christof entered the room, fury striking his face. "You fucker!"

Brent sat up.

"You killed him!"

"Who?" Brent asked.

"Chet! He's dead!"

"I've been *here*."

Christof held his father's whip tight, shaking as he continued, "You've gotten into her head! She didn't have magic until you fucked her; you raped her! She was an innocent little flower before you came and—and filled her with your magic and vagrancy and lies! You fucking demon!"

"Is that what you believe?" Brent shook his head. "You don't know anything about her. Or me. You've got some messed up view or something. I mean, Bria's not some innocent flower if that's what you think."

Christof cracked the whip, though it limped at the end like a wet noodle.

"If she killed Cadet Lawry..." Brent winced. "It means...I mean...it means that he was going to hurt her."

"He was a good man!" Christof sent the whip inches from Brent's legs. "An admirable guard. A bit of a floozy, but a good man! He did what was right for the Order!"

Brent chuckled.

"Shut it!"

The whip slammed down on Brent's body.

Again.

And again.

"Cadet Carver!"

Brent exhaled and brought his knees to his stomach. *Still alive.*

"Father! Elder Don Van!" Christof pivoted. "I only was administering Level Four, per your dictation and—"

"It must be controlled," Elder Don Van said calmly. "Malice does naught to eliminate the demons. They thrive on that." He joined Brent on the floor. "Well boy, what say you? Are the demons stirring in your core, or have you come to accept the Effluvium's light?"

"I think..." Brent spat. "I think you don't really know the Effluvium."

"You believe you do, boy?"

"Better than you," Brent snorted. "I can see it. It's surrounding you now, Elder Don Van. It's telling me...it's telling me about..." He shook his head and squinted into the mist. It showed a story of a man, decades younger, working in a stone building, hooking children up to electric buzzing machines. Brent furrowed his brow. "Why would you need to use electricity, Elder? What good does hooking children up to machines like that do? I mean, that could...did you kill those children, Elder?"

Smack.

Brent hit the wall. His back screamed.

"You are telling stories!"

"The Effluvium says—"

"That demons are crawling all over you, distorting reality and disrupting our land of peace," Elder Don Van hissed. "You shall learn soon enough of the Buzzing. With this magic of yours, it would have been smart of you to stay to the shadows."

"Kinda difficult when...I mean, you've been watching me since I was a toddler."

"It's a shame the first three levels did naught to set you free," Elder Don Van snarled, ignoring what Brent said. "So, while ill-performed, we attempted Level Four. We shall try again in the morrow...but if even a more ritualistic method fails, then Level Five may be appropriate."

"A fifth level?" Christof asked.

"I shall tell you after the evening prayer. Now is not the time. We need to discuss *your* behavior." Elder Don Van ushered the Captain and Christof from the room, looking back once at Brent to say, "I recommend you try to sleep, Mr. Harley. A well-rested body does better in the fight against the demons."

He closed the door. Overhead, the gas lantern shook, dancing with shadows on the wall.

Or were there two lanterns?

Brent couldn't tell.

CHAPTER FORTY

Broken Walls

A musky yellow light filled the room. Bria woke to it, clutching a blanket against her chest, fighting the headache that had haunted even her sleep. Caroline sat across from her at the kitchenette, reading a book scribed in a foreign tongue.

Caroline didn't look up as she spoke. "Good morning. Sleep well?"

Bria shook her head. Nightmares lingered in the forefront of her mind, of hands against her body - pressed, forced - and then empty stares, setting like the sun. Captain Carver's voice echoed in the terrors. *Count the lamps. How many are there?* Bria struggled to remember.

Her thoughts returned to more than her. She remembered Brent begging her to leave, the vagrants being pushed through town, and the droves of vines following her steps.

"I would like to truly apologize for my comrades' stupidity," Caroline interjected. "They are old and bitter and often do not think things through enough...which is spectacular, as I never think anything through as it is."

"They tried to kill me." Bria shivered.

"No. I think Ningursu, our leader, was trying something he has not done in a long time. He was using his puppeteering. He usually reserves that for extreme circumstances."

"I'm sorry?"

"I am babbling, yes, I apologize. I suppose the word I am looking for is control. Ningursu tapped into your powers with his magic. He caused *you* to act."

"Control?" Bria reached behind her ear and pinched her little branch. "Is he still—"

"No. Brent made sure of that." Caroline frowned. "But the worst of it already took place. The Council used you as bait to lure the Diabolo here."

"With my magic?"

"Yes."

"So, this is all my fault, and Brent's taking the blame." She sat up. "He's going to die..."

Caroline slammed the book closed. "I swear, how do either of you get anything done? *It is my fault!* That's all I ever hear from Brent, and now you? Malarkey if you ask me! Both of you are to blame!"

Bria's head fell.

"Neither of you knows what is going on; you cannot control your powers because emotions get the better of you. I know—because I am to blame, too. My emotions prevented me from giving Brent a proper training. You would not have been dragged into this, because he would not have made the mistakes that—oh consarn it, this is my fault."

"No, you're right." Bria gulped. "We're *all* to blame. We've all made mistakes. You're right."

Caroline pursed her lips. She was quite a beautiful woman with shining eyes and well-rounded lips that surely haunted those who saw her in their final moments. Like one of Brent's stories, she might have been a siren, a lure, or a creature of dreams. Yet, there she stood, the caricature of Death.

Bria started to laugh.

"What is so funny?" Caroline inquired.

"Just the thought of Brent taking *your* place," Bria laughed. "He's a klutz. Him...as Death? I never realized how stupid that is!"

"I am quite the clod too, to be frank." Caroline grinned. "Like Master, like Apprentice."

Bria smiled in relief more than happiness. After using the lavatory, she joined Caroline at the table and grabbed a piece of bread. "How long was I asleep?"

"Almost a day."

"A day!?!" Bria shot up, "Why does everyone let me sleep like that!?! I don't have time! I need to go—"

Caroline grabbed her wrist. "From what I have observed, you do not sleep enough. So, it is necessary."

"Brent could be dead!"

"The two of you have single-track minds, I swear. Brent was going on and on about you. I hope you understand there is more at stake than—"

"I do!" Bria turned away. "The monster is out there, your Council thinks Brent will fail, and you do not trust me! You used me."

"*I* did no such thing."

"The Council did! You are a part of the Council, right?"

Caroline heaved.

"It's not my job to save the world." Bria rose. "I'm still young; I have no business taking sides or saving the world or any of that. But if I can save *someone,* that's enough for me."

"Where are you going?"

Bria stopped by the front door. "Like I said, I'm going to find Brent and get him to safety. Then I'm turning myself in for killing Cadet Lawry."

"He deserved it, as I am sure you are aware," Caroline asserted. "I locked him in Hell."

Bria shook her head. "I still killed him. I don't want the Order terrorizing my family over a petty death."

"You killed him by *accident*."

"Like they will care!" Bria opened the door. A yellow musk ripped over the clearing, sending slithers of light through the trees. Her magic spurred at her feet, mimicking the shifting of leaves and the hum of the wind. Control returned to her fingertips, up her spine, and to the little root behind her ear. She called upon her mask to hide her face.

"Bria."

She faced Caroline again.

"The Diabolo is near."

"I know."

"The Council is loitering in Newbird's Arm. Alojzy, Jiang, even Tomás and Aelia. They might attempt to use you as bait again."

Bria glanced back to the sky. "I can't hide forever. I'll find Brent, then I'll deal with everything else. He's my damsel in distress after all." She clutched the doorpost and smiled. "You could help, Caroline. Go against the Council, help Brent, and stop the monsters."

"I am not brave enough to tackle something like that," Caroline replied. "Helping you was my act of rebellion for the decade."

"You have to help! Brent's one of you...unless you think he's going to fail too?"

Caroline said nothing.

"Fine. I get it. You're all the same." Bria didn't look back, hopping into the trees and away from the abandoned cabin.

Logs cluttered the ground, vines wrapped about the trunks, and branches snapped at her touch as Bria navigated the dismantled forest. She did well to avoid where the Cadets had ambushed her, taking a detour through the dilapidated homes on the east side of town. She ducked beneath bushes upon seeing Mrs. Harley and Alexandria walking home with their heads down. Every part of her wanted to yell out to them, but she gulped down the desire.

The path into town lay strewn with leaves and dead branches. The yellow sky took hostage the flowers, sending petals floating through the air. Despite the confusion the day before, she managed not to destroy—only create.

Instead, the destruction arrived from the wind billowing through the yellow-tainted Effluvium. Bria could not see her own fingers as she held them out. The trees told her where to go, and with confidence, Bria walked through the grass, listening to the bellows of the wind.

Shouts drew her east to the fences of the Pit. A crowd formed outside the hedges. Senator Heartz stood before them with her arms crossed, a sanguine smile resting on her lips that masked her fatigue. Bria recognized most of the townsfolk: mothers of school children, vendors from the market, young and old alike. Even a group of lieutenants and cadets joined the mob. But of course, her grandmama led the pack.

Their shouts, though many, had a unifying theme:

"How could you let them take our home like this!?!"

"They took my child! Humiliated 'em!"

"I haven't seen my son in the weeks since they locked the Pit."

"You saw that damn demon vagrant boy? How d'you let him happen?"

"I'm surprised the vagrants ain't knocking down them walls!"

"Fix this!"

"We'll kick ya from office, ya hear me?"

"Vote her out!"

"Maybe Elder Don Van is right!"

"No, he ain't!"

"This ain't my Order!"

"Enough!" Senator Heartz boomed, raising her hand, looking for once like a leader rather than the woman in the castle who traveled to the Capitol to eat cakes. "I have heard your complaints, your sobs, your tears. I shall not let this go on anymore."

"Then what will you do!?!"

The Senator turned to the Guard. "Lieutenant Randall. Are your men loyal to me or to your Captain and the Order?"

"We serve Newbird's Arm, ma'am, not one person."

Senator Heartz beckoned for the Guard to come to her side. They removed their pistols from their holsters and positioned them on their shoulders. "We must," she stated, "be...delicate. Take this one step at a time."

The townsfolk jeered.

Bria shoved through the crowd, commanding her branch to tighten over her face. *This isn't like you. This isn't your fight. You don't have to save these people.* She glanced at their weary faces. *But who else will? It's all intertwined somehow...my life, the Council, the Order...it's all knitted together.* She gulped. *This is my home. I can't just...abandon it.*

"Pardon me." She climbed on the stage to face Senator Heartz.

Murmurs followed her arrival; they knew her without seeing her face. But no one budged.

The Guard readjusted their pistols.

"Senator, I think the time for diplomacy passed a while ago," Bria announced.

"What are you doing here?" Senator Heartz hissed. "Leave. You're a child. This is bigger than you."

She shook her head and turned to the Pit fence behind them. A branch lifted her upon it. Vagrants had gathered at the other end, peering through the fence at the Senator. Now their attention fell on Bria.

"It's the terrorist!" one vagrant screamed, pointing at her.

"The little witch!"

"A demon!"

"Listen!" Bria clenched her fist. "Please! We can't keep acting like this is okay! You're right! But ranting changes *nothing*! Madame Gonzo," Bria turned to her grandmama, "you say when life gets a little petty, we should replace it with something pretty. But, maybe that's not enough. We can distract the world with flowers for ages, but that will not fix our problems. Real demons will return, children will continue being stamped, and we will suffer. Let me tell you a story..."

Gasps and more murmurs struck the crowd, but Bria waved it away.

"I know! Stories! Terrible, right? That's why we have a *demon*. But is he a demon? What has *he* done? What have *I* done? Think about it." Bria inhaled. "You watched him grow — he tried to be good! He tried to get a job. He tried to listen. But everyone spat on his shoes. So, he turned to the stories for help. Instead of decorating the world in popery, he saw the problems. Then he turned to a witch and asked her for help to save the world. So...so she fought the villains and killed them, but even that didn't stop the madness. It was only when she saw the townsfolk crying, she realized there's strength in the hearts of mothers, of children, of old and young men. Every one of you can fight."

Bria looked towards the trees.

"It's not a good story. I'm not a storyteller. But it's not over yet. If we go together and decide to not shed blood and act as one...we may just get our town back. There's strength in numbers. We must work together. We shall not let fear govern us, for that's what they're trusting will hold us back. No, we shall disregard this petty...*petty* world and make it *pretty*. But not just with flowers. With our voices. With our *unity*. Let's show the Order we aren't their puppets anymore."

She closed her eyes, half expecting someone to throw something at her. But instead, her grandmama joined her upon the fence.

"She's right!" Beatriz Gonzo rallied. "This is no longer the Order here in our town! It never was! They've been prying into our lives for too long now! These vulgar men from Knoll, Elder Don Van's torturous cleansing, and Captain Carver's persistence is not the word of the Effluvium!"

"Then what is?" someone called back.

"Hatred! Destruction!" Beatriz argued. "This radical idea of theirs has been hiding in the shadows since the Smoke Riots! They have corrupted you to see their ways: magic and stories are wrong, colorless eyes belong to demons, stories taint the Effluvium, and the vagrants belong behind walls. But the world is changing! It starts with our children." She squeezed Bria's hand. "So, don't disregard their voices. Let them carry the torches and ignite the flames!"

"Madame Gonzo," the Senator begged, "we cannot have a riot."

"We will not riot!" Bria stated. "We're going to...show unity! We're stronger as one. With the vagrants! With everyone!"

"How can you promise that?"

"I can't!" Bria stomped her foot. "But damn it, it's better than letting the Order think they control us. They don't."

The Senator peered towards the Temple. "My daddy always said I'd have to protect this town...but I don't know if this is what he meant."

"We must try, Helga," Madame Gonzo urged as she hopped from the wall.

"The Order has too much control. That is true. This hasn't been my town, or your town, for a long time, and it is my fault." The Senator's face fell. "I let them lead while I relished the lavish life of the Capitol."

"Then do something."

"You're right. Yes, you are. Perhaps now is time to change." the Senator straightened her back again, her head on her shoulders like a woman ready to lead and said, "Newbird's Arm will no longer stand with the Order. Today we take back our town."

Cheers followed. Bria turned to look at the vagrants and then back at the citizens of Newbird's Arm. Just beyond them, masked by the yellow smog, she saw Jiang, Alojzy, Tomás, and Aelia watching with jars laced about their waists.

It didn't surprise her; Caroline warned her they'd be watching.

Bring it home, a voice cooed in her head.

"Let's start this as equals." Bria reached for the nearby oak tree. The moment she touched its branch, the tree grew, expanding at the trunk, so its roots fledged outwards and buried beneath the wall. It aged a hundred years and then eroded the ground, cracking the wall beneath her feet.

The Pit's wall fell.

The sky rumbled.

The vagrants emerged.

And Bria fled into the trees.

CHAPTER FORTY-ONE

HIDDEN IN THE PEWS

Brent passed the time floating between stories. He spent moments recanting the life of the woman in Yilk, then off into the tales of those out in Mert. He clung to a single thread that contained his own past, and when he descended too deep, he used it to hoist him back. Yet often it grew cumbersome to hold on, the pain in his side too unbearable. He slipped from the edge. Down, down into a different story, he tumbled, only to resurface again with a whiff of his past.

Elder Don Van returned sometime later with Jemma and Christof at his heels.

Christof pulled Brent to his knees by a fistful of hair. "Sit up, Harley."

"Sister Jey Ma," Elder Don Van motioned for her, "as we discussed."

"Yes, Elder." Jemma still made no eye contact with him, kneeling before Brent with a pair of shears.

"What's happening?" Brent asked her.

"For the Buzzing, we must keep your hair short," Elder Don Van remarked. "No need to set your head ablaze."

"Stay still." Christof kicked Brent's back.

He bowed his head, letting Jemma cut away at his locks. Still, Brent managed to summon the next words. "What is the Buzzing?"

"Shut it, Harley!"

"No, no, Cadet Carver, it is quite alright." Elder Don Van's smile slithered. "Mr. Harley deserves to know what will become of his mind."

"My mind?"

"Level Five of the Cleanse, the Buzzing, is to rid your mind of the last demons and make you pure. It severs the ties to your magic and storytelling. Obedience and Order, by way of the Effluvium, will reign."

"Buzzing..." Brent repeated the word a few times.

Elder Don Van continued, "We only established it about twenty years ago. A man from the country of Perennes arrived here with a history of child molestation, multiple wives, and burned domiciles. Like you, Mr. Harley, he had a set of silver eyes. Magic of the monsters followed him. After being in the Province for a couple years, he performed a deadly enchantment on an elderly woman that turned her next of kin into donkeys. He claimed her fortune and bolted towards Knoll's Gully. Thus, the riots began–the Smoke Riots, yes? You've heard of them?"

"Smoke Riots," Brent muttered.

"One of our Elders came up with a new idea–inspired from the Eastern Land of Delilah–to shock away the man's demons with wire and *electricity*. After the cleansing, he lived another ten years devoted to the Order, the demons vanquished from his body. A model citizen at last."

Brent watched the mist trickle over Elder Don Van's body. The story it told was different, of a young man experimenting on an old enchanter to test the prowess of his magic. The young man, upon success, celebrated, and children from lands far and wide were brought to him for cleansing.

A chuckle escaped Brent. "That's a fascinating—fascinating *story*, Elder..."

"Pardon?"

"I'm a story—storyteller. I know about the Smoke Riots...and I see the truth." Brent smirked. "I can tell when something—something is...exaggerated...or fake...or a story. Seems like you—you're good at it."

Elder Don Van lunged at Brent. The shears slid, slicing away a good chunk of hair. "Listen here, *demon,* I speak but the truth. It is your *lies* and *fictions* that taint the Effluvium!"

Christof hit Brent with his club and laughed.

"Cadet! Not now. Go report to Lieutenant Randall."

"But sir!"

"I have no additional use for you at this time. Sister Jey Ma, come. We shall resume the cleansing presently."

They left the crevasse, locking the door behind them on the way out. Jemma glanced back once at Brent, but her expression told no tale.

Brent slid to the ground and picked up his locks of hair, holding them towards the lanterns. His tears came as a surprise. *They're taking everything from me.* He dug his fingers into his head and shuddered. "I probably look like a fucking alpaca."

As the minutes ticked on by, Brent once again fell back into his stories.

Fight them when they come, boy!

Give 'em Hell.

Or give in. Cry. Beg for mercy.

Just tell them you've changed. Lie. Save yourself.

Brent groaned, "All of you stop. I'm just gonna—I wanna lie here."

Useless.

He shut his eyes, "I'm me...not you. This is what's right..."

The stories kept arguing. Brent drowned in them.

Down.

Going.

Gon —

He managed to come up for air when the door opened.

"No, no, please." Brent choked as the light filled the room. "I don't want to...please...I wanna...I don't wanna lose my mind. It's all I have."

"Mr. Harley, relax." Brother Roy Al walked forward and placed a hand on Brent's shoulders.

Jemma trailed in behind him. "We're going to get you out of here."

"What? Why?"

"Because I am opposed to this on all counts," Brother Roy Al informed him. "If you have done something wrong, the cleanse is not supposed to be for punishment."

"Who's saying magic is bad, anyway?" Jemma asked. "I saw how everyone smiled when you told that story. It was...healing, almost."

"You don't need to get in trouble for me," Brent remarked. "I'm not worth it."

"I told you, if you *cared* to listen, that I don't want to be a part of *this* Order. Not one that tortures children at least. If that means rebelling a bit and breaking a few rules, so be it."

"But—"

"Do not argue with me, Brenton Harley."

"Sister Jey Ma and I have discussed this at length." Brother Roy Al helped Brent off the ground. "Here, put this on."

Brent fumbled with the light blue robe and veil, putting it on backward at first. Jemma turned it around and cast the fabric over his eyes.

"Keep your head down," Brother Roy Al said, "and stay quiet."

Brent slumped forward, shaking as he walked. Jemma used the back of her hand to keep him standing, guiding him up the stairway to the atrium.

The early evening cast a dim yellow glow through windows. It transformed the pews into a golden abyss, dancing with the red gems glowing from the Year Glass above them. A group gathered in the aisles, praying as Elder Don Van hummed hymns at the front of the room. Captain Carver and his guards waited to the side.

"We'll head out the back." Jemma ushered Brent forward. "No one should notice."

Their footsteps might as well have been gongs.

Captain Carver perked up as they walked through the atrium, eyes narrowing. Only when they reached the back door did he speak out. “Roy! What goes there?”

Elder Don Van’s hymns ceased, eyes narrowing.

“Ah, Brother!” Roy Al turned to the Captain. “How are you this fine evening?”

“Who’s this?” The Captain glared at Brent.

“Madame Hillcrest of Grover’s Marsh. She visited from yonder today.”

“She seems rather tall for a woman.” Captain Carver approached Brent. “What say you?”

Brent kept quiet.

“Speak!”

He shook his head.

“Pathetic.” Captain Carver pushed up Brent’s veil. “You could have tried a better disguise, Mr. Harley.”

“Glenn, let him go,” Brother Roy Al pleaded. “This is not the right. Your loyalty should be to Newbird’s Arm.”

“My loyalty is to humanity.”

“Then this is inhumane! Look at him! He needs a doctor!”

Do I really look that bad?

“Brother Roy Al! Sister Jey Ma!” Elder Don Van called from his podium. “I find this behavior abhorrent. Return the demon to his cell immediately, and I shall be kind with your punishment.”

The patrons murmured.

"Please don't hurt them," Brent begged. "They only did this because I—"

"Brent, don't try to be a hero," Jemma spat. "We did this because it is *wrong!*"

A crack of thunder sounded off above the Temple. The Year Glass trembled, and a few of the benches shivered beneath the call of the storm. The yellow tinge from outside had not ceased with the storm, becoming brighter and wreaking of sewage. A child cried.

The Diabolo is coming. Brent bit his lip. *We should've stayed below.*

"C'mon Harley." The Captain grabbed Brent's arm. "Back down you go. Don't think you're getting free so easily."

"Elder," Brother Roy Al begged, "you are disregarding everything the Effluvium stands for. This is not the prosperity we seek!"

"You have much to learn, Brother." Elder Don Van joined them. "This boy has magic and demons all over him because he chose to open his life to lies and stories."

"No, sir, I beg of you, there's a scripture—"

"I know the Scripture!"

"It says," Brother Roy Al insisted, "the Effluvium grows with a message in the sand. It says that magic has a destiny to grow and bring us life. Can you not understand, Elder? That is the truth. And if you keep locking away boys like Mr. Harley, or children with passion, or old women who tell tales...you're not helping the Effluvium grow. You will only dismantle it."

"Enough!"

The windows shook, another flash of lightning rallying in the sky.

Seconds later, the front doors to the Temple swung open. Rain and dust blew through, followed by a whirlwind of leaves leaving a path in their wake. Roots crept forth next, and once they made a home on the wall, there she stood, looking larger than life.

A goddess, perhaps.

Or a queen.

"Bria!"

CHAPTER FORTY-TWO

DISORDER

Bria stormed the Temple, the foliage following her with the arms of warriors and the passion of lovers. As she twisted through the trees, the smog thickened, reaching for her with a hundred fingers. She soared. Her trees attacked the Temple from all sides. A distant song broke from the walls of Shanty Town.

Ey oh
We have come back
We have come back
We have come back
Ey oh
The sky is gold
Or so we're told

Bria commanded her branches to pull open the steel doors of the Temple. It was dramatic, with flair, but as the dust cleared and the sky boomed, her grasp of the world won control. Her presence screamed like a tornado ruffling through the plains, and her branches climbed through at all angles and careened through the pews.

"Bria!"

His voice brought solace, and she calmed her storm. A rain drizzled behind her, while the dim lights of the Temple cast a glow across the mist seeping about her ankles. Bria did all she could to keep her head up, riding on the chants filling the market square behind her.

Ey oh
We sing like knives
We'll cut and fight
Ey oh
We have come back
We have come back
We have come back

At first glance, Bria didn't recognize Brent. His hair stuck out in uneven directions, his curls snipped away and left with random flurries about his head. A frilly blue robe layered his body, while blood stained his eyes and made his irises shimmer.

"You!" Captain Carver barked. "I've had enough of you."

Bria flicked her wrist. The vines lassoed around Captain Carver and dragged him by his waist into the pillars, tying him against one of the columns. As he shouted vulgarities, the vines covered his mouth and muffled his words.

Bria glanced back to the atrium, locking eyes with Elder Don Van. "Anyone else?"

The few townsfolk who remained in the Temple rushed out through the back, fear striking their faces down.

"My dear," Elder Don Van cooed, "I understand your mind has been corrupted by this young man. He caused you to free some phenomenal power. We can lock it away again. Do not turn your back on the Order."

"I've had this power since I was a child," Bria spat, clutching her fists. "I'm Madame Gonzo's granddaughter born with the flower on her head! I'm still alive! I'm still here! So, don't blame anyone for *me*. I've always been here."

"My girl, you are delirious. Come, we shall cleanse—"

"Forget it!" A branch broke through the window and whacked Elder Don Van into the pews. He landed on the ground with a grunt, gripping the bench as he climbed to his feet. After stumbling a few paces, he fell again to his knees.

Bria took no chances. Her vines climbed over him, locking him to the ground like a fly trapped in the spider's web. It'd be so easy to suffocate him and watched him squirm...but then she remembered Cadet Lawry's lifeless body. She couldn't let this happen again.

She loosened her defenses, pivoting as the additional guards rushed at her. A gust of wind road with her fear, picking up the guards like bushels of leaves and sending them flying into the walls.

Outside, the chants grew louder.

Bria retained her defenses as she rushed through the pews to where Brent hid with Brother Roy Al and Jemma. He was worse than she thought, with long red marks branding his skin, cuts along his sides, and hallowed cheekbones. His new hair cut resembled patches of grass. Yet, his eyes still sparkled.

He reached for her as she approached, pulling her into a shaky hug.

Finally, Bria cried. "I thought—"

"I know," Brent croaked. "I did, too."

Bria longed to hide in his arms, washed away in stories and tears. But the chants kept growing, and despite her pleas, the tension grew. It was still difficult, though, to squirm out of Brent's grip.

She turned to Brother Roy Al and Jemma. "Thank you."

They responded with smiles. Bria swore she'd never seen Jemma at such peace.

"We should get out of here," Bria whispered. "I might have, um...I might have broken down Pit's walls I was hoping there wouldn't be a riot, but..." She glanced back toward the window.

"People are irrational," Brother Roy Al recited. "Go. Get to safety. Both of you."

"You both should, too. There's a monster loose. It might be near."

"That's probably why people are misbehaving," Brent mumbled, "It's everyone's nightmares wrapped in a thousand...I mean, it's a prick who just...it's terrible."

"We'll be fine," Brother Roy Al promised. "We are in the house of the Effluvium, after all."

Bria objected, "It might not protect—"

"Go."

Bria hoisted Brent from the ground. She stumbled slightly, maintaining her defenses while guiding Brent forward. *Just a bit farther, then you can rest.* Her body ached already, eyes heavy, with fatigue drifting through her muscles. *Brent needs you to stay strong.*

The trees started receding. Captain Carver's voice returned first.

"DON'T MOVE, YOU FUCKING VAGRANTS!"

Brent glanced up at him, smirked, then took another mocking step.

Bria slapped his arm.

Elder Don Van stirred as they rushed past him. A few minutes and he'd wake up. By then, they would be long gone. Or so Bria hoped.

At the door, Brent stopped, digging his hand into Bria's shoulder. "Wait."

"What?"

"The others..." Brent glanced to the staircase and to the pews. "The others getting cleansed, I mean. They're still here. We need to get them."

"Brent, go!" Jemma shouted, "Roy and I will take care of them."

"Are you—"

"They're our responsibility, not yours. So, get out of here, a'ight?"

Brent exchanged a nod with Jemma. Betrothal had brought them together, but chaos formed friendships. That much Bria knew.

She wished she knew more. Like what lay beyond the Temple door as it swung open.

The scene belonged to a nightmare. While vagrants aligned with townsfolk, the market square experienced the consequences. Carts flipped, horses ran loose, and fruits lay strewn about the ground. Smoke from the train plumed overhead. Gaslights flickered and burned. The guards—both loyal to the Senator and not—pulled back those who fought, dragging naysayers away. But it didn't matter if they threw them into the Pit; the vagrants continued to pour out of the hole Bria created. They carried torches and trampled over hedges. Of the blackened trees still standing, many climbed into their branches and rallied their comrades.

The chants unified them as one.

Tearing through the sky, the storm fueled them further. Its glow transfused with the landscape, stinking of rot, tobacco, and the dead. If it bothered Bria, it hit those around her harder. As Brent said, it fueled misbehavior. Bria had at least dabbled in its presence.

Brent gripped Bria's shoulder, his eyes drifting over the chaos, mouth ajar. He mouthed something to himself, before releasing her shoulder and whispering, "There's so much...I—I don't know who is real."

"Then let's get out of here." Bria helped Brent down the steps. "Get you to safety."

"And you."

Bria didn't have the heart to tell him her intentions.

She clung to his arm as they entered the fray. People crashed into them. Brent fell twice. His breathing worried her, but if they reached the edge of the square, get to the trees, then they'd be free.

Bria paused at the center of the square. Cadets gathered by the roadway towards the gardens, led by Christof himself. His eyes blazed as they locked onto her. "You!"

She backed up.

"You fucking little—"

Brent shot his arm out in front of Bria. The mist thickened. A story of a crowd hurled out around them, tripling the number of people standing about.

"This way," Brent muttered. "We'll be safe from beasts over yonder."

It wasn't Brent speaking, she realized. A story had taken place, capturing his tongue and thoughts, and he fought through the commotion like a warrior in battle.

"Ay there be the dragon," Brent motioned to the sky. "I'll take 'er down, I swear thee."

In the sky, Bria saw it: the Diabolo had taken shape, towering over them, as menacing as ever. Its white hair cascaded over its face while its jaw unhinged wide in a profuse smile. One of its eyes hung to the side, both glowing like the sun in a gray sky.

It landed on top of the Temple, producing a roar like thunder. The townsfolk slowed, peering towards the sky. They finally turned towards its as the Year Glass snapped in two beneath the Diablo's body.

Glass shattered. The blood-like liquid from inside the Year Glass coated the Temple in crimson. Chaos followed.

Shrieks.

Sobs.

Screams.

They can't see it. They're in danger.

"Ay, it's the beast." Brent crossed his arms.

"Brent! Snap out of it!" Bria pulled him forward. "I need you back to normal again."

"I ain't a lad named Brent. My name is—"

"Stop it!" she shouted. "Your name is Brent Harley. Say it. SAY IT!"

"Me name is..." He flinched. "My name is Brent Harley."

"Who am I?"

His brow knitted together.

"Who AM I?"

He blinked a few times. "Bria...hey..."

"Good." She gulped. "You're back then."

"I think so."

“Well you better be. Because it’s here.” She pointed to the Diabolo.

The Diabolo shrieked again, clawing down the walls of the Temple. With each step, it tore apart the bricks and the glass. It ripped away the branches, vines, and roots clamoring up the sides. Wind blustered behind it, shaking the remaining structure. The stairs leading up to the atrium crumbled.

And then the Temple fell, taking the Order’s prowess down with it.

“Shit...” Bria sank to the ground. “We have to do something. It’s here because of me...”

Brent nudged her. “That’s not our only problem.”

She glanced up. Christof had climbed out of the mist, half his face bloodied, his rifle missing, a limp in his step.

But Brent was pointing to something else.

The Council surrounded them, camouflaged against the smoke.

CHAPTER FORTY-THREE

THE DIABOLO

As the Council surrounded them, Brent cowered on his knees, gripping Bria's shoulders to calm her tears. His heart raced. His head hurt. And the stories continued spinning. Bria kept opening her mouth to speak, but no words came out, and she shrank to the ground. They had nowhere to go.

The monster moved towards them, sniffing the air with its lopsided nose, each snarl emulating a horrid gas like that lurking in the Capitol and neighboring cities. Poison, pollution, death; if the gas could speak, that would be its chant. Christof approached from behind them, inching forward as Aelia, Tomás, Alojzy, and Jiang, continued to tighten their circle.

The riots in the market ceased as the monster joined the fray. Some fell to their knees, while others broke into prayer. Sobs poured. Children cried. Mothers wailed. Fathers moaned. A Hellish sensation dragged them down; Bria even quivered.

Brent found himself unphased. Had his own journeys through Hell dulled the blade? Or did the stories outweigh the onslaught of terror?

One story.

Two.

Three.

Hundred.

He saw all the monster's tales: a story of existence and collection. Terrible stories, wrapped in the songs of children, begging to exist, then locked away in a jar to collect dust for eternity. No one to speak to, no one to sing to, no one for comfort. Until light returned, and it screeched, begging for food and a bed.

While the monster thrived on terrible pasts and eating of magic, it had its own song.

Loneliness.

"Brenton!" Tomás called over the storm. "Time to come home. Let us handle this!"

"Harley!" Christof spat from behind him. "Get away from her!"

"You're going to put it back in a jar..." Brent gawked, tightening his grip around Bria's hand. "It needs to end."

"Brenton!"

"Harley!"

Stories...just stories in the air...

"Brent." Bria glanced at him. "You need to run. I can take care of this, but you need to get out of here and find a way to break your curse."

Brent stared at her. "You're giving up? You don't ever just...you don't give up!"

"I can fight the Order, but the Council and the Diabolo? I don't know if I can. And you aren't strong enough, so you need to go! Please, Brent...please." She kept shrinking towards the ground as if the world closed in on her. "Please. I'll try and hold them off so you can run. Get back to Mert. I'm sure somewhere there can help."

Brent narrowed his eye and scowled. "No. This is our fight."

Stories, just stories...

"Brent, please—"

Brent cut her off. "Wait. I have an idea. Come on."

"What? No, Brent, stop."

"C'mon!"

As the Council and Christof reached them, Brent dragged Bria forward, straight into the heart of the storm. He pushed through the townspeople, using the strength he had to keep Bria close. Already, the Council disappeared with the storm, and Christof's screams mingled with the thunder

He took refuge beneath a sideways cart and cupped Bria's cheeks, speaking over the wind, "I think we...we need to destroy the Diabolo...or something. If we don't destroy it, then it can come out again. They'll lock it away in a jar and won't...I mean, it won't stop. It'll just keep attacking and hunting and...and...it won't stop! Someone could use it or something, and I don't know. We need to destroy it."

"But what can we do?" Bria frowned. "My magic doesn't work on it much, and we're surrounded."

"I—I have an idea." Brent cleaned her face with his sleeve. "A stupid idea, but an idea."

"Brent..."

"Can you use your powers to lure it down? Enough so it's in reach? With the branches or something?"

She stared out towards the Temple stairway, where the monster lingered, sniffing over each person hiding in the shadows. Then she replied, "Yes...I think so."

"A'ight, good." Brent straightened his back. "That'll give me enough time to release it."

"Release it? What?" Bria grabbed his wrist. "What are you going to do?"

"The stories...they're all intertwined. I think if I can reach into the monster's core, I can set all those past lives free, into the Effluvium and all. It's a shite plan, but what else do we got?"

"You might die!"

"I'll get better. Probably." Brent grimaced. It was a weird thing to say, but the Mist Keepers existed on the sole premise that they got better. He knew that.

"No, no," Bria pleaded. "There has to be another way."

"Do you have any other ideas?"

"No," Bria sniffled, looking away as she spoke, "but I told you, you're not allowed to die. So, you better survive this, okay?"

"I'm not going to make a promise I can't keep. But I'll try." He turned, avoiding his own tears, but the floodgates opened when Bria pulled him back. "Bri..."

She kissed him. Brief. Fast. Tearful. Then, she hiccoughed, "I love you."

He took a strand of hair and pushed it behind her ear. This wasn't what he wanted. Why couldn't they be back by the fields, naming cows and drinking like they used to do? It might as well have been a dream long ago. At least he knew one thing, though, and he voiced it even now in the terrorized market. "I love you, too. Constantly."

They kissed once more. Brent longed for it to be a magic kiss, like in a story. The type that would make everything better. By the time Bria released him, and

Brent peeked over the cart, he knew that would never be the case. The Diabolo towered in the center of the square.

The Diabolo's prowess washed over him the moment he stepped into the square. He gagged. A branch from the nearby tree lowered to keep him steady. At its touch, he relaxed, able to call upon the stories flowing through his blood. He once again abandoned his identity, riding on the masquerades of the characters in his head. How truthful were these stories now, so ingrained with his identity? Was the ridiculing woman from Yilk all that mocking, or did she disagree with Brent because that was what Brent wanted to believe?

Whatever truths existed, he used their confidence to stand now.

"Oi!" He waved his arms to grab the Diabolo's attention. "Thought we'd hang out again if that's a'ight with you?"

It snarled.

"Don't wanna talk? That's a'ight, that's a'ight...you can just listen. But why don't you come down a little closer so we can see eye to eye?"

The Diabolo launched itself towards him. At the right moment, branches vaulted from the neighboring trees, wrapping about the monster's arms and legs. It screeched, trying to fend off the attack. They grew tighter, entangling themselves with the creature's body.

As it lowered to the ground, the mist joined, a wall of clouds blocking Bria and the townspeople from view. Together, Brent and the Diabolo stood alone at the same level.

Brent walked towards the monster. Up close, he saw its ravaged humanity, piecing together bits of what it once was, like a child with clay. Each piece of the story came from someone else, like a patchwork experiment made by some stuck-up doctor in another tale. The hands belonged to a woman who suffocated her sisters, the jaw belonged to a leader who led by murder and not by virtue, while one eye once belonged to a seer who lied and lured children to a house in the woods. More and more stories pulsed from its body. It breathed the smoke, its eyes glowing a feverish yellow, while two separate sized jawbones constructed its face.

"Harley," it breathed.

"That—that's new," Brent gulped.

"You should be dead," it hissed. "Like me."

"Yeah...a'ight."

"Your bitch killed me."

"What?"

"A tree, a tree fell on me..."

"Cadet Lawry?" Brent flinched, taken aback by the sudden revival. "But how are you—"

The Diabolo shrieked, recomposing its monstrous self as the noise tore open the sky. It mingled with thunder and lightning. As it pulled against the vines, muscles flexed, blood dribbling from its lips.

Brent shook back his fear and stepped towards the Diabolo. He unclenched his hand, using an invisible rope of stories to pull him towards the creature. At his touch, the monster screamed again.

"You poor...you poor thing," he frowned. "Created out of hate...suffering...too much in one creature..."

It growled.

"I'm here to help." Brent placed his other hand against the monster's cheek. "You'll be at peace soon."

He ignored its squirming and focused on the children singing—no, screaming—behind the terrors of a thousand stories. As he delved into the tales, he saw the children reaching for him, begging for a helping hand. Where did they come from? Why did their souls live etched in the Diabolo's decaying body?

As he reached, the tales grew. He saw a cadet chasing a girl in the forest, tripping and screaming as a tree came down. His last sight was the girl's fright. The cadet smiled.

Another tale, nonetheless, the same: a woman carving a meal made of her own husband's flesh.

Then another. A child with a blade, blood dripping down as they cut their peers.

Again, a man marching his comrades to certain death against their wills.

And another.

Another.

Another.

One more.

Each tale overpowered the last. They weighed down his consciousness, dragging Brent Harley deeper into his own mind. None of it came as a surprise. It was a risk, and he did what he could to save his mind.

He recited his name. But it belonged to a stranger.

At the mention of his home, he no longer felt any remorse.

And his one constant? There was no name.

Only a phrase, recited, over and over again as the stories collided in his psych.

I don't know who I am anymore.

CHAPTER FORTY-FOUR

Something Pretty

Bria watched Brent disappear into the Diabolo's embrace. Gone, just like the mist. Nothing happened at first, and after a few seconds passed, an odd tranquility rested over the market that made Bria even more uneasy. Then Brent stumbled back from the Diabolo, arm outstretched, mist trickling out from his fingertips. Stories spun around him, fast and without any reasonable plot: nightmarish tales of children screaming, of parents gone into hiding, and of leaders burning the world circled his body. Bria felt stuck, unable to help him as he curled towards the ground.

The stories continued in a cyclone, wrapping around him and picking up with the wind. At first, the monster did not change, continuing to pulse with nightmares.

But as the tornado picked up and Brent became overwhelmed with mist, the monster started to shrink.

Bria rushed forward. She still couldn't see Brent, but her magic flourished again, and so did her courage. She commanded the roots and branches of the nearby trees to grab the Diabolo and force it to the ground. The monster cried out, almost pathetic and hopeless.

Empty without a story.

With a final bit of dismay, the Diabolo hit the ground, disappearing into vapor. The cyclone stopped, and a rainbow cascaded over the few clouds floating over the ground. It lasted but seconds before dissipating into the now blue sky. Bria exhaled, her control over the trees leaving her as she abandoned her spot and rushed over to where the Diabolo had stood. In its place, Brent wobbled, stumbling like a drunken fool.

"Brent!"

She raced over, catching him before he collapsed. His eyes rolled backward.

"Come on, you're okay, you're okay." She lay him on the ground and pushed back his hair, "You did it...we did it..."

A smirk rested on his lips, but he didn't open his eyes.

Bria looked away from him, squinting as the dust settled in the town. People hid behind carts and buildings, hugging each other–strangers and friends alike–and gazing towards the sunlit sky. At the foot of the Temple, Brother Roy Al and Jemma led others away from the destruction, climbing over rubble and ash. While most of the guard stood, gawking at the sky, Christof sat on the ground a bit back, holding his knees and wheezing while staring at Bria.

"Come on!" Tomás shouted over the settling dust, "He's gone. We should reconvene with Ningursu—"

The commotion muted his voice, and with a whiff of mist, the Council vanished.

They're gone, Bria gulped, *We're safe.*

The sunlight did not reassemble the town. Destruction reigned. The Diabolo had destroyed the temple, unhinged the roofs of home, and crushed the gates to the Pit. Blackened soot covered every tree, the grass turned brown, and the flowers died. Even the Senator's Garden had wilted. The mountains, though breathing in the springtime air, were painted with the colors of autumn.

A child's cry broke the silence.

It ruptured a hollowness in Bria's core. She couldn't place it, but it broiled in the core of her heart and flushed through her body. She wanted to find Elder Don Van, Captain Carver, Christof, the Council, and rip them limb from limb. But...she also wanted to just lie on her bed and sob for hours. Even still, it was something else. A sense of emptiness and dissatisfaction? A sense of heartbreak and loneliness?

After all this time, she had not answered the question: why was she born with a flower on her head?

And why did the trees keep following her?

And why–*why*–did this happen?

Why her?

She cried towards the garden, bringing Brent closer to her chest. It beckoned her, begged her to return, to get away from the death and destruction flooding through her home. A town covered in ashes took away her hope. Newbird's Arm would be the symbol of demons and demise across the province.

Beautiful Newbird's Arm with its gardens, green hills, and bolstering market had died.

In times of death and horror, when life seems a little petty, why not replace it with something pretty?

She dug her fingers into the dirt. Somewhere, she saw children playing, lovers kissing, and mothers protecting their children to the end. How could she leave her home so scathed?

It could not end like this.

She visualized a world untouched by hatred and disdain. A world where magic and love reigned. She felt it through her fingers, in her heart, and in beating in her soul.

Why not distract them with something pretty?

Long ago, Bria realized she was connected to nature. In her garden, she used to run to flowers crying out for water and used to sing songs to bushes who wallowed in loneliness. When the trees wanted more sun, she'd blow away the clouds and tell the branches to cling to it. When a drought touched the edges of the Newbird Mountains, she guided the tree's roots deeper into the ground. Usually, it was but one plant at a time, one cloud at a time, one lake at a time. But this time, the trees screamed for her, and the entire town of Newbird's Arm cried in agony.

Make it pretty.

She saw each seedling, each tree, and each bushel and each bud. They called for her as the fire ripped them to pieces, as they wallowed in the pain from the Diabolo, as they sang the songs of a death blossom. Parched, they yearned for water. Wilting, they pleaded for life. They needed help.

Newbird's Arm needed help.

Bria dug her nails deeper into the soil. The world called to her, not just the plants, though. Men, women, children, animals, fungi, wind, and rivers...for a fleeting moment, she felt it all. It brought her back to a time in her childhood where she thought she listened to the water talk or the sky sing. She'd buried those memories, but now she heard them all. She pictured a world where everything lived together, and death came to conduct deals with kindness.

And Death looked like a kind man with silver eyes and a crooked smile.

She smiled at Brent, a raspy breath escaping his lips.

Make it pretty.

The world is petty.

She hugged Brent's body. Only then did she realize that grass had gathered beneath them. Covered with wildflowers, the grass spread out beneath her hands and through the market. The trees blossomed, the hedges grew tall, and the charred trees reached the sky with fresh blooms. It didn't stop there, though. The town was lathered in bustling greens, trees and flowers filling the dusty roads. Overhead, light rain fell, washing away the dust.

Through the rain, everyone stopped. It cleansed them of their anger and dismay. The smell of a spring rain had an enchanting way of stopping people in their tracks and sending them back home. Even the most versatile flames couldn't resist a gentle mist.

She gazed at her audience. Her grandmama sat on a bench, mending the wound of a vagrant with eyes as silver as Brent. Others gazed at her. Even the Guard remained frozen, a few of them keeping Senator Heartz on her feet.

Bria licked her lip then assured them, her voice loud, "If people ask what happened today, tell them that Rhodana the Forest Queen returned. And tell them that they can come with their armies, their Order, and their hate...but no matter who comes: Newbird's Arm is protected!"

She didn't expect the applause that followed.

"I'll be back, I promise." She locked eyes with her grandmama. "I promise."

Bria tapped her heel to the ground. On her mark, a sinkhole opened, swallowing her and Brent whole.

The taproots lowered them into the tunnels while the ground closed above their heads. She collapsed against the ground, staring at Brent's unconscious body. Her heart raced, her head spun; it was hard to hear the trees, replaced with the sullen drip of water against the stalagmites.

"Brent..." She shook his shoulder. "Brent, we did it. You did. We—we will be okay. The Council's going to leave us alone. The Order is gone from Newbird's Arm. We can go back to Mert and open that little shop. The Diabolo is gone. Brent, please..."

His body trembled.

Bria laughed and wiped her eyes, “See...see...it’ll be okay.”

Another gasp ruptured his lips. A thick yellow smoke poured from his mouth.

“Brent?”

One at a time, his eyelids flickered open.

Two yellow eyes stared back at her.

ACKNOWLEDGMENTS

To all the following, my thanks, for your support, friendship, and kindness throughout this process:

First to my parents for their ongoing supporting in this project, by fueling my imagination and creativity.

To my beta readers, thank you for all your insights in helping make this book the best story possible.

To Kimmi and Nicky, without either of you I never would have developed these characters in the first place.

To Dee and Mae, for encouraging me to keep on pushing forward with this story.

To Moira, my cover artist, for putting up with my continuous revisions in order to make this cover beautiful.

To Charlie, my editor, for not only helping polish this book, but also for helping me reach deeper into my character's emotions.

And finally, to Matthew, for letting me talk your ear off countless times as I worked through this project. Without your support, I wouldn't have been able to finish.

ABOUT THE AUTHOR

E.S. Barrison has been writing and creating stories for as long as she can remember. After graduating from the University of Florida, she has spent the past few years wrangling her experiences to compose unique worlds with diverse characters. Currently, E.S. lives in Orlando, Florida with her family. *The Mist Keeper's Apprentice* is her first novel.

CPSIA information can be obtained
at www.ICGtesting.com
Printed in the USA
FSHW010025090620
70734FS

9 781734 367027